P9-DUJ-381

DARK TALISMAN

STEVEN M. BOOTH

Azimuth Books • Carlsbad, California

DARK TALISMAN

Published by:
AZIMUTH BOOKS
6965 El Camino Real
Suite 105-212
Carlsbad, CA 92009
www.azimuthbooks.com

Cover and interior design by TLC Graphics, *www.TLCGraphics.com*
Cover: Tamara Dever; Interior: Erin Stark

Main front cover image: ©iStockphoto.com/jsnyderdesign

Printed in the U.S.A.

ISBN: 978-0-615-79725-0

Library of Congress Control Number: 2013937217

This book is dedicated to my father,
without whom none of it would be possible.
He was the most patient man I've ever known,
and someone I could always talk to.
Thanks, Dad, for all you did.

For we wrestle not against flesh and blood,
but against principalities, against powers,
against the rulers of darkness…
against spiritual wickedness in high places.

EPHESIANS 6:12

Anora Fel
Akadian
Plain
Torinth
Ssithian
Archipelago
Calasta
River
Pillars
of Zor
Plains of
Arborath
Anaerith
Darrow
Forest of
Valinar
Finiath
Arcaan
Mountains
Porinta
Malas
Feruban
Desert
Xancata
Island of
Fu
Dark Forest
Telfall
Fairn
Nar'oo
Caltra

SALUSTRA

CHAPTER ONE

SILKS

THE SULTAN OF FU WAS INCREDIBLY FAT. HE WAS ALSO A VAIN AND merciless tyrant, more interested in hoarding his riches than in the suffering of his penniless serfs. He truly deserved to be robbed.

In spite of his girth, or perhaps because of it, Al`Taaba was obsessed with jewels and they bedecked nearly every garment he owned. He displayed them copiously—and because of his girth, there was a great expanse to cover. His vast wardrobe was contained in a vault the size of a barn and smelled nearly as bad. Stall-like closets lined the outer walls of the place, each packed with tent-size chemises that glittered and glowed in the subdued light from Altira's glowing, lucent shawl. The Dark Elf could barely navigate by its feeble glow, however, and even with her magisight engaged the bright greens and yellows of the royal attire seemed faded and devoid of allure.

Not that Altira was interested in either the stylishness or the hue of the corpulent ruler's clothing. She was after the gems. The Sultan had spent the better part of his tenure as despot of the tiny island of Fu squandering the taxes he extorted on jewels of every size and description. He took meals adorned in his riches, including formal dinners attended by hoards of fawning ambassadors and lesser so-called royalty. In addition he consumed numerous daily snacks alone, draped in gems of every size and description.

Altira was here to reduce his inventory. Her purse had been depleted as a result of acquiring a bracer of sildars—magical daggers that mysteriously returned to their sheaths after being thrown. In addition, she needed to silence the other applicants in her guild. She'd had enough of being the bottom rung. Last time, that twit `Talim had been given half of *her* loot simply because he was the cousin of the Cali and needed a new sabre. Altira wasn't about to make that mistake again; no one knew about this little excursion. She would just liberate a few of the Sultan's less frequently worn trappings. With some care, the loss would not be noticed for many months, if ever. `Talim would turn a most excellent shade of green when she showed up wearing a bracer of knives worthy of only the finest of rogues! That should silence the idiot once and for all. Altira was still the best thief in Nar`oo; she just needed to prove it.

Standing in the center of the massive vault, she reached into her belt-pouch and removed a pinch of salt powder with two fingers. Crouching, she tossed the dust at the floor in front of her with a practiced flick of the wrist. A ghostly cloud settled onto the polished black marble surface.

"Scurry into that, you horrid little vermin," she whispered.

Last time Altira had come, she'd stepped on one of those cursed, nearly invisible black scala beetles that crawled about underfoot. They couldn't hurt you themselves, but squishing one brought the entire hive up from below, and it caused a horrible racket—the wicked things had a most annoying screech when they were enraged, and it was easily heard by the guards. They had almost been her undoing last time and she wanted no part of that frantic escape ever again.

Seeing her way clear, Altira crept deeper into the vault, carefully strewing the salt powder in her path. As long as she kept the beetles at bay she'd be safe, despite the five levels of guards above her, the patrolling nagisets, the secret doors, the intervening gateways, the three moats, and the innumerable other obstacles placed around and within the vault—which was, after all, the most closely guarded enclosure in the known world. The Dark Elf smiled. She always enjoyed thwarting the Sultan's pitiful protections. Getting into the chamber wasn't a problem. Getting out, though, would be the real trick. It was one thing to pass through the walls of the castle unladen, but dragging out a half-hundredweight of jewels would be harder than sneaking in. Still, these fools were so inept, soon she'd be home free.

Altira crept into the first stall on the left and sliced off an emerald the size of a lime from the hem of a sea-green evening gown. She inserted it into the softly glowing satchel on her hip and muffled a cough. The smell of the place was stifling—the man clearly had no commitment to personal hygiene. She tiptoed back to the center aisle, being mindful to remain on the salty path.

Stall by stall, she filled her bag. The walls of each closet were paneled with thick cedar, but still this was like mining in a very real sense—she had to descend through grime in order to extract something of value. In any case, she was almost done. The bag at her waist was starting to slow her down. There was no need to be greedy; she could come back any time. Just one more nice diamond should do it ... something impressive to round out her collection ... *hmm, which should it be?* Altira delved farther into the capacious vault. Her eye was drawn to an alcove in the back. There was a new cabinet that hadn't been there before.

"What have we here?" she whispered, then squinted back to make sure her exit was clear. One of the nasty beetles was at the very edge of the salty path leading to the door, clearly testing the validity of her protection, but it scurried quickly away. Her retreat was still safe. Altira turned back to the cabinet. It was tall and constructed of embellished ebony, its gentle whorls of dark grain nearly invisible in the faint light but speaking still of significant artistry. Not that she cared about the form of the case; the design of its golden lock was her entire focus.

Closing her eyes, she cast her mind toward the reflective metal plate in the center of the left door. Yes, there were magical wards in place—an enticing challenge that piqued her curiosity. The Sultan had placed significant protections around the chest. Its contents must be worthy of her attention. And this was a recently acquired treasure as well since the cabinet had not been here on her last visit.... The time had come to see what was inside.

Altira squinted at the runes delicately engraved into the lock's gold façade and executed an intricate motion with her left hand. *Yes*, she thought, *it's the ward of Balthor.* Nothing she couldn't handle, but still... it required substantial skill and further aroused her curiosity. She extracted a tiny wand from its sheath inside her jerkin and traced the proper counter-sigil over the lock. She could sense the extinguishment of the protections. Replacing the wand, Altira executed another complex figure with her right hand. There was the faintest click from inside. She smiled and carefully turned the latch-handle. The door swung outward, revealing a sparse enclosure with three nearly empty shelves. A small silver chest sat in the exact center.

"Well, well," she whispered. "And what have we here?"

Once again, she sent her mind toward it and, as before, sensed additional magical protection. Impressive—two sets of wards, and this second series was much more elaborate. It took her several moments of delicate probing to determine the extent and nature of the second set and to disarm them. At last the mysterious treasure was within her grasp.

Altira gingerly raised the lid, ducking just in case. Nothing happened. She looked around nervously, a reflex acquired in her classes on thievery, but there was no instructor to whack her for her uncertainty. She peered into the velveted enclosure. A pendant of deepest azure lay within, anchored to an elegant silvery chain. Although she sensed no further protective spells, the gem itself seemed to possess a subdued power that was most intriguing. The pendant was clearly magical, but it was beyond her skill to determine its precise nature. Altira considered her options. The Sultan had gone to exquisite lengths to protect this treasure; surely he would miss it. On the other hand, something rare might also be seldom viewed. And when `Talim saw the amulet, he'd be envious for a month. This would prove her abilities, once and finally.

"Come to me, little trinket." As she reached for the softly glowing bauble, her skin tingled. She felt an outright electric rush when she lifted it from its enclosure, trailing its luxuriant platinum tail. Slipping the pendant over her head, she tucked it inside her blouse next to her midnight skin and flicked her raven hair from underneath the delicate chain. There was no time to admire her acquisition, though—she had many obstacles to evade in the few remaining hours of night. Fondling a talisman would get her no closer to safety.

She reapplied each ward, relocked both the chest and the cabinet, and then carefully retraced her steps to the front of the vault, ever vigilant against the scurrying beetle menace. She reached the massive door in short order.

Closing her eyes, Altira focused. This was one of her favorite skills. Those who had no knowledge of the Alo`Dara foolishly believed that Dark Elves could walk through walls—as if anyone could pass through a solid object. She smiled. No, the secret lay in the 'Shadowed Passage.' There was simply a way *around* any object. You just had to be able to visualize where you were going and what was on the other side of the obstruction. Therein lay the true secret of the skill: you had to project your sight some distance ahead, and Altira was a master of that art. Still, she was careful to stay focused, for to pass into a wall or floor would be instant death.

She drew the magic and cast her vision through the door. *Yes.... There it is ...* The corridor was two strides away. She could sense the uneven flagstones lining the floor. *A cabinet to the left.... Better move ... there.* She needed to shift up a bit as well, as the ground was slightly higher on the other side. Keeping her eyes closed, she changed her focus and drew the passing magic. A small vortex of natural force swirled about her and she fell into welcome blackness.

Altira kept the image of her destination uppermost in her mind and let the Darkness envelop her. Holding her breath, she experienced an instant of utter cold, became weightless for a moment, and then reappeared in the hall on the other side of the vault door, a hand's breadth above the floor. Flexing her

knees as she dropped to the cold flagstones, she invoked invisibility. Her form became slippery, the light bending around her, making her almost impossible to see. Now to find that secret door to the upper level.

"Nice visiting with you, Sultan," she whispered. "Next time, we simply must do tea." She turned and crept silently down the hall.

CHAPTER TWO

ESCAPE

ALTIRA HELD HER BREATH AS THE SENTRY PASSED, NO MORE THAN a cubit away. The deep shadows cast by a single flickering torch halfway down the corridor should hide her well. Still invisible, she crouched behind what must have been the gaudiest statue ever created. It depicted a massive horse at least twice the size of a normal animal, mounted by a rider enwrapped in flowing gilt-edged crimson robes. The entire statue was festooned with so many rubies, it was nearly impossible to imagine how the stallion could bear such a weight. It would be easy enough for her to pluck a jewel from the thing, but impulse thievery was almost always a bad idea, and it really wasn't her style. Besides, she had nowhere to put one of the massive gems, and also, it would be nearly impossible to fence. Altira silenced her avarice and shrunk deeper into the alcove as the stumpy guard stopped and scratched his beard, yawning rudely. Altira scowled and shifted her weight to the other foot. “Get on with it, you fool,” she whispered to herself. “I don’t have all night.”

The hour of appropriation had come and gone—the deepest part of evening when most were safely tucked underneath sheets and blankets. Altira was more than ready to get back to her pode and tuck herself in just as snugly. Waiting for this lazy dolt to move was worse than watching grass grow.

The sentry tugged on his sword belt and resumed his beat, shuffling round the corner. *Finally.* Altira crept from the alcove and stole in the opposite direction. She was almost out. Just one more locked door, the portcullis, and then the three drawbridges spanning the moats. Those wouldn’t be a problem. She just needed to get to the base of the huge iron gate. She crept to the final door and sent her mind forward. *Drat!* There were guards on the other side.

She waited, but the fools were arguing about some stupid serving wench in the local tavern—something about ale and sleeping space. Meaningless prattle. Altira tapped her foot and fumed. If she passed beyond them, she could probably make it to the passage to the portcullis, but she’d be within view because she couldn’t pass while invisible. The hallway was well-lit, and with three guards.... It would be risky.

Sighing, she suffered their interminable drivel until she thought her very ears would fall off. The shuffling gait of the returning sentry echoed from the turn in the corridor. She had no time left; she must risk passing. Altira closed her eyes, focused, and stepped into the Darkness.

The jump itself went well, but the moment she appeared in midair on the other side, a foot above the floor, a shout of challenge accosted her. Altira fell to the ground and whirled to face the men, her hand darting defensively to her sildars.

This was not her way. She could easily kill all three, but the whole point was to remain undetected. She didn't have time to go invisible. The guard on the right drew a short-sword and sprang forward. With lightning speed, one of Altira's sildars leapt into her hand and she skewered him in the leg. The middle guard, shocked at the swiftness of her attack, froze in indecision. The third man, an officer by insignia, whipped a pearl-handled dagger from his own belt and threw as Altira's second blade took down his befuddled companion.

Ordinarily, she could have easily dodged his attack, but she was releasing her third sildar. Altira was committed to the throw and couldn't dodge properly. The weapons passed, midair. The captain spun and crumpled to the ground, her blade sprouting from his shoulder. Altira tried to move right, but she wasn't fast enough. His knife would find her heart.

She grimaced, ready for piercing pain, but felt instead a moment of intense cold exploding from her side. There was a bluish flash followed by… nothing. There was no sting of steel, no flutter from a skewered heart. Nothing.

Altira rose from her protective duck and opened her eyes. The captain's dagger lay on the floor at her feet, its wickedly pointed tip encrusted with frost. As she stared in utter amazement at the weapon, she noticed a mysterious glow penetrating the midnight silk of her blouse. Fishing out the pendant, she beheld a bluish-white luminance still radiating from deep within the gem. What was this thing? There was no way the guard's blade could have missed at this distance; and why was his dirk tipped with ice?

A second shout yanked her from her quandary. What was she doing, standing here staring at some stupid bauble while she was discovered yet again? Time to get out of the cursed place.

She went invisible and raced down the final corridor, passed through the portcullis, floated over the three moats, and in a matter of moments, disappeared into the forest of Cantira as the sounds of cavalry rushing over the drawbridge echoed over the turgid waters in the three moats surrounding the great Fortress of Fu.

ALTIRA PRESSED THROUGH THE LAST STAND OF KNEE-HIGH SUMMER grass edging the Dark Forest. The early morning dew dampened her well-oiled thigh-length boots and drew the earthen aroma of sedge into the air in a welcoming embrace. The dawning light from the east revealed the forest surrounding the Alo`Daran forest of Nar`oo as a bulwark of shadowed sentinels, standing against the light. Safety was near. Altira squinted and cast her vision ahead. There was something askew in the arboreal shadows to the right of the path. Yes, someone was lurking in the lower branches of one of the trees—someone she knew.

Altira lifted her chin and continued down the path, striding confidently into the forest.

"Where have you been?" The high-pitched voice seemed superior and condescending. Altira stopped and turned around as she rested a hand on her dirk.

"What business is it of yours, Ca`tra? I suppose you don't have anything better to do than skulk around in the trees all night?" She hooked a thumb in her belt and sunk into one hip as the other Elf dropped to the ground at the base of his Midnight Elm. He seemed annoyed at her lack of perturbation.

"Master Fal`Tallan was ... miffed ... when you didn't show up for passing tests this morning," he said.

"And why would I care what Fal`Tallan thinks? Name me another acolyte who can best me at passing." Altira turned her back on the smaller Elf and continued down the path. Ca`tra was forced to keep up.

"It's not a question of how good you are, and you know it," he replied. "It's about being accepted into the Cala. If you `Tang off the Masters, you'll never make it. He'll have you doing grunt work for a week now."

"He'll have to find me first." Altira sneered as she continued down the path. "I don't care about the Cala; they won't accept me, anyway. They've had it in for me ever since my mother was killed. Now go away and leave me alone."

Ca`tra was a peon. He only gained stature amongst the acolytes by informing on others. Altira couldn't remember when he'd actually done anything to merit the advancements he'd achieved by being second cousin to the Dar.

"So perhaps I should mention your little excursion to Fel`Soon," he challenged. "And what's in the bag?"

Altira spun on him—he was nearly a hand shorter than she. Ca`tra almost ran her over in his haste to keep up. She plucked his own dagger from its sheath and pricked his chin with it in a single, fluid movement. Her companion yelped and leapt back. She pressed her advantage.

"Mention whatever you want, you little twit, but don't expect any mercy from me next time we have dueling practice. You've already lost the lobe off your left ear; perhaps you'd like a matched set?" She flicked the dagger into the tree next to him, turned on her heel, went invisible, and passed without looking back.

What a complete idiot, Altira thought. *Slicing off his other ear-lobe would be too good for him. I should do the Guild a favor and lop off his tongue instead.* She'd no doubt suffer as a result of the encounter, but it had been a long night and she was tired. All she really wanted was to lock the door to her pode and hibernate for a week.

A night owl hooted a welcome an hour later as Altira wearily ascended the stairway leading to her remote dwelling in the treetops.

CHAPTER THREE

REPRISALS

ALTIRA FINISHED COUNTING, RETURNED THE LAST OF THE GEMS TO their pouch, and smiled. It had been a nice haul, in spite of the drama. This should seal her position in the Cala, if anything could. Na`talim's theft from Porinta was a distant second both in terms of difficulty and value. Her critics would be forced into silence once and for all.

She pulled the drawstrings of the leather bag tight and reached for the amulet. By all rights she should turn it over to her Demi; it was clearly magical. But it had somehow saved her life. She felt a strange kinship with the glittering trinket. No, the talisman was hers and she had no intention of relinquishing it to some selfish tyrant because of a silly rule.

She turned the glowing gem in her fingers, feeling the electric chill emanating from its aqua depths. She obviously couldn't wear it in the city. Although it was a symbol of her victory over the Sultan, there would be too many questions—it was hardly inconspicuous. She slid the leather pouch aside and cleared the table in front of her. Made of deeply polished maple, it was half a hand thick, solid and comforting. She found the right place in the grain and gently traced one of the dark fibers with the tip of a finger. The surface parted, revealing a capacious hollow. Altira wrapped the amulet in a handkerchief and deposited it within, resealing the opening with another touch. No one would discover it. None in Nar`oo had her command over the wood. It was a strange ability—one that would no doubt taint her reputation further if it were discovered—but it had its uses from time to time.

The bag of gems was too large for the hollow in the table so Altira rose to secrete those in the wall behind her bed. She was interrupted by an insistent knock at the door. Pocketing the bag, she disengaged the three iron latches. Outside stood a tall Elf, tapping his hand upon the hilt of an elegant black sabre. It was the Dar's First Aide.

"You've really done it now, you idiot," he said.

"What are you talking about, `Tan?"

"Get your coat. The Dar demands to see you. And bring the rocks from Fu."

"What rock—"

"Don't!" He cut her off with a chop of his hand. "I trusted you, and you've made me look bad. I'm the only one who defended you in that whole thing with the gold, and now you pull this stunt."

"'Stunt'?" Altira smiled crookedly. "Who else could have pilfered the Vaults of Fu? Tell me that? This will be sung at erafest."

"You'll be lucky to make it out of the forest alive, you little fool. You've no idea what you've done." Ac`Tan stepped around her to yank a jerkin from her closet, then tossed it at her. "Come on, get going. He wants you … now."

Altira donned the garment, considering her friend for a moment. Then, without a word, she turned and sauntered through the open door. She heard `Tan close it behind as she led the way down the bridge, suspended high above the forest.

Because Altira enjoyed living on the outskirts, the traversal to the Dar's apartments, located in the heart of the city, took quite a while. When they reached his pavilion, she paused.

"Come on," Ac`Tan said. "There's no point in delaying the inevitable." He took her arm and unlatched the door.

She jerked free and glared at him. "Leave it, `Tan. I know the drill." She stepped around him, and led the way into the Dar's apartments. Her friend growled at her and followed.

The head of the Alo`Daran nation was housed in a huge two-story tree house, a monstrosity that spanned three of the largest elms in the forest. Polished mahogany walls and walnut floorboards were supposed to give one the impression of standing in the middle of a midnight cloud of swirling mists, and the vastness of the ceilings and the circular walls were designed to bestow a feeling of endless expanse, as if the office enclosed all of Nar`oo. But to Altira it merely spoke of the Dar's insecurity. He was trying to make up in architecture what he lacked in charisma.

Ac`Tan retired to his desk, nestled amongst the bookshelves that lined the wall to the left of the door. He unbuckled his sword and hung his elegant satin cape on one of the pegs behind the desk. Pointing to a crude wooden bench across from him, he went to the door leading to the Dar's office.

"Sit. I'll announce you."

Altira crossed her arms and leaned against the doorjamb. In response, `Tan shook his head and scowled again, then opened the door to the inner office and disappeared inside.

Altira considered her options. This was certainly not the first time she'd been called, so she knew what to expect. Only, there was something in `Tan's demeanor this time that hinted at a greater transgression, something more significant than what that snitch Ca`tra could have reported. But what? It was hardly unusual for someone to pilfer a few gems—she had done it many times without censure. And the Sultan was as valid a target as anyone else. Skies! Jen`Tar had stolen from the very Lord of Scale in Finiath, and he was three times the tyrant Al`Taaba was. No, something big was afoot. Otherwise, her friend would never have been so abrupt.

Ac`Tan returned, and she lifted an eyebrow. His aspect evoked distance, as if he were veiling some emotion. Another jibe rushed to her lips, but she bit it back. Something was very wrong with this. He gestured impatiently and she slid past him and into the Dar's office. The door slammed shut behind her with the finality of a dungeon.

Altira surveyed the familiar enclosure. The Dar's sanctum was adorned in marble, gold, and ebony. Fel`Soon himself was perched behind a huge walnut desk, elevated just enough to make it difficult to see him from the handful of high, backless, three-legged stools arrayed in front. She stepped to the left, crossed her arms, and half-sat on a writing table at the back, watching the huge Elf as he wrote. He was clearly agitated, although that was not unusual for Fel`Soon. It took him several moments to finish. He threw his quill into a nearby inkwell with practiced precision and stared at the top of his desk for a moment. Pointing at one of the stools, he spoke without looking up.

"Sit, you cur, or I'll force you."

Altira sauntered to the outer wall and pulled one of the scribing chairs forward. The wooden legs squealed in complaint as she drug it across the naked floorboards. She stopped in front of the pitiful stools, took some time arranging her chair, then plopped into its relative comfort, lounging against the back. Yes, that was most satisfactory.

Unable to see her from his position, Fel`Soon growled in response and rose. He circled the desk, kicked one of the intervening stools aside, and stood in front of her. The Dar was an imposing man, blessed with a stockiness that made him look almost human. He was nearly as tall as Ac`Tan, but had twice the girth. There was no one in Nar`oo that could best him hand to hand, and he used his reputation to bludgeon what he wanted out of most of his citizens. Altira, on the other hand, had never been impressed with his fighting. He seemed clumsy and inept, using force when elegance was required. She crossed her legs, knitted her fingers, and waited for him to explode.

The Dar, however, seemed to lose some of his fire for a moment. He crossed his arms and considered her narrowly. "I expect you're proud of what you've done."

Altira gazed into his eyes and said nothing.

Fel`Soon held out a hand. "Give them to me. I want to see the pitiful loot that caused all of this."

"I don't know what—"

With amazing quickness, the Dar kicked her legs aside. A wickedly curved dagger appeared in his right hand and hovered a span from her chest.

"Shut it! Hand them over, you spawn of a traitor, or I swear I'll slit your throat right here."

Altira jerked away, shrinking at first from the point of his blade. She flicked her eyes from it to his face, judging the Dar's intent. She could jump to the outer office—few had her ability with the Shadowed Passage—but it would just mean more trouble. No, it wasn't worth it; she could always get more loot. Altira let loose the arm of the chair and slid her hand inside her jerkin, taking great care. She noted the taut muscles in the Dar's upper arm as she extracted the weighty satchel of gems. Fel`Soon yanked it from her grasp and stepped back, his blade weaving in her general direction.

The bag filled his sizable hand. He hefted it a couple of times then tossed it onto his desk. "Where's the rest? That can't be all of it."

"Have you ever tried to escape from the Fortress of Fu?" she asked.

This caused the Dar a moment's hesitation, but he quickly recovered. "*My* exploits are not at issue here. The fury of the Sultan would not be incurred by this pitiful haul. What else did you take?"

"Anything else would be impossible to pass through the walls. You'd know that if you'd ever been there."

"You are pathetic. I give you the chance to redeem yourself and you choose the route to certain death." He sheathed his blade angrily. "The Sultan is our ally, you pink-skinned excuse for a `Dara! We don't steal from our allies. If you'd asked your Demi, like you're supposed to, he never would have given you permission. But you never ask, do you?"

"I didn't think—"

"No, you never do! You just do whatever the skies you want and the rest of us can just fall into the bottomless pit of Tarak`Nor, can't we? Well, now you're going to get exactly what you deserve." He lifted a parchment from his desk. Scanning it a moment, he smirked at her. "Oh yes, you will indeed."

"What? The Sultan's henchmen couldn't find a knife if you stuck it in 'em."

The Dar barked a mirthless laugh. "It's far worse than that, you little skype. You've managed to enrage him to a degree I've never seen before, and he's a dangerous adversary when crossed. You're a disgrace in so many ways, I can't count them." He tossed the parchment on his desk. "I'll not have you in my land any longer. You are banished." He paused to let the significance of his pronouncement register.

"You can't kick me out for stealing some gems! I was born here. I have a right—"

"You have nothing! You have what I give you and naught else. As for being born here, you weren't. I've let you stay because of your mother, but that is over and done with."

His mention of her mother confused Altira. "What do you mean? All right, look. I took some cursed gems from a fool who has so many he can't count 'em. I'll give them back, all right?"

The Dar barked again. "It's far too late for that, you little twit." Fel`Soon was enjoying this. "I've always said you'd come to no good end, and now all your arrogance has finally come back upon you. Your mother was a disgrace. I never should have let her talk me into letting you stay, in spite of her … friends. You don't deserve to live in the hovel you call a pode; you're not really Alo`Daran."

"Look, I don't understand why the Sultan is so mad. It's not like I'm the first person who's stolen from him. Just two moons ago Jen`Tar extracted that gold—"

"Ac`Tan!" Fel`Soon's voice boomed amongst the dusty rafters of his office, cutting her off. His aide rushed in, alert for some attack.

Before she could react, the Dar grabbed Altira by the jerkin, yanked her from her chair, and nearly threw her to the floor in the general direction of the door.

"Take this pitiful excuse and throw her out of the forest. I don't want to see her self-serving, ignorant, condescending carcass ever again. And you!" He pointed at her. "If I EVER see you inside Nar`oo, I'll have the skin peeled off every inch of your pitiful frame, twice, then have you bleached and thrown to the Dwarves. Now GET OUT!"

Altira leapt to her feet to put some distance between herself and the head Elf. "Fine! Who needs this place, anyway? I've been alone my whole life. I'll just go somewhere else. I don't need you!"

The response from Fel`soon was unsettling. He smiled crookedly and retreated to his desk. "Loot is the last thing you have to worry about, you pitiful excuse for a `Dara. I'll be astounded if you're still alive in a week. Ac`Tan, drag this swine out of my office. She's dirtying up the floor."

Her friend took Altira's arm from behind. She started to resist, but the intensity in his eyes bade her stop.

"And after you've tossed her to the narthaks," the Dar barked, "come straighten out these chairs. I have an inquisition in half an hour."

Altira saw him turn toward his desk as `Tan dragged her through the door.

CHAPTER FOUR

BANISHMENT

ALTIRA TRUDGED DOWN THE SWAYING BRIDGE, HAPPY TO PUT SOME distance between her and the cursed Dar. A dark cloud of anger swirled about her. This was the last straw. *I need this place like I need a dirk with no blade,* she fumed. Ac`Tan followed at a distance, silent until she had reached the other side of the bridge and had started across the weather-worn planking of the intervening platform.

"You really screwed up this time, little one." Her friend's voice was tinged with a finality that was both disturbing and liberating at the same time. Altira stopped and turned on him, making him come up short.

"I don't get it," she said. "Why is he always so … so—" She could've throttled a dragon bare-handed, she was so livid.

The slight elevation of her friend's left eyebrow, followed by an imperceptible rotation of his head, demanded silence. He twitched the third finger of his left hand. He was using Cal`Tali—the silent speech.

"Not here. We'll talk on the way out. There are too many ears." He gestured to the next bridge with his head and spoke a bit too loudly. "Keep on moving, you cur. You're lucky I don't toss you off the platform and be done with you, here and now."

Altira grimaced and turned toward the next bridge. They reached her pode eventually and `Tan waited outside as she gathered a few belongings. She grabbed some clothes, extracted the amulet from the table and shoved it in her pack, then cast about for something else that was portable. There was nothing. She sighed, slung the all-too-light kit onto her back, and left her home for the last time.

They circled round to the back and stole across the bridge to the next Midnight Elm. Few knew where she lived and Altira liked it that way. They encountered no one during her expulsion from Nar`oo. She raced down the final spiraling stair to the ground and stalked away from the city. With each step her anger grew. She had suffered nothing but rejection, abuse, and trial among these people her whole life. She was *glad* to leave the cursed Dar and his oppressions in her wake. The path turned north and entered the gloom of the central forest. The First Aide kept his distance and followed several strides behind, clearly avoiding discussion.

"`Tan?" she called over her shoulder.

The tall Elf dodged around a sapling and kept his distance as they descended into a leafy depression, saying nothing.

Finally, she spun on him. "All right, enough! Talk to me, or I'm not going another step." She stamped a foot at the top of the hollow, her arms crossed.

The well-equipped Elf bounded up the rise and grabbed her arm. "I'll not bandy words with you, Altira, now go! I saw the parchment—I delivered it, in fact. You've no idea what you've gotten yourself into." He began to drag her down the other side of the hill.

"Stop it. Give off!" she cried and twisted her arm free but still followed. "What are you talking about? What parchment?"

"You saw it. The Dar was reading it. Have you ever heard of the Assassin of Sur?"

"No … well, wait, I think my mother mentioned him once. Isn't he a Cirrian?"

"Yes. An outcast, like you. A reprobate of the worst sort. A light-dweller gone bad."

Altira snorted. "Well how bad can he be? Cirrians can't wield weapons. They're made out of air. What's he going to do? Blow me to death?"

"Don't underestimate a Cirrian assassin. If you do, you'll be dead. Cirrians are nearly invisible and can wield great magic. He's a master of poison, for one thing. He can taint water by sheer force of will. If he touches you, you're done for. His tentacles can envenom your blood and it doesn't act quickly; it can take days to die—weeks if he wants."

"Marvelous. So how do I fight him, then?"

"*Fight?* Lords, you can't engage him, you little fool. You run, and you do it fast. You scamper and you hide and you hope he gives up before he sniffs you out. Weapons and spells are nearly useless against Cirrians. He can see you when you're hidden and though he can't pass through walls, he can still seep through the cracks. They also have some kind of enhanced smell. He can detect you a league away."

Altira scowled at this revelation. "Great."

"The only thing that will stop him is cold—it slows 'em down. And dark. They can't take being underground for more than a day. They derive strength from light; it's their food. They can be destroyed by an explosion if it's big enough, but the only ones who could muster enough magic to do that are the Guardians, and you can hardly expect any help from them—wretched birds. No, you run and you hide, preferably somewhere dark and cold. And you keep your eyes open."

They reached the edge of the forest quickly and Altira paused, gazing into the lazily rippling, late afternoon grass of the rolling southern plain. Standing beside her, Ac`Tan laid a hand on his sabre and sighed.

"I've been expecting this for a long time," he said. "It was inevitable, really. The Dar's been looking for an excuse to get rid of you for anna."

The gently swaying grass seemed to beckon to Altira, calling her to some greater purpose or mission. She tore her eyes from the soothing meadow to consider her friend. "That's crazy, `Tan. Why would the Dar want to kick me out? What did I ever do to him? What makes me so incredibly dangerous that I can't even be allowed near Nar`oo?"

"Let's just say the Dar's not in the habit of permitting dissent, and leave it at that." He took her arm and impelled her into the plain. "Off with you now, I'm sure we're being watched."

Altira jerked free. "Fine. May the lot of 'em fall into the bottomless pit. I don't need 'em, anyway." She set her jaw, turned, and marched away from `Tan into the tall grass. She was tempted several times to turn back and gaze longingly into the forest that had been her home for as long as she could remember, but she refused to give the watchers in the trees the satisfaction of seeing it. Instead, she lengthened her stride, marched up the first hill, and descended into the depression on the other side. Only after she was well out of range did she hazard a backward glance. The tallest denizens of the Dark Forest still stood, silhouetted against the salmon clouds reflecting the light of the setting sun, their leafy arms swaying gently in the breeze off the ocean, waving as if to say good-bye. `Tan was nowhere to be seen.

Altira gazed upward. There were a few tattered remnants of orange-tinged clouds high above, but naught else. How long would it be before the Cirrian found her and descended from the skies? Altira shuddered and pushed the thought from her mind. Turning away from the light, the forest, and everything she knew, she strode into the velvety grass of the open plain.

It would be night soon and she had no idea where she was going. To the west was the fishing city of Fairn and beyond it, the Island of Fu. Going in that direction would be sheer insanity. East was Telfall, the underground capital of the Dwarves. She'd never be able to survive in the subterranean hovels those stumpy excuses for half-men called homes. They were more filthy mines than any kind of proper place to live.

She could always venture to Xancata, in the north. The Dark Overlord would surely have something for her to do, but she'd heard stories and she wasn't at all sanguine about the prospect of spending the rest of her life as a minion of the Undead Master. Once you went into Xanath Xak's service you never got out. Besides, she hated the desert; the Dark Forest wasn't much, but it was a far sight better than the endless expanses of desiccated sand that surrounded the once-verdant, former Elven capital.

Nor was Porinta and the horrid, green expanse north of it any better. The entire region was infested with those insufferable, holier-than-thou Alo`Kin. She wouldn't last two seconds in Porinta. In fact, the whole of the north, with the possible exception of Finiath, was completely overrun with perpetually smiling imbeciles whose idea of fun was to yank dirt clods out of the earth and chew on them. And besides, the farther north you went, the closer you got to Anora`Fel—the cursed Guardian City. No, east was the best option, and the more she thought about it, the better the Dwarves sounded. A hole in the ground couldn't compare with her pode in the trees, certainly, but for the time being darkness was preferable to sunsets and the aroma of pine needles.

Altira trudged into the deepening twilight, wondering if she'd ever feel safe gazing into open sky again.

CHAPTER FIVE

REFUGE

THE DARKNESS WRAPPED ALTIRA IN A COMFORTING EMBRACE. THE night was her home now and she welcomed its protection. The waning three-quarter moon cast ethereal shadows upon the meadow, revealed as a gently rolling quicksilver carpet in her magisight. The glistening hoary blades of high grass swayed gently in the southern zephyr as if to welcome her to her new home. Fine. If this was her fate then so be it, but she needed to find a covert. The clouds in the east looked like rain. Lying in a sopping, dew-covered lawn under the moon might be something one of those prissy Alo`Kin might enjoy, but a Dark Elf required a proper pode to sleep in, somewhere shaded and secret and safe.

And what of the cursed Cirrian? `Tan was pretty astute and had never led her astray. If the First Aide was right, her adversary probably wouldn't attack at night, when the sun was hidden and he was weakest. It was frustrating though, not knowing anything about this assassin. Altira needed intelligence but had no clue how to get it. The Cirrians were a distant, superior race that had little to do with the "dirtlings," as they supposedly called those who lived on the ground. The only ones that had any contact with them were the Guardians, and she wasn't about to go find one of those—she'd be eaten in an instant.

If worse came to worst, she could probably evade a Cirrian face-to-face, given her skill at passing, but how could she ever sleep? Resting during the day and traveling at night seemed the most prudent course, but if she slept when the sun was up she'd be vulnerable when her adversary was strongest. Altira kicked at the grass and scowled as she walked. There was nothing for it but to press on without rest until she could find somewhere deep and dark to retreat.

She hitched her pack higher on her shoulders and lengthened her stride through the calf-high, silvered sedge. The words of the Dar returned, haunting her steps. What had he said again about her mother? Something about a secret. And how had Antarra convinced Fel`Soon to let her daughter stay when clearly the Dar despised her whole family? And when he said she wasn't Alo`Daran—what was that all about? She had lived her entire life in Nar`oo. How, then, was she not of the Dark Forest?

There were many questions to be answered—too many—but they all must wait. Altira had to first deal with that overweight chunk of meat in Fu. Yes, the Sultan needed to discover the business end of a dirk. Or wait. No, even better—she needed somehow to convince him that she hadn't stolen the amulet, that it was someone else. The Dar! Yes, that was perfect; what noble irony that would be, to have the Sultan's hordes come after Fel`Soon. But how could she accomplish that? A trip back to Fu seemed in order. She needed to sneak about a bit and gather more intelligence. Something would turn up, but she must deal with the Cirrian first. Altira couldn't have him chasing her all over Salustra; it would cramp her style. So fine, she'd burrow into Telfall for a few days, a week at most, lose the Cirrian, and perhaps even learn something from the Dwarves that would reveal a weakness in her adversary. Yes, that was the trick. Telfall, and then Fu. That cursed Cirrian and the Sultan would regret the day they took on Altira, the darkest of the Dark Elves.

She tilted her head toward the ever-watchful pinpricks of light that domed the sable covering above her. The "eyes of darkness" were silent to her mind, though there were those of the Alo`Dara that claimed the ability to hear the whisperings of the stars. Altira shook her head and continued on, the gentle breeze wafting through a few strands of her jet-black hair. The prevailing winds were generally from the east, which was fine—this worked in her favor. She would be downwind of the monster. It was a three-day trek at least to the Carthakian Mountains that cradled the Dwarven capital. She had never been to Telfall before and had no idea how to find the entrance to the vast underground catacombs. She should shadow someone. Yes, locate a Dwarf traveling in that direction and just sneak in behind. She could find a haven in some little-used nook in the metropolis. Once she arrived it would be easy; Dwarves were no match for her abilities in stealth. Getting there in one piece was the problem.

Altira continued east for the remainder of the night. As the horizon hinted at the first charcoal hues of morning, she discovered a sparse but welcoming forest adorning the foothills of the coastal range. She found a large oak that had been scoured by a bolt of lightning, and took refuge within its darkened bole. The cavity formed a natural cave, shelter from the elements, at least, and the best retreat she could find. It felt good to be enclosed in the relative safety of the wood, almost as if the tree were embracing her as a wayward cousin. She remained in the bowel during the daylight hours, trying to stay alert for any sign of the Cirrian, but since Altira had never seen one of the air-dwellers, she had no idea what the cursed things even looked like, let alone the proper tactics in evasion. She'd heard that they appeared as flimsy yellow clouds, but that was pitiful intelligence upon which to base one's existence. 'Tan had said they were nearly invisible; perhaps magisight would help. The thing was, magically enhanced sight was mostly useless during the day—the brightness hurt her eyes. She could always hope Cirrians had an obvious scent, but that also seemed an optimistic leap of faith, considering it was a life-and-death decision. No, if her current luck held, the Cirrians were probably invisible, undetectable, irresistible, and omniscient. Their mere touch was no doubt universally—and painfully—fatal. She should just throw herself on her sildars now and deny him the kill.

This was so maddening! The indecision was no doubt exactly what the Cirrian wanted—to give her days of terror and worry to dim her senses and make her thinking sloppy. Well, she wouldn't give him the satisfaction! Repressing the fear that swirled inside, Altira forced herself to relax. She took a few catnaps in her covert and managed to rest a little in the late afternoon, constantly casting her vision about, on alert for any signs of approach. The sun finally descended into the plains to the west after what seemed an interminable wait. She was still alive, but cramped and stiff from crouching in her burrow.

Finally rising, she stretched and foraged a bit for some herbs in the sparse forest, gleaned a bit of moisture from the nearby leaves, and continued east, just inside the glen. She discovered the southern coast in the early hours of the morning. This close to the Ocean of Storms there was a pleasant onshore breeze with the invigorating scent of salt and sea. It lifted her spirits a bit and she quickened her pace.

Just before dawn she came across a moderate size, hard-packed road leading south to what must be a fishing village on the coast. Deeply gouged wagon tracks spoke of frequent commerce. Her lack of rations motivated a detour. Perhaps there would be somewhere to hide in the town, and during the day the odors from the wharves would mask her scent. There might even be a thieves' guild to take advantage of. She could pose as a freelance wharfie and perhaps gain some measure of protection. Altira desperately needed a decent rest.

The descending road welcomed her weary step. The crescent of sky over the white-painted cliffs to the east turned a dismal shade of slate as she came upon the first rude outbuildings of the village. The masts of several largish schooners could be seen over the stumpy, ramshackle buildings of the town. The many shops and stores suggested that commerce here involved not just fish but produce and overseas goods as well. For the first time since leaving her former home, Altira's spirits began to rise. The greater the population, the more opportunity there would be to take advantage of her particular skills. Surely she could find some advantage here. First, however, it was nearly morning and she needed a hiding place well away from traffic.

If the Cirrian tracked by scent, the safest place would be somewhere smelly. As she entered the town, the road crested a small hill. From the top she could see a good portion of the harbor and the docks to the left. Two large ships and a smaller fishing trawler were securely tied. In the middle of the bay, some distance from shore, was anchored an old decrepit vessel with a

single tattered sail. Swaying in the gentle swells of the protected harbor, the dark and gloomy cabin seemed inviting, even though it looked filthy—the perfect place to hide from an experienced tracker. And if she floated over the water it would be nearly impossible to follow her. The problem was, she wasn't at all sure she could make it that far. Altira could levitate over short distances, but the fishing boat was a good quarter-league out.

Lovely. I walk all the way here and the perfect hiding place is just out of reach. She cursed the Dar for the thousandth time then made her way down the hill. She had to figure a way onto that ship.

There was some activity near the fishing trawler, but otherwise the village was still asleep. The closest point to the dilapidated boat was the far end of the docks, past the schooners. She went invisible as she approached the ships. It was a simple matter to evade the few morning workers. Her invisibility was effective in the dawning half-light, and she quickly traversed the heavy planking that separated the vessels from the warehouse shops and offices on the left.

Reaching the end, she scurried up the low hill abutting the beach and made her way to the point closest to the anchored boat. It seemed larger now that she was closer, and she noticed from her vantage point several implements scattered on the deck. The vessel appeared deserted. She had halved the distance, but it was still too far. Even with a running start she'd only be able to make it a little more than halfway. A gentle breeze ruffled the frills on her charcoal blouse, stirred by the burgeoning offshore wind. *Perhaps....*

Looking around, she located a length of silk entangled in one of the bushes at the top of the hill. She used her dagger to fashion a makeshift sail from a couple of fairly straight branches.

When she was finally ready, the first light of dawn had started to etch a pinkish fringe on the clouds to the east. She must hurry. As Altira waited for the wind to build a bit, she prepared the levitation spell, and—

What the—? Just as she was about to race off the edge, three Dwarves appeared from one of the buildings on the dock, walking in her direction. Although she was invisible, the sight of a makeshift silken kite mysteriously floating over the water would surely garner unwanted attention.

"Stupid, stumpy little dorfs," she hissed. "Get away!" She took cover behind a bush, waiting for the workers to get wherever they were going. The absurd twits certainly took their time, laughing loudly as they trudged up the gangplank of the closest ship and disappeared below. Altira waited for a moment to be sure they weren't coming back and then rose. Without waiting for more interruptions, she held her silken spinnaker high above her head and raced off the edge of the hill just as the wind picked up.

The sail was anything but stable, and twice it nearly threw her into the dirty brine, but with the advantage of her magic and after struggling with the inconsistent wind, she finally tumbled onto the foredeck of the boat moments before her levitation ended. Rolling to her feet, she whipped a sildar out, braced for action. But it was unnecessary. No stirring came from within. No sounds of rushing footsteps. No shouts of challenge. The boat was still, rolling gently side to side in the waves.

Smiling to herself, Altira scampered around the low forward cabin and in a moment had the locked portal open and was descending the well-worn stairs into the darkness. Even with magisight, it was difficult to see the interior. The boat was fairly large, perhaps fifty cubits from bow to stern. There were living quarters,

a small galley, cleaning rooms, perhaps enough space for a Dwarven crew of a dozen men or so. Altira continued down, seeking the lowest and most inconspicuous part of the vessel.

There was a cargo hold below that reeked of dead fish and worse. Just forward was where equipment was stored, but the holds were empty. Clearly the boat had not been used in many weeks—maybe even moons—and perhaps would not be for many more. She located a compartment that looked like it was used to store nets. The floor was littered with chunks of cork, bits of mesh, and uneven lengths of hemp. She rummaged around in one of the cabins, found an old blanket and some bedding, and dragged them into one corner of the compartment. After arranging things as well as she could, Altira surveyed her nest.

"Well, it's no tree house, but it'll do for the moment."

The rising sun etched a thin line of brilliance across the decking as Altira settled into one of the corners in her makeshift cradle. She had done the best she could. Now all that remained was to wait for dark and hope for the best.

CHAPTER SIX

TYKE

ALTIRA RUMMAGED THROUGH THE DESOLATE PANTRY OF THE SHIP, looking for something to drink. She fetched an ancient, grimy bottle from a dusty corner, then, discovering it was empty, discarded it with disgust.

"Skies, what a mess. Don't Dwarves have any sense of tidiness at all?" she mumbled.

Grimacing with stiffness as she walked, Altira hobbled back to her makeshift bedroom. She had arisen with a stiff back, a raging thirst, and a hunger that would shame a barbarian. Her accommodations left a great deal to be desired. The angling light of day was gone, replaced by a palpable gloom. Squinting upward, Altira could barely make out a dim burgundy strip of sky through the cracks between the decrepit deck planking above the cabin. It was nearly night.

She tossed an empty tin aside and winced. Her makeshift mattress had wreaked havoc on her body during the day. Stretching, she tried to work out some of the kinks. Sleeping on ropes and smelly bedding was hardly her idea of comfort but that was the least of her worries. Water was her main concern now—water and food. She reached down and fetched her pack. As she swung it to her shoulder, something tumbled out and rolled to the corner of the compartment.

"What the—" Altira scowled, then fished around in the dust for a moment. It was the pendant! The dirty, cobwebbed trinket still glistened in the half-light, its allure undiminished by its shroud of grime. She had forgotten about the cursed thing in her haste to get out of Nar`oo.

Wiping it on her leathers first, she blew off the remaining dust and turned the softly glowing gem in her fingers, considering its depths. She was now an outcast from her people, a hunted Elf hiding like a frightened field mouse in the empty hold of a decrepit vessel in some unknown city. All because of this stupid bauble. The Sultan had thousands of jewels; why all the fuss over the amulet? She hefted it, sorely tempted to chuck the thing overboard and be done with it, but she couldn't quite bring herself to do so. The trinket held a strange attraction for her somehow, as if it was pulling her along with an irresistible power in some unknown direction. For better or worse, Altira was bound to the gem. She had stolen it and it had saved her life. She was bound to accept the path it dictated, whatever the consequences.

The Cirrian had no doubt been charged with its retrieval in addition to exacting vengeance upon her. Altira would need to deal with him if she was to have any chance at a future, which at the moment looked pretty bleak. She slipped the platinum chain over her head and tucked the gem inside her blouse. The thing had saved her from the captain's dirk in Fu; perhaps it would shield against the assassin's touch. Altira reshouldered her pack and trudged up the stairs leading out of the cabin. She slid open the portal at the top and cast about for some way to get back to shore—she surely didn't want to swim for it.

The boat seemed empty in the fading light. The rapidly setting sun was only visible as a golden shimmer in the high, flimsy clouds to the west. The evening was warm but not uncomfortably so. Wandering aft, she lifted a weathered tarpaulin to discover a small skiff lashed to the stern.

"Well, well, what have we here!" she mumbled, betraying a moment of optimism before she recalled the condition of the remainder of the boat. "With my luck, it's probably rotted through." She yanked the weathered covering off the tiny vessel. "Or cursed, at the very least."

The skiff was filled with cork floats and netting but otherwise seemed seaworthy. Altira emptied the contents and worried at the knots in the weather-worn rope that bound it to the aft railings. After wrestling it over the side—it was horribly heavy for such a small vessel—she was finally able to slide the boat into the water and climb inside. Throwing her pack in, she fitted the oarlocks and commenced rowing toward the shore.

She heaved upon the oars but they struggled through the water, as if she were plowing through molasses. Was there some sort of anchor attached to the craft? Stashing the oars for a moment, she leaned over the stern of the boat. There was nothing attached, but just below, scrawled in bleached, weather-worn ink, was the tiny vessel's name: *Last Chance Lucy.* She laughed out loud for the first time in days—no, *weeks.* It felt so good she did it again. At least Dwarves had a sense of humor, however minute.

She went back to the oars, convinced it was just exhaustion and a lack of food. The exertion of getting the skiff off the boat and through the leaden seas had redoubled her hunger. Her thirst, which before had been a mere annoyance, was now beginning to gnaw not only upon her stomach, but on her outlook as well. Altira's brief amusement at the name of her vessel was soon subsumed by more basic requirements. She needed to get to the shore and find some food, and soon.

The moonless night hid her well, and it was easy to steer for the pair of lanterns on the near end of the dock, but it was taking forever to reach land. She finally ran aground on the gravel beach, hauled the skiff up a bit, then tied it to a large chunk of driftwood in the unlikely event she'd want to return to her mattress of ropes in the morning. She rested for a moment against a convenient rock and then breathlessly hiked up the hill that separated the beach from the docks and went invisible before descending the far side.

There was little traffic on the wharf. The sounds of laughter and the clatter of dishes issued from the far end. When the smell of greasy onions and fresh ale reached her, Altira's stomach growled loudly enough to wake a hibernating bear. She quickly ducked into the shadows of a darkened alley, alert for discovery. *Great, all this way to be given away by my own hunger!* Yet all seemed quiet. She willed her innards to be still and went off in the direction of the marvelous aroma.

The alley seemed to lead to the back of a warehouse. She made her way behind the stores until she was close to a noisy and clearly well-attended tavern. She crouched behind a large stack of wagon wheels and waited. The back door to the inn was just a stone's throw away. When no one approached, she crept to one of the dingy windows, mired with grease and soot, and peered inside. There were two cooks busy at the fire at the far end of a large kitchen. Fresh vegetables, a side of pork, and numerous other cooking utensils littered a large preparation table in the center.

Altira watched for as long as she could then crept to the door as one of the cooks carried a steaming tray through the swinging doors to the front room. If she didn't do something soon, her stomach would give her away. Testing the knob on the back door, she nearly shrieked with joy when she discovered it was unlocked. *My luck may be turning … finally*. She silenced the rusty hinges with a wave of a hand, cracked the door, renewed her invisibility, and snuck inside. The aroma of the well-prepared food hit her like a battering ram. Driven by a need that challenged her normal reticence, she scurried under the large table. The other cook was busy at the stove, stirring a huge iron pot. The dumpy woman (or was it a man? she could never tell with Dwarves) was wrapped in gravy-stained linen and wielded a huge wooden spatula as if it were a shovel. Silent as a church mouse, Altira reached up and snatched a large slice of black bread from a cutting board then scampered under the far end of the table, next to a large storage locker. She bit into the still-warm piece and nearly passed out from the sheer joy of the taste. How long had it been since she'd had a decent meal? At least two days now, she figured, with only a few foraged herbs and some dew for sustenance. The bread tasted like the finest delicacy ever prepared, fit for the Grand Coronation Ball for the most opulent King of Torinth.

Altira hunkered under the table for a bit and devoured her humble meal. *Water, definitely need water,* she thought. She waited for the second cook to leave, then popped out and snagged a flagon from a serving tray. She flipped up the cover and downed

half of that, then pilfered some fruit, several vegetables, and a handful of tarts. Stuffing them into her pack, she crouched low and stole out the back door with the cooks none the wiser.

There was a moderate hill behind the shops. She headed up, stopping below a large poplar near the top, and attacked her plunder with gusto. As she reached for the covered flagon of water, her eye caught movement behind a darkened shipping office two buildings down. Someone was skulking in the shadows behind a stack of casks to the right of the door—and he was very bad at sneaking.

Her suspicions were amply confirmed when the rogue, who clearly didn't know the first thing about thievery, crept right through the light cast by a lantern outside the warehouse on his way to the porch.

"What an idiot," Altira muttered as she nibbled on a carrot. She was riveted, though. The short form crept up the stairs and bent over the lock. It took him forever to get the latch undone and she winced as he pushed it inward. The squeal from the rusty hinges was audible from even her remote location. Altira shook her head and reached for the water flagon, captivated by the sheer ineptitude of the dolt. It didn't take long before a series of shouts issued from inside the building followed by the pounding of several sets of boots, probably rushing toward the door. She chortled to herself. This was better than dinner theater.

The useless burglar tore through the back door and vaulted over the porch railings, two other Dwarves in close pursuit. The thief dodged to the left to avoid some crates stacked behind the warehouse. Altira giggled for the second time that day and then clamped a hand over her mouth—the idiot ran as if he was being chased by a herd of wild narthaks. The first of his pursuers, a balding clerk girded with a leather apron, had leapt over the railings and was nearly upon him, grasping wildly for his quarry as the thief stumbled over an intervening box. The burglar leapt over another impediment, pulled over the same stack of wagon wheels Altira had used earlier as cover, and then darted up her hill.

She scowled. "Not *right* at me, you imbecile." She quickly wrapped her remaining food in a cloth and crammed it in her pack. She went invisible and hastened lower on the hill, taking cover behind a bush to observe. The simpleton wouldn't last much longer—they were almost on him. The burglar was still heading right for her, though some distance down the hill, careening through the underbrush and shrubbery as if it didn't exist. She almost laughed again—the fool *was* a herd of narthaks.

"Have you no concept of stealth, you idiot?" she mumbled as she cast about for a nonlethal weapon; the fool needed some deterrence. She scampered a span up the hill to a nice collection of stones at the base of a ficus, and snatched a handful of the smooth, round projectiles. The thief was continuing his pell-mell ascent of the hill as his pursuers tried to stumble through the wheels. The heavy, spoked obstacles on the ground were huge and randomly spinning, making them an effective barrier to the Dwarves.

The first of the burglar's pursuers, the clerk with the apron, had almost cleared the wheels.

"Git 'im, Talen," the other Dwarf shouted, "or I swear you'll never work agin!" Altira figured him for a manager, with his thin black visor and finer clothing. He took a step, slipped on a wheel rim in the darkness, and fell backward, swearing.

"Yes, he's got to be the manager," Altira muttered. He sounded just like the Dar.

Even as the clerk-Dwarf escaped the wheels along with his obnoxious boss, Altira crept lower, still invisible. She hefted the stone in her hand and squinted, gauging the distance. But instead of launching her missile at the burglar, she threw it at the clerk as hard as she could. The projectile struck his upper thigh and he cried out, grabbed his leg, and nearly fell to the ground, glaring at the back of the burglar who was still ascending the hill. The clerk looked confused—he was clearly trying to determine how the thief had launched the rock whilst scrambling up the steep ascent.

"Stop!" he screeched, rubbing at his leg. "Dat's assaul', ya fiend. Git back down 'ere or we'll 'ave da sherrif! Git down, I say!"

The manager Dwarf had nearly made it through the wheels. He had acquired a large stick somewhere and raised it to whack the clerk from behind, presumably to force his employee to pursue the burglar up the hill.

"Oh, no, you don't." Altira launched another stone, which hit the manager in the shoulder. The stricken Dwarf yelled and dropped what now looked to her like a fishing pole. The clerk turned to his companion in surprise and then refocused on the burglar who by now had reached the top of the hill, behind Altira.

"Dat's it!" the manager yelled. "Ye'r in for it now, Tyke! Ya, I know who ya are, and I know what ye'r tryin'. I'll be tellin yer master 'bout all dis, and da sherrif'll be throwin' ya in jail! Now git back down 'ere! Or I swear …"

For a moment, the two squinted into the darkness, clearly uncertain of the location of their quarry now that he had stopped crashing through the undergrowth. The manager gestured in Altira's general direction and shoved the leather-clad Dwarf toward her.

Oh, no, no, this won't do, she thought as the clerk stumbled toward her. Altira plunked him in the center of his leather-bound chest. He fell backward across one of the wheels, clutching his apron. His companion, clearly beyond sense at this point, kicked the clerk out of the way with a force that sent him rolling, and then bound over the wagon wheel with a shout. Altira had had enough. She struck him in the side of the head and he collapsed into the spokes and lay there unconscious, splayed like a mounted hunting trophy.

The clerk, however, was done. He rose, ripped off his apron, yelled something unintelligible, and then threw the leather garment over the recumbent form of the manager.

"That must be Dwarven for *I quit,*" Altira murmured, smiling as she watched the clerk storm away. His boss finally stirred and sat up, confused and alone. Altira dropped all but one of the remaining stones and retreated to the top of the hill. She'd managed to avoid discovery, though she'd no doubt enhanced the reputation of a pitiful burglar who didn't deserve it.

"I should carry these all the time." She chuckled to herself and stuffed the final smooth rock into her pack. "Better than daggers—you don't have to retrieve 'em, and they're free!" She reclined against a large fir at the top of the hill and fished around in her pack for the remaining food. She was just polishing off the last of a really wonderful blackberry tart when she heard someone stumbling through the brush behind her. A branch snapped loudly and then the movement stopped. The noise was enough to wake half the town. The fool of a burglar hadn't escaped, as any self-respecting thief with half a mind would. What an unbelievable, incompetent idiot! Altira angrily shoved the rest of her food back into her pack and went invisible.

The stumbling recommenced.

"You sneak like a four-hundred-stone ogre," she called, her anger overcoming her good sense. "Get away from here if you value your life, or I'll gut you like a wet fish."

The burglar's stumbling approach halted at the sound of her voice but then continued.

Who was this dupe? Did he not know common speech? She tossed the crust of the tart away, shouldered her pack, and leapt into the tree, confident in her retreat. Dwarves were notoriously bad climbers. The fool continued his bumbling approach—she could smell him a league away. Her magisight finally revealed a disheveled, pitiful figure emerging from the undergrowth on the backside of the hill. He wore ragged, dark brown overclothes that looked to be made from leather, but it was a material that seemed to have been worn at least ten times too many. The sleeves were irregular and the trousers stained and creased from ill folding. The whole outfit was pockmarked with a myriad of burns, as if the pathetic figure had been pelted with a torrent of incendiary hail. The overall effect was as if he had been stuffed into a too-small traveling bag a fortnight ago with a legion of fireflies and then extracted after a distance of several hundred leagues.

"Hullo?" His voice was subdued and gravelly, as if he'd been yelling for an hour. At least the dolt could whisper. "Where'd ja go? Come back, please. I've nay come ta harm ya. I wish ta thank ye fer ya aid. I'm a poor thief, I know, but dis pilferin' thing ain' my expertise. I been forced into it and I kin really use yer 'elp if ye will… Lass? Hullo?"

Altira lounged on a branch and considered her options. She was in a strange town, hunted and without supplies. She could possibly use this village idiot to garner provisions, but the Alo`Dara didn't assist others. It wasn't in her nature, and she'd always detested Dwarves. They were a clumsy, short, smelly, inept race. Still … she wasn't in a position to be picky. Altira grabbed her branch and swung to the ground—partially hidden behind a scraggly bush—and went visible. She was still a safe distance from the burglar.

"And why should I help you, you dorf? You seemed to be doing quite well on your own."

The forlorn robber chuckled. "Ya … right. Nearly got meself skewered by Colm. Drat him and his late hours."

"*Late?* It's barely dark, you complete skype. What did you expect?"

"As I said, I ain't no burglar. I dunno 'bout thievery 'n' such." He raised a hand to his eyes and squinted in her general direction. "Come closer, lass, will ya? Where I kin see ya? I won' 'arm ya, I give ya me word." He cast about, trying to find her from her voice. Couldn't he see someone standing right in front of him? Altira stepped from behind the protective shrubbery.

"Arr, there ya are." He stuck out a well-muscled, calloused arm in her direction. "Tyke's da name. Journeyman weaponmaster at yer service."

Altira raised a delicate eyebrow and crossed her arms. It didn't take long for him to get the idea and lower his hand. "Well, no matta. I've had dealings with ye shadowed ones afore. I know that ye'r aloof-like. I thank ye for yer aid. Might I know yer name, lass?"

"I am called … Sinthe." It was the name of the Dar's pet nagiset.

"Right then, Sinthe, let me tell ya da problem. Me master, Smith Transon, he ordered a very special shipmen' o' shanks from Porinta a week ago. He paid in advance and needs 'em ta finish a pair of swords for Lord Arshem. He promised delivery in a fortnight's time. Well, he comes to collects dem from da

shipper dere …" The Dwarf gestured with some angst at the back of the store from which he had recently escaped. "An' dat cursed supervisor, Colm the cheater, asks for an additional five gold in shipping charges! Imagine dat—when Transon had already paid da true and fair price. Well ya can imagine, me master was not pleased and 'e storms out, ya see. He gits back to da shop and he orders me ta get 'em or git another sponsor, an 'e tells me dat I needs ta get 'em dis very night. Since 'e's da only smithy in town, I gots little choice. As I say, I'm no burglar, but I tries me best to get in—I have some skill wit' locks and picks 'n' such—but ye saw da result."

The Dwarf bowed to her. "Sinthe, I know ye of the shadowed forest be skilled in the dark arts. If ye will help me get dose shanks, I'd be happy to pay ye whatever I have—it ain' much, but perhaps ye might be in need of supplies—ye are pretty far from home."

The hopeful look on the pitiful thief's face was more annoying than anything else, but still, Altira had few options. "What kind of supplies do you have?"

Tyke's thick eyebrows shot up. "Why … anyt'ing ya might need. Me sister Marta is a great cook. Ye could have food, blankets, weapons, whatever ya need."

"And what might these—what did you call them—these 'shanks' look like?"

"De're steel shafts 'bout a cubit long." He stretched his arm out, demonstrating the length. "An' … 'bout a finger thick. Dey be forged by a great smith in the north—Grannok by name—and shipped overland to Porinta. Dey're 'specially embued and dur'ble and used in sword-makin'. The bundle of six is just inside da door—or dey were when I went in." A frown crossed his brow. "Dey pro'lly moved 'em."

Altira considered him for a moment then nodded curtly. "Oh, all right. But *stay here*." She cringed at the memory of his prior attempts at stealth. "Don't move, don't do *anything*. You'll have to wait a while; now is not the time to acquire. We wait till everyone has gone and the moon has set, at least. Just stay here and wait. I'll be back." With that she went invisible and bounded down the hill, leaving the Dwarf smiling broadly. He sat and propped himself against her tree. At least he could do one thing well—rest.

CHAPTER SEVEN

TURNING

ALTIRA CROUCHED BEHIND A STUNTED MULBERRY BUSH MIDWAY up the hill. The moon's amber orb sunk slowly into the shimmering seas to the west, leaving the landscape dark and welcoming. The bright, friendly inn had fallen silent as the last of its inebriated patrons wove wearily home. The hour of appropriation drew near. She had watched the back of the warehouse as the manager-Dwarf looped a chain and padlock through the iron bars bolted to the back door and then left for home, limping and with his head bandaged. As if a chain and padlock were any obstacle to her.

Rising, the silent Elf made her way to the back of the store, bounded up the stairs in a single leap, and opened the padlock with a twitch of one finger. The chain took even less effort, for all the twisting and turning and grunting the stumpy Dwarf had put into it. Altira was inside in moments. With magisight she found the bundle of shanks propped up behind the front counter. She tried to snatch them away at first, but nearly threw out her back when the bundle didn't budge. *Gah*, she thought, stepping back to eye the thick, blackened rods. They must weigh twenty stone, at least; nearly as much as she. This time bracing herself first, Altira managed to wrestle the monsters through the back door with a modicum of stealth, but there was no way she'd be able to drag them down the stairs without waking half the village. She needed help and, unfortunately, there was only one option.

Returning to her spot at the top of the hill, Altira discovered Tyke snoring loudly under her tree, sprawled in his singed leathers like some great hibernating sloth—a sloth that had rolled too many times in a campfire. What a fool. If he rasped any louder it would wake the Lord of Scale in Finiath. She kicked him unceremoniously in the shin.

"Wake up, you dolt," she whispered heavily. "What in the skies do you think you're doing? This isn't a camping expedition! Get up and help me drag this horrid iron down the steps. And be quiet while you're at it, oaf!"

Tyke rubbed his eyes and smiled in spite of her insults. He levered himself to his feet and followed down the slope, with Altira wincing at his bumbling traversal the entire way. They stumbled to the back of the building and up the steps of the shipping office. When Tyke saw the bundle, he gasped and did a pathetic little dance, hopping from foot to foot, then apologized profusely under his breath when Altira hissed and drew a sildar. He slung the steel to his shoulder as if it were a sweeping broom and they retreated up the hill.

"Sinthe, ye have nae idea how much dis means ta me," the ersatz burglar said as he lowered his bundle to the ground. "Me

master woulda kicked me halfway to Xancata fer failing dis. Let's git over to ma place. We'll get ya all set up and my sister'd like ta meet one of da shadowed ones fer sure."

Tyke waited for some response but when Altira said nothing, he reshouldered the shanks and backed clumsily down the hill, gesturing for her to follow. Altira reached up to retrieve her pack from the tree branch. *This fool couldn't find his nose if you cut it off and handed it to him wrapped in Michaelmas paper.* "Why am I doing this again?" she mumbled to herself, even though she knew the reason—her pack was empty. Fine, if this idiot dorf had supplies, she could take what she wanted and be on her way. She looked up and saw the imbecile click his heels as he turned the corner of the tavern. *What a simpleton.* She sighed, shook her head, and followed.

They took a circuitous path through the town, weaving through dark and empty alleys, finally arriving at what appeared to be a leather shop. The Dwarf disappeared into the open space between the store and a millinery on the other side. Before she followed his bounding form up the stairs to the second story, she cast about for an escape route. Cirrians may sleep at night, but only a newly initiated acolyte would let her guard down with the setting sun. After determining the openness of the alleyway—there were large streets on both ends—she warily ascended.

"Well, dis be it," Tyke whispered as she approached. "Tanner Bilda gave us dis place for a fair price till I can build me own after I've finished me 'prenticeship. Come on in."

They entered the second-story apartments—Altira had to duck down to make it through the door—and Tyke dropped his burden to the wall with a thud. There was a low fire in a hearth across from them, its meager glow revealing a small but clean domicile. A muffled grunt came from one of the chairs facing the fire. Another Dwarf, virtually identical to Tyke in Altira's eyes—perhaps a bit shorter, if that was possible—rose and accosted them.

"Caw, Tyke, you beamer. What's with coming 'ome at this hour! Where have you been—" The Dwarf, who could only be Tyke's sister, choked as her eyes found Altira. She closed and opened her mouth several times then backed toward the tiny hearth. "What? Who 'ave you got? What do you want with us, you evil thing? Tyke, what is this? Why have you brought *that* into the house? What are you going to do with us?" There was real fear in her eyes as she clutched her apron to her breast.

"No, no, sis." Tyke hurried to his distraught sibling. "It's not like dat atall. Sinthe 'ere isn't about evil, in fact she helped me get dose shanks fer Transon." He gestured toward the bundle propped near the door. "I promised 'er somewhere ta sleep an' some victuals. She'll not 'arm us, ya 'ave me word. Right dere, Sinthe?" He glanced up at Altira and then gestured for her to come closer. "Dis be Marta, me sister." He tried to smile and look welcoming. It only partially worked.

Altira crossed her arms and raised an eyebrow.

The Dark Elf's reaction did little to stem Marta's apparent terror, but at least she didn't cry out or make further fuss. Her brother hustled to the door and closed it, then busied himself with lighting some of the oil lamps. After a golden glow had warmed the room, Marta seemed to calm a bit.

"Well, I guess if ya helped Tyke an' all, dat be somethin'. Are ye 'hungry m- miss? Would ya like some brisket or perhaps an ale?" Marta seemed to relax further as thoughts of food crossed her mind.

Tyke collapsed into one of the chairs and started to lever off one of his boots with the toe of the other. "I'll have a spot o'

dat if'n ya don' mind, sis. I'm not sure what kinda food Sinthe here likes." He stopped worrying his boot for a moment and motioned for Altira to take the other chair.

She lowered her pack to the floor and glanced around the room. Everything was three-quarters its proper size. The hearth was a bit too small and the chairs too wide and just shallow enough to be uncomfortable. The ceilings were low enough to engender a longing for trees and open sky instead of comfort and hominess. The overall effect of the dwelling was one of awkward crampedness, not to mention the smell. She took shallow breaths to avoid inhaling the noxious blend of boots too long uncleansed, overused Dwarven cooking spice, and eau de Dwarf.

Altira wanted to get what she could and be done with this pair. She dropped her pack on the far side of the chair and sat, squirming on the too-hard surface to put maximum distance between herself and Tyke, ready to leap for the door if the need arose. Marta considered her for a moment and then, appearing satisfied that this Dark Elf meant no harm, she turned toward the kitchen.

Altira, realizing Marta's intent, called out, "I've already eaten, but I could use some water or fruit … or something." She turned back to Tyke and continued. "And a traveling flask, if you have one."

"Yes'm. Right away," he said. Finally pulling off his boot, he rose from his chair. "Jus' stay 'ere. I'll fetch it from the back." He tottered down the hall, his remaining covered foot drumming a strange, lopsided rhythm on the floorboards.

Marta was busy in the kitchen placing some flatware on the stocky, too-short table when Tyke returned. He went to the kitchen for a moment then limped to Altira, offering her the filled water flask and a small bundle, wrapped in oilskin.

"Dat be some Elvish bread dat Marta picked up at da market las' week. We been savin' it as a treat for a special o'casion, but methinks ye could use it more." He sat and grabbed his other boot with both hands and yanked it off. The smell was almost too much for Altira. Her eyes began to water as the aromatic Dwarf continued. "Oh, and we have some mulberries in the kitchen. I'll wrap some of dose for ya." Tyke threw his boot in the direction of the hearth and headed to the kitchen; the shoe nearly tumbled into the fire. Altira rose and backed away from the thing as though it were cursed.

How in the skies had she come to this place? Kicked out of Nar`oo, banished and chased by an unknown assassin, what had she ever done to deserve all this oppression? Well, she wasn't dead yet, and at least her luck hadn't completely abandoned her. These Dwarves might be ignorant and smelly, but Altira had to admit that they seemed willing to help when no one else would.

She glanced at the packet in her hands, confused by her feelings, then shoved the wrapped toma and the water flask in her pack. She stood just behind the chair, holding her kit by one strap, and stared into the hearth. The familiar dancing yellow flames spoke to her. They were a point of commonality. Fire was universal. It cleansed and renewed. The flickering ballet of golden dancers cavorted above the glowing coal embers as if they were there solely to entertain her. The fire was charismatic. Perhaps it wouldn't be such an awful thing to remain here after all. But no, it wouldn't take long for the Cirrian to find her. She needed to move on, and quickly. She who stands still too long lies still for eternity.

"Sinthe? Missie?"

Altira started and looked up as Tyke's sister edged toward her. "Yes, what?"

"Dere be a bedroom we 'ave for guests in da back, mistress. Ya look like ya could use a res'. Da bed be extra-long an' soft. Wouldja like to see it?"

A wave of exhaustion swept over Altira the moment Marta mentioned rest. The only sleep she had caught had been a short nap in the dirty hollow of a tree over two days ago, followed by a fitful rest in some filthy hold on a rotting mattress. She had been running mostly on fear since she had left Nar`oo and naught much else. The prospect of having to hike back to that cursed dinghy and having to paddle all the way back to the cold, decrepit ship, figuring out how to get back on board and then sleeping on that horrid bed for *another* night, seemed incredibly absurd in comparison to a warm apartment with a roof over her head and a decent mattress—in spite of the smell.

She nodded curtly at Marta. The odor would have an advantage, too: who could detect her delicate scent amongst these bath-starved creatures of dirt?

The wide woman-Dwarf smiled at last. "Come then, dearie. Let's get ya settled."

They went down the short hall to the rear of the apartment. There was a small but comfortable room with a window overlooking the back alley. Altira ducked through the doorway, tossed her pack on the bed, and immediately pulled the window open, admitting a cool, refreshing breeze. She turned to see Tyke elbowing round his sister, who stood uneasily in the doorway. He crossed to Altira, carrying another bundle.

"Here ya go, lass. I've added some wheat stalks for yer journey. I've heard dat Elves like dem. Can we git ya anyt'ing else?"

"No. Th—" Altira stammered, at a loss for words. Finally, she just nodded and bowed ever so slightly toward the pair. Amazing. If she had invited these two to her pode in Nar`oo, at the very least they'd be thrown out of the city the moment they were discovered, and at worst … well, Altira didn't want to imagine what tortures the Dar would think up for them in order to extract whatever pitiful intelligence they possessed. Yet here they were, welcoming a mortal enemy into their home without a care. What a strange and confusing race were the Dwarves. At the same time, inept and incredibly free with their trust and possessions. As if to confirm this impression, Marta hastened over and retrieved a single errant stalk that had fallen to the floor. She proffered this to Altira and then scurried back to the safety of the doorway when it was accepted.

Altira stared at the golden thistle as if she'd never seen a stalk of wheat. This was so strange. Life wasn't supposed to be like this. People didn't *help* you; they did everything they could to make your life miserable. The only one she'd ever considered a friend was `Tan and he would never have given her anything. Advice, yes. Chastisement, certainly. Perhaps a good word with the right people from time to time in exchange for loot or knowledge, but never anything like this. Never food when you needed it, or a bed to sleep in when you had none, or a roof over your head when you were far from home and hunted.

"Come on out, Tyke. Let mistress Sinthe git som res'." Marta plucked at Tyke's ragged sleeve. "She looks a fright."

Tyke started and smiled crookedly at Altira. The two bustled out and closed the door behind them.

Altira flicked a dead leaf from her cloak. Marta wasn't so far off about her appearance—two days on the run had taken a toll on her exterior as well as her insides. She sat on the edge of the comfortable bed and carefully returned the errant stalk to Tyke's bundle, placing the lot into her kit. As she buckled the flap, the full weight of her predicament descended upon her.

"It does not end here," she said grimly. "I'm not going to give them the satisfaction. That Cirrian has a weakness and I'm going to find it." It's going take more than a pitiful creature made out of air to kill Altira the Dark Elf. She pushed her worries aside and tumbled onto the bed, careless of the coarse, gritty feel of the woolen blanket. Marta was right about something else, too—the bed was actually the perfect length. Altira hugged her pack and instantly fell asleep.

CHAPTER EIGHT

THE CIRRIAN

"GET AWAY FROM 'ER, YOU! GIT BACK!"

Tyke's gravelly shout ripped through Altira's dreams, instantly waking her to a room awash in sunlight. Something wooden clattered across the floor in the front room, accompanied by the sounds of a scuffle. The Dark Elf leapt from her bed, a sildar filling her right hand by sheer reflex. She heard a thud and felt a shudder through her boots. Was that a body hitting the floor?

"Marta! You fiend!"

Tyke's voice seemed more distant now and the terror edging it raised the hair on the back of Altira's neck. An unnatural odor seeped through the door, permeating the room with a smell like fresh lightning mingled with a sickly sweetness that made her stomach turn. The hair on the back of her neck tingled as she locked her eyes on the door and reached for the pack.

Her bag now on her back, Altira ducked low and crept toward the strange amber glow coming through the cracks in the door. She silenced the hinges with a wave of a hand then cracked it just enough to see through. The only thing visible was part of the hall and the bedroom opposite hers. The ceiling and walls were illuminated with a strange golden glow, like that of an oil lamp with a wick turned up much too far. Something hard hit a wall then clattered to the floor; a steel weapon, to her trained ear. Altira slipped through the door, gazed down the hall, and froze.

Hovering over the crumpled form of Tyke's sister and haloed by the ample sunshine from the double bay windows beyond was the strangest creature she'd ever seen. It looked like one of the jelltars that sometimes washed up on the beach late in summer, only this thing was much more flimsy. It was translucent, tall, and elongated—impossibly thin, in fact. Its insides were visible through its skin, and it shimmered in the lucid sunlight, seeming to glow from within. A slender yellow line bisected it vertically, and two tiny, jet-black ovals floated in a hairless, impossibly pointed pinnacle that must be its head. Its mouth was no more than a horizontal slit. It had no limbs, at least not in the normal sense, but rather golden-tipped appendages or tentacles that seemed to ebb and flow at need. One of these was hovering over Marta's unmoving corpse.

It was the Cirrian.

A chair flew at the apparition, passed entirely through it without apparent effect, and shattered against the iron stove.

"Git out, ya murderer! What 'ave ya done?" Tyke appeared now, sidling from the hidden corner of the living room, moving warily toward the front door. He saw Altira standing in the hall.

"Synthe! Git out, it's killed Marta!" He whipped one of the steel rods from the bundle of shanks near the door and prepared to throw it, javelin-like, at the monster. With blinding speed, one of the tentacles flashed toward the Dwarf but Tyke somehow deflected its golden tip with the steel and dove to the right, out of its path. The tentacle whipped back and, in the process, knocked the oil lamp from its chain by the door. The lantern crashed explosively to the floor, its glass shattering below the Cirrian, engulfing the monster and everything around it in choking orange flames. The creature hissed and leapt to the ceiling, lashing another tentacle at Tyke, fast as lightning.

But already the Dwarf had leapt to his feet and was dodging again, with even greater speed this time. At full force he shouldered through the closed front door, shattering it into a thousand splinters, then continued through and jumped off the railing outside, and out of sight.

The naphtha fire had taken purchase in the floorboards. Altira coughed and backed down the hall, away from the thing, as thick, acrid smoke filled the room. The horrid stench of burning flesh and worse assailed her as she wiped her eyes to see through the choking blackness for an escape. She laid a hand on the wall and tried to back toward her room, watching for the monster, but it was impossible to see anything through the fire and smoke.

Almost faster than thought, one of the flimsy yellow tentacles pierced the flames, its golden tip a blur of speed. Before she could think, it struck her chest. There was a moment of intense cold and a blue flash. She was blasted backward, crashing against the wall at the end of the hall, stunned by the impact.

Stunned, but miraculously still alive.

Sheer reflex kicked in even as her dizziness lingered. Visualizing the alley she'd seen through the window of her bedroom, Altira drew the passing magic and leapt into the Darkness. As the utter cold embraced her, she desperately prayed she hadn't jumped too low. Passing into the ground would be fatal.

She popped out several feet above the alley and merciful luck placed her above a stack of hides waiting for the `Tanner. She fell into these back first, rolled off, leapt to her feet, and nearly collided with Tyke, who was racing around the far corner of the building.

"What in the name of da Five Lords of da Felshar was dat thing?" he yelled, skidding to a halt. He turned to look up at the orange flames starting to curl from the attic of his house.

"A Cirrian," Altira said. She palmed one of her sildars.

"A *what*? That's impossible. How could … but they—"

The window of Altira's room exploded outward in flames, showering the alley with shards of glass and wood.

"Caw! Marta's still in dere!" Tyke turned and tore around the corner of the building.

"Tyke! You moron, are you insa—" But he was already out of sight. *Skies!* Now what was she supposed to do? She should leave him behind and get out, and fast. "You stupid, suicidal Dwarf!" she shouted. Then she shoved her sildar home and raced after the thief. The stupid little man would no doubt kill himself trying to drag his sister from a house threatened by more than just fire.

Altira spotted the racing Dwarf halfway down the back of the building. "Tyke … stop!" she yelled as shouts of alarm echoed from down the street. She had only moments before they'd be discovered by the fire brigade.

She reached the opposite end in time to see Tyke bounding up the outer stairs as thick, pluming smoke poured through the shattered doorway. Try as he might, though, there was no way he could enter. The courageous Dwarf only made it halfway up the stairs before the heat and vapors drove him back. He tried several times to brave the inferno and was about to dive into certain death when Altira grabbed his arm.

"Listen, dorf, if you want to throw your life away, I'm not going to stop you, but look at that fire. Do you really think there's any chance, even after the Cirrian's strike, that Marta's still alive?" She locked her eyes with his. "You can't avenge her if you're a toasted cinder."

Tyke tore his arm from her grasp. "Leave off! Ya ain' got no idea—" Tyke turned away to rush one last time up the stairs but his gaze was drawn skyward and his soot-streaked face turned an ashen shade of gray. Altira saw it as well. The Cirrian was swirling around the corner of the fully engulfed house and descending directly at them like a narthak rushing prey.

Altira instantly leapt over the banister and ran from the horrid creature as it approached, rippling in the stiff breeze from the harbor.

Tyke thudded to the ground behind her and caught up, yelling as he came. "'Ow in the fracas do ya fight dat thing? My sword did nutin' and flames din' give it pause."

Altira tried to remember what `Tan had said. "Dark," she blurted out. "Dark and cold is the only thing." She reached the end of the alley and stopped, unsure of the best way. The Dwarf reached her and rushed past.

"Dis way! I know! Follow me!" He turned into another alley and raced down the street. Altira hesitated then looked behind. The monster was nearly upon them, but it wasn't moving as quickly outside as it had indoors. Without thinking she fol-

lowed the Dwarf. Tyke ran across the road and into another alley.

"Where are we going?" Altira yelled as she raced down the passage, alert for others. Running into the town sheriff would be all she needed. For the second time, she nearly collided with the lumbering midget who had come up short, just inside the passageway. "Get on with it!" she screamed. "He's right behind us!" They both glanced back, trying to see around the corner of the alley.

"'Ere! Git down 'ere." Tyke ran to what looked like an outhouse and yanked the door open. The darkened, ramshackle enclosure covered a steeply raked stairwell descending downward.

Altira ran to him. "What are you doing? What's this?"

"Escape route. Earthen tunnels." He looked back. "Hurry! It be plenty dark a hundred cubits down."

She squinted into the pit below her. For someone completely inept at burglary, this Dwarf was showing impressively quick thinking. She hesitated. `Tan always said, "Allies are just enemies with their swords sheathed."

"Go!" Tyke shouted, and pointed behind. Altira didn't need to look. Throwing caution to the skies, she grimaced and leapt down the steps two at a time. *One enemy at a time, just deal with what's in front of you.*

A large room greeted her at the bottom, carved from the bedrock. Several casks were stacked behind the stairs, and there were a number of crude, dust-covered cabinets. One of the doors was open slightly, revealing tools. Tyke leapt down and took in the cave.

"Dis way, quick!" He beckoned to her and then raced into one of the tunnels framed by thick timbers. The passage was a snug fit even for the short Dwarf, which meant Altira had to try to keep up half bent over to avoid ramming her head into the numerous support beams. The way was illuminated by evenly spaced globes of ghostly luminance embedded in the rocky roof. The Dwarf was some distance ahead. While she was falling behind, Tyke was clearly in his element.

"Where does this go?" Altira shouted. The Dwarf didn't stop. "Where are you taking me? Tyke, wait, you imbecile. TELL ME WHERE WE'RE GOING!"

The Dwarf finally halted to let her catch up. "Da entire town is underlaid with escape tunnels," he replied, then dashed away, toward a split in the passage. Without pausing for a moment, he turned left as Altira scurried after him. "I t'ink it best if we head north, eh? Toward da plains?"

Altira turned to peer behind, trying to sense pursuit. She couldn't detect the Cirrian, which had a most distinctive feel. It would be nearly impossible to locate them underground, even if the monster could fly down here, which Altira seriously doubted.

"Sinthe!" Tyke's gravelly call echoed off the rough stone walls. "Dis way." He popped his head from a tunnel junction ahead, motioning for her to follow.

"All right, all right, don't get your britches in a bunch. I'm coming, you twit!" She scowled and ducked down the tunnel, trying as best she could to follow the nimble denizen of the depths.

Tyke finally slowed a bit. "Don' you worry dere, Sinthe, that ting'll never find us in 'ere."

"Stop calling me that!" Altira nearly rammed her head into a timber, ducking just in time.

The Dwarf came up short again. "What? Call you what? What'd I say?"

"Sinthe. Stop calling me Sinthe. It's not my name."

"An' 'ow'm I 'sposed ta know dat, eh? You said—"

"I know what I said, you half-height, stocky version of an ogre. Do you think I go around telling everyone my real name?"

The Dwarf responded by placing his fists on his hips and rooting himself to the naked stone of the floor. Altira waited to see what he would do, but it was pointless. She glanced behind and tried to sense pursuit, then turned back. Could she find her way out of these horrid tunnels alone? Doubtful. Her glare returned to the Dwarf.

"Go!" she urged, but clearly he had no intention of continuing until she was more forthcoming. "Oh all right, you annoying little twerp! It's Altira. A-l-t-i-r-a. All right, you happy now?"

Tyke didn't say anything, just nodded once, spun around, and recommenced his mad dash down the tunnel. Altira was forced to fume in silence and follow as best she could. At least they were putting a good deal of distance between them and the murderer of Tyke's innocent sister.

CHAPTER NINE

THE WAY TO TELFALL

THANK THE LORDS OF LIGHT FOR THE FRESH AIR! ALTIRA WANTED to fall to the ground and hug the warm and welcoming grass. Escaping from the horrid tunnels was like emerging from a grave. Tyke stood a few paces away, at the top of a shallow ravine, gazing south, toward his city.

"Holy Lands of the Felshar," he mumbled in amazement. "It's killed the brigade. Caltra is done for." Tyke's voice was tinged with a fear that Altira had not before heard.

A huge pillar of gray-black smoke billowed skyward in the distance. Altira scrambled to the top of the mound. The view confirmed the nightmare. More than half the town was engulfed in a horrific inferno that threw plumes of orange and red hundreds of feet in the air. Thousands of dwarfs had swarmed onto the three ships and were clustered about the railings. The vessels had been hastily pushed into the bay where they were trying to tack against the wind, attempting to put some distance between themselves and certain doom. The remaining population was streaming past the wharf to the safety of the hills, south and east, along the coast, carrying whatever possessions they could.

"We need to get out, Tyke," she said. "We're too exposed up here. He'll find us for sure."

The Dwarf scowled and started down the hill. "Dat fiend will answer fer dis, I vow it." Reaching the base of the mound, he looked around, perplexed. "But where do we go? All my stuff was back dere."

"Listen, Dwarf. Unless you have an army, you need to get as far away from that thing as you can. It's after me, anyway, not you. You should get as far away from me as you can."

"An' where, exactly, am I supposed ta be goin', eh? I canna go back ta Caltra! I say dere's strength in numbers." He took a step nearer.

Altira backed up and waved him away. "Are you insane? I'm telling you, you can't come with me. Find somewhere else. Surely there's a Dwarven city nearby."

"Only Telfall, an' dat's over four days' hike, way into da mountains."

Altira fingered a sildar and considered her options. Doing the annoying little man in was certainly one choice but something in her heart forbade that alternative—he was here because of her. Still, she didn't need any more complications in her life right now, and the annoying little twit would only slow her down. She felt an almost irresistible desire to pass, and quickly. A subtle thought popped into her mind.

"Wait a minute. Did you say you knew the way to Telfall?" Altira bit her tongue the instant the words fell from her lips. What was she doing?!

The question lit up the Dwarf like a firefly in Ferubah. "Of course!" he beamed. "Da Dwarmak must be tol' about dis atrocity." He paused a moment, considering. "I've never act'ally been meself, but me cousin, Baldor … 'e 'as been many times an' he told me da way."

Altira sighed and rubbed her face with a tired, dirty hand. She was such an idiot! How did she ever let that slip? She should just go invisible and jump away. But then, if the Dwarf could take days off her journey, the annoyance might just be worth it. At least till they got to Telfall. And as much as she hated to admit it to herself, the reality was that they were in this situation because the Cirrian was chasing her and not through any fault of the Dwarf.

The journeyman smith took her confused silence as acquiescence, glanced at the hazy sun to get his bearings, and lumbered past her, going east. "Right, den. We'd best be getting on. I wanna put as much distance as we can b'tween us an' dat thing before ni'."

Altira stood, staring at his back, arms crossed as he departed. Eventually the Dwarf realized she wasn't following. He was halfway up the rise at the end of the ravine when he turned back, a confused look beclouding his simple features. She stayed rooted as he jogged back.

"Whassa matta dere, missie? We got ta git goin' or he'll be catchin' us!"

Altira sunk into her right hip and put on her most condescending look. "Tell me, *Dwarf,* how many times have you risked your life in a chase?" A scowl that would shatter wrought iron was ample response. "And who do you think knows more about the monster that is chasing us?"

Tyke grimaced and crossed his arms, but didn't reply.

"So … we'll not be *lumbering* around in the middle of the day, when the Cirrian is strongest and when he can easily see us from any vantage point in the clouds." She waved her arm for effect. "We wouldn't get half a league before he'd be on us. Oh, and what weapons do you have, or supplies, or anything?" She knew by the collapse of his scowl into a worried frown that she had him cowed now. "So, we won't be 'getting on' as you put it, we'll be …" She bounded up the hill and cautiously peered over the crest. "We'll be heading toward those woods over there." She pointed to a dark thicket to the southeast. "And we'll be takin' cover until it's dark, when the Cirrian is weakest and unable to see."

With that, she shifted her pack and marched toward the welcoming woods. A subdued mumble and the scuffling sounds of her companion followed her.

Skies, she thought. *This Dwarf just may be the death of me yet.*

They entered the forest. The trees were dark and seemed welcoming. The sweet aroma of pine needles and peat embraced her like an old friend. Tyke remained sullen, clearly less comfortable amongst the living denizens of the forest than he had been dashing through his underground tunnels.

After about a league they came to a large depression filled with needled scrub surrounded by fir and pine trees. The light of the late afternoon sun cast a dappled, cobweb pattern on the leaves and branches. Altira could easily hide in the thick brambles, but they would need somewhere more covert for the Dwarf or they'd be discovered. Maybe she'd just go invisible and creep amongst the branches and let the Dwarf find his own hiding place.

"'Ere, miss. Methinks dere be a cave behind dese rocks."

Altira tore her eyes from the welcoming thicket. "What? Where?"

Tyke had continued on and was standing at the base of a small hillock with a jumble of moderate size boulders at its base.

Altira plodded over to him with some reluctance. "There's no way we can squeeze in there. The cracks are way too small." It would be sheer insanity to attempt a Shadowed Passage into the unknown space. For all she knew there was solid rock behind the pile of rubble.

Her companion grunted in response and laid a calloused hand on the foremost boulder. It was half Altira's height and must weigh at least two hundred stone. The Dwarf cocked his head a moment, staring at the huge chunk of weathered limestone, then he moved around it, gripped it with both hands, placed one foot against the face of the cliff, and heaved. Altira leapt back as the great impediment came free with a sucking sound and tilted away from the hill. Tyke wasn't even breathing hard as he shifted the stone aside, revealing a promising, narrow abyss bracketed by two other boulders.

The Dwarf looked at her and wiped his hands on his trousers.

"It's still not big enough," Altira complained. "There's a nice thicket back—"

Tyke silenced her with a raised, dirty finger. She put on her most indignant glare.

The equable Dwarf smiled and turned to work on the leftmost rock. It was smaller and he shifted it with less effort.

She had to admit that the opening was starting to look promising. "No, no. Don't roll it that far. We'll need to replace it when we're inside or he'll see." Her companion stopped and Altira moved around the lumbering midget. The opening was big enough for her to squirm inside. "Leave it and let me look."

Altira cast magisight and squeezed through the opening. It was thoroughly dark inside, and even with enhanced vision, it

was still difficult to see at first. There was water trickling somewhere in the back, but the echoed sound of her footfalls on the scree covering the floor told her that the cave was of moderate size. When her eyes adjusted, she beheld a small enclosure with a pool of water at the back. A mat of exposed roots descended from above, forming a `Tangled, irregular domed ceiling over her head. There appeared to be another fall of rocks at the back as well, perhaps an additional exit. It was perfect.

"Right. Come inside and pull that thing back where it was," she called.

After a moment, Tyke wriggled backward through the crack and, reaching through the opening, he walked the boulder back in place. He stepped away to investigate the cave himself.

Curious, Altira leaned on the stone he'd rolled into place. Then she pushed it, hard. She couldn't budge the thing. For the second time that day, she considered the puzzling little man.

Even as she watched, Tyke took a step in the darkness and fell flat on his face, tripping over a rock embedded in the floor.

"Krakas, how can ya see in here?" He pushed himself upright and brushed his hands on his trousers. Altira gestured at him with a hand and mouthed the vision magic. Tyke came to his feet and considered her, amazement suddenly written on his face.

"Wha'? Wow, dat be great. Wha' did ya do, missie? I kin see!"

"Stop calling me missie, you imbecile. My name is Altira, if you recall."

"Ri', sorry, den … Altira." He scanned the enclosure. "A nice bit o' space, dis. Hey! Dere be firewood e'en. I'll get us a nice blaze goin'."

"Dwarf, have you completely lost your mind? You want to send up a pillar of smoke to lead the Cirrian right to us?"

"All right, now, da name be Tyke, an' I'd appreciate if'n ya use it, A-l-t-i-r-a. I'm sorry, all right? I ain' used to dis sneakin' and hidin' and carryin 'bout like we's afraid." He went to the far corner and plopped down in a sandy spot, looking glum.

"Well, we *is* afraid, at least we'd better be if we're going to live through the day. Do you have any concept of who's chasing us? You saw it kill your sister. You saw what it did to the town. Doesn't that terrify you?"

"Nay, I've nae got fear." He picked up a nearby weather-worn chunk of obsidian. "Da chil'ren of da rock don' fear death, nor do we b'leve in vengeance as ye of the Dark Fores' do. Marta has crossed ta be wit' our family in a betta place. Dere be nae reason fer anger or grief. But I'll say dis to ya. Dat thing had nae right to come into our house after you, nae right ta kill da fire brigade an destroy da town. 'Tis a blight an' a curse on da land and it needs be dealt wit', and that harshly. When we git to Telfall I inten' to be talkin with the Dwarmak hisself. We'll see how well dat t'ing does agin' a legion of Dara`Phen. Dey be immune ta poison. We'll see how well it does agin' the thousand silver'd magic cleavers of the `Phen."

The concept that the Dwarves might have a force capable of defeating the Cirrian was an interesting revelation. Altira was none too certain, however, that they would fight in defense of some Dark Elf that happened upon an innocent Dwarven city and brought destruction in her wake. More likely they'd chop her into a thousand bits and consider the problem solved.

She found her own sandy spot on the opposite side of the water and bent to fill her flask from the shallow pool. The liquid was clear, cold, and invigorating to the touch. "So, how far is it to Telfall?" She tapped the cork in her flask and propped herself against a rock next to the pool.

"Well, as I say, I've not been there afore, but it took me cousin maybe three days ta make it, strollin' casual-like. That was wit' proper victuals and gear, mind—none of which do we 'ave."

"What's between us and the city? Open plain? Mountain passes?"

"Got no idea, tho' da north road from Caltra do follow da mountains den east. It be a well-traveled path. I'm sure dere'd be an inn or two." The stocky smith rubbed his stomach. "I could do wit' a bit o' ale an mutton or some of Marta's—"

At the mention of his sister, he stopped and stared into the rivulet of water winding its way under the far wall of the cave. A forlorn look passed upon his face at first, to be replaced with a strange air of peace. "She had a way wit' cookin', did sis." He shook himself from his memories. "Anyway, I'm sure we kin find vict'als tomorrow."

"There is no way I'm going to follow a common road—he'd expect that. Is there a back way into Telfall?"

"Aye, dere be seven ways to the great city, tho' most know of only two or three. If'n we follow da coast to da east, there is supposed ta be a wharf 'n' road through da mountains."

"Will there be many at the port of Telfall, then?"

"Nay, not at dis time'a year. Most of da traffic do come through Caltra 'cause da road be more passable. The Telfall wharf be mostly for warships and da like." Tyke stirred from his spot and dipped his cupped hand into the water. "Should take less den a day ta get dere."

"Good. We'll wait till it's dark then, and make for the wharf." Altira got comfortable, hugging her pack and feigning sleep for a moment to see what the Dwarf would do. Tyke finished drinking, returned to his spot, and curled into a ball at the base of the cave wall, apparently content to make the sand his mattress.

They rested in the cave for the remainder of the day, Altira taking quick naps interspersed with attempts to detect the Cirrian. No telltale sounds or scents came to her. Apparently, as a result of their subterranean escape, or perhaps as a consequence of the smoke and haze from the destroyed city, they had managed to evade the assassin, at least for the moment.

Just after dark she nudged her companion awake and jumped through the rock wall to the outside. Her ability with the Shadowed Passage amazed the simple Dwarf, who had to shift the stones enough from the inside to squeeze out of their hiding place. Altira ignored his questions and, navigating by the stars, made her way toward the coast and hopefully a safe path into the Dwarven capital. She had no idea what she was going to do after that.

CHAPTER TEN

BACK DOOR

WHERE WAS THE STUPID DWARF? ALTIRA PEERED THROUGH THE shrubbery and across the corrugated, sandy beach dotted with brittle, windswept marram. Below her, a rude cluster of buildings hunkered at the end of a weathered pier, as if they were the only anchor holding it to the continent. It had been *hours* since Tyke had left, promising to return "ri' away" with supplies and intelligence. She should just leave. Why had she ever trusted the stumpy little man, anyway? Altira shifted her weight to her other elbow and looked up the twisting road behind as it weaved into the hills. The shadows were starting to lengthen. It would be dark in a couple of hours and she needed to be well into the mountains by then.

Enough of this interminable waiting, already! She pushed to her knees, casting one last glimpse down the beach. A small form emerged from one of the buildings and turned in her direction. Altira squinted; it was Tyke, and he was carrying something on his back. The stocky figure waddled up the road, his shadow angling through the golden grasses. The crescent bay behind contained three Dwarven warships swaying in the gentle waves. There didn't seem to be many sailors about; the wharf was quiet, with only a single wisp of gray smoke curling from the chimney of the inn.

Altira sighed and settled back into position. It took the Dwarf forever to ascend the hard-packed dirt road that edged the beach, trudging along in his annoying side-to-side wobble. How could someone that could outrun a Cirrian be so abominably slow when unchallenged? She had worked up quite an annoyance by the time Tyke reached the top of the hill and peered into the waist-high brambles.

"Missie, you dere?"

Altira passed into the Darkness and popped out right behind him. "You certainly took your time, blockhead! What took so long?"

Tyke turned slowly, as if expecting her. "Din' take long atall, missie. I got ta talkin' wit' one of da pilots in da inn, an' I had ta barter me ring for some victuals an' dis pack." The stocky Dwarf shifted the huge bundle on his shoulders. It must easily weigh as much as Altira herself.

"Have you no sense at all?" she asked. "We're supposed to be *sneaking* into Telfall. How do we do that with you lumbering all over the road with a kit the size of Tandara the dragon? We are climbing *into the mountains*. Do you intend to lug that up these hills?" She gestured angrily at the jagged purple mountains.

"Don' you be worrin' 'bout dat, miss—"

"Stop calling me missie, or I swear I'll shove a dirk in you and leave you here to bleed to death!" Altira palmed a sildar and tossed it in the air once, putting on her fiercest look.

Tyke eyed the glimmering point of her knife and smiled. "Now, now, don' be getting yer elbows all akimbo. All right, I'll call ya Alti, like ye prefer. Dat better?"

"It's Alti-*ra*." She glared in resignation and shoved her sildar back in its sheath. "Just follow if you can, but I'll not be waiting around for you to haul that monstrosity up any of these hills." She marched up the road.

The former smith shifted his enormous pack and lumbered after her. Altira glanced back at him now and then, surprise turning to begrudged admiration. What had looked like a waddle from a distance turned out to cover quite a bit of ground, and efficiently at that. Though the Dwarf shifted his weight from foot to foot, he didn't seem to tire doing it and easily kept up with her as they ascended into the foothills of the massive Carthakian Range.

The first portion of the road was steep and they climbed steadily until the evening sun descended into the rippling cobalt waters far below. The light was fully gone when the road angled left and meandered down a jagged ravine cut from the towering mountains, hiding the magnificent vistas from them.

"Alti, can I git yer magic sight, please? I kin 'ardly see where I'm goin' 'ere."

Altira waved a hand in the Dwarf's direction, casting vision for herself as well. The umber and black shadows were transformed into ghostly images in shimmering teal. "How far is it, do you know? To the entrance?"

"Dunno, never been on dis road. Though da innkeep said it was a day's walk to da service gate on the south, I'm nae sure where dat be."

"Remind me again … Why did I bring you with me? You don't seem to be much help."

"Me sparklin' personality?" He flashed her a toothy grin.

"Yes, that's it, no doubt," she muttered, turning and continuing up. They ascended through a myriad of switchbacks and massive granite bridges, climbing ever upward, getting ever closer to the Dwarven capital.

They took most of the night, ascending into the silent, darkened pinnacles. In the wee hours they stopped to rest and Tyke revealed that the monstrous pack he'd been lugging up the hills contained mostly food. There were several tiny casks of ale, black bread, some vegetables, and what looked like most of a side of pork. Altira wondered idly what kind of ring the Dwarf could possibly have possessed to barter for all of it, but it was none of her business. She accepted a carrot and two apples with a nod and watched in amazement as her companion polished off an entire cask of ale, three meat pies, and several slices of pork, burping loudly afterward. She scowled and shook her head. Dwarves were such barbarians.

They rose and continued upward. The air, chill at first, became downright cold after a while and Altira had to pull her coat from her pack. The Dwarf, however, didn't seem to require additional clothing and trudged on without complaint. It was nearly dawn when the well-traveled road finally descended into some sort of valley. The moonless night made it impossible to see more than a few score cubits even with magisight, though she sensed they were coming to a large open space. When they discovered a stunted beech tree clinging to the sloping, rocky

ground to the right, Altira decided it was time to stop. She led them into the rocks at the base of the cliff some distance behind the tree to wait for dawn. As the sky over the jagged peaks began to brighten, she finally saw that the path descended into a gentle valley carpeted with grass and diminutive trees. The road hugged the right wall of the canyon and terminated at a pair of huge granite doors on the northern side, embedded in the bare rock of the mountain. She turned to her companion and whispered.

"Is this it?"

"Aye, reckon i'tis."

"What do we do? How do you get in?"

Tyke threw his pack to the ground and sat on it, wiping his brow in spite of the chill. "We need ta wait fer da day-guards. Knockin' will do nutin'—I doubts dey will e'en hear it."

Altira scowled and settled down amongst the boulders, taking cover behind a blue and black chunk of granite. As if she would actually knock on rock—how crude and pointless. On the other hand, not knowing what lay on the other side of the doors precluded passing. Knocking might be the only way to actually get the doors open. Waiting to check things out was definitely the right plan. She fished some bread and fruit from her pack and waited to see what transpired by the light of day. At least they had a good view of the valley from their protected vantage point.

Not much happened. The silvery light of dawn evolved into a glorious morning and yet there was no stir in the silent valley, save for the occasional buzz of a bumblebee or horsefly. This must be a little-used entrance.

Tyke was snoozing some distance away, clearly unconcerned about discovery—he was a Dwarf, after all; they wouldn't skewer him with a thousand arrows on sight. Could the absurd little man snore any louder? She poked him with a foraged stick and was rewarded with a grunt. The fool frowned at her, rolled onto his other side, and promptly went back to sleep. Altira retreated to her rock and chewed on some toma. Occasionally she would cast about with her mind, seeking for signs of pursuit, but there was nothing. The occasional chatter of chipmunks or the call of a wild eagle soaring high amongst the purple crags were the only significant sounds that permeated the silence of the valley. Would the stupid Dwarves ever come out? Did they sleep all day long, the lazy dolts?

The morning was half spent before the creaking sound of an approaching wagon echoed off the canyon walls behind them. It seemed to take forever for the vehicle to breach the hill and descend into the valley. It was a huge, four-horse conveyance driven by a shabbily dressed pair of dwarfs sporting gray, soot-ridden clothing. As the wagon drew nearer, Tyke stirred and wiped the sleep from his eyes. Spotting the cart, he came closer to Altira. The wagon passed below them. It was open and heaped to overflowing with coal. Dust clouds swirled behind the vehicle whenever it hit a pothole or stone in the road. Altira coughed in spite of herself.

"Must be da daily delivery," Tyke said. "From da mines in da south. C'mon, dey'll have ta open fer it."

The Dwarf grabbed his pack, rose, and started toward the gate but Altira hissed and gestured to him.

"Get back here," she whispered. "I'm not going to just wander up to some sentries and hope they don't mind one of the Alo`Dara coming for a visit. You get in and I'll follow behind, hidden."

This confused her traveling companion at first and Altira had to give him a shove before he started back toward the doors. She went invisible and crept amongst the shadows of the cliff base as far as she could.

The wagon lurched closer to the great stone portals then ground to a halt. The two drivers didn't do anything—just sat and waited. After a few long moments, a horrid rumbling was followed by the sound of stone grating on stone as the gigantic barrier parted. When the gap was sufficient, two guards in shining armor stepped out and took position on either side of the opening gateway.

Tyke was still some distance away and had reached the main road, some ways behind the wagon. Altira matched him on the east, creeping among the boulders scattered along the base of the cliff. As soon as the portal was fully open, the lead driver clucked to the team and the huge draft animals heaved the laden wagon through the doorway. When it had passed inside, Tyke came into view of the guards, following the wagon. The Dwarf on the right raised a restraining hand and stepped forward.

"Stay, there! What b'iness have ye 'ere. Dis be not the ri' entrance fer visitors. Git ye roun' ta the main entrance on da wes' side. Dis be only fer coal wagons an' da mil'try."

"I've come ta visit me cousin Bardok, an' I have some dire intelligence fer da Dwarmak. Da city of Caltra 'as been destroyed. I also needed ta get some t'ings from da wharf, so's I tooks da southern ro'. Can't ya let me in dis way? I don' wanna have ta go all da way roun' da mountain!"

"I have me orders—an' dere from the Dwarmak hisself. Ya canna come in dis way. It be barred for anyone but da supply wagons and mariners. Ya 'ave ta go roun' to da front. Now git on wit' ya!"

The surly guard gestured sharply and rested a hand on his short-sword, tilting it forward. He was clearly not going to budge. Tyke was displeased with this development, and clearly showed it. During this exchange, however, Altira had sidled along the cliff base and had managed to sneak from rock to boulder until she was just behind the guards. It would be a simple thing to scamper inside. She cast her sight forward. Or even better, she should jump around the guards, avoid the slim chance of being detected, and leave the annoying Tyke behind. Yes, that was an excellent notion; pass right past them, all the way into the corridor! She sent her mind forward into the gap past the gate. Simple. She sensed an unusual feeling of power just inside the corridor, but otherwise the way was clear.

The wagon had passed through. Tyke looked around, clearly dejected, then scowled and trudged away, toward the other entrance. The guards were retreating inside, following the wagon. There was no time left to ponder. Altira waited till the sentries were inside and the doors had begun to close. Focusing well within the corridor, she passed. The welcome Darkness embraced her and she reappeared in the center, well inside the great passage, just as the doors boomed closed. It was a dimly lit, cavernous tunnel. Excellent! Now to find—

A strange, ominously painful hum filled the air. Altira clutched her head with both hands and collapsed to her knees as the sound increased in force until it seemed the walls themselves were screaming. She cried out and fell to the ground. The last thing she heard was the shout of the guards and boots pounding toward her as oblivion descended.

CHAPTER ELEVEN

CAUGHT

IT WAS WET. FOR AN INSTANT ALTIRA THOUGHT SHE WAS BACK IN Nar`oo. Had she forgotten to latch the shutter on the window above her bed? Had the thatch on her roof developed another gap? No, she wasn't on her comfy divan … She was somewhere hard and cold. Her cheek was half dead with chill and her head was pounding as if someone was smacking her with a tree limb the size of an ancient oak. Why was she lying on stone? And where was the light? She couldn't see a thing!

Altira groaned and pushed herself to her knees with arms that felt more like rubber than flesh and bone. She nearly passed out as a sparkling wave of dizziness spun through her head. She barely held back a retch.

"Oh, stop," she mumbled to no one in particular, as if trying to impede whoever it was that was whacking the back of her neck. It felt like her skull had been split in two by a bolt of slimy green lightning. There were tiny little stars now, dancing in the dark like a cloud of putrid gnats just out of reach. She rubbed her eyes and tried to calm her churning stomach.

"Wha … where am I?"

Her voice echoed sharply off walls that were far too close for comfort. This wasn't her pode! She was in some kind of horrid rocky room, pitch-black, damp and cold. Blearily, Altira wove magisight … but nothing happened! This cut through her haze like a knife. She'd never failed that spell, even as a first-year Greenie she'd gotten it right on the first attempt. Her inability to execute this most trivial of skills swept the swirling mists from her mind in an instant as an electric chill shot up her spine. She had … she was in Telfall—she must be!

Groaning, Altira squinted, shook her head, and tried to focus. Mercifully, the dizziness receded, to be replaced by a palpable emptiness. It felt like someone had sucked half the life out of her. She laid a hand on the floor and rolled to her knees. The movement caused the darkness to recede a bit, not from any act of hers but as a result of the increased glow emanating from a grimy yellow sphere set into the wall on her left. She was in a cell. There was a stone bench with a single blanket, presumably some kind of crude bed, and she faced a huge, black-banded door on the far side, accessed by three stone steps. The floor was comprised of black stone, worn smooth by untold pacing. Altira shivered, then rose and stumbled to the bed-platform. She nearly fainted with the effort, but at least the nausea was receding.

From her seat she could see her pack lying on the floor in the back of the cell. Gathering some strength, she fetched it and returned to the bench. There was food and a few belongings inside, but her sildars and spare dagger were missing. She found the water flask and took a drink, then nibbled on some toma. It

did wonders. Her head felt almost normal, and her strength was returning. How long had she been in this horrid place? What had happened? How did she get here? Altira focused. The last thing she recalled was passing through the wall from outside, into the corridor. Then, the screaming walls and blackness. Of course! The entry had been warded. In her haste to get inside, she'd foolishly ignored the telltale signs of magical protection.

"Stupid, ignorant, smelly, inconsiderate Dwarves. I hate you all!" Her voice bounced back at her from the unyielding stone but produced no discernible result.

Well, fine. *Enough of this, then.* There wasn't a cell made that could hold Altira of the Alo`Dara. She shouldered her pack, shook her head to clear it further, then crossed to the iron-bound door. It shouldn't be hard to pass beyond. She tried to cast her vision through the wood but couldn't. Try as she might, she was unable to sense anything outside the cell. This second failure of a fundamental skill shook her to the core. Something was horribly wrong. Never before had she been unable to jump. What *was* this horrid place? What cursed, damp, cold lifeless magic prison had she been thrown into?

The walls began to press in. Altira wasn't used to being confined in closed spaces. She gritted her teeth and forced herself to calm down. Fine, she'd just wait for them to come and then she'd go invisible and walk out. As an experiment, Altira next tried the invisibility spell—and failed that, too.

Frigid tentacles of terror started to snake into her mind. She stepped back from the door. "Ohhh, you are so going to pay for this, you horrid, stumpy, useless, smelly, ignorant little band of turds!" she screamed at the unyielding wood, as if it could hear her tirade. "When I get out of here, I'm going to strangle every single one of you then feed you to the narthaks of Kelicost—in bits!"

The only response she got back was the sound of dripping water in the far corner of her cell. The lifeless black granite walls watched with eternal dispassion, utterly unaffected by her tirade. She returned to the crude bed and collapsed upon it. Well, at least she was out of reach of the cursed Cirrian. If she couldn't sneak into the city, there was no way under the seven skies some horrible, floating jelltar could. So fine, the one thing she *could* do was wait. She wouldn't give them the satisfaction of seeing her break. Her chance would come. She still was a hundred times faster than any stupid, smelly Dwarf.

She dropped her pack and pushed back on her cot, then crossed her legs and sat upon the scratchy wool blanket. They had to come for her eventually, and they would be sorry. Oh yes, she hadn't even begun with the ignorant underground rodents in this place.

ALTIRA HAD NEARLY REACHED THE END OF HER THIRD SERIES OF centering exercises when the sound of muffled footsteps approached from outside her cell. She closed her eyes and focused, forcing herself into relaxation. It was four steps from the cot to the door. She could easily vault over the heads of the guards if they came close enough. *Bide your time … Fear is the destroyer … Patience.* There was the audible clanking of keys and a click as the door lock disengaged. Altira fetched her pack and readied. The door swung inward and the glow-light brightened, casting the cell in stark illumination. She blinked in the brilliance.

A Dwarven soldier stepped in, clearly someone of rank from his attire. Two other stumpy men were behind him. When the officer entered, he was scowling. He wore an elegant short-sword at his side and cast an appraising look in her direction as Altira sat on the stone bench across from him, then gestured for his companions to enter. They did so, closed the door, and positioned themselves on either side of the stairs leading to the slab of oak. The officer-Dwarf approached.

"I be Lorin, capt'n of da third regiment of the Dara`Taen," he said, his hand upon his weapon. "What were ye doin', tryin' to sneak inta Telfall? An'don' be tellin' me no lies. I'm fermil'r with the dev'ous nature of ye Dark Elves."

Altira considered him narrowly. The time was not yet; the door was closed.

Her silence didn't impress him. "C'mon, you. Out wit' it, or do I need to call a mage to extract da truth from ya?"

"Bring him," she replied, her voice dripping with disdain. "You will find the Alo`Dara are made of firmer stuff than you imagine. No pitiful Dwarven dabbler in magic is going to extract anything from me."

The captain squinted at her for a moment then tried a different tact. "Okay, now look. We know ya was tryin' ta sneak in. We watched ya all mornin' wit' that Dwarf ouside da south'rn service gate. Why would one of ye Dark Elves be friendly wit' one o' us, and why would ya be tryin' ta sneak inside if ya already had someone ta vouch for ya? What were ya tryin' ta steal?"

The fact that they had detected her and Tyke didn't surprise Altira—her inept companion was hardly inconspicuous. The question was, how much else need she reveal?

"I wasn't here to steal. I was trying to hide."

"*Hide?* Why in the fracas would you *hide* in Telfall? That makes no sense, missie!"

Altira chuckled, in spite of herself. "You know, you're absolutely right. It makes no sense at all. Nothing makes sense these days. I've no idea why I'm inside this dank, depressing, horrid city. Only because he can't kill me in here, I guess."

"He, who? Who are ya talkin' about?"

"The Cirrian, of course."

"Oh, come on. What do you take me fir, a flyin' imbecile? Cirrians don't *kill* people. Dey're creatures of light, of culture an' finesse. Dey are the consorts of Guardians, not evil like y'all! Tell the truth now!"

"I *am* telling the truth, you little twit!" she yelled back. This stunted little man was starting to get on her nerves. "Slay me if you can, and be done with it. I'm sick and tired of running all over Salustra and having to deal with you stumpy excuses for real people."

"Now hold on dere. I'd not be givin' offense if I were you, or I'll jes' have ya thrown in da firey pit. We'll see how well ya do da backstroke in molten lava!" He paused a bit, calming himself. "Now look, as far as I kin see, yer only crime so far is tryin' ta sneak in by da back way. Don' be makin' it worse by throwin' roun' insults."

"Whatever. I told you the truth, you ... *Dwarf.* All I got back was more questions. Kill me or go away—just stop boring me with pointless queries."

Lorin caught her gaze, challenging her to look away first, but was disappointed when he didn't succeed. She sat there and stared him down. Finally, he seemed to come to a decision and stepped closer, glancing at her pack. "You say some Cirrian is chasin' ya?"

She raised an eyebrow and considered him with a bit more interest, then replied very slowly. "Yes, as I *already* said. An *assassin*. Hired by the Sultan." She cocked her head.

"Al`Taaba hired 'im?"

"Are you deaf as well as short?" She glared at the Dwarf, willing him to step closer and for the door to open so she could bound over his head to freedom.

"There may be—" He turned to one of the guards. "Feltok, fetch my cousin. Tell him we may have news regarding that Celthoth creature."

"Sir!" The guard on the left saluted smartly and ascended the stairs, cracking the door just enough to slip through.

Altira scowled and continued to wait as Lorin turned back to her.

"What's yer name, lassie? An' be truthful or I swear I'll leave ya in 'ere ta rot into blackened bones."

She considered him for a moment. There was no advantage in hiding her identity. Perhaps a bit of honesty would prove useful. "I am called Altira."

This seemed to satisfy him. The Dwarf captain began to pace back and forth at the foot of the stairs. "Right, now we're makin' progress. So how did ya come ta be outside wit' dat other Dwarf?"

"He asked to accompany me to Telfall."

Lorin stopped his pacing and pointed threateningly in her direction. "I said be truthful, Elf. No Dwarf'd accompany an Alo`Daran willingly. 'E had ta be yer captive. Now what did ya do ta make 'im come wit' ya? Did ya threaten 'is family?"

"Of course not, you idiot. Why in the Five Lords of the Felshar would I drag a Dwarf to the steps of Telfall? Tell me that. Are you crazy? I did everything I could to get rid of the annoying little twerp but he just wouldn't go. I have no need of—"

She was interrupted by the return of the guard, who was accompanied by another Dwarf dressed in a red robe. They cracked the door and slipped through without presenting any opportunities … *again*. The new arrival was clad in an impressive crimson garment with golden stitching at collar and cuff. He spoke with a refined tenor and was clearly well educated.

"All right now, Lorin," he said, "what's so important that you have to drag me from Borin's lecture?" The red-robed Dwarf peered at Altira through bushy eyebrows. "And who is this Dark Elf?"

"'Er name is Altira. She's been tellin' us 'bout a Cirrian assassin dat was 'ired by the Sultan of Fu."

"You don't say. That is most interesting. But what makes you think she's telling the truth? The Alo`Dara are notorious liars, you know."

Lorin measured Altira with a knitted brow. "I believe 'er, least 'bout da 'ssassin'."

Altira glared right back at him. "Oh, thank you *so very* much. Your faith in the obvious is just staggeringly impressive."

The robed Dwarf smiled quizzically. "She has quite a tongue, doesn't she?" He descended the stairs and came closer. "All right now … Altira was it? Tell me of your encounter with this alleged murderer. And leave nothing out, please." He glanced over his shoulder. "Corporal, get me something to sit on. This may take a while."

Altira was intrigued. What a strange development this was. Why in the seven skies would this red Dwarf care about her predicament? Well, no matter. She had all the time in the world, and the more they talked, the greater the chances were for

escape. Altira recounted the whole revolting tale from the Sultan to the cell, all the while seeking some opportunity to get away. She recounted her banishment by the Dar, and as she told the story, a strange feeling came over her, as if a huge weight was being lifted from her back. She wasn't the only one in the world that knew of her dilemma now, though she doubted these incompetent Dwarves could offer any aid. When she told how Tyke's sister had been attacked and the city destroyed, a look of fury o'ershadowed the red-robed Dwarf called Gentain.

"You mean to say this monstrosity attacked a Dwarven female … and it was he that impeded the fire brigade in the protection of Caltra … and that he was the cause of that inferno?"

"Precisely." Altira was surprised at how angry it made her to recount this part of the tale.

"And you saw it prevent the fire brigade," Gentain said, "with your own eyes?"

"Well, no, not with *my own* eyes. You'll have to ask Tyke about that. But after we escaped from it, the city was already half destroyed and the fire was threatening the ships in the harbor. The only thing that could have prevented the brigade would have been the Cirrian."

"The fiend!" Gentain clutched his robe in a fist, his eyes wicked slits. His gentility and easy manner fell away for a moment, revealing an inner fury that was most impressive. "And let us be clear," he said, mastering his anger, "you did not force yourself into this home or sneak in, you were invited by Tyke?"

"Yes."

"And you had no part in the fire?"

"None. It was started by that yellow ball of slime."

The mage considered her narrowly. Altira sensed that some kind of magic was being employed, but it was beyond her ability to discern its nature. Finally the Dwarf rose and paced to the rear wall and back, fuming. Altira could feel the arcane power gathered about him.

"No creature—man or beast—can destroy an entire Dwarven city with impunity. We will deal with him, you can rest assured of that."

Lorin, who had been standing behind the mage, near the door, growled. Gentain raised a single finger, silencing the captain, and then returned to his stool. "Now. When he attacked, you say he *grew* a tentacle, and then struck at you?"

Altira nodded. "He was floating in the smoke."

"I've never heard of one of the air-dwellers attacking anyone. They are a generally peaceful, introspective, altruistic race, although your description of this creature is most compelling. I don't think anyone could manufacture a Cirrian from sheer imagination. There is a serious flaw in your story, however. If this monster struck you, then why are you still alive?"

Altira shrugged. "Frankly, I dunno, but I think it may have been the pendant."

"Pendant? What pen–"

Lorin stepped forward and extracted Altira's necklace from a pouch at his belt, dangling it in front of his cousin's face. "We took dis from 'er before we locked 'er up—an' it took some serious magic to get it off 'er, I can say."

A look of complete astonishment overtook Gentain. He reached for the amulet. "You had— This can't be—" He took the glittering gem from his cousin and examined it carefully. "Incredible. The Azure Amulet of Malchrist. How in the seven skies did you come by this?"

Altira smiled crookedly—so the pendant *was* special. "Well, it was just lying around in Fu. I picked it up on a trip there."

This evoked a grunt from Lorin. "Lying 'round … Of course it was."

His cousin was more circumspect but was also visibly impressed. "Let me understand. You got this from the Sultan?"

Altira nodded.

"And this is why the Cirrian is after you."

"Yes, the horrid thing."

"You have no idea what it is, do you?" When Altira didn't respond, he continued. "This pendant was stolen from the Dwarmak's private vault over two moons ago. We suspected one of your people was responsible for its theft, although we've not been able to prove it."

"Well, it wasn't *me,*" said Altira. "Why in the seven skies would I steal the thing and then bring it back? It makes no sense at all."

"Agreed. You would be a fool to do so."

Tiny amber rainbows of color, refractions from the light in the cell, danced across the mage's hands as he turned the gem in his fingers.

"So," Altira asked, tentative for the first time in this grilling, "what is it for?"

Shaking his head, Gentain clutched the amulet, rose, and moved toward the door. Then, seeming to change his mind, he turned back. "It is a shield," he told her. "It protects the wearer from a single strike, physical or magical."

"What do you mean … *single?*"

"It takes the gem a while to regenerate. It will protect you once, but if an opponent strikes a second time before the gem is refreshed, the blow will reach its target." The mage nodded to Lorin, who gestured for one of the soldiers to open the door.

Gentain herded the others out and stood on the top step for a moment, considering Altira from the doorway. "If your story is true, you may have performed a great service to us, strange though that may be." The red mage squinted at her. "A bizarre turn of events, to have one of the Alo`Dara return something stolen by one of their own kin. We shall see what the Dwarmak says."

The mage left and the door shut with a resounding boom.

The sound of the portal closing jolted Altira. Lords! She'd been so astounded at discovering the true nature of the amulet that she'd completely missed her golden chance to escape! She rose, climbed the steps, tested the solid door, and then gave it a resentful kick. The probability of getting another chance to escape was about as great as surviving a bath in Lorin's pit of lava.

CHAPTER TWELVE

ALLIES

ALTIRA TRACED THE BORDER OF THE HEAVY WROUGHT-IRON HINGE for the hundredth time with her finger, looking for some weakness in the metal. It would be a trivial thing to use magic to slice through it were she a mage, but even if that were the case, it would still be impossible given the enchantments in this wretched place. In the days she'd been in this cell, she hadn't come up with a single working spell. She punched the solid oak in sheer frustration.

"Ow, you horrid thing!" Altira winced as she pulled a splinter from her knuckle, then kicked the door in retaliation. "Stupid Dwarven wood. The trees in Nar`oo would never—"

Her mention of the Dark Forest sparked a moment of clarity. The door was *wood!* Altira pondered for a moment. Would her mastery over the arboreal also be suppressed here? She couldn't recall ever specifically drawing upon the cha`kri when she opened her table at home, nor had she used a sigil, as was always required when drawing upon arcane forces. She just *did it.* Which meant … could she part the wood in the door without the cell's protective magic sensing it?

She shifted to the opposite side and placed two fingers gently on the rough surface of the oaken portal. It was ancient, hewn eons ago and nearly petrified from breathing the air in this awful place. There *were* fibers, though. She traced the grain until she found the right place, then focused. Bending closer, she tried to reach into the wood with her mind. It was difficult—the stiff fibers were resisting—or no, not the door, but some magic woven into it. The enchantment was fighting her invasion. The wood wanted to bow to her will but was restrained by the magic. Altira focused, pushing harder with her mind. The natural struggled against the arcane, and the wood slowly prevailed.

Several tiny cracks issued from inside followed by a satisfying snap as a finger-wide gap opened in the door.

"Yes!" Altira leapt for joy then bent to continue, but hesitated—there was someone coming. The footsteps stopped right outside. A key was inserted in the lock followed by a grunt and a dull thud. Altira hurried to the bed and assumed a meditation pose, sitting cross-legged, willing herself to calmness.

"I can't. It's stuck, drat it!" A complaining voice permeated the thick wooden timbers. Someone was not pleased.

Altira smiled.

"Whaddaya mean, stuck? It was all ri' da las' time."

"Tyke, if you would, please …"

There was a rattling followed by a boom that shook the hinges. The door didn't budge, as if the wood itself was revolting from centuries of abuse.

Altira chuckled to herself. "Serves them right." She closed her eyes and smiled more widely.

The next impact evoked a shower of dust from the door casement—she could even feel the impact through her sleeping pallet—but still the door held. That was followed by silence for several heartbeats. Finally there issued forth some sort of battle cry and the door exploded inward, splitting in two at the point of her division, leaving a hands-width chunk of wood including the lock and latch still clinging tenaciously to the door frame.

It was all she could do to not laugh out loud. She closed her eyes once more and forced herself into calmness.

There was a stunned, dusty silence for a good while followed by the sound of someone kicking through the debris at the top of the stairs. She squinted in the direction of the door.

The red mage was framed in the remains of the jamb, surveying the destruction. He turned his accusing look upon her.

"All right, then, what did you do, Elf?"

Altira smiled benignly and considered the magician. "I have no idea what you're talking about. It's your cell, not mine. If you can't maintain your prisons, it's certainly not *my* problem. It does look like you'll need a new door, though." She smiled faintly and returned to her centering. They wouldn't be using the door to slip in and out anymore, that was for certain. A chance to escape was approaching. She could feel it.

Gentain scowled at her, and Lorin shouldered around the befuddled mage. "All ri', now, ya elfie. We got plenty o' cells ta spare. We'll jes throw ya in one with a steel door!"

The mage grabbed the captain's tunic. "Hold a moment, Lorin. We can't move her. Her powers will return the moment she's outside the wards."

"Well, tha's jes fine. I'll be knockin' her out den." The stocky captain drew a narrow club from his belt and hefted it.

The fire kindled in Altira's eye as she judged the distance to the door, but her anger was replaced by astonishment as none other than Tyke stepped into the cell, blocking the portal yet again. He was carrying the mage's three-legged stool. "'Ang on dere, cap'n. Let me talk to 'er," he said, descending the stairs. "I don' think force'll be required. 'Specially when we tell 'er what da Dwarmak said."

Lorin exhibited a strange deference to Tyke, paused, and lowered his club, clearly disappointed. "I nae trust dis one, sir. Methinks she's better off a-sleepin'."

The red mage laid a restraining hand on Lorin's arm. "He is right, captain. Let us speak to her before we resort to violence. Tyke, bring the stool."

The captain clearly wasn't happy, but he sheathed his club and stepped to the foot of the stairs. "All ri', but I'll be watchin' da door so she kin nae escape." He backed up the steps and took position in the broken jamb as Tyke handed the mage his stool. Altira finally noticed Tyke's attire. The former burglar was adorned in a much-improved outfit. The singed and wrinkled leathers had been replaced by a thick, well-formed burlap-like set of garments and a leather jerkin. A short-sword hung at his side and he was wearing new, shiny black boots. He appeared nothing like the bumbling thief Altira had encountered behind the inn in Caltra. Who was this Dwarf, anyway?

Gentain accepted the stool and sat, adjusting his robe. Altira took a deep breath and tried to center. She pulled her legs up and focused. The wool blanket was starting to itch, but she ignored it and watched Lorin like a hawk. They were just a bit too far away to leap over and the cursed captain was blocking the exit now. The time was not right, but it would come. They had shattered the door, after all.

The mage continued, seemingly unperturbed. "So … mistress. Much has transpired since our last meeting. Would you care to know of the Dwarmak's decision?"

Altira turned her attention to the mage. "Why would I care about the opinion of the leader of a bunch of ignorant, smelly half-men?"

The red mage dismissed her insult with a wave of his hand. "We know that it was not your intent to return the amulet. You did not part with it willingly and further, you were caught trying to sneak into the city. You had no intention of relinquishing anything. It seems illogical, however, to conclude that you were the one who stole the talisman—there was no gain for you in returning to the site of a former crime. Also, had you pilfered it from us you obviously would have been able to enter the city without being caught. The fact that you stumbled into the tunnel wards is powerful evidence of the truth of your story—which does, in fact, interest us. In addition, the fact is, the amulet is now back in our possession as a result of your actions, whether or not you intended it, and the Dwarmak accounts that to your credit. He is a generous man—more generous than I would be, given the same circumstances."

Gentain extracted a scroll from an inner pocket of his robe and scanned it.

"You are to be relocated. And clearly"—he twisted to survey the shattered door—"that is advisable." Returning his gaze to her, he continued. "We have made a small dwelling available. It has taken a bit to prepare it so it will be proof against your particular skills." He gestured at Altira with the scroll. "Know that even though your new quarters will be comfortable, your magic will remain suppressed for the time being and you must agree to remain confined within."

Altira smirked and narrowed her eyes as she considered the cracks in the opposite wall. "I'm actually rather comfortable here. I think I'll stay indefinitely. You can keep your pitiful Dwarven hovel."

"I must say, I don't appreciate your attitude. We've gone through quite a bit of trouble to get you released from this cell. I would think a little gratitude would be in order."

"You knock me out, you throw me in here, you feed me slop for days, you take away my magic, and then you expect me to be *grateful*? You're lucky I don't slit all your throats and leave you for dead!"

This drew the captain from the door, growling. He nearly drew his sword, but was brought up short by the mage, who raised a hand.

"Mistress, you have three alternatives." He ticked them off on his fingers as he continued. "A number of the Dwarmak's advisors would have you thrown unceremoniously into the pit of Tarak`Nor. Others favor locking you in a cell and throwing away the key. Myself, Tyke, and a few of the Dwarmak's closest advisors believe you have intelligence and abilities that will be helpful in a particular effort of great importance to us. It's your choice, of course, but I would think that cooperating would be to your benefit." The mage knitted his brow now, displaying a firmness that was impressive. "Understand one thing, however. You will not escape from this cell. If you harbor some thoughts that you would be successful in accosting us and fleeing, please dispel them."

The red mage gestured casually over his shoulder at the door. The remnant of the portal was ripped from its thick iron hinges as if it were weightless. The door flew across the room and slammed into the back wall, then slowly disintegrated before Altira's eyes into a pile of steaming sawdust as if it was being attacked by a million invisible termites. Tyke, who had been standing on the landing at the top of the stairs, vaulted off at the mage's first gesture, diving out of the way of the careening wood.

As the last remnants of the door were reduced to yellow detritus, Gentain turned back to Altira, smiled, and replaced the scroll in his robe. He then brushed a few stray bits of sawdust off his garment and looked up.

"So, what is it to be, mistress? Will you help us, or do you wish to be encased in enchanted steel for the rest of your life?"

Altira gritted her teeth and considered the remains of the decimated door. Her estimation of these Dwarves changed markedly in that instant, but she was not about to relinquish a life's worth of distrust in a single moment, in spite of the capability of the elemental mage.

"Fine," she said, mastering her emotions. "But I will need *real* food, not the rancid victuals I've been given. I need fresh vegetables at the very least."

Gentain smiled, clearly pleased with her decision. "That should not be a problem, mistress."

"And … at least one plant, and … and some fresh water."

"So, I gather you've decided to accept your new accommodations and aid us in our quest?"

Altira frowned at him. "I seem to have little choice, do I?"

"That is a perceptive observation."

She slid to the front of the bed and the mage raised a hand.

"There is one other thing," he said. "The only way to ascertain the validity of your intent is for you to be questioned by one expert in the art of detecting perfidy. Now, before you object, know we do not intend to cause you pain. We simply wish to determine your motives with certainty. We have communicated with one of exceptional … sensitivity, and he has agreed to journey here at speed."

Altira shifted back and stared at him with some anger. "I have no intention of submitting to some stupid inquisition." She retreated to the back of her bed. "If you don't believe me, that's your problem, not mine."

Tyke, who had been silent during this exchange, now stepped forward. "Alti, now look. I know dat ye've been nae treated well, but it's yer own fault. If'n ya had come wit' me to da fron' entrance instead of tryin' ta sneak in like ya did, well everyt'ing would 'ave been fine. Ye'd be in a nice place wit' food 'n' water, 'n' everyt'ing. Please do wha' Gentain 'ere asks. Dere be stuff happenin' dat ye don' know, an' dere's a lot ye can do ta show yer value to da Dwarmak."

Altira squinted at her former traveling companion, her doubt obvious.

"What Tyke says is true," offered the mage. "And the alternative is hardly desirable. Without some assurance of your intentions, we cannot permit one who is not a Dwarf, and worse still, an Alo`Daran, to roam these caverns alone. I'm sure you appreciate that. If you will submit to the interview, you will be free to roam the city. And again, I promise, no coercion will be employed."

Altira scowled. "And how long will it be until this so-called investigation takes place? I'm not sitting in some cell for weeks on end, waiting. The cursed Cirrian will find me for sure." At the mention of her pursuer, she squirmed on the scratchy blanket in spite of herself.

"You need not concern yourself with Celthoth. You are quite safe as long as you remain in the city. For one thing, there are magical wards of exceeding potency that guard not just the entrance but the passageways—as you well know—but in addition, no Cirrian would be able to descend into the city. Not only do they require sunlight to survive, but the air in here is quite toxic to them. Something about sulfur and the metal vapors from the forges in the lower levels. No, as long as you are inside Telfall you are quite safe, and the interview should take place in only a day or two, in any case."

Altira fumed in silence. She hated the situation, but a couple of days wouldn't be too bad, and Tyke's words did hold some prospect of a brighter future, at least. She certainly was well done with this damp, cold, confining, minuscule cell with no green and little prospects of escape.

"All right, then." She slid off her pallet and stood. "Let's get on with it."

The red mage smiled and rose from his stool. "Excellent! I will escort you to your new quarters. Please put this on."

He reached inside his robe and extracted a silver neck-collar, offering it to her. Altira took it and turned the shiny circlet in her hands.

"What is this … thing?" she asked, holding back a comment about the crudity of Dwarven jewelry.

"It is a device to maintain control over magic. I will remove it when we arrive at your new quarters."

Altira gasped and dropped the cursed thing to the floor in horror, then backed away from the glittering monstrosity. "Are you insane? I won't touch the horrid thing! I'd rather sit in an iron prison for a thousand years."

Tyke came forward and retrieved the circlet from the floor. "A warded metal cell or an enchanted silver circlet—it's all da same, Alti. Eh? An' dis collar is only for a momen'." He looked at her, kindness in his eyes. "It's all ri' dere, missie. It won' hurt, an' it's only till we git to yer new place, which is real nice—I've seen it. I know ye Elves of Nar`oo are skittish 'bout yer magic but trus' me, dis is da only way. Da clasp is on da back, see 'ere." He opened the circlet and offered it to her.

Altira scowled at him for a long moment, undecided. She glanced at the remains of the door and back to the circlet. Finally, she snatched the horrid band from the Dwarf and snapped it around her neck, quickly lest she change her mind. "All right, fine. Now what? What other atrocities are you intending to foist upon me?" She crossed her arms and stared at the mage.

Gentain ushered her past Lorin, who was clearly none too happy with the situation. His sword arm twitched as they passed and his fingers gripped his weapon with white-knuckled intensity. Clearly the captain would have preferred her to put up a fight and Altira was none too certain that was not the better option. As she exited the cell, she was sorely tempted to rip free from the mage's grasp and bolt down the corridor in a mad dash for freedom, but Gentain's demonstration of his arcane abilities had convinced her against it. If she ran, he would simply exercise some form of cursed elemental magic to restrain her.

The passage was brightly lit by several glowing spheres embedded in the ceiling and was immaculate. At least these stumpy people had a decent sense of cleanliness. It was also strangely capacious—very unlike the tunnels under Caltra. Seemingly, the passage was designed to accommodate more than just Dwarven traffic. The red mage led to the right and down the corridor to a set of ascending steps. They climbed. Altira had always prided herself in being able to remember the intricate pathways to and from objectives, but it wasn't long before she was hopelessly lost in the myriad twists and turns.

"Who designed these horrid tunnels?" she complained after a while. "Some half-asleep, drunken Dwarven architect with a broken quill and no ink? There's no sense or logic to any of 'em."

The red mage chuckled in response. "They weren't *designed* really. They follow the veins of ore, mined eons ago by our ancestors. Afterwards they became the tunnels we know an' love. You'll get used to 'em after a while. It took me ten years to master all of them."

Altira snorted and followed closely. Ten years? It'd take her a few days, if that.

Eventually they came to a door on the right. Two square pillars of cut limestone and an elegant cornice framed an entrance cut into the wall. There was a single guard standing on the left. He nodded to the red mage and saluted Lorin.

Altira and Gentain entered. Inside was a brightly lit, fairly spacious room containing numerous potted plants. The ceiling arced over them in a smoothly plastered dome, which glowed pleasantly, illuminated from its circumference. The exits, one each on the left and right, were framed with cylindrical pillars festooned with verdant ivy. There was the faint sound of trickling water issuing from somewhere. The mage reached for Altira and she recoiled.

"It's all right, lass," he said. "I just want to remove the neckband. Come back. Yes, that's right."

Altira permitted him to approach and Gentain executed a complex sigil with one hand. The band released and he deftly plucked it from her neck as Altira stepped back.

Gentain pocketed the circlet and gestured toward the glowing amber dome above. "These are actually rooms reserved for ambassadors of the Alo`Kin," he said. "I trust you won't be too offended. I had hoped the plants and water would be more acceptable. Methinks you'd not be comfortable in a traditional Dwarven domicile. We prefer crystal and rock to vines and potted plants."

"It's fine, I guess," replied Altira, somewhat surprised at the health of the vines.

"All right. Now lass, when I leave, a magic barrier will form at the doorway. Please don't try to breach it, nor … um, *tamper* with the wood? No more shattered doors, please?"

Altira graced him with a crooked smile.

"I will return this afternoon and see how you are doing." He turned to exit and his eye was drawn to a potted ficus, standing to the left of the door. Gentain reached out and traced the edge of one of its emerald leaves. "So delicate, they are. So unlike the bounty of the mines …"

The red mage shook himself from his reverie and moved to the door, then turned back to her. "Food will be brought later. They will inquire as to its acceptability. Oh … by the way … the bath is down there, to the right." His cheeks turned a rather amusing shade of pink at his implied suggestion.

Altira realized that she did, indeed, need to avail herself of soap and water. She picked at the jerkin she'd been wearing now for what, a week? "Are there, perhaps, other clothes, as well?" she asked.

Gentain seemed amused. "Indeed, although I'm afraid the colors might be a bit too ebullient for you. There are garments that should fit in the bedroom to the left, in any case, and also a place to eat and write if you feel so inclined." With that the mage bowed and exited.

Altira looked about the room. It certainly was an improvement from that nasty, tiny cell—and there was even green! The air was nearly breathable as a result. She supposed she could

endure this place for a while, especially if she was safe from the Cirrian. She crossed to the door and traced a fiber in the wood with a finger. It was young and pliable, but also hummed with hidden wards that were even more powerful than those binding her former prison.

She was still a captive, in spite of her improved environment.

CHAPTER THIRTEEN

INSPECTION

IT WAS TRULY EMBARRASSING. ALTIRA SUNK DEEPER INTO THE STEAMing tub and peered through the pinkish foam floating upon the water as if she were gazing over a range of strangely buoyant, sudsy crimson mountains. She desperately hoped no one could sneak into her bath.

Apparently the Alo`Kin didn't believe in proper soap, like any self-respecting Elf. They had degenerated into using this frilly, absurd method of cleansing themselves—foaming pinkish crystals, tossed into the water. Although, she had to admit, it certainly was relaxing. And the bath was really hot, warmer than she'd ever thought possible. She scooped up some of the foam and scrubbed at her hair then ducked underneath to rinse. This was certainly better than lying on the cold ground in some forsaken forest, all alone.

Altira sprawled back and sighed. It was amazing how being clean changed your outlook on life. She grabbed another handful of the bath crystals from the urn next to the water inlets and tossed them into the tub. There was a hissing sound followed by a nearly volcanic-like eruption of pinkish foam that spread across the water like magic white lily pads. If anyone from the Dark Forest caught her at this, she'd be the object of endless ridicule, if not instantly labeled a traitor. It was one thing to be fastidious, but only those prissy, do-good, holier-than-thou, frill-loving, tree-hugging, empty-headed Alo`Kin would ever take a *bubble bath*. It was just … just … so *mindless!* But still, she was locked in here; no one would find her, and Altira had surely earned a bit of decadence. She'd spent the last two weeks trudging all over Salustra, being abused by Dwarves and lying around in a dungeon. And she wasn't Alo`Daran anyway; she'd left that life behind. Why not live a little? Besides, a long, warm soak in pinkish fluff was just plain relaxing, in spite of what they might think in Nar`oo.

After lounging in the soapy water till her fingers resembled sun-dried figs, she stepped out, wrapped herself in a soft towel, and found the clothes closet. Gentain hadn't been kidding—the clothes within were truly Alo`Kin monstrosities. She mumbled a luck-prayer to the Dark-Elven God of Fashion and delved deeper into the wardrobe.

She lifted the hem of a pink cloak trimmed with some sort of awful, fuzzy crimson fur and shivered. "You are kidding, right? Greenies are such prima donnas. How could anyone make, let alone wear, something so horrible?" She dropped the cloak as if it were infected with the mange and hunted further through the frilly foolishness, finally finding a dark green blouse and accompanying black trousers and jerkin. The silk shirt was a bit too loose and the trousers didn't fit exactly—the legs were too long—but all in all it wasn't bad. She yelped for joy when she pushed through the clothing and discovered a pair of black dragonhide boots, stuffed way in the back of the closet, as if they had been hidden. They were just her size and would make the whole outfit worth the work.

She sat on the bed to pull on the boots and was astounded at the comfort of the mattress. She'd not had a decent sleep in—well, in ages! She lay back, secure in the knowledge that for the first time since the nightmare in Fu she was relatively safe. It took only a moment for her to fall into a dreamless slumber with one boot on and the other foot dangling lazily over the edge of the bed.

ALTIRA AWOKE TO THE SOUND OF SOME SORT OF CHIME. NOT SURE what it meant at first, she sat up, rubbed the sleep from her eyes, and cast curiously about the unfamiliar room. The movement caused the overhead glow-lamps to jump to life. Embarrassed that she'd slept so soundly—and with one boot on—she quickly donned the other boot and stood.

"Altira? We're coming in." The muffled sound of the red mage's voice came from the front room, through the door. It was followed by a rattle of keys and the squeak of iron hinges. Altira rose and sauntered into the front room as Gentain and Tyke entered.

"Ah, there you are," said the mage. "We thought you'd escaped! We rang three times."

"I was … sleeping." Altira scrunched up her nose and stretched, then plopped into one of the chairs arrayed along the back wall. "So, what? Have you come to drag me to yet another dismal dungeon?"

"Ya doin' all right in here, Alti?" Tyke asked as he sidled around the red mage to finger the leaf of a plant, as if to verify it was indeed real.

"The name, as you well know, *Tickles,* is Alti-RA."

"'Tickles'?" Her nemesis from Caltra jerked around, yanking the leaf off by accident. "Ye'r kiddin', ri'? TICKLES?" This amused Gentain no end. He chuckled and produced the familiar silver choker from an inside pocket of his robe. "The days of your confinement may be nearing an end, *Altira.* The examiner has requested your presence."

The Dark Elf stood and reluctantly accepted the collar, tempted for a moment to throw it at them and rush through the open door. She had the advantage of a bath and a good rest. It would be easy to escape this prison. But then where could she go? At least she was safe from the Cirrian for the moment. It might be worth putting up with a few indignities if it meant she could gain the trust of the Dwarves—assuming this wasn't some sort of elaborate ruse to cheat her of her freedom permanently.

On the other hand, the prospect of being forced to tell the truth was frightening on so many levels it wasn't even funny. Well, she didn't have to answer their questions if she didn't want to. They couldn't drag a response from her—she'd just jump away. And if they didn't like her answers, the worst thing they could do was throw her out. She doubted very much they would kill her at this point. In any case, she was curious about this "examiner" person. Who was it, and what techniques would he use to discern the mind of an Alo`Daran? That might be intriguing, and she might learn something to boot.

Altira clipped the silver circlet about her neck with some disease. "All right then, let's get this over with."

They exited her apartments, turned right, and started up through a maze of tunnels. Although it wasn't long before she was lost again, the twisty corridors were beginning to make a little sense now. It took a long time to ascend to the huge atrium that was the showpiece of Telfall. The chamber was nearly two hundred cubits from the marble floor, inlaid with the gold and silver sigils representing the twelve Dwarven tribes, to the apex diamond far above. The huge jewel was apparently open to the sky, for it glittered with refracted sunlight and projected a cascade of tiny amber rainbows into the massive chamber.

Surrounding this great space were circular terraces extending from the ground all the way to the crown of the cavern, connecting to numerous doors and passages. Great marble stairs with silver banisters spiraled through these on the periphery, leading from one level to the next. Thousands of Dwarves hurried to and fro on myriad errands. The sheer size of the enclosure took Altira's breath away for a moment.

"Come, lass. We mustn't keep him waiting. This way, if you please." Gentain crossed to the great spiral stair and started up, gripping the banister tightly.

They went round and round, ascending to the very top of the massive space then turned right, into a tunnel. This continued upward in another spiral, corkscrewing into the pinnacle of the mountain. Altira began to wonder how long it would be before they popped out the top of whatever peak they were in. They had already climbed thousands of cubits—there couldn't be much more of the mountain left. Eventually they reached a pair of large pearlescent doors set into an elegant archway. Positioned on either side were honor guards clad in brightly polished silver armor over black leathers. Their hands rested on

the hilts of a pair of glowing axes with impossibly thin handles—clearly magical, those.

The red mage gestured with a hand, and the doors gracefully opened. They passed into some sort of huge audience chamber. At the far end perched the biggest bird Altira had ever seen—it had to be twenty cubits tall or more. Stationed in front of the huge red eagle sat a thin human dressed entirely in green. There was no one else in the hall and two chairs had been positioned opposite the man, who sat with his legs crossed.

A chill of terror crept up Altira's spine. She knew very well what the huge avian creature was—one of those cursed Guardian things. And not just any Phorin`Tra, it was the crimson one, the chief bird … What was its name? Norak, or some such. They were nasty, vicious creatures that could gobble you up in a heartbeat. And that man—it must be the bird's Companion. She'd heard stories. There was some kind of unholy bond between them. There were tales that the birds fed upon the life force of their captives, discarding the husks when they were finished before finding another victim to sup upon. Tyke and Gentain seemed unperturbed, but Altira wanted nothing to do with either the bird or its man. She froze just a step inside the door and instinctively cast invisibility—which of course failed due to the cursed collar. She swore under her breath and crouched protectively.

This caused Gentain to stop and turn toward her. He discerned her panic and came quickly to her side. "I know what you're thinking, mistress." His voice seemed unnaturally calm, given the circumstances. "You must trust me; you are safe here. You are under the protection of the Dwarmak. No evil may befall you in this hall, or anywhere else inside Telfall. You know my power—you have seen it. I give you my word as Dara`Chakrin. You are secure."

"I'm not going anywhere near that thing." Altira gestured sharply at the huge eagle. "Your assurances will mean little with my head bitten off!"

Tyke came to join them. "Bite yer head off? What are ya sayin', missie? 'E's not gonna 'urt ya. What could make ya think sumfin' like dat?"

"You're a Dwarf, you idiot. I'm Alo`Daran! That's reason enough for that cursed, overgrown excuse for a buzzard to gobble me up."

Altira noticed over Tyke's shoulder that the man in green had risen from his chair and was approaching. He was nearly twice the height of the Dwarves, thin and gangly, dressed like some sort of forest warder. He wore a wickedly curved ruby-capped sword that looked supremely vicious. Altira started to back toward the door, feeling for the latch as the man came near.

He stopped when Altira retreated. "Is there a problem?" he asked, his voice sounding more like it belonged to someone three times his size. It was deep and sonorous and, Altira had to admit, it carried no tenor of aggression, just polite curiosity.

Gentain turned to him. "Ah, no sir, Farthir, our ward here seems a bit apprehensive about Naroc, is all. Could he perhaps wait outside?"

The man seemed genuinely apologetic. "Unfortunately, it is necessary that he see Altira in order to perform this task." The warder approached further and stepped around the stocky mage. Altira was now pinned to the door. She gripped the handle in back of her tightly, ready to do her best to escape.

"Ak`ta e`olith, Mistress Altira," the tall man offered softly. "I'm afraid I do not know your clan. As Gentain said, I am

called Farthir." He rested one hand on the hilt of his sword, bowed with some grace, and flourished with his off-hand.

"Ak`ta—" The ancient greeting formed on Altira's lips without thought, but it was fundamentally wrong that this Guardian pawn would use the Elven appellation. Still, it was a magical greeting that assured the peaceful intent of those who employed it and required a response.

Still wary, but admittedly curious about how such a one would know the ancient tongue, Altira replied, "Ak`ta e`olith, Farthir of the Phorin`Tra. How do you know the tongue of the Ana`Ala?"

"The greeting is a phrase used by both Dark Elves and the Alo`Kin, as you may know, mistress. I use it to testify that I bear you no ill will."

This gave Altira some pause. She hadn't known that the prissy Alo`Kin used the ancient greeting, but it wasn't surprising. Both races shared a common heritage, after all.

"Come and sit, Altira. I assure you, you are safe here." The tall man—Farthir—gestured toward one of the chairs positioned near the huge bird.

Altira released her death grip on the door handle as her panic tapered to an unsettling disquiet. There was nothing for it. She had gone over all the options with Gentain back in her room. In any case, it would be far better to die here quickly, the prey of some giant bird, than to linger on death's doorstep for weeks, the victim of some cursed Cirrian poison. Besides, if she was to stay in Telfall she needed to get through this. And both the green man and the red mage had told her she was safe, for whatever that was worth. Altira squared her shoulders, gritted her teeth, took a deep breath, and stepped forward with renewed resolve.

Gentain and Tyke followed closely, lending their support. Farthir gestured again to the cushioned chair and sat himself across from her. The two Dwarves moved behind as Altira sat. Maybe she could use them as shields if the eagle struck. Surely it couldn't move very fast—it was the size of her pode, after all—bigger even, more like the size of the Dar's apartments. She perched on the edge of her chair, like a doomed sparrow under the steady gaze of a falcon.

When she was relatively settled, Farthir rose and bowed to her. "Altira of the Alo`Dara, I introduce Naroc, Phorin`Tra, Lorath de Narim." He half-turned to the great bird and gestured upward with a sweeping movement.

Altira's gaze was forced toward the gigantic eagle towering behind the man. She nearly leapt from her chair as the bird bowed toward her. It was a weird movement, not quick and aggressive, but rather much like the graceful motions of the man—not the kind of thing a predator would do at all, and entirely out of character for an eagle, or a Guardian for that matter. It was almost as if the bird sensed her fear and was moving slowly, so as not to alarm her further. Altira stared at the huge eagle, uncertain of what to do, then just nodded curtly.

Farthir turned back to her and spoke strangely now, with a completely different tenor in his voice. "I perceive ye bear some trepidation toward us, daughter of the night. I say unto you with the truth of the wind that no harm shall befall you whilst in this nest."

What was going on here? "Truth of the wind"? And who called a room a "nest"? These were not the words of a forest warder of the south; it was almost as if this Farthir person had two different personalities. She scowled and looked over her

shoulder, toward the door. Perhaps the time had come to make an excuse to leave.

"What is wrong, mistress? You seem confused," the man said, now apparently back in his original character. His seemingly effortless jump between personalities became even more bizzare.

Altira looked at him askance. "Ah … nothing. I think I left the water running in my room," she said, trying to think fast. "I need to go check. I wouldn't want to cause a flood." Altira started to rise from her chair.

The warder tilted his head to the right, as if listening to some strange, internal voice. It was the final straw. Altira rose to her feet and sidled around her chair. She glanced up nervously at the huge eagle. He was looking at the warder at the moment with some intent. She might be able to reach the door in time if she left now, while they were occupied. These Dwarves were all right, but if this was the price she had to pay—to be interviewed by some crazy person who was operating with half a bowstring—then she'd rather face the Cirrian alone, outside. At least he wasn't of dubious mental stability.

Her two companions registered shock as she started to retreat toward the door. Her hand crept to the collar. Could she yank it off? Doubtful. It was probably sealed magically. She'd have to make it back to her apartments visible, and figure out some way to cut the cursed thing off.

She had only backed a span from her chair when the bird sang. The Guardian stretched forth its neck and filled the chamber with a marvelous melody. It was at the same time both a single note and an entire symphony. It echoed from the walls and hummed through Altira's bones. But it wasn't just music; the song held a message, more powerful than words. It was the most eloquent tune she had ever heard and it carried with it the irrefutable assurance of comfort, peace, and safety.

The song went on for what seemed an eternity as every bit of tension in Altira's body was drained. All thoughts of escape, all confusion, all terror were instantly dispelled in the radiance of the magical music. The bird finally stopped and a vast silence descended upon the entire mountain. Altira realized then that there had been a myriad of near and distant noises—people shuffling through halls, the murmur of conversations on the periphery of her perception, distant hammering, the breathing of the mountain itself—all of these fell quiet in the wake of the eagle's song, as if bearing humble obeisance to its power.

She looked up at the great bird as it settled back into its perch and considered her with its onyx eyes. Gazing into them confirmed the truth of the song: there was no animus, only a deep, unwavering sense of justice, truth, and vast power. She stared at the bird, unable to break the spell of its gaze, lost in the bottomless pit of Naroc's consideration. It was like he was holding her aloft through sheer force of will, communicating the truth of her safety. The Guardian finally blinked and broke the connection. Altira nearly collapsed to the floor. Grabbing the back of her chair, she used it for support. The warder considered her calmly, his hands folded in his lap.

It took Altira several moments to find her voice. "What … what in the skies was that? What happened?"

The man looked up with a faint smile. "Naroc perceived that you did not believe my words and took matters into his own hands, I'm afraid. It is rare that he would act in this way. Few there be that hear the song of the Phorin`Tra. They use it only when the need is great."

"I don't understand. What need? Why is it so important that I trust you?"

"I can't say I understand fully," the warder said, glancing up at the bird for a moment. "But he only uses 'truth of the wind' when he's very serious about what he is saying."

"What do you mean? He didn't say that, you did. Are you … err … confused?"

Her implication that he was "slightly off" seemed to amuse Farthir, for he smiled and shook his head. "No, mistress. It wasn't me speaking, it was Naroc."

"I'm quite sure it was you, not the bird. If the eagle wanted to say something, I'm sure he could speak for himself, given that song. You appear in need of some … serious counseling."

Now he laughed outright. "No, mistress. The Phorin`Tra have not the capacity to speak as we do. Please, do sit."

Feeling somewhat recovered, and now without trepidation, Altira moved around her chair and perched again on its edge. "Well all right, then. What are you saying?"

"Naroc and I share a special bond—he speaks to me in my mind and I repeat his words. The Guardians have great power in song but lack many of the abilities we take for granted, including speech. That is why Companions are required."

"So you actually do this by *choice*?"

"What do you mean? Do what?"

"Submit yourself to the will of some bird. Don't you find that degrading?"

The warder seemed truly bewildered by her question. "Not at all. I think you misunderstand. We are *companions*, like you and Tyke. I am not subservient. We treat each other as equals. I have the greatest respect … why are you laughing, mistress?"

At the mention of the name of her Dwarven torturer from Caltra, Altira had been unable to restrain herself. The concept that Tyke was her … it was too much. "I'm sorry. Tickles isn't my *companion*. Hardly that." She saw the Dwarf scowl out of the corner of her eye and fume in silence.

"I see," Farthir continued. "Well, regardless, Naroc would never harm me. In fact, to do so would cause him the greater pain." He looked up at the bird with a fondness that was quite disarming, then turned back to her.

"In any case, let us get to the point of this meeting. The time has come to verify your intent regarding the Dwarves."

The penetrating gaze from both bird and man rested upon Altira as if she were made of glass. Even using all her Alo`Daran skills at subterfuge, she doubted just how much—if anything at all—she could hide from this pair.

CHAPTER FOURTEEN

A PLAN

AFTER ALL THE ANGST ALTIRA HAD EXPENDED OVER THE LAST TWO days, worrying over what crucial state secrets she might be forced to reveal, the actual inspection turned out to be rather innocuous, or at least it certainly started that way. Farthir, the vaunted Head Companion from Anora`Fel, began his "inquisition" by asking her what kind of food she liked. Then he moved on to a truly critical discussion of where she grew up and how she felt about her education in her Cala. They discussed her parents, how she felt about being banished, her relations with the Dar, and the benefits of living in the Dark Forest.

This was why they dragged her all the way up here? To make chitchat with the Companion of the notorious Chief Guardian bird? The longer it went on, the more cheerful she became. This was going to be a walk in the woods.

When they came to discussing her family, however, she really couldn't say much—her mother had not been forthcoming at all regarding her father, and Antarra herself had been killed by the horrid Greenies when Altira was just a youngling. She did the best she could on the difficult subject, and was about to mention her mother's death when the warder stopped abruptly and stared into the space over her head, caught in the middle of a sentence.

He was no doubt conversing with his bird, but the effect was still disquieting—as if he wasn't completely … well … sane. The man refocused. "Interesting," he commented. "Naroc says, 'The daughter of the earth doth possess a destiny that reacheth beyond the horizon. She shall yet be the instrument of great trial and pivotal change in her people.'"

Altira raised an eyebrow and considered the huge avian presence looming over them. "Okay now, look. I know the eagle is supposed to be really smart and all, and don't take this the wrong way, but what exactly is that supposed to mean? 'The instrument of great trial and pivotal change'? I mean, how in the seven skies could I affect anyone in the Dark Forest? They kicked me out, remember? I'm banished? And what's all this about reaching 'beyond the horizon'?"

Farthir seemed mildly amused. "I know Naroc's prophecies might seem rather … arbitrary at first, but I assure you, he is seldom wrong in these matters. Sometimes the true meaning of his pronouncements are not understood for many anna."

"Um, all right." Altira tapped the arm of her chair absently with a fingernail and watched the flames dancing in the hearth. "So is that it? Are we done? Can I leave now?"

"Not quite," said the warder. He cocked his head and considered her with a degree of intensity that was unsettling. The

Great Bird also bowed now toward her, its penetrating gaze boring into her. She squirmed a bit as the warder continued. "Altira of the Alo`Dara, is the account you gave Gentain regarding the attack in Caltra true?" His gaze narrowed to an intense consideration that seemed to bestow physical weight. "Were you in fact assaulted by the Cirrian and did you escape with Tyke and flee for your life?"

Altira set her jaw and stared at him evenly. "I would prefer to call it *evasion*." She couldn't help but notice out of the corner of her eye that her former traveling companion seemed very pleased with himself at the moment. "But that's basically what happened, yes."

The warder did the unsettling stare-into-space-and-ignore-you thing for a moment then continued, his inspection undaunted. "And were you a party to the original theft of the Amulet of Malchrist from the Dwarmak, a moon hence?"

"No. I never saw the thing before I found it in the Sultan's vault."

"Do you intend any deviousness during your stay here? Can the Dwarves trust you to behave yourself when in Telfall? Do you bear them any malice?"

Altira smiled, in spite of the weight of the questioning. "You mean other than bringing Tickles down a few notches? No, I have no vendettas or vows against the Dwarves at the moment." She glanced at her companion from Caltra. His prior smugness had evolved into a frown of annoyance.

Farthir consulted with Naroc for a moment then spoke with a strange lilt to his voice. "'The daughter of the earth beareth truth in her wings. She doth not intend evil and may be trusted to aid in our quest.' Thus sayeth Naroc."

The feeling of immense weight vanished and Farthir executed a strange sigil with his left hand. The silver circlet snapped from around Altira's neck and floated to him. He plucked it from the air and tossed it to Gentain, who caught it deftly.

"We are assured of your intent," asserted the warder. "Now on to weightier matters."

Altira let out the breath she had been holding and relaxed a bit, though she had to wonder what else the man might have to talk about. She needed to do something about the Cirrian, and quickly. The Dwarven city was a nice temporary resort, but she had no intention of making it her home.

Altira felt her cha`kri returning as a result of being freed from the silver circlet and went invisible to test the return of her arcane abilities. The red mage drew a sharp breath and rose from his chair. The warder and the bird, however, continued to gaze at her as if nothing had happened.

Farthir raised an eyebrow and seemed moderately amused. "I trust our faith in you has not been misplaced," he said, fingering the top of his ruby sword, which was propped against the chair.

Altira became visible. "Sorry. No, I was just … testing." She graced him with a thin smile. "What is this *quest* you were talking about?"

The man blinked. "Quest?" he asked.

"You … or the bird I guess, said I could be trusted to aid in some sort of mission? What's that about? When Gentain told me I was to be interviewed, he didn't mention helping with anything, only that my truthfulness would be tested."

"Oh! He didn't tell you? I'm sorry, he should have." Farthir scowled at the Dwarven mage, who seemed somewhat embarrassed. "This was the second purpose for our meeting. Let me explain. Your stalker may be someone we have been seeking for nearly five anna. We know only his name—Celthoth—garnered

from some rumors in the thieves' guild in Fairn. Until now, we've had no idea who this might be, or what capabilities he might possess. He is suspected of the murder of the Dwarven ambassador in Porinta, the death of two Elf-lords in Anerith, the obvious assassination of the former ruler of Cantira, the near destruction of a fishing village in the north, and who knows how many other atrocities."

Altira rose from her chair and paced to the fire then back. "What makes you think it's the same thing that's chasing me—this Cirrian?"

"First, the victims have all been poisoned by an untraceable venom. Second, the assassin breached remote chambers and locations, inaccessible by all but the most devious of assailants. Finally, the meager descriptions we have of his escape are consistent with the assassin being a Cirrian—an inconceivable notion, were it not for your report. You and Tyke may in fact be the only ones who have ever survived an encounter with this beast. He has left a trail of dead and dying all across Salustra."

Altira pulled a sildar and absentmindedly cleaned a fingernail. Tyke squirmed uncomfortably in his chair, but she ignored him. "If it wasn't for the protection of the amulet, I would also be dead," Altira admitted.

"Perhaps, perhaps not. But survive you did, and it may permit us to finally apprehend the monster."

She returned her sildar to its sheath and sat again. "So how can my mere evasion allow you to catch him? I don't see that. And besides, I thought Cirrians were all about light and truth and such. How could this thing be an air-dweller and also a deadly assassin?"

The warder seemed impressed. "Excellent questions, mistress. When Gentain first told us your tale, we flew to Cirrus and talked with the Azimuth. He confirmed the identity of the assassin. There *is* a Cirrian named Celthoth. He is an outcast from their society, an aberration renounced by the Cirrians and despised as a traitor to their beliefs. The problem is, as a race they have no concept of anger or violence, and therefore no way of prohibiting this deviant from doing whatever he wants. The Azimuth was most anxious that we do what we can to 'inhibit' his activities."

Altira kicked the leg of her chair with a foot and fingered her sildar again. "I'd love to 'inhibit' him. I'd like to make sure he never threatens anyone—Elf, Dwarf, or man—ever again. The problem is, you can't kill the horrid thing with weapons; they pass right through it. How do you kill something made out of air?"

"You got a throw off?" Farthir was clearly impressed. "That's astounding. Cirrians are fast. Most of his victims were struck before they could even cry out."

"Well, I didn't hit him *myself*." She glanced at Tyke, who had his hand on his short-sword and seemed annoyingly smug. "But I saw him in battle, and yes, they are really quick."

Once again, Farthir seemed impressed. He took in the Dwarf's demeanor and then consulted with his bird for a moment. Altira rose and walked to the window as he resumed. It was raining outside and the gentle patter of the raindrops on the glass was rather soothing.

Farthir spoke to her back. "Well, by whatever means, you two managed to evade him and that's far more than anyone else has accomplished. I shall mention all this to the Dwarmak." He glanced at Tyke and nodded.

Altira turned from a consideration of the mountains outside and crossed her arms, slightly chilled. "So what was he offered to kill me, have you any idea?"

"Cirrians have no use for money," replied Farthir. "According to what we have managed to piece together, the payment for your demise may have been arcane power. According to a Dwarven spy, the Sultan purchased an ancient scroll from Xanath Xak describing a truly dire spell. Since the Sultan—Al`Taaba—is not a wielder of magic, it is reasonable to deduce that this scroll, or more likely the knowledge it reveals, will be the payment for the contract on your life."

"A spell? That's it? It had better be one pretty impressive incantation to be worth my skin. And also, why is the Dark Lord meddling in the affairs at Fu?" She considered the carpet, clearly woven in that distant city, as she wandered to the serving table and idly fingered an unripe pear.

"I can certainly assure you regarding its worth," continued Farthir. "It is a curse that taints the very air we breathe, something a Cirrian reprobate would appreciate and, further, use. It would permit him to kill with a word from a distance. We cannot allow him this knowledge. It would incur a blight on all Salustra. None of our leaders would be safe. We must do whatever it takes to stop this monster, but as you point out, he's nearly impossible to kill."

Altira returned to stand behind her chair. "Assuming we can even find the cursed thing."

Farthir agreed. "Quite. He can hide in the clouds. The only way to catch a Cirrian is to lure him into a trap. Naroc and I should have the power to destroy him, but we lack the means to …" at this point the warder looked her square in the eyes, "… to *lure* him. The Phorin`Tra are hardly inconspicuous."

Altira smiled ruefully. "Ahh, *now* it comes together! You want to use the evil little Dark Elf as bait in some nefarious plot to catch the air-dweller. I should have known!"

"I assure you, mistress, we are not unaware of the risks. We would not ask this if there were any other way. We cannot *require* you to help us. We can only ask. But remember—the Cirrian's demise is as beneficial to you as it is for us."

Altira frowned. The idea of participating in some Guardian-hatched plan went against everything she had been taught in Nar`oo. It flew in the face of who she had been her entire life. On the other hand, there were precious few other options. Basically, it was either help these people, or go it alone on the plains of Salustra. And the red bird was supposed to be the most powerful of the Phorin`Tra. If anyone could destroy the assassin, it would be Naroc and Farthir. It was do it by herself, or do it with them and the Dwarves. The decision was obvious.

"Very well. But after it's over, I'll be free to go, right? This is a onetime arrangement?"

Farthir seemed amused at the question. "Of course, mistress, but let's just deal with what's in front of us, eh?"

"All right, fine then. What marvelous plan have you hatched with your bird?"

Hearing this, the red mage rose, stepped forward, and fished around in the pockets of his robe. "The Dwarmak said if you agreed to assist … where did I put it … ah! This should help a bit, anyway."

Gentain extracted a large black velvet case and handed it to Altira. She raised the cover to reveal the familiar amulet, its platinum chain glittering in the light from above. She lifted it from the case. Her strange attraction to the azure jewel had not diminished, nor had the sense of imminent doom it evoked.

"The Charm of Malchrist may help protect you if the assassin strikes again," the mage said.

Altira stared at the bauble, captivated by the facets in the jewel. She ducked her head and donned the talisman, then stood.

"All right then." She rubbed her hands together as if before a feast. "So how do we get on with killing this cursed thing?"

CHAPTER FIFTEEN

TO CATCH A CIRRIAN

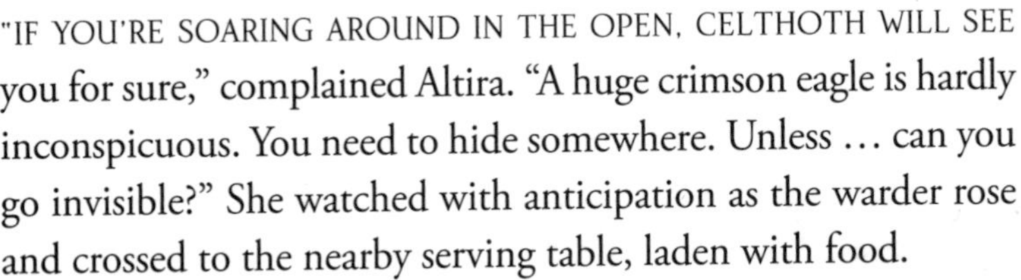

"IF YOU'RE SOARING AROUND IN THE OPEN, CELTHOTH WILL SEE you for sure," complained Altira. "A huge crimson eagle is hardly inconspicuous. You need to hide somewhere. Unless … can you go invisible?" She watched with anticipation as the warder rose and crossed to the nearby serving table, laden with food.

"No, alas," he replied. "The ability to bend light is a latent talent, unique to you Alo`Darans, not the result of magic." Farthir broke off a chunk of cheese and popped some into his mouth as he returned to his seat by the fire and mumbled through his food. "I can be 'hidden,' but it's not like true invisibility and Naroc has no such skill. Also, if we're somewhere out of view, how do we know when you're attacked? Guardians can't see through mountains, after all. And if we're leagues away we won't be able to hear when you call, if you need help."

Gentain poked one of the logs in the ample hearth, creating a shower of sparks that flew up the chimney. "And neither Tyke nor I can be near for the same reason—he'll see us. We've been over this a hundred times. Celthoth views everything from above. If we get far enough away to be hidden, we'll never get to you in time when he attacks."

"Getting to her isn't a problem," said Farthir. "Naroc can pass right to her. We only need to enchant something—a weapon or trinket, your amulet maybe—and he can sense you. It's a simple enough spell."

The Dark Elf brightened with this intelligence. "Can you tell what's going on? Can he hear me if I call?"

"No, alas. He can only find you, not tell what's going on, or see what's near."

"Then we're still left with the issue of communications," said Gentain. "I'm going to go talk with Borin. Maybe he can come up with something."

"Borin?" Altira stopped fingering her amulet, and tore her eyes from its aqua depths to consider the Dwarf. "Who is he?"

"The Chief Elemental Mage—a scholar versed in varied arcana. If there's a magical solution, he will know of it."

"Well, lovely then. Ask him how to see through mountains. Meanwhile, I'll be here deciding which jerkin I want to ruin by painting a big red target on it."

The red mage chuckled, tossed his poker into the stand by the hearth, and left without replying.

The room was silent for a minute, save for the occasional pop of the embers in the fire. Farthir's sharp features were cast in flickering red-orange relief in the glow. Finally he broke the silence. "Where is your friend, Tyke?"

"Skies, stop calling him my 'friend.'" She waved her hand at the door through which Gentain had left. "How should I know where Tickles is? I think he said something about going to see one of the smiths in the forgery. Something about lava vapors or some such."

"Really? I wonder what that's about. I met him in the corridor after your examination. He seemed rather agitated. Apparently he sought an interview with the Dwarmak and was refused."

"Refused? Why? That thing killed his sister. You'd think the Dwarves would be a little more considerate, given the situation."

This caused the warder pause. He squinted at Altira for several moments before proceeding. "You are indeed an enigma, mistress. At times you seem very much the Dark Elf, and at others, something entirely different."

"What are you talking about? Not a Dark Elf? That's crazy, what else would I be?"

Farthir rose and filled a goblet with wine. "To be honest, I'm not really sure what you are. Naroc sees many conflicting futures and 'portents' swirling about you."

Altira turned around to look over her shoulder at the huge Guardian. The eagle gazed implacably back, his unblinking raven-like eyes unreadable as he perched on his stand near the wall. Naroc flexed one of his golden-tipped talons and broke the connection with her.

Altira leaned back into her chair and smiled. "Oh, didn't I tell you? I'm really the cursed princess of an outcast ancient ruler of Anea`Na`Silithar, forced … um … forced to live under an evil spell cast by her wicked sister's brother's stepcousin who's a witch. And … and all I need is for some handsome prince to

rescue me from my imprisonment in this horrible shell of a body." Altira batted her eyelashes at the warder in mock allure.

Farthir nearly choked on his wine and still managed to spill a substantial quantity on his shirt in a fit of coughing. Finally he managed to gain control of his mirth. "Really? I didn't know princesses snuck into dungeons and stole mysterious amulets as a form of amusement."

Altira just smirked. "Now don't take this the wrong way, Farthir, but your bird is crazy. There's no way I could 'portend' anything. I'm an outcast, remember? If I set foot inside Nar`oo I'll be mulch in a heartbeat. The Dar will have every sentry peeled and then whipped to death if they allow me to pass."

Farthir sat, leaned forward, and tried to brush some of the wine off his shirt. "Perhaps … perhaps not."

Typical. Altira was starting to believe the man took lessons in obfuscation. He never gave you a straight answer if he could bend it to look like cragweed. Perhaps it was the bird's influence. She decided to change the subject. "So tell me then, how do you enchant the pendant, anyway?"

Farthir set down his cup and gestured for the gem. Altira slipped the chain over her head. It caught for a moment on a strand of her jet-black hair. She untangled it and handed the amulet over with a twinge of cupidity. The warder turned it in his palm then held it to the light. The deep blue crystal glittered in the warming glow from the fire. Altira heard a scratching sound from behind. She turned in her chair to discover the huge eagle standing right behind her. It towered over them, its head nearly brushing the ceiling. She almost leapt out of her seat. *It's just a big stupid bird, you twit,* she thought. *He's not about to bite your head off, sitting here in the middle of Telfall.* Altira forced herself to turn to Farthir and willed calmness into her heart. It only partially worked.

Her alarm increased fourfold as the huge creature bent over, its beak descending to the warder and amulet. Altira gripped the arms of her chair, her knuckles going white, and gritted her teeth. It had a strange odor up close, like exotic spices mingled with pure, unbridled power. It was not altogether an unpleasant scent and bore no hint of aggression. Altira relaxed a bit and watched the warder. Farthir squinted at the amulet and performed an intricate gesture with his hand. Naroc bent farther and there was a faint flash of crimson light that surrounded the warder's hand and the trinket. The Guardian rose and returned to his perch, his great talons clattering across the naked stones of the chamber. Farthir handed her the necklace.

Altira accepted it gingerly and held it at a distance. There was a faint crimson glow surrounding the gem. "So how close do I have to be for this thing to work?"

"Naroc can sense it and pass to you from anywhere in Salustra." He gestured at his large companion. "Although, obviously you need to be somewhere with enough space."

Except for the slight reddish glow, the amulet seemed unaltered. Altira considered it for a moment longer then shrugged and donned the pendant. As she did so, the door to the chamber burst open and Gentain entered, clearly excited.

"I'm a complete idiot!" He rushed across the floor, halting for a moment to give way as Naroc returned to his perch. "Why didn't I see Borin at the start? Took him only a heartbeat to solve the problem, didn't it?"

"What did he say I should do, then? Yell really loud?" Altira smiled as she tucked the amulet inside her blouse.

Gentain barked a laugh and plopped into his chair. "No, silly. Can`ties. I don't know why I didn't think of it earlier."

"And what in the seven skies is a Canty?" she asked.

"Can`tie. They are rare and special gems, formed in the netherworld of the mines—the deepest part. They always come in pairs, formed when the crystal lattice splits into twins under great pressure. When magically separated and imbued with power, the two crystals remain linked at a distance. Any sound impinging on one will be heard in the other."

"Interesting …" Altira admitted.

"Indeed. With them we can monitor every step of your mission and Naroc can pass to you when you call—as long as we can enchant something, as Farthir said."

"Already done," replied the warder, gesturing to Altira. "Her amulet."

The Dark Elf raised the pendant from her blouse and dangled it for the red mage to see.

"Excellent!" said Gentain. "Borin is preparing a pair of Can`tie and will have one mounted as the pommel-stone in a long knife. The other will remain with us. The assassin won't suspect if you carry an additional weapon, will he, mistress?"

"Not if it's appropriate—not horribly heavy or ugly. It needs to look like I chose it."

Gentain nodded. "Borin is aware. We'll have to see what he comes up with in the morning."

"Fine then." Altira rose and stretched. "I'm going to bed. All this thinking is making me tired." She started for the door and got about halfway there before the bird squawked. Altira ducked and spun around, prepared to jump away. But the Ruby Guardian was still on his perch. To her utter amazement, Naroc bowed to her. It was accompanied by an unspoken air of acknowledgment, as if Altira had somehow crossed an invisible threshold between uncertainty and trust. Somewhat embarrassed at her instinctive reaction, she rose from her protective crouch and bowed in return to the bird, who seemed to acknowledge her response. Altira wasn't sure how she knew—there was just a feeling surrounding the Guardian, as if she could almost read its mind. She cocked her head and then backed from the room slowly, trying to understand what had just happened. Farthir chuckled to himself as he watched, his eyes enigmatic.

It would have been infinitely easier for her to actually *be* a cursed princess. Then all she'd need to do was find some vapid prince, instead of having to consort with all these Dwarves and Guardians and such, in order to survive. If she was royalty, she'd be the queen of relentless persecution.

CHAPTER SIXTEEN

ON THE ROAD

ALTIRA HEFTED THE DWARVEN LONG KNIFE, TESTING ITS BALANCE. It was a poor throwing weapon—too heavy at the hilt—but an excellent offensive dagger. The quillions were substantial, and the blade was well forged. Its edge glittered with a razor sharpness that seemed almost eager to divide flesh asunder. The intricately carved ebony handle was inlaid with gold and silver filigree and wrapped in black dragonhide. A smooth translucent orb of deepest ruby perched atop the pommel, gripped in six fingers of platinum. Floating inside the gem was a multipointed silver star that glowed with an unearthly crimson luminance. The wicked point at the end of the slightly curved blade looked like it could pierce solid granite. It was clearly magical and one of the finest weapons Altira had ever seen.

"This is not too bad." She nodded to Gentain and stifled a smile as she retrieved the jewel-adorned scabbard from the table and slid the blade home. "It won't look too out of place."

This clearly amused the red mage. "I'm so glad you approve. That's no ordinary dirk, mistress. It has a long and shaded history, too lengthy to recount. It was made by a great Dwarven smith for the Elven race centuries ago and has been retained in the deepest weapon vaults for nearly a thousand anna. The Dwarmak exhibited a great deal of trust in choosing the Blade of Karthak for you. We hope it will not be used against those who created it."

"Karthak?" Altira's eyes grew wide. "*The* Karthak? As in the ancient winged Elvish warrior?"

"One and the same."

"Well …" She held the sheathed blade in front of her with greater reverence. Slowly she rose and, with some formality, attached the scabbard to her belt. She then bowed to the red mage with a look of solemnity. "I am honored to wield a blade with such a noble heritage. The Dwarmak need not be concerned, for I vow it shall never be used against Dwarven-kind." This seemed to impress not only Gentain, but Farthir as well. Altira turned and leaned casually on the back of her chair. She considered the warder, who was seated at the dining table. "So then, how do we start this little dance, Farthir?"

The man tossed his fork on his plate, then rose from the remains of his breakfast. He glanced at Naroc for a moment. The Guardian was nestled on his perch at the far end of the chamber. "Good question." He wove around the table and came to stand next to her, facing the fire. "Prudence is indicated. Celthoth must believe you left Telfall of your own volition. No hint of our purpose can be suggested by your escape, or by subsequent events, or the trap will fail."

Altira shifted the dagger out of the way and sat in her chair. The hilt of the weapon felt warm in her hand and strangely familiar, as if the dirk had chosen her and not the other way around. "Then why don't I just sneak out? Tell no one that I'm leaving and let me find my own way. If we announce that I'm on a mission, it will no doubt get to Celthoth."

"Agreed." The red mage was sitting in an opposing chair. "Although I would suggest not leaving by the front entrance—it's too obvious and it would send the wrong message."

"Clearly." Altira recalled the path to the back door—she had worked it out two days hence. It felt good to know she wasn't losing her touch, having been buried underground for so long. "The best way to leave would be the way I got in—by the coal gate—but how do I avoid the wards? I don't want to be thrown back in that horrid cell."

Gentain smiled. "There's little chance of that. It's going to take a month to fix the door that you … that was shattered." He paused for a moment then continued. "Anyway, all you have to do is hide in the back of one of the wagons. The wards are dropped when they pass through."

"That would have been good to know on the way in, but never mind. That should work." She rose and made her way to the door. "I'll get my stuff and call by the stone when I'm well away."

Gentain rose from his seat and came to her. He moved as if to embrace her, then thought better of it and simply offered his arm. "Good luck, mistress. Be careful."

Altira cocked her head at the man for a moment, then took the proffered arm, gripping it firmly. She gazed into the mage's eyes, nodded once, then turned and left before the moment became awkward.

ALTIRA HEAVED THE PACK TO HER SHOULDER AND SMILED. IT WAS wonderful to finally be *herself* again! The time in Telfall had ultimately proved diverting, but she had missed the sun and the open air, and the trees. Yes, to be outside would be marvelous, even if she was forced to act as bait in some devious Guardian trap.

She went invisible, snuck out of her quarters, and crept down the corridor outside, delighted to finally be able to use her magic. The few residents she passed were oblivious to her presence and the traversal to the back exit went smoothly. She reached the proper level and snuck through a cavernous furnace room lined with huge smoking pots of bubbling ore. There were a score of Dwarves about, clad in thick leather aprons and caps, but she snuck past without incident and into the next room—an equally large bunker lined with heaps of coal. She crossed this toward what was clearly the exit to the outside. As she approached, she could feel the now-familiar hum of the wards that had been her demise last time. She scampered to a small alcove on the right and hunkered down. Now all she needed was a wagon.

It took nearly two hours for the creak of an empty conveyance to echo from a side passage. She almost laughed aloud when the drivers executed a sharp right turn and made for the exit—they were the same two that had "escorted" her into Telfall the first time! Altira rechecked her invisibility as the empty wagon rumbled closer. Flattening herself into the shadows of the wall, she waited until the vehicle passed then leapt upon the back gate and clambered into the dusty bed. The powder nearly made her sneeze, but she forced control, wrinkling her nose and covering her face with an edge of her coat. Scrambling to the front of the bed, she crouched in a corner and willed herself to stillness. She was not going to mess up her exit like before.

Her departure went flawlessly. The wagon lurched through the great stone doors and into a bright noon day. Altira winced at the brilliance. *Now, time for phase two,* she thought. As the wagon passed under a large oak by the side of the road, Altira leapt upward, snagged a thick branch, and pulled herself into the tree. The wagon lumbered down the road, jostling the drivers as it hit a pothole. When it was well out of sight, she sneezed loudly and went visible.

Altira lounged for a moment on the tree limb and breathed in the pristine mountain air. It felt like she hadn't taken a breath in weeks. A glorious summer day greeted her. The wildflowers and mountain grass fairly shouted their health and vibrancy. She had forgotten how wonderful fresh air tasted. And the tree, it was fabulous. She nearly hugged it, in spite of her heritage. Its bright emerald leaves embraced her in a welcome that was as much a homecoming as any parade. How could anyone choose to live underground in that horrid crypt of a place?

Altira leapt down and found the road leading west. When she was out of sight, she rested a hand on her elegant long knife and casually tilted the pommel stone forward.

"I'm away," she said quietly. "Can you hear me?"

Farthir's voice responded almost instantly. It was thin and possessed a strange echo, as if he was yelling at the far end of a lengthy tunnel.

"Aye! We can hear, mistress, though you seem far away. Where are you?"

"Just left the valley, headed up and west. No sign of the Cirrian."

Gentain's voice replaced the warder's, a bit stronger, as if he was holding the stone closer. *"Altira, there's something I forgot to tell you about your knife. Borin wove an enchantment about it to protect you. When the Cirrian draws near, it will hum. The closer he gets, the louder will be the sound."*

She scowled. "And you didn't think this was important last night? Will this give me away? I'm not sure it's a good thing."

"My mind has been on other matters recently. I'm sorry, Alti—"

She sighed. "Oh, never mind. At least I know. I can cover it if it's too loud. I'll tell you if it sings. Farthir, can Naroc sense me?"

There was no response for a bit and then the warder responded faintly. *"Yes. He can see you in the valley. You seem like you're enjoying yourself."* There was a hint of amusement in his voice.

This response troubled Altira for a moment but the feeling passed quickly as she sprung up on a nearby rock at the crest of the hill to survey the winding path descending the mountain. The day was glorious, and she was alone at last! No Dwarf to drag along, thank the Lords of Light. At least she'd shed that part of her bizarre new existence. She leapt lightly to the ground and continued walking, unconcerned for the moment about the Cirrian. The blade would alert her if the miserable thing was near.

Her job now was to be the lure, so bait she would be. If anyone had told her a fortnight ago that she'd be depending on some Guardian and his lackey for her safety, she would have laughed so loudly they would have heard her in Finiath. What an ironic turn of events—to be banished from Nar`oo and now to be the consort of Guardians. What had she become? Well, it would make little difference who her friends were if she were a corpse lying in some road. The only thing that mattered now was to lure the Cirrian and manage to evade him long enough for Farthir to kill it.

How he'd do *that,* however, was a complete mystery.

CHAPTER SEVENTEEN

AN IMPERFECT STORM

"THIS ISN'T GOING TO WORK—IT'S TAKING WAY TOO LONG. I'LL BE in Malas by tomorrow." Altira trudged up another endless hill to peer into the shimmering afternoon sky, seeking for signs of the Cirrian.

"We must be patient, mistress." Farthir's plaintive voice echoed from the pommel stone attached to the Blade of Karthak. She was about ready to pry the cursed thing off and throw it into the bushes. The Can`tie had started out a blessing and had evolved into a curse. Absent the condescending advice bestowed by the warder, the elegant blade would be worthy. With the horrid thing attached, the knife was reduced to being yet another albatross she was required to drag around Salustra. Clearly she'd been cursed to forever be the collector of magical trinkets that only made her life more miserable. First the amulet, and now the knife. It was time to be done with this pitiful scheme.

"Patience?" she said, grabbing the hilt and raising it to her lips. "What do you know of patience? You just sit there, safe in Telfall. All you ever do is think up other people's tortures and wave your hand and make them miserable. You never have to *walk* anywhere, anyway. You *pop* all over Salustra on that wretched bird! Tell me something, Farthir. Have you ever waited three days in sewer water for an iron grate to be opened? Have you endured the sting of a thousand anticles while being tested by your Cali? Don't you *dare* talk to me of patience, *warder.* You know nothing of it!"

"Now Alti—"

"And what's with this '*we*' thing? *We* aren't slogging all over Salustra in the middle of the hot summer waiting to be attacked by some putrid cloud of yellow slime. It was a bad idea from the start. The cursed thing is never going to show. I'm telling you, it's figured out the trap. I've wandered all over the landscape for *five days* now, and nothing. Do you hear? *Nothing!* No sleep, a thousand hills, up and down, up and down, all the while wondering if my next step will be my last. You want patience? Then you come out here and do this yourself!" Altira reached the top of the latest hill and halted. "I'm telling you, it isn't working. Come pick me up. Let's figure out something else."

"There isn't anything else. We've been all through this, mistress. It's either draw him to you, or hide for the rest of your life. We can't get him otherwise. He could be hiding anywhere. He's too slippery."

This was absurd. She was getting nowhere. "All right, *fine* then, I'm walking back to Telfall." Altira turned around and started down the hill.

"Stop."

"Shut up!" She tilted the long knife forward and reached for the gem, intending to yank it off.

"We—you've been down the road behind. You know what's there; there's no place to hide. Do you want to suffer another five days of skulking about in the open? At least there's cover in Malas, and it's less than a day's journey—as you just said."

She stopped. He was right, the cursed man. No way she wanted to endure four more nights without sleep—and there *weren't* any places to hide on the road back to Telfall, that much was true. She had passed the point of no return. With a glare that would melt lead, she gripped the knife more tightly, turned around, and trudged back up the hill. She reached over and tugged once at the pommel stone, but it was much too firmly attached. Yet another reason to hate those stupid Dwarves.

Farthir fell silent—a good thing for him—and the air became cooler as the sun descended into the rolling plains behind. Altira turned from the road, looking for a good retreat for the night. She absolutely refused to spend another sleepless evening creeping down the middle of some dusty road, watching for an assassin that never showed up. Tonight she would rest, even if it killed her.

Eventually she located a small copse about half a league from the highway, sat and propped herself against a comforting beech. She dozed until a bit after midnight when she was awakened by a rustling in the grasses to the west. Clearly, it wasn't the Cirrian; this was a four-legged creature.

Altira leapt into the tree, cast magisight, and peered into the darkness. It was a narthak. The offshore breeze had carried her scent into the forest and the creature had come seeking prey, the foolish monster. And it was a big one, too, nearly to her shoulder. Narthaks resemble dogs at first. Their heads and snouts are wolf-like, but when viewed from the side they are clearly something nastier. Huge front shoulders taper to a narrow waist and hindquarters and the fangs are four times the size of any wolf's teeth. They have razor-sharp talons and mostly prey upon the wandering grass-eaters of the southern plains. It was unusual to see one this far south, though. It must be very hungry—or it had been sent.

Altira smiled. The narthak's motivations were immaterial at this point and besides, she was in the mood for some fun. It was past time to test her new weapon. She drew the knife, leapt to the ground, then sauntered through the knee-high grass, directly at the beast. The narthak saw her at once and froze, obviously confused as to why this pitiful creature would show no apparent fear. It hunkered lower and prepared to leap, tracking her with its glowing crimson eyes. Narthaks could see in the dark, but then so could she.

"Come on then, grunt, let's dance." She stopped a few paces away. The beast stalked closer, wary of this prey that did not flee in terror as it ought to. It snuck toward her as if shadowing an oblivious victim. Altira could see the tension in its huge shoulders as it rippled slowly closer, its grayish coat glistening in the starlight. She feigned a lunge and it froze, its anger building.

Altira sunk into one hip and crossed her arms. "So, are you going to skulk around in the grass forever or—"

"What was that?" Gentain's distant voice echoed from the Can`tie clutched in her fist.

The narthak leapt. Glistening claws raked through the air, prepared to rip Altira's flesh asunder, but they found nothing.

The moment the beast launched, she passed, ignoring the tinny voice issuing from the stone. Darkness embraced her and she reappeared just beyond the creature, whirling in midair and already slashing. Her blade seemed to possess a mind of its own. It leapt at the monster, seemingly of its own volition, parting

the leathery hide as if slicing through butter. The beast screamed and spun around, aiming a swipe at her head, a huge bloody gash opening in its hindquarters.

"Altira?" Gentain called through the stone. *"What's that? Are you all right?"*

She passed again, this time to the side, and scored another wound on the narthak's shoulder. Knowing what it would do, she didn't use the Shadowed Passage but instead leapt entirely over the beast as it swiped at her again. She nearly sliced its left leg off at the joint. The knife didn't seem to distinguish between bone and sinew, but passed through both with equal fervor.

"Altira?! Speak now or we come." It was Farthir this time.

"Silence! I'm fine, it's a narthak."

The beast had had enough of this unreachable opponent who vanished into thin air. It started toward the distant forest, limping on its three remaining legs and weak from the loss of blood. Altira palmed one of her sildars and dispatched the monster quickly. The magic blade reappeared in her bracer as soon as the beast was dead.

She knelt to clean the ancient knife but it wasn't needed. The blade glistened as if new. She held the weapon to the sky and inspected it in the starlight. Not so much as a spot on it. Karthak would be pleased. Smiling, she returned it to its scabbard and tilted the pommel forward.

"Hey, little Can`tie people. Please don't yell at me when I'm trying to fight, unless you want to get me killed. If I need your help, I'll call, all right?"

"Well, please tell us if you're going into battle, and we won't be needing to yell at you," replied Farthir.

"Certainly, *warder*. When the Cirrian's envoy delivers his formal invitation, I'll be sure to pass along the information." She started for a clump of trees down the hill. "I'm Alo`Daran. I can handle myself, thank you *very* much. Rest assured that if you're needed, you will hear about it."

All she got back was silence. Fine. Maybe she could finally get some sleep.

THE LATE MORNING SUN SHONE BRIGHTLY ON THE HARD-PACKED highway. In the distance, Altira could barely make out the sketchy form of a bridge spanning a large chasm. After their little exchange of the previous night, Farthir had been taciturn, which pleased Altira no end. She had finally obtained a good rest thanks to the silence. Refreshed from her sleep, she had risen early and returned to the road, ready to face the last day of this interminable journey. The morning had passed uneventfully.

It was becoming rather warm, though.

The heat caused the image of the distant bridge to ripple and dance, making the span seem miles away. Funny, it didn't feel *that* hot really. She peered at the distant, flickering image. It could be a mirage … though those illusions were generally the consequence of scorching summer days. A shrill cry came from above as a pair of sparrows swooped and darted, contending over some perceived breach of territory. Strange, if it was hot enough for a mirage, the birds should have been driven to the shade of some tree instead of cavorting around in the clouds. And it didn't smell that hot either. There was no aroma of the road dust and mingled meadow flowers that accompanied travel during the sweltering summer days on the roads to and from Nar`oo.

Altira stepped over a tall stone, then another, then—nothing! Careening forward, she fell *through* the road. Lords! It *was* a mirage. Instantly she levitated, whirled around, and grabbed one of the ragged rocks forming the wall of the vertical cliff, stopping her fall.

Farthir must have heard her cry as she fell through the road but with impressive restraint he remained silent. She found a foothold and gazed down. The river glittered back at her, nearly a thousand cubits below, an azure snake winding amongst the huge, jagged boulders at the floor of the chasm. "I'm all right," she reported, her foothold secure.

"What happened?"

"I fell through the stupid road. The Cirrian created some sort of illusion that looked like the highway and I managed to walk right off a cliff."

"Shall we pass? Do you need aid?"

"Aid? I'm an Elf, stupid. I can climb a pitiful hill. Besides that, the blade is still. The Cirrian's far away. This is probably a test to see if I'm really alone."

"Well … all right, Altira, but we're ready. For him to do this instead of a direct attack means he suspects something. If he's close enough to form a vision he may strike at any time, seeing you're alone. Or, he may attempt some ranged assault. Cirrians have great control over air and water. Be watchful for unusual weather or strange-looking clouds."

"Right." She replied and began her ascent of the cliff, watching the heavens for any signs. She reached the top in short order. The mirage had vanished. It was clear now where the road veered to the right and she had continued forward, nearly falling to her death. Altira glared at the sky, which was adorned with abundant cotton-puff denizens.

Raising her fist, she shrieked at the heavens. “Get down here and finish this job, you putrid cloud of dra`cata piss!” She whirled to look behind her and whipped out her knife. “You’re a sniveling, spineless pile of bat guano and you smell like the deepest cesspool beneath the ogre lairs of Najarak! You don’t deserve to desecrate whatever cloud you’re hiding in! COME DOWN AND FACE ME, YOU SLIME!”

Tinny peals of laughter issued from the Can`tie, held aloft in her fist.

“Shut it!” she hissed through clenched teeth. “He’ll hear.”

Farthir’s merriment was cut short by a distant crash, as if he had fallen off his chair or knocked over a table.

“So much for the elegant manners of the Guardians,” Altira mumbled. “Let’s hope the Cirrian is as deaf as he is ugly.” She sheathed her knife with a snarl when nothing happened. Apparently, her tirade to the heavens had failed to entice her adversary. Altira scowled and made her way back to the road, one eye on the heavens and the other, eagle-like, on the path. She’d not make that mistake again.

Although she fully expected the assassin to swoop down upon her at any moment, nothing happened for the next two leagues. Farthir remained quiet but she could tell that he, and Naroc as well, had been focusing on her with great intent. As she commenced the ascent of a moderate size hill, she noticed a cloud on the other side of the rise. It was leaden gray and pregnant with moisture—an aberration in a sunny sky with white, cottony puffs.

“Farthir. Stand ready. There’s a cloud coming.”

“Understood. You might want to seek shelter. Cirrians can wield lightning.”

"Why does that not surprise me at all?" Altira noted a copse to the east, but hunkering under a tree was the worst place to be in a thunderstorm, so she continued her climb up the hill. The cloud floated right at her, traveling much more quickly than it should by nature and, what was worse, against the wind. She cast about for some cover but there wasn't any, just a scattering of rocks and a few scraggly bushes. She needed to get off the stupid hill; she was far too exposed. Altira ran down the back of the mound as a jagged bolt arced to the ground from the cloud, now half a league away. Thunder rolled over the grassland and echoed off the hills to the east.

If she lay in the ditch beside the road she'd provide the smallest profile, but that presumed the lightning strikes were random, and that was unlikely. Lying on the ground might very well play right into his hands. As she rushed down the hill she noticed a rock outcropping some distance to her left and swerved for it, running as fast as she could over the uneven terrain. The cloud veered toward her. It would be on her in a moment.

An ear-shattering crack threw her into the air as a sizzling bolt split a nearby tree in half, but Altira managed to roll to her feet. How long had it been between the strikes? Not very long. The jagged smell of the lightning-sundered tree wafted to her from behind as she dove into the rocks. Altira went invisible, sent her mind forward, and discovered that the cluster hid the top of a rock field, extending downward for half a league. She chose a spot and stepped into the Darkness.

Popping out perhaps twenty cubits down the hill, she was just regaining her feet when a huge discharge struck her last position. The ground rocked with the force of the explosion. Fortunately she had landed just behind a large chunk of granite that deflected the brunt of the blast. She cast ahead and jumped again, landed, and then passed a third time. This final passage placed her north of the rock field, at the top of the hill. She crouched behind a fallen log and searched for the Cirrian.

The cloud seemed to have lost her track. Another blinding flash of blue destroyed a tree south of the rocks in an immense, acrid fireball of hissing sap and ignited leaves. The Cirrian had lost her scent amongst all the sizzled air and wood. The coward had no intention of facing her one-on-one, but was trying to hide in the air and cast lightning about. He clearly suspected something.

As the thunderstorm meandered south, Altira held the talking stone close.

"I'm all right. The cur is hiding in the cloud, trying to fry me with lightning, but I've lost him for the moment."

"Did you see him? Do you think we can find him in the cloud?"

"Not a chance. It's way too big. You'd never know where to look."

"Drat. Can you continue?"

"I'm fine. It takes a lot more than a little rain and some noise to kill a Dark Elf. I'm glad of this, actually. He knows now that he'll have to do better than throw some lightning at me. We need to find somewhere enclosed so he has to descend, like Tyke's house in Caltra, but somewhere … bigger."

"Malas will be your best bet. Where is he now?"

"Drifting away to the south. I'll sneak back to the road invisible. It'll take him a while to find me."

"Very well, but be careful, my friend."

Altira passed several more times to be sure, and went invisible for the next league. That should demonstrate that sneaking about and hiding in the sky wouldn't work with her. The problem was, Altira wasn't entirely sure she could evade the Cirrian

again in close quarters. Celthoth was fast. He had been able to strike her in Caltra—she'd only been saved by the amulet—and by the fire. Next time he'd have time to strike at her more than once and that meant the amulet couldn't save her. That meant her only hope for survival would be praying that the cursed Guardian would protect her. Why didn't that give her warm and tingly feelings of comfort and peace?

CHAPTER EIGHTEEN

MALAS

MALAS WAS QUITE AN IMPRESSIVE CITY. COMPARED TO THE SLEEPY Dwarven village of Caltra, the place was huge. It was also well protected by a great stone wall nearly thirty cubits high. A pair of giant wooden gates barred entry at the moment, closed against the darkness. Altira went invisible, approached the huge doorways carefully, and passed through the portal without incident. A pair of sleepy guards dozed at their posts on the other side. She was sorely tempted to pilfer their spears, lying propped against the ramshackle guard hut, but she resisted the temptation, found the first abandoned alley, and scurried down it.

Altira wound through the sleeping city toward the north. Skirting the ramshackle harbor district, she sought a remote and spacious enclosure. The first rays of the rising sun caressed the very top of the great wall surrounding the shadowed metropolis as she continued north. It was fully morning when she reached the far edge of the city. Many of the shops and homes were dusty and unused. The town may be well protected, but clearly it had seen more prosperous times. Trudging down yet another deserted lane, she came upon a huge warehouse abutting the outer wall on the eastern edge of the city near the ocean. It was abandoned and thickly coated in dust. It was perfect.

She crouched in an adjacent alley for a while, casing the location. The street was deserted. Altira rose, passed through the huge sliding doors, and refreshed her invisibility. Inside was a cavernous enclosure. A few crates and an ancient, decrepit wagon were the only residents of the warehouse, and everything was covered in dust and cobwebs. The windows on the south wall admitted almost no light. A shadowed glimmer of the morning sun was all that penetrated the grime and encrusted dirt built up on the sills.

Altira enhanced her vision and followed the outer wall toward a dilapidated two-story office structure on the far end of the space. A pitiful weathered door with peeling paint was nailed shut but she passed inside and carefully ascended a set of creaking stairs to the second story. The only furniture in the first room was an ancient rolltop desk. It, too, was coated with a thick patina of dust. She sneezed and made her way into the next room, seeking a covert with some privacy. She discovered an empty office with somewhat less dirt and settled into a corner to wait.

"Gentain?" she whispered, afraid if she made any noise at all, the the rickety ceiling would crash down upon her.

"No, it's Farthir. How are you doing?"

"I'm inside Malas. I've found a place. It's big enough for the bird and away from prying eyes. I'd say it's time to let him find me. Are you and Naroc ready? It shouldn't take long to catch my scent. The wind will shift to the west as soon as the sun clears the wall."

"We're ready. Just call and we'll come."

Altira placed her hand on the knife and tried to rest. She managed to nod off for a bit and awoke near midday with a powerful thirst. The warehouse was still quiet, but now much brighter. She stood and wiped the grime off a window with her elbow. Thin shafts of brilliant amber light revealed a scattering of unfilled crates on the floor of the nearly vacant warehouse. She went to her pack and fished out the water. It was almost gone. She'd have to find more soon.

As she sipped the last of the drink, Altira absently swatted at a mosquito buzzing near her ear before realizing it wasn't an insect at all. It felt more like a vibration—the knife! The ruby gem on the pommel was dimly glowing and the buzz coming from it grew louder, now sounding more like a thousand honeybees gathering nectar in a distant field. *Here we go,* she thought, crouched in her corner and whispered into the stone, "Farthir? I think—"

"We hear the blade. Naroc is poised. Give the word and we pass."

Altira tossed the empty flask on her pack and sent her mind through the wall. She surveyed the exterior of the office, cataloging every door and nook, preparing to jump in a heartbeat. The hum grew louder, now like the imminent approach of hornets.

She risked a peek through the office window. The humming increased. She scanned the dusty floor, the walls, the ceiling, sent her mind into every corner, but there was no sign of the Cirrian. A familiar putrid odor wafted to her—from above!

"He's here."

"On our way."

The lightning-like scent grew more oppressive as Altira retreated to the far corner of the room, her heart racing. She cast through the wall at her back and found a place to jump as a thin tendril of yellow—like a wisp from a smoldering corpse—snaked through the broken ceiling planks and oozed into the room. It wafted to and fro, seeking some contact, and then coiled toward the floor. The Cirrian oozed through the ceiling like some impossible, putrid serpent made entirely of rancid smoke. The ephemeral reptile slowly curled upon itself on the floor as it became both more substantial and more ominous. The tendril coalesced into a vapid pool of eerily luminous, translucent slime.

Not about to give the nasty thing time, Altira passed through the wall into the next room. A faint wail permeated the partition. It was incredibly stupid. Hadn't it figured out by now she could jump through walls? Well, no matter. Its days of terrorizing Dark Elves were about to be terminated with malice.

She moved back as it oozed through the intervening door. She gave it time to commit to the traversal and sent her sight ahead, to the floor of the warehouse. A strange note echoed from outside, as if someone had struck a giant church bell with a brazen hammer encased in cotton. She barely perceived it, however, for she was preparing to jump through the wall. *That looks like a good spot ...*

An instant before she was about to pass, the partially formed Cirrian lashed a tendril at her. She jerked and it missed her by a hairsbreadth and swirled into the wall by her head. Skies! That was sheer luck. It wouldn't miss again. Altira jumped to the warehouse proper.

She dropped to the dusty floor and spun to look at the office. This time the scream of frustration was audible. The beast really was stupid … or wait, was it? She now stood in the center of a nearly empty, cavernous enclosure with nowhere to hide and nothing to impede her opponent. Krakas! It had been *herding* her!

Altira backed toward the massive front doors, looking for something to hide behind, as Celthoth passed through the front wall of the office. The transition was unlike its previous passages; this time the beast slipped through all the cracks as if they weren't even there, using every fissure and crevice at the same time. It took only a moment. It *had* been toying with her!

Altira raced for the exit but the warehouse was huge. Where *was* the cursed bird? It had been ages since she'd called. The Cirrian hissed and grew in size, now nearly five cubits long, and flew after her. Altira looked over her shoulder as she raced through the dust. The creature was forming an impossibly thin filament of energy. It was time to get out of this death trap.

She reached the huge doors, cast sight through them, found a spot outside, and prepared to jump. At the same moment, sunlight from above hit the Cirrian and there was a blinding flash of energy.

A crack of energy threw Altira against the doors and to the floor. Momentarily stunned, she tried to get to her feet but her legs wouldn't work. The beast was nearly on her, the tentacle drawn back like an immense whip. She gathered the passing magic for a desperate jump but she was still dizzy from the flash.

"Altira, have you used the amulet?" Farthir's voice called from the talking stone. It was loud. He was close.

"No! Help!"

The whip was in motion, its golden tip a blur of speed. The floor rocked beneath Altira and the wall behind her detonated in a horrific blast of crimson energy. A deafening explosion of splinters, shattered glass, and iron fragments skewered the Cir-

rian with a million deadly darts. The whip was torn apart midair; it never reached her.

An oval of blue-white energy saved Altira. The sheer force of its protection pinned her to the floor with an irresistible power as the horrific hail of debris impacted the amulet's shield. The thing saved her life yet again.

The shield relented, showering her with dust and debris. Brushing the wood chips and bits of glass from her hair, Altira finally was able to look up. Hovering just outside the obliterated wall was Naroc, his great wings sweeping broadly. Farthir stood in front, hands outstretched with a fierce look that frightened even Altira. Beside the warder stood a Dwarf carrying what looked like a pair of bandoliers. It was Tyke.

The tremendous explosion had blasted the Cirrian into myriad tiny tendrils of slimy yellow mist that swirled and circled aimlessly in the air. Yellow slime coated the chunks of wood and glass that littered the floor on the far side of the warehouse.

Altira levered herself to a sitting position and tried to focus. Tyke bounded through the remains of the doors and ran to her.

"Alti! Are ya all right, missie?"

"I … I think so—" Her words were cut short by a horrific creaking from the roof. The rafters groaned and fell several cubits, lacking most of the supporting timbers from the wall. The entire roof threatened to collapse. Tyke drug Altira to her feet and they stumbled away from the decimated wall, taking cover near some empty casks.

The warder, followed closely by Naroc, stepped through the devastation, navigated around several burning timbers, and came to them. He gazed appraisingly at the disparate cloud of yellow, now drifting toward the ceiling. "That was too easy. Cirrians are supposed to be almost impossible to kill."

Altira propped herself against a large barrel and shook the dust from her hair as the three watched the cloud of slime. She fetched the amulet from inside her blouse. Its color remained unchanged, but its allure seemed greatly diminished. She could sense its power slowly returning, but guessed it would be hours before it could protect her again.

She looked around at the remains of the Cirrian. The cloud didn't seem to be coalescing, but neither did it dissipate. The tiny yellow tendrils were darting amongst the rafters, perhaps thirty cubits above the floor.

"Dat isn' right," complained Tyke. "'Tis nae disappearin'. If we'd killed it, it'd be lyin' charred, on da floor, not floatin' roun' da ceilin'."

"What in the seven skies do you have to do to kill one of these things?" complained Altira. "If that explosion and skewering it with a million shards didn't work, how in the name of the Five Lords of the Felshar do you destroy it?"

Farthir just shook his head. "Something a lot more deadly than a hail of wood and glass, it would appear."

CHAPTER NINETEEN

CELTHOTH DESCENDS

"'ERE, ALTI, TAKE DESE."

Tyke offered her a bandolier containing six crude daggers. The handles were bound with stained pigskin, and they weren't even steel—they were made out of some kind of revolting blue crystals.

Altira grimaced. "Why in the seven skies would I want those horrid things? They look like they were made out of bat guano by a one-armed goblin. They'd probably fall apart if you used one."

"Not likely, Alti." Tyke proffered the bandolier. "Dey are sulfur daggers, missie. Special-made by Borin."

"Sulfur?" She turned her attention back to the cloud of floating slime. The Cirrian was in pieces … but was it dead? "What's sulfur, and why should I care?"

"Didn't Gentain tell ya 'bout da Cirrian? That it nae can come inta Telfall?"

"I guess so." One of the chunks of slime detached itself from a bit of wood and oozed onto the floor. "What of it?"

Farthir drew his sword and stepped toward them, eyeing the swirling cloud. "It was Borin's idea, actually. Cirrians can't venture inside Telfall due to the sulfurous vapors in the air. It's a deadly poison to them."

Altira was distracted by the cloud. Several of the larger chunks were now rising from the floor. "So what? Weapons just pass right through the thing, and I hardly think the Cirrian is gonna take a bite out of some stupid dagger. Honestly, sometimes—"

"No, no, Alti. Um … can ye explain it, sir?" Tyke looked to the warder.

"Yes. Here's how it works. Naroc and I create a vortex of flame. You toss the daggers into it …"

"… and the fire kills the Cirrian," Altira replied, immediately getting the idea. "But won't he just fly out the top? He got out of Tyke's house pretty quick, and that was some inferno."

"Not if da t'ing be surrounded, on all sides, like a big ball. Doncha see? Once da sulfur is in da flames, it be dire an' he can nae penetrate 'em … at leas' accordin' ta Borin."

"Give me one of those." Altira gestured for a bracer. Tyke handed it over and slung the other one over his head. Altira pulled a blade and tested the weight. The balance wasn't too bad—the handle was light enough to provide decent stability. It was throwable and the edge was wicked sharp, but the thing was so thin it was translucent. It would be useless in a real fight—the flimsy blade would shatter the moment it struck anything—but they might very well melt in flames.

Farthir gestured toward the rear of the warehouse. "We better move back, it's starting to re-form." Several more chunks of yel-

low had parted from the debris on the floor and were floating upward to join their companions.

Tyke and Altira went to Farthir in the far corner of the warehouse, Naroc towering over them protectively. It was a strange feeling, to take shelter near a beast Altira had always despised. But it was stranger still to watch the nearly indestructible monster recover from an explosion that would have obliterated her and had nearly vaporized the far wall of the warehouse.

The bits rising from the floor incorporated into a cloud that grew darker and more substantial. The Cirrian would be back soon.

"All right," said Farthir. "Here's what we do. I envelop it in flames and keep it surrounded. Tyke, you go left, Altira, right. When I yell, throw the daggers. Let's hope this works. If not, we're going to be in real trouble. Naroc can pass, but he has to be in physical contact to take you, and we can't all sit on him and throw daggers at the same time. Once you've tossed yours, get close so we can shield you."

"Don't worry about me. I can take care of myself." Altira hoped her voice didn't betray the trepidation gripping her heart. She moved away, donned the bandolier, and palmed two of the daggers. If this didn't work, she wasn't going to hang around to see what the creature would do. She'd be out of here in an instant.

Farthir backed under his bird and sheathed his sword, freeing both hands. "Just lob the daggers. Otherwise the blades may not melt in the fire."

Altira nodded and refocused on the cloud. "Should I throw them all?"

"Nae," replied Tyke. "Borin said two or three should do the job or it won' work atall. Let's save some for, well, for later."

"There isn't going to be any later, Tickles. Either we kill this thing now, or it's everyone for herself." Altira judged the distance and flipped a dagger in the air to test its balance.

There were no more bits left on the floor now and the top of the cloud had begun to coalesce into the Cirrian's head. His beady, coal-black eyes considered them balefully as his lower body formed. A tendril emerged.

Altira glanced at the warder. He was watching the Cirrian intently, his bird bent over him. She could feel the crackling energy as vast arcane power began to build around the Guardian. Several strands of her hair arose, attracted by the immense, natural force. A translucent crimson bubble popped up around Farthir and the eagle. Altira was outside it.

The warder gestured to them absently, still focused on the re-forming Cirrian. "Get closer, you two. You're too far away. Naroc can't protect—"

The forming tendril whipped at him, a blur of speed. A loud crack and a blinding flash of crimson light erupted from Naroc's shield as the bubble intercepted the tentacle, deflecting it upward. At least the Guardian's defenses worked.

Altira ducked and scampered inside Naroc's bubble, but the warder wasn't about to wait for the next assault. In a huge, circular motion, Farthir gestured at the beast. Swirling fingers of red-orange flame erupted around it, rapidly building into a massive vortex of fire. Even from a distance and inside Naroc's shield of protection, the heat was nearly unbearable for Altira. She backed closer to the bird and protected her eyes with an arm. Farthir bent toward the Cirrian, his hands describing a sphere. The inferno intensified. The creature screamed and a tentacle popped out the top of the ball of fire.

"Now. Throw NOW!" yelled Farthir. "He's escaping!"

Altira tossed both daggers, as slow as she could, to give them maximum exposure to the flames. It was all she could do to resist the instinct to throw with all her strength. The weapons flew in a gentle arc, entering the flames from above. Tyke stepped forward—Altira was amazed that he could stand the heat—and tossed a blade underhanded, then grabbed a second and threw it as well. He backed away and raised an arm to ward against the heat.

The inferno turned a brilliant blue for an instant and yellow smoke swirled amidst the orange flames. Choking fumes emanated from the vortex. It smelled like a thousand rotten eggs burning. Altira gagged and covered her mouth with a hand. Beads of sweat etched lines through the soot on Farthir's face as he grimaced and bent toward the huge ball of fire, expending every bit of focus he could muster. Altira felt Naroc grunt from deep inside.

A horrific, piercing scream issued from the flames, becoming higher and higher in pitch. The inferno became a dark brownish color and the screech increased. Altira thought her head would shatter with the sound. She cowered under the eagle and covered both ears.

Suddenly there was an enormous thud and then a huge detonation from inside the vortex; the flames turned nearly black for an instant and then the tornado exploded, showering them in a hail of detritus that coated everything with caustic, smoking black slime.

The blast threw Altira into Naroc, in spite of his shield. The feathers of the eagle's chest felt cool compared to the scorching heat from the fire. She placed a hand against the bird for support and then stumbled forward and shook her head, trying to clear the ringing in her ears.

The Cirrian was gone.

Farthir wiped his dripping brow with the back of an arm. "Is everyone all right?"

"Ya," Tyke replied, the sleeve of his shirt still smoking. "So dat's it? Did we kill it?"

"What do you think all this snot is?" Altira crossed their pristine oval of protection and nudged some of the horrific-smelling black slime covering the floor with a toe. "That thing is worse in death than it was in life."

Farthir sat on a crate and surveyed the devastation. It looked like some despicable god of filth had sneezed. Everything was coated in putrid, steaming black goo. Altira grimaced and held her breath. "Let's get the skies out of here. I need to take a bath—for about a week."

"Aye," agreed Farthir. "I think Naroc can carry us all, if Tyke doesn't mind being grasped in his talons, but let's get outside. Otherwise there will be a real mess when he takes off."

"Oh, we wouldn't want to make a mess, it's so tidy in here at the moment." Altira began to search for an escape, but it was hopeless. They stood in the only island of clean in a vast ocean of filth. "I'm not slogging through this … this *stuff*. I'll meet—"

"Here," the warder interrupted. He rose and gestured at her, making a strange corkscrew motion with his arm.

Altira shrieked as she rose into the air, reached for the floor with a hand, and flipped over. She ended up floating upside down, the amulet dangling in her eyes.

"What in the skies are you doing, you idiot?! PUT ME DOWN!"

"You want to avoid the grime?" asked the warder. "Well, just be still."

"DROP ME THIS INSTANT, or I swear, I'll skewer you with four sildars!" She palmed two and prepared to throw.

"Very well, as you wish, *mistress.*" Farthir motioned and she fell to the floor at his feet.

Altira scrambled to her feet, furious. "Don't you ever … EVER do that again! I don't care who you are. I'm perfectly capable of jumping outside, thank you so *very* much! If you want to levitate someone, go practice on Tickles, but leave me alone." She glared fiercely at him, shoved her sildars home, and stepped into the Darkness, popping well outside the warehouse. She turned and looked back through the opening in the devastated wall.

"Are you coming?" she yelled. "Or are you planning on staring at the muck for an hour?" Her call drew their attention outside, and the three turned toward her, the warder seeming surprised. Didn't he realize she could pass, stupid man? Farthir floated himself, Naroc, and the Dwarf above the grime and over to her. When they were well clear of the devastation, he vaulted to Naroc's back and reached for her.

Altira was still intensely miffed at the warder for his attempt at levitation. "That's all right, *companion,* I'll just walk back to Telfall, thanks." Altira turned to start the weeklong journey rather than be carried around on the back of some huge red bird.

Farthir seemed confused. "What? Why? We can be back in a moment. Come on, it's easy. Naroc will grasp Tyke and we'll be gone."

"I prefer to make my own way, thanks."

"Altira, I'd feel much better if you came with us. Celthoth is gone but the Sultan is still after you. There's no telling what else is out there. It's better to come with us now. If you're out wandering in the wilderness somewhere, we can't protect you. I'm sorry about the levitation thing. I was only trying to help."

The thought that Al`Taaba would have hired more than one assassin gave her pause. Altira turned back, sunk into a hip, crossed her arms, and stared at the annoying man for a moment. "Oh all right, but you'd better not drop me."

"I give you my word." Farthir leaned forward and offered his arm again.

Altira sighed, grasped the warder, and leapt to Naroc's back. The worst part was having to wrap her arms around the cursed human—but it was the only way to hold on. She stifled a yelp as Naroc leapt into the air. The still-smoking roof of the warehouse fell away with alarming speed. Altira buried her face in the warder's jerkin, closed her eyes, and willed herself not to scream.

CHAPTER TWENTY

JEN`TAR

RETURNING TO TELFALL WAS A UNIQUE EXPERIENCE TO SAY THE least. Altira was intimately familiar with the Shadowed Passage, of course, but she had never felt anything like the kind of power Naroc wielded when he jumped home. It was as if the Guardian pulled the very essence of the world into himself, so vast was the vortex he wielded to pass them into the Darkness. The weightlessness and the utter dark and cold were familiar, but they seemed to last an eternity. When they popped out, soaring high above the mountains, Altira shrieked in spite of herself. She wasn't afraid of heights generally, but they were *thousands* of cubits up and it was *freezing!* They spiraled down and within minutes had alighted on some sort of terrace cut into the side of the mountain.

The moment Naroc landed, Altira leapt off and hugged herself. It was horribly cold to start with, and the frigid drafts caused by Naroc's descent had cut through her overcoat like a thousand razor-sharp bodkins.

"Where … where is the door?" she asked, stammering and hopping from foot to foot. "How do we get in?"

"'Ere, Alti, dis way," said Tyke.

Naroc had deposited them on the cold flagstones some distance from the side of the cliff. The Dwarf gestured for her to follow and hustled to the rough stone wall at the back of the large flat area. Tyke grasped what looked like nothing more than a chunk of protruding granite, and pulled upon it. The rock wall swung out to reveal the passage to the audience chamber—apparently the entrance was camouflaged to look exactly like the mountain. Altira shouldered by him in a mad dash across the chamber and nearly jumped right into the blazing hearth, she was so cold. But common sense prevailed, and after warming her hands and back for a while, she was somewhat thawed. It was then that she noticed the odor emanating from her clothing. She smelled like a three-week-old corpse drowned in the sump pool of a tribe of ogres. Wrinkling her nose in utter disgust, she quickly excused herself and hurried down to her room.

The moment Altira closed her door, she nearly collapsed from exhaustion. Only through sheer force of will did she manage to crawl into the bath for a while—she wasn't about to sleep in slime-coated clothing—although the temptation to nod off in the tub was almost irresistible. Only the fear of being discovered kept her awake. Finally, she slogged out of the soapy pool, threw on the first comfortable thing she could grab from the closet, and crept between her covers. She didn't care if the air was stale or that there were no real trees about. The mattress was soft and she was safe; that was all that mattered—at least for the moment.

Those few thoughts were about all she managed to push through her mind before she fell into a dreamless slumber.

IT WAS DARK. AT FIRST ALTIRA COULDN'T QUITE TELL IF SHE WAS awake or still asleep. But then the faint sound of steel slipping through leather came from the front room and her acute senses went instantly alert. She was not alone.

But that wasn't the worst part. Her bedroom was dark as pitch, and that was wrong. The crystal lamps the Dwarves employed were never fully extinguished. Even when quiescent—like when you were sleeping—they emitted a dim, star-like glow. Altira silently mouthed the spell for enhanced vision but it did no good—even magisight was useless when there was no light at all. Yes, something was horribly wrong. The Dwarves hated total darkness. Someone had extinguished the lamps.

Altira sent her mind through the nearest wall and into the hall on the other side. The lamps there were glowing with a friendly golden luminance. The faintest sound of a footfall snapped her perception back to her foyer. Someone—or some-*thing*—was skulking in the dark just at the door to her room, and it was no Dwarf. The figure froze, as if perceiving its detection. The sound of slipping silk impelled Altira to pass instantly, just as a poison-tipped dart buried itself in her pillow.

She popped out in the corridor and started to retreat toward the door at the end of the hall, casting her vision back, trying to see her attacker. An instant later an Elf, dressed entirely in black and with veiled face, popped into the air at the far end of the corridor, facing away. He was carrying a nitado in his left hand. Altira didn't hesitate; she ducked and instantly passed through the door behind her even as the assassin spun and raised his weapon to his lips in a single fluid movement. She raced down the hallway as another dart buried itself in the wooden door with a dull *thwup*.

Altira turned left, yanked open another door, then raced up a random set of granite steps, cursing silently. She knew who her pursuer was. And that knowledge rattled her more than facing the dread Cirrian ever had.

The stone passage was cold under her naked feet. As long as she kept moving she should be okay—she knew these tunnels way better than her pursuer did. She would need that advantage. The Elf on her heels was surely Jen`Tar, the Prima of her Cala. Only the Alo`Dara employed the nitado, and it was Jen's favored weapon.

Altira cursed as she flew around a corner. Jen was really, *really* good—the Dar himself had snuck out of a duel with the master assassin. Skies, how in the Five Lords of the Felshar had he managed to sneak into Telfall? What about Gentain's vaunted Dwarven wards? This was not good. Not good at all.

Altira reached for her long knife and swore once again—she'd left everything back in her room. She'd been in bed, after all. Now here she was, racing through a Dwarven dungeon with the foremost Alo`Daran assassin on her tail, completely weaponless, barefoot, and nearly naked. Not exactly a promising scenario. She needed help. Where was the cursed warder when you needed him? Without her knife and the Can`tie, she couldn't call, even if Farthir had been listening, which he probably wasn't.

Altira detected the faintest whir of steel through air and ducked a second time. Intense pain shot through her leg as a sildar embedded in her thigh. Krakas! She collapsed to the floor,

clamping her hand over the wound to stem the flow of blood as the blade vanished and returned to its master.

Jen`Tar sauntered up as if walking in the park. "You little fool," he said, shaking his head slowly. "First law of battle—never do the same thing twice. I thought you were supposed to be good. The Dar vastly overestimated your ability. Down in three, it's so sad. What a pitiful little shadow of a Dark Elf you are." He pulled his nitado from his belt and shoved a dart into the chamber with finality. "Die slowly, kin of a traitor."

Altira smiled. "Guess again, twit." In a heartbeat she drew all her strength and passed upward through at least twenty cubits of solid granite, into a hallway far above. Falling to the floor of the empty corridor, she bit her lip and grimaced against the pain. She'd just bought herself a few more moments of life. "Follow that, you cur," she muttered. Altira had wandered these tunnels long enough to know her neighborhood. Jen`Tar would have no clue where she'd gone, and she doubted he could even make the jump through so much solid rock. Twenty cubits of granite would be nearly impossible for anyone without an intimate knowledge of the city's passages. It would take him precious minutes to sense the layout.

She groaned and levered herself to her feet, still gripping her leg tightly. She placed a bloody hand on the wall to steady herself and focused. She knew this passage. If she went left and then up two stairs, she'd be in the corridor to the anteroom—the one to the Guardian. She tried to take a step and cried in pain, in spite of herself. *Not that, idiot. Pass, you fool, just pass.*

She grimaced, focused, then started passing down corridors instead of hobbling. Five jumps later she popped out a few cubits in front of the great alabaster portals and collapsed to the ground. The honor guards jumped back at first, not expecting an injured Alo`Daran to materialize from thin air, a stone's throw from the doorway. When they realized who it was and saw the blood, one leapt forward.

"'Ere, Skymistress, what's wrong? Ye'r 'urt? Wha 'app'ned? Daltra, summon the Companion quickly!"

The other guard turned to open the door.

"No!" Altira cried. "He'll be here in moments. Raise the alarm! QUICK!"

The Dwarf let go of the door and turned toward her. "What are ya talkin' 'bout? Who's aft—"

A red-feathered dart materialized in his muscled forearm. The guard plucked it out, as if it were some sort of curious insect. For a moment Altira thought the poison would have no effect. But then the Dwarf's eyes glassed over and he toppled to the ground.

"INTRUDER!" yelled his companion, leaping to his feet, his now brightly glowing axe raised like a shield. A distant bell of alarm began to sound from somewhere above. Altira wasn't about to wait to see how he'd fare against Jen`Tar. She cast ahead and passed through the great doors, popping out on the far side of the hall, near the fireplace. Her leg gave way and she fell to the floor, entirely spent. Naroc's perch to the left of the fire was vacant.

"Help!" she cried and tried to crawl behind a chair, leaving a bloody trail on the marble tiles near the hearth. She attempted to summon the strength for yet another jump but could not. Only a moment later her pursuer popped into the center of the room, landed lightly on the elegant Fuan carpet, and smiled. He pulled another dart from the ample quiver at his side and reloaded the nitado in a single, flawless movement. The gun was at his lips and the missile was flying at Altira before she could think.

CHAPTER TWENTY-ONE

ERLINI

ALTIRA CLOSED HER EYES AND BRACED FOR THE PAIN. SHE WAS completely spent from passing and loss of blood, her leg throbbed, and she had nowhere left to run. Outside, there was nothing but terrace and a sheer fall down the mountain. It was over; she was done. A strange ethereal hum seemed to surround her for a moment, followed by the sound of a dart rattling across the marble floor.

Jen … missed? Impossible; he never misses. Altira opened her eyes. Some kind of weird green bubble enveloped her. The assassin cursed, whipped out a sildar, and threw it. The blade ricocheted off the glowing sphere and shattered a vase on a nearby map table.

"You can't hide behind the cursed birds forever, you little spawn of a traitor!" Jen snarled, backing away. "The Dar will have your skin, you little plink, and I'll be the one to deliver it.

Enjoy the few days you have left, forever looking over your shoulder. You're mine, do you hear?!" He cursed her in Cal`Tali and vanished.

As Jen`Tar passed, Altira finally noticed a strange bird in the shadows on the far side of the room. It wasn't Naroc; this one was green. As it moved closer, the thing fairly glowed in the half-light from the fire. In front of the green Guardian strode a tall, auburn-haired woman, elegant in stature and bearing. She held a brightly glowing two-edged blade—the same hue as the bird. Her fiery eyes were veiled with concern.

"You appear to have acquired a few new enemies, mistress." Her voice was softer than Altira had expected, but it still held great power.

The Dark Elf grimaced and tried to rise. "I'm all ri— oww!" She nearly passed out from the pain. "On second thought, the floor is nice." She gripped her leg more tightly and took a few deep breaths, sizing up the woman crossing the room to her, followed closely by the great eagle. "Who—"

"I am Danera, and this is Erlini, the Emerald Guardian." The woman bent over. "Be still now, child, let me look."

Altira shrunk from her touch. "I'll be all right. No, really—don't!" The room began to spin around as Altira pushed the woman away with a bloody hand.

"Don't move, you little hero, lie back. Moving will only make it worse. I promise I won't hurt you. We're here to help."

Altira was gripping her leg with a crimson hand, trying to keep from bleeding to death. She gritted her teeth and suffered the inspection—she didn't have much choice in the matter. The tall woman held a hand over Altira's injury for a moment with closed eyes and then turned to silently consult with her bird. Nothing

happened at first, but after a moment, the great eagle leaned toward them both, stretching forth its neck, and began to sing.

Altira had heard Phorin`Tra song before, of course—when she'd met Farthir and Naroc—but this one was completely different. It wasn't a tune of power and assurance, but rather of healing, of binding. It was a symphony of sustenance. Even through her pain she sensed that it could mend any tear, join any schism, make anything whole.

The song ended and Danera wove a strange sigil over Altira's leg. The pain vanished. A wave of comfort flowed from the injury, radiating outward, filling her with peace. The bird rose and the woman completed her incantation with a flourish. Altira felt a mild shock deep within her leg and then nothing—no pain, no weariness, and no dizziness whatever.

The woman fetched a goblet of water from the serving table. "Here, mistress, drink a little. Can you sit up now?"

Altira frowned, at first uncertain. The last time she'd tried to rise she nearly joined the world of spirits. "Is that a dare, or what?"

The woman raised an eyebrow and regarded her quizzically.

"Yeah, right," Altira said. *This woman has no sense of humor...* "Sitting up." Miraculously, Altira managed to lever herself up without passing out. She scooted over and propped herself against one of the divans near the wall. No pain! She *was* feeling better. Accepting the goblet from the woman, Altira drained it in one gulp. Turning her foot experimentally, she gently explored the jagged tear in her gown with a bloody finger. There was no scar on the skin underneath. In fact, there wasn't even a mark! Her leg had been made whole. "What did you do? How—"

"Healing be our particular calling, little raven. It was most fortunate we were present, and not my mate of the crimson skies. Farthir doth possess a dearth of skill in the art of binding."

It was clearly the bird that was speaking and not the woman—like Naroc and Farthir, except for some reason Altira got the distinct impression this eagle was a girl-bird.

"What happened to Farthir? How long was I asleep?"

The woman—Danera—answered. "Farthir sent word a day and a half ago. He was called to Porinta on a matter of great import and asked us to watch over you—a precaution which clearly was well advised. You have slept for three days. It would appear you were greatly taxed in your battle with the exile of Cirrus."

"Three days?" Altira was stunned—her rest had seemed to last only a moment. She considered the woman. This new Companion had a most elegant way of speaking. It was clear she was highly educated, and perhaps even of royal blood. "Have I really been aslee— Wait a minute! The sentries!"

Using the arm of the divan, Altira pushed herself to her feet and rushed to the door to the chamber, hobbling at first on her uncertain leg. She yanked it open to reveal the still form of one Dwarf, and another down the hall being assisted by a corpsman with a hand pressed against the soldier's bleeding shoulder. A fourth Dwarf was jogging down the corridor toward them. He stopped when he saw Altira.

The kneeling Dwarf looked up. "Dis one'll be all ri', but 'elp dat one. Help Daltra, Skymistress. It looks li' dire poison, it does."

"Danera!" Altira yelled over her shoulder as she knelt next to the Dwarf at her feet. But it was unnecessary; the Companion was right behind her. The tall woman shifted her sword out of the way, knelt next to Altira, then placed a delicate hand on the brow of the fallen soldier. She closed her eyes in concentration.

"He is alive but we must act quickly. It's some sort of toxin."

"Probably cum`ala," said Altira. "Jen`Tar prefers that. It's slow but sure."

Danera paused in her ministrations for a moment to consider Altira narrowly, seemingly surprised that a Dark Elf would aid the fallen Dwarven soldier.

Altira cocked her head. "Well, Jen was attacking *me,* not the Dwarf. The least I can do is help him if I can. But cum`ala is nearly always fatal unless the antidote is administered quickly, and I don't have any."

Danera smiled warmly and returned to her patient. "The taint is dire indeed, but not beyond our skill, little one. Step back now, that I may reach him." It was the bird speaking through Danera. Altira scuttled to the right as the tall woman pushed open the other section of the door.

The great eagle squeezed her neck through the opening, toward the prostrate Dwarf. The Guardian gently probed the chest of the fallen soldier with her massive beak. His body was surrounded by an emerald glow for an instant. The bird withdrew and Danera knelt and executed several sigils. These ministrations produced no discernible result at first, but after several tense moments the guard stirred and brought a shaky hand to his brow.

"*Errg.* Me 'ead. Who be hammerin' so loud? Feels like someone be poundin' on me noggin wit' a spiked mace."

"You were struck with dire venom. Be still and rest," replied Danera. Then, turning to Altira, she gestured toward the far table. "Can you fetch some water please, mistress?" The Companion placed a restraining hand on the Dwarf's shoulder as he tried to get up. "Lay still for a bit, corporal. It will take a moment for your strength to return."

Altira filled a goblet and returned to the fallen Dwarf, navigating around the huge bird who filled the doorway. Erlini shuffled back to let her pass. The guard was sitting now, his back to the wall. Danera was helping the second Dwarf.

Altira knelt and handed the goblet of water to the reclining Dwarf.

"Thank ye, Skymistress," he said, drinking deeply.

"'Skymistress'?" She chuckled as she accepted the empty flagon from the soldier. "You cracked your head when you fell, did you?"

Daltra seemed mildly offended. "An' what be da matter wit' 'Skymistress'? Was Tyke's idea act'lly, an' I kinda like it. Da cursed Cirrian 'as been the bane of the Dara`Phen now for nearly two anna. Destroyed all of Caltra, killed da Fuan ambassador to Telfall, Dwarves in Fairn, a farmer in Darrow. Certainly … Skymistress! Ye be da 'ero of da day. Slayer of Cirrians, mistress of da sky. Dere's been talk o' a medal and an audience with da Dwarmak hisself!"

"A medal? Skies, now I know you've cracked your skull for sure." But there was no dizziness evident in Daltra's hazel eyes, only honest Dwarven fervor. Altira sat back on her heels. Dwarves might be strange, ignorant, and peculiar but they were also forthright and true—something she couldn't say of most of her so-called friends in Nar`oo, especially the cursed Dar. Something needed to be done about that Elf. "Well, all right," she relented, "but I didn't kill the Cirrian, you know. If anyone deserves the credit it would be Farthir and Naroc. If it weren't for them we'd all be lying dead in Malas."

This drew an objection from the Dwarf and Altira didn't have the heart to argue. Still, "Skymistress" seemed rather a preposterous appellation.

Danera had completed her ministrations to the second Dwarf now and was returning.

Altira rose. "I need to get back to my room. It won't do for the *Skymistress* to scamper around wearing next to nothing." She turned to the woman. "Can your eagle sense the assassin?"

Danera closed her eyes for a moment. "He flees to the southwest, hounded by a squad of Dara`Phen. He will be hard-pressed to escape. Telfall is now on high alert. You should be safe for a while."

"Good!" barked Daltra, rising to his feet. "I 'ope they chop that cursed Elf into a t'osand bits and feed 'im to—oh, sorry, Skymistress, no 'fense."

"None taken. Jen deserves whatever he gets, the cur," Altira replied angrily. "He's no friend of mine. None of them are. I hope you all chase him back to Nar`oo and do in the cursed Dar as well."

The fervor of her response drew a surprised smile from the Dwarf.

"Well, they kicked me out," she replied. "I owe them nothing." She nodded to the corporal and turned to leave. "I'm going back to my room."

"Erlini would like a talk when you are ready, mistress," Danera called after Altira as she strode down the hall. "There is much you do not know."

"There is much I wish I never knew," Altira replied, waving her hand behind in acknowledgment before hastening down the stairs. She had a few hundred questions of her own about Guardians and the Alo`Dara, but they would have to wait. From now on she wasn't going anywhere without that amulet—and her knives. No more sleeping for three days either; she didn't have the luxury. The time had come to take back her blessed life.

CHAPTER TWENTY-TWO

FEL`DARA

ALTIRA PULLED ON HER BOOTS AND KNELT TO FISH HER PACK OUT from under the bed. She had been a fool. She should have worn the pendant when sleeping, even if it did get tangled in her hair. She was no safer here in the bowels of Telfall than she would be lying in her pode in the Dark Forest, under the nose of the Dar. Altira shook her head and rummaged in the pack. Where was the thing? It had been on top … where had it gone? Ah!

She fetched the talisman out and sat on the bed, entranced by its glitter. The gem had always held a strange allure. Its magic was fascinating, certainly—it had saved her life three times now. But there was something more to the amulet than mere protection. Altira sensed a deeper magic hidden in the facets of the azure jewel. Yes, she was convinced that shielding her was only the most superficial of its capacities. As she turned the glittering crystal in her fingers it caught the light like the teardrop of some ancient, mournful god. Her attention was drawn to its center; there seemed to be a flaw in the gem.

Wait. It wasn't a blemish. There was a spiderweb of darker blue that she hadn't noticed before. Altira held it up to the glow-sphere, trying to discern the form of the imperfection. As she rotated the gem, the filaments aligned into what looked like a sigil. Yes! It was *Ver*—the symbol of truth! She recognized it from the spell used when sealing a vow. How did a glyph come to be embedded in the gem … and more important, why?

As she considered the jewel more carefully, the complex character seemed to take on a three-dimensional form, now appearing more spherical than flat. It was enclosing something. The sigil beckoned to her; it needed to be opened, like some missive from an ancestor long dead. Almost without thinking, she mouthed the words for the incantation of access, one of the most basic of spells. The moment Altira executed the magic, a gentle force began to tug on her mind, lightly at first and then with some insistence.

The gem was drawing her inside. She dove into the aqua crystal and passed through the sigil into a darker indigo pool. At the very center swirled a mist of gray like a fog that obscured something else. Altira dove deeper, passed through the mists and out the other side.

The fog parted and a glittering city was revealed. A vast metropolis was buried within the gem! Bright pinnacles and minarets of pure crystal reflected the sunlight like a thousand brilliant stars. She passed through the last of the mists and beheld the city in its pristine glory. How beautiful it was. The perfect walls were an unbelievable shade of alabaster. The gates were purest gold, and the thoroughfares paved in sapphire and emerald. It was a city unlike any in Salustra, and somehow Altira sensed she was looking into the distant past.

She descended toward the sand—for the city rested in the midst of a great desert—and suddenly she recognized the place. It was Xancata! Or wait—not the current city of the Dark Overlord, but the ancient home of the Elves that he overthrew. It must be Anea`Na`Silithar, the City of the Stars—the ancestral abode of all Elven-kind.

Altira soared above the massive battlements toward the very center of the city, circled the highest minaret once, then swooped through a great, pinnacled opening into an inner sanctum. She floated above and beheld two Dark Elves sitting in an empty amphitheater. This must be the hall of the Ancient Council. But the patriarchs of the Ana`Ala—the ancient race of Elves—were not present. Just the two figures, sitting next to each other at one end of the semicircle of twelve chairs.

"This is not the way of the light," one said, his voice old but firm. "We have not the right to dictate—"

"We have every right!" The second chopped him off with a calloused hand. "The place of the Cali is to *lead,* and what better way than to show the people the best and easiest path?"

"The easy path is not always the best, Fel`Dara. If time has taught us anything, it is that through trial comes the greater wisdom."

Altira gasped. The second Elf must be the very first Dar, the great-great-grandfather of Fel`Soon!

"Bah. What do you know of trials?" the ancient Dar said, rising. His shoulders had not the same breadth as his latter-day descendant, but he possessed the same condescending, superior tone. "You have lived your life being served on, hand and foot!"

he barked. "You know nothing of conflict, nor of the forces outside the city that would tear us apart."

"I know that unity is a greater defense than division," the older man said, undaunted by the brutal physicality of the younger Elf facing him. "What you suggest would make us weaker, not stronger. I foresee the great battles that are to come as well as you, Fel`Dara, and we must remain united if we are to survive."

"No." The ancient Dar shifted closer to his adversary. "We will only prevail through diversity, Sen`Tana," he said. "Too long have we lived in this city. Too long have we allowed the other races to gobble up the lands of Sa`lea till we are left with only this single pitiful city in which to survive. What happens when they decide that the gold of Anea`Na`Silithar is too good for the Elves? What happens when they are jealous of our wells of purity, of our protected spires? Where will we run when we are backed against the wall? Tell me that!"

"The magic that envelops us is greater than any other," replied Sen`Tana. "No race can breach the barriers we have imposed."

The Dar raised a heavy hand and jabbed a finger at the seated man. His golden ring of ascendance glittered in the sunlight. "You are as foolish as you are ignorant, Sen`Tana. Have you not seen the visions of Talamar? Do you not know of the prophecies? Are you as completely uninformed as you are arrogant? How can you sit there, a ruler of an entire Cala of Ana`Ala, and in your blind stupidity condemn them all to destruction because you refuse to admit the obvious truth?"

Sen`Tana leapt from his chair. "How dare you speak to me thus?! You think that fleeing like a frightened youngling will save us? We all know whom you have chosen to follow. Your selfish lust for power and your fascination with the dark secrets will be the undoing of us all, do you hear me? *Us all!* As long as we are united, the magic will prevail. The lord to whom you ascribe seeks only our destruction. Of course I know of Talamar's visions, you fool. Do you forget? I was *with him* when he first penetrated the veil of future days. His predictions were intended to warn against a division that would render us vulnerable to the netherworld. What you propose will create the very schism that he warned against. It will result in the destruction of every Elf in Sa`lea! Without unity we will succumb to the Lord of the Undead. I have seen it. Your heavy-handed rule is well known. You would have us all bow and scrape to your 'greater wisdom' and at the same time you drive a wedge into Elven-kind that will prove our utter destruction! You are a traitor to your people and should be removed as Cali, and I shall make that motion tomorrow. You must not be permitted to lead, and the council will agree. Of this I am certain."

Fel`Dara did not hesitate for an instant, but growled once and leapt at Sen`Tana, dagger in hand. The elder statesman had no chance against his younger, stronger opponent, even if he had been armed, which he was not. A crimson stain besmirched his linen robe as the frail Elf collapsed at the foot of his golden seat.

The mists swirled around a stunned Altira, obscuring the vision for a moment, then cleared, revealing now a packed assembly. It was the same vast amphitheater she'd just witnessed except now the full council—minus two chairs—was present along with a multitude of Elves, both dark and light. Fel`Dara was speaking.

"And thus, my spies have discovered the truth of the matter," he said, his voice slow and deep—vastly different from the strident anger she'd seen only moments before. "Sen`Tana was slain by none other than Cara`Tan. Cara`Tan has long been a hater of Dark Elves, and was unwilling for Sen`Tana to continue his long and honored tenure as one of the chiefs of our houses." Fel`Dara gestured at an empty chair. "His absence is more than sufficient evidence of his guilt."

"But Cara`Tan is missing!" cried another council member. "None of his family can find him. I'm certain he would be here if he could. The assertion that he is the cause of the death of Sen`Tana is unthinkable! Cara`Tan has always been one to assert peace and calm debate. He would never—"

"He has!" cried Fel`Dara, his calm gone in a flash. "And here is proof." The Dark Elf shook the wrappings from a bloody blade, which clattered onto the table in front of the elders. "This is his ancestral dagger. Note the pommel-gem and the distinctive etchments on the blade. And it is covered in the very blood of Sen`Tana himself! Let the seekers come and verify. Let enchantments be made. What I say is true."

"This is inconceivable!" cried another Cali. "You have stolen the knife and used it yourself. We see through your subterfuge, Fel`Dara. You do not deserve to lead your family. You should be banished from this council and city!"

The Dark Elf turned upon him. "ENOUGH! I am through with this council, with your prevarications and divisions. I have had enough of this cursed place. You can keep Anea`Na`Silithar, I want no part of it—it will fall soon enough, anyway. My family—and the family of Sen`Tana, for that matter—are done with this abuse. You have ever despised those that are skilled in the arts of evasion. We have always been seen as aberrations and looked down upon by those of higher birth. Well, enough, I say! We will make our own way, and you all can rot in your 'City of the Stars'!"

With that Fel`Dara tossed the bloody cloth over the dagger and stormed out of the amphitheater, followed by fully a quarter of the assembly, which was by now in utter chaos.

Altira felt herself withdrawing from the crystal, its message now delivered. Her sight returned and the more familiar Dwarven glow replaced the brilliance of the ancient city. She sat on her bed, the amulet clutched tightly in her fist, utterly speechless.

Her mother had been a historian. Altira knew well the storied legends of both the Alo`Kin and the Alo`Dara. The Green Elves had been driven from their city in utter defeat by Xanath Xak and had fled to the forests of Valinar nearly three millennia hence. They were a hunted people, and the Lord of the Undead sought their destruction with a passion bordering on insanity.

The Dark Elves, under the leadership of the Dars, had fared no better. Hated by all that knew them, they had retreated to Nar`oo, to skulk and cajole an existence from the world. They were the occasional servants of the Lord of Xancata, although many of Altira's countrymen considered that service beneath them and an abandonment of their essential nature. Altira had discussed this with her mother many times and Antarra had always been adamant. She had claimed that regardless of what may have happened in the past, regardless of the alleged atrocities of the Alo`Kin, the time would come wherein the Alo`Dara would be forced to ally with the Green Elves or face complete annihilation.

And … and this was all caused by Fel`Dara and the Dars! The entire tragic history of the Dark Elves, the bedtime stories, the hushed legends of betrayal, the vaunted tales of deceit and trickery told amongst her people—they were all lies, told to keep them in subservience. It had not been the Alo`Kin that were responsible

for the plight of Altira's people. It had been caused by the selfishness of five generations of Alo`Daran rulers themselves.

And what of the future? This thought chilled Altira to her core. If the vision in the amulet was true then imminent doom hung over not only her own people, but all Elven-kind. Without the strength engendered in the unity of the races they would not have the power to resist the Undead Lord. A miraculous truth dawned upon Altira in that moment. The two races of Elves reflected two very different but essential components of existence: the sensitivity and forthrightness of the `Kin balanced the fearlessness and stealth of the `Dara. They were two sides of the same coin and both essential to life. Torn asunder, neither race could survive. Unified, they could not be defeated.

If the Elven races were to prevail, they must be brought together against the forces dedicated to their destruction. Altira had now become an unwilling servant of that very unification.

CHAPTER TWENTY-THREE

TO KILL OR NOT TO KILL

ALTIRA HAD TO FIND DANERA AND ERLINI. EVERYTHING HAD CHANGED. The Dark Elf leapt up the stairs two at a time, nearly colliding with a startled Dwarf as she raced down the corridor at the top. She called out an apology and hurried on, the remnants of the vision swirling in her mind like the smoky aftermath of a great explosion of insight. She'd been lied to, they all had. If the crystal held the truth then the Alo`Dara were not outcasts, as everyone believed. They'd been tricked out of Anea`Na`Silithar by the first Dar, not kicked out by the Greenies as all the legends claimed. They were as much modern-day victims of the Dar's treachery as Sen`Tana the Ancient had been. What's more, if some way to unify the races was not devised, then all the Elves—both green and dark—were doomed. Altira's banishment from Nar`oo had now become a nearly trivial footnote in the eventual destruction of everyone she'd ever known.

But where exactly did this put Altira? At the moment she was the only one who knew the truth. Unless … Could the Dar know of the vision in the amulet? Doubtful. If he did, he would spare no effort to see the thing destroyed or at the very least he'd twist the vision to his own purposes. Fel`Soon would have ordered it stolen from the Sultan weeks ago. But that begged the question: How did the Sultan get it in the first place? And for that matter, how did the Dwarmak have a talisman containing a critical truth about the Alo`Dara locked up in his personal vault? Oh yes, there were a myriad of questions, and Altira was going to get to the bottom of them. Her life, indeed the lives of all the Elves, depended on it.

But what should she do? She'd been saying for two weeks now that she was no longer of the Dark Forest, that the troubles of the Alo`Dara were not her concern. But that was before the vision, before she realized the truth behind what the Dar was doing. When it came right down to it, Altira realized that it wasn't the citizens of Nar`oo that she despised, it was their leader. `Tan was all right, certainly her mother was a noble Alo`Daran, and there were also many amongst her former people that she respected. Amazingly, Altira couldn't bring herself to hate them all because of the wickedness of one Elf. Fel`Soon must be exposed and the rest of her people must know the truth. One moment of revelation had changed everything.

The honor guard was barely able to salute as Altira rushed down the corridor and burst through the doors of the audience chamber. The green bird ruffled her feathers and nearly flew from her perch, to the right of the door. Danera leapt from her chair and instinctively whipped out her emerald sword before Gentain and Tyke could even move from their chairs. The Companion relaxed when she saw who it was.

"Altira, skies! You nearly scared the life right out of me!" Danera resheathed her glowing blade. "I'm glad you've come. We have much to dis—"

"Gentain, where did you get this pendant?" Altira strode across the elegant Fuan carpet and dangled the glittering talisman in front of the startled mage.

"What do you mean, mistress? I didn't get it—you did, from the Sultan."

"No, no," she replied crossly. "I mean, where did the Dwarmak get it? Why did he have it in his vault? Where did it come from? Did you make it, or was it fashioned by the Elves?"

The startled mage was clearly taken aback by the sheer intensity of her inquiry. "I'm sure I don't know. It's been in his private collection for eons. I'm not sure of its origins. Why do you ask? What's wrong?"

"Who would know of its history?"

"Balfor I would assume. Altira, what's going on?"

She stared into the fire. The dancing flames seemed to hold some comfort. "I saw … There is a vision inside it."

"What kind of vision?" Danera asked, stepping closer. "What have you seen, mistress?"

Altira turned toward her, the fire kindled now in her own eyes. "Can you bind your sight to mine?" she asked Danera. "Is there a spell that permits you to see what I see?"

This gave the Companion some pause. She turned to her bird for a moment. The Emerald Guardian had been observing Altira with some interest. "Yes," Danera said finally. "Erlini has this ability."

"Do it." Altira crossed to a chair and perched on its edge. She held the gem lightly in her fingers and stared into its aqua depths. "Tell me when you're ready."

"A moment." The woman sat next to Altira and traced a strange figure in the air with her hand.

"Is it done?" asked Altira. "Can you see?"

"Yes, proceed."

Altira frowned and turned the amulet so the sigil aligned. "Watch."

She passed into the gem, opened the lock, and shared the vision. Danera gasped as Fel`Dara struck, and fell into a stunned silence as the revelation ended.

"Incredible," said the Companion. "This … if this is true, it would change the world. If the Alo`Dara knew the truth, if the Dar knew this existed—"

Gentain was now beside himself with curiosity. "Will someone *please* tell me what the fracas this is all about? Danera, what did you see? What's in the talisman?"

"It is a recorded vision revealing the truth behind the schism between the Alo`Kin and `Dara," Altira replied. "It predicts the destruction of all the Elves if they do not unify against Xanath Xak."

The mage went pale. "Are you sure of its veracity? You're certain it's not something fabricated by someone to sow discord amongst the Alo`Darans?"

"No, it has to be true," said Altira. "The vision is contained within *Ver*. One cannot embed a false vision within that sigil, and no one but a Dark Elf could open it."

"I see." Gentain rose and paced to the window and back, scowling. "I must visit with the Dwarmak. He must know of this. Surely the pendant would have been of Elven manufacture or it could not contain such a vision." He turned to Altira. "I honestly have no idea how it came to us, mistress." Then to Danera, "I believe this answers your previous question, Companion."

Danera cocked her head. "Perhaps …"

"What question?" Altira was becoming rather annoyed with all this discussion. Someone needed to *do* something. "What are you talking about, and how does it affect the Elves?"

Danera replied, still looking pensive, "I've been confused about what's happened to you. The response to your theft of the jewel has been completely disproportionate. Fuan law provides specific penalties for thievery. Death is not one of them. Regardless of what was stolen, the Sultan had no right to hire an assassin; it violates Fuan law. In fact, the price he paid for the magic scroll alone far exceeds the value of all the gems you stole. It makes no sense, especially given the current political situation in Fu. That he would hire a second assassin—a Dark Elf, at that—is even more inexplicable. Al`Taaba is a miserly man. Regardless of his anger, it's unlikely he would incur so great an expense merely in retribution. It lends power to factions in Fu that would see him deposed. He'd be playing right into their hands, which again, he'd never do. Finally, what is the chance that the foremost Alo`Daran assassin would accept a mission from the Sultan to slay one of his own kind?"

"Oh, Jen`Tar would kill his own mother if you offered him enough gold," replied Altira. "Or, if the Dar commanded—oh."

Tyke grunted. "'Xactly. That's what we were thinking. Who is it dat's tryin' ta kill ya, anyways? Is it really da Sultan, or is it da Dar, or is it both? How do ya know it was Al`Taaba dat hired da air-dweller an' da Dark Elf?"

"I think the Cirrian was definitely engaged by him," said Altira. "The Dar was reading a scroll from the Sultan when he banished me. As for Jen`Tar—I'm not so sure."

"If Fel`Soon had the slightest notion of what was contained in that crystal," observed Gentain, "he would move the sky and the oceans to get it back so he could destroy it."

Altira moved her long knife out of the way and sat back in her chair, deep in thought. "That's assuming he knew about it." She came to a decision. "Look, there's no point in worrying about the Elves now. We do know that the Sultan hired the Cirrian, so I'm going to deal with that swine first. If I have both him and the Dar on my tail it's going to be rough, but I have no choice. I'm no longer safe in Telfall, that seems obvious. I need to get out of here and get on the road. At least I don't need to worry about constantly watching the sky for that cursed Cirrian." Without another word, she rose and started toward the door.

"One moment, mistress, if you please," called Danera. The tall woman rose and crossed to her. "I really feel that we should tell the Dwarmak about this. If it's true, as you say, that only an Alo`Daran can open the vision, then we need your help. He held the amulet safe without knowing its contents for a very long time; I think he deserves to hear about the destruction that is hanging over the Elves—it could affect his people. In addition, he may be able to shed some light on how it came to be here and perhaps even offer some help."

Altira stared at the whorls in the carpet for a long moment. She had just finished saying that they needed more information. "What possible aid could the Dwarves be? This is an Alo`Daran problem. I'm quite certain he wouldn't mind if the Undead Lord wiped out every Dark Elf on the face of Salustra."

Danera scowled. "But that's the whole point—it wouldn't *be* just the Dark Elves, would it? The Green Elves in Valinar are equally threatened, and they are allied with Telfall. Besides, as you just finished saying, you're going to have half the Dark assassins in Salustra after you as soon as Jen`Tar gets back to Nar`oo. Further, if the Dar knows about the amulet, then you'll never be able to sleep soundly for the rest of your life. The chances you'll be able to sneak back into Fu are slim at best and going anywhere near the Dark Forest would be sheer insanity. So what are you going to do? Hide somewhere like a frightened field mouse, and hope the Dar forgets about you, about the amulet? That's not you, Altira. Besides, where could you hide? Certainly not anywhere in the north, and you definitely can't take cover in Xancata, under the nose of the very person that seeks your destruction. No. I know it may be difficult to admit, but this is not something you can do alone; there are just too many forces arrayed against you. It seems to me that you need us. You need as many allies as you can get."

Altira frowned. It was clear her options needed some review, but she wanted out of this death trap of a city. "Well I know one thing for sure—Telfall is no longer safe. I'm not lying around for Jen`Tar to come back and visit me again in my bedroom!"

Gentain stepped forward. "Nay, mistress. We discovered how your attacker got in and he won't succeed a second time. That's one of the reasons Danera and Erlini are still here. The guard has been tripled and reinforced with Dara`Phen. Great magic has been employed. The elite are on all-day alert and can see through invisibility now. Also, Borin has greatly enhanced the entrance wards under Erlini's direction. I think you are safe—at least for the moment."

This gave her some pause. "All right, but you're going to have to convince me how the Dwarves can possibly help with either the Sultan or the Dar. You have no relations with either. Won't helping me just start another war?"

"Whaddya mean, 'no relations'?" Tyke replied, with a gleam in his eye. "Where do ya t'ink da Sultan gets all 'is gems, eh? We be da only ones dat know da secrets of da mines. 'E's been barterin' wit' us fer decades fer his glitter an' methinks a few

hundred stone of diamonds might go quite a ways in convincin' 'im ta leave off chasin' da elfie? I mean, whas' da mos' importan' t'ing to da Sultan, eh? A silly am'let, or his weight in rubies?"

"Listen, Tickles, it would be much simpler to just arrange a convenient accident—and a lot less expensive. Give *me* the rubies, I'll make sure Al`Taaba never bothers anyone ever again." Altira glared menacingly at her friend. "That man needs to discover he can't sic some Cirrian piss-cloud on me and get away with it!"

Danera sighed and shook her head. "Mistress, trust me. The Sultan will get his just rewards, but killing him now will only make things worse for you. Let's suppose you do manage to arrange some 'mysterious' mishap. Do you really think they'll have any doubts as to who was responsible? In the end you'll have the entire nation of Fu and Prince Al`Nuan on your tail as well as the Dar and all the assassins in the Dark Forest, not to mention Xanath Xak. Then what will you do? Let's try the financial enticement first. If that fails, then we can consider other options, but I agree with Tyke—Al`Taaba would sell his soul for a chest full of jewels. And don't forget, we still have the issue of the vision to deal with, and in my mind that is the more critical issue. Don't you think your people deserve to know what's in that crystal? Isn't that more important than killing the silly ruler of a tiny island? Would you sacrifice every Elf in Salustra just to satisfy a vendetta?"

Altira fell silent. She probably could argue the vendetta question, but the truth was, Danera was right; she needed the help. She was pretty sure that if she stepped outside the protection of Telfall, her life would be measured in minutes. Jen would find her eventually—that's what he did, and he was the best. The only thing that had saved her the last time was the green bird and her Companion. And it was true that there was always safety in numbers. Also, the prospect of sitting on top of a shipment of Dwarven diamonds did have some very intriguing potential side benefits. Who would miss a gem or two out of an entire chest?

"All right," she relented. "I'm getting tired of being chased everywhere anyway. It'll be nice to be on the offensive for once." Altira turned on Gentain and jabbed at him with an accusing finger. "But you had better see to your defenses, mister mage. Jen snuck in here way too easy last time. Your vaunted wards and magic had better work. I don't want to wake up looking like a pincushion with a thousand of Jen's poison darts sticking out my butt!"

Tyke laughed and the red mage turned … well, red. "Aye, Skymistress," he avowed. "That would be … uncomfortable."

Altira did a double take. Had the red mage made a joke? She considered him for a second then continued. "All right, fine. We'll play nice with the Sultan, but no holding back when we get to the Dar. That cur is going to get what he deserves, that I can promise you. I'll not let him oversee the obliteration of every Elf in Salustra just to satisfy his lust for power. He's going to rue the day he banished this Dark Elf!"

CHAPTER TWENTY-FOUR

THE DWARMAK

THE DWARMAK'S PRIVATE STUDY WAS AN EXERCISE IN CONTRADICTION. It was, at the same time, capacious and cluttered, solemn and gregarious, opulent yet unassuming—much like Balfor himself. Spectacular floor-to-ceiling windows graced an entire wall, permitting a magnificent view of the mountain peaks to the north. Between the leaded crystal openings were huge bookcases containing a vast array of leather-bound tomes, vellum scrolls, stacks of paper, odd knickknacks, and mysterious, clearly magical devices.

The center of the room was dominated by a huge walnut table surrounded by comfortable chairs, its highly polished surface nearly buried in maps, scrolls, open books, and correspondence. It was clear that Balfor cared little for neatness. Either that, or he was constantly called to deal with crises of one sort or another.

The Dwarven leader himself stood in front of the huge crackling hearth opposite the windows, his back to the warming fire. He was not pleased.

"This is most dire news," he declared. "You say the Undead Lord is about to wage war upon your countrymen?"

Altira sat in a chair to the leader's left. "Not exactly, sir. The vision predicts the eventual demise of the Elves, but we don't know exactly when that will be."

"So nothing is imminent. You say that you discovered this vision in the amulet? How did that happen, and why didn't we find it ourselves, ages ago? It's been here for a very long time."

Danera perched on the edge of the table across from the Dwarmak, her arms crossed. "The vision is enclosed in an ancient Elvish sigil, only visible to a descendant of the Alo`Ana."

"Not only that," Altira added, "it's accessible through an incantation only Dark Elves use—or at least I've never heard any of the Greenies using the spell of binding. It is employed when you want to assure someone's intent. Only an Alo`Daran would know of the sigil and spell."

The Dwarmak considered her narrowly. "So the message was specifically hidden and intended for one of your people."

"Yes. You say it's been here for ages," said Altira, "where did it come from? How did it come to be in your vault?"

The Dwarmak shook his head, his displeasure growing by the moment. "Its past is not fully known. There is lore recorded in the archives that speaks of an Alo`Kin named Talamar—one who brought the gem to us centuries ago and begged the Dwarmak Malchrist to keep it safe and hidden. This Elf had been of great service in his day, and the Dwarmak swore an oath that the gem would never leave his possession until one of Talamar's descendants would come to retrieve it. I felt it was appropriate to loan it to you for your protection during your battle with the Cirrian—that cursed monster had to be stopped, and we needed to keep you alive for that reason. Besides, you're a Dark Elf, and the gem was clearly destined for your hand."

Altira didn't question his frankness. She'd had her own reasons for joining forces with the Dwarves—most alliances stem from selfish motivation. "Other than that," the Dwarmak continued, "I have no idea of the amulet's origins, but it is not of Dwarven make. Our gem-masters say it is of ancient fabrication and is highly magical, but they were unable to further discern its nature and purpose—other than to discover its protective abilities, of course."

Tyke had been sitting quietly at the table next to Danera and was clearly confused. "But sir, dere's sumfin' I don' understan'. Why would an Elf give us da amulet? Wouldn' he be hidin it in his own city, or givin' it ta another Elf ta keep safe?"

"A reasonable question, captain," the Dwarmak granted. "In the distant past we had little intercourse with the Alo`Ana. Remember, this was before the destruction of the City of the Stars. I imagine Talamar foresaw that devastation and wanted to secrete it far from the conflict. Telfall would be the perfect place to hide it. An Elf would never think to look here for a precious treasure, if anyone knew about it at all. Clearly Talamar was wise in that regard." The husky Dwarven leader shook himself and turned back to Altira. "It would appear the amulet possesses significant value to the Alo`Dara. I assume the reason you requested an audience was to ask if it might be returned to them. I will happily grant this, especially since we are indebted to you, Skymistress." He nodded to her and turned to leave.

"Pardon, sire. There is one other matter," interjected Danera. "Something of significant importance to the Dwarven Empire."

Balfor turned back to the Companion, somewhat miffed. "Very well, but make it quick. I have a council meeting to attend."

"What will happen when Xanath Xak succeeds in destroying the Elves?"

This question drew the Dwarven leader back. "I thought you said that would not happen for ages?"

Altira rose from her chair and came to stand next to Danera and Tyke. "No, I said we didn't know when it would occur, but The Dar's been preparing for war against the Greenies for years. If he knows about the amulet—and we have some reason to think he might—he'll want to commence hostilities as soon as possible, before the vision in the talisman is known to his people."

"And Xak knows this will be the perfect time to strike," Danera added. "A victory over the weakened Elves would turn him upon the Dwarves. We must do everything we can to keep that from happening."

Balfor's demeanor became more intense, a cloud forming above him. "And how am I supposed to do that? The Elves have been fighting ever since they left Xancata. I've already pledged aid to Shathira; what more can I do? She'll not allow Dwarves inside Valinar, nor would we want to get involved in some skirmish between the Elven factions. I don't see we have any choice in the matter."

"May I suggest, sire," said Danera, "that the first objective is to determine the situation in Fu. We have some intelligence that implies some very strange goings-on with the Sultan."

"Al'Taaba, too?" This new revelation seemed to disturb Balfor greatly. "Skies, what's going on out there? Has everyone lost their mind? Elf against Elf, Xak considering attack, Fu unstable. What's the matter with you all? Can't you just get along? All we

Dwarves want is to be left alone in our mines. Why must we constantly be gettin' involved in other people's messes?"

Danera smiled knowingly. "The other races do not have the same calm and noble nature as do the Dwarves, sire. We do not need your intervention though, only a little help dealing with a … diplomatic mission."

"I'm afraid our ambassador to Fu was asked to leave some weeks ago, Companion. We currently have no relations with Fu."

"'Tis a bit simpler dan dat, m'Lord," offered Tyke. "We's jes lookin' ta req'sition a few baubles ta tempt da Sultan. We's plannin' on offerin him a bit o' enticemen' ta loosen his tongue firs'."

"Baubles? Captain, I know you've only recently been commissioned, but the riches of Telfall are hardly considered 'baubles.' Our mines are the envy of all Salustra. Take more care with our wealth, if you please. And what exactly do you expect to gain by 'loosening his tongue,' as you put it. How would this benefit the Dwarven Empire?"

"All right, look," admitted Altira, "this isn't about loosening the Sultan's tongue, it's about me, all right? The man clearly is angry over my taking the amulet—a trinket that was never his in the first place, but still … some appeasement needs to be made. We have to do that before we can deal with the Dar and the Dark Elves. I … *we* need to get the Sultan off my tail, and do it in a way that doesn't start a war. And, well, we need your help. All right?"

Altira's candor startled Balfor for a moment. He considered her before responding with a quizzical smile. "So, dark one. You seem to have acquired some degree of Dwarven forthrightness during your stay in Telfall. I admit, I'm impressed. Given your help with that cursed Cirrian, I'd be happy to provide the necessary gems. Tyke, see to it."

The smaller Dwarf rose and assented as the Dwarmak continued.

"However, I will need your assurance that you will continue to provide us intelligence regarding the situation in Fu and in the Dark Forest. Also"—he glanced at Danera significantly—"we need to avert a disaster with the Elves. A catastrophic battle is the last thing I want. Do I have your assurance that every means will be engaged to avoid that?"

"Trust me," Altira blurted out before Danera could respond, "after we deal with Al`Taaba, my first task is to make sure that the cursed Dar never issues the order to attack anyone ever again."

CHAPTER TWENTY-FIVE

NAJAL

AN EBULLIENT OCEAN BREEZE CAUGHT THE SPRAY FROM THE BOW wake of the ship and spattered Altira with a refreshing rain of foamy droplets. She giggled, raked her shimmering hair from her face with dampened fingers, and breathed in the ocean air. Sailing was such a glorious endeavor—no restrictions, no treacherous roads, nowhere for assassins to hide. Yes, she could very well stand to live the rest of her life sailing the seas. If it weren't for the complete absence of green, it would be a most excellent endeavor. But she did miss the forests. Nevertheless, this was an acceptable trade-off for the moment—the relative safety of an invigorating ocean voyage for the danger of a slower overland journey. It was a welcome change indeed.

The prospect of finally being done with the Sultan tempted her to succumb to Tyke's eternal optimism, but Altira had been through too much in the last moon to let her guard down for even a moment, especially after Jen`Tar. It was all well and good to be carrying a chest of gems that weighed more than she did, but Altira was far too jaded to believe a ransom was ever the end of any vow of vengeance. Even though Danera had agreed to act as intermediary, which was fine enough, Altira wasn't about to succumb to irrational confidence. They were sailing into the mouth of the dragon and they had best realize it. Nothing short of a miracle was going to make things right and Altira still had a pair of sildars with the Sultan's name written on them.

"'Ere, missie, don' be standin' so far out. If'n ya fall off, ye'll be plowed under!" Tyke wasn't enjoying the trip nearly as much as she. His face had a definite greenish tint, and he had spent the better part of the last two days in his cabin.

Altira danced farther up the bowsprit, flexing her knees as the great keel of the vessel ascended one of the moderate swells. "What's that, Tickles? You think I can't stand upright on a beam twice the size of my arm? Don't be absurd." To flaunt her Elvish balance, Altira grabbed one of the lines to the foremast and leapt into the air, circling it entirely and landing lightly again on the great jibboom of the ship as it descended into the trough of the next swell.

"Stop dat!" cried Tyke. "An' stop callin' me Tickles, or I swear I'll cut that cursed line meself."

Altira ignored him, went invisible, and passed to the deck of the ship, appearing immediately behind the stocky Dwarf. "You'll have to do better than slice a few ropes to get at me, you clumsy little oaf." She poked him in the shoulder, and as he turned she passed again, this time to the top of the fo'c'sle. Unfortunately, the ship had crested the current swell and was descending into a larger than normal trough. The deck pitched

down just as Altira appeared, and she fell to the deck, nearly hitting her head on one of the belaying pins circling the foremast.

Tyke barked a laugh. “See? Serves ya right! Don’ be passin’ roun’ da ship. Ye’ll end up inside some decking or a bulkhead and that’ll be da en’ of the sly little Dark Elfie, it will!”

Altira rolled lightly to her feet and was about to counter with a remark about Tyke’s frequent trips to the aft railings when she noticed Danera emerging from a forward hatch to stand amid-deck, looking up at the great billowing sails. Altira took careful note of the rise of the ship this time and passed again, appearing on the other side of the great mainmast. Steadying herself on the corner of the cargo hold, she approached the Companion.

“Danera, what makes you think the Sultan is going to accept this ransom? Why won’t he just steal the treasure and kill us all?”

The tall woman turned about and swiped several strands of her auburn hair from her face. “I have some influence with the court, mistress. I am … I know the Prince.”

“Al`Nuan? What’s he like, then?”

A strange, wistful smile flitted across Danera’s face and Altira detected the faintest hint of embarrassment.

“He is quite nice,” she said. “Tall, and an excellent horseman.”

“Is that so? And how exactly does knowing Prince Sure-in-the-Saddle guarantee my safety? Does he have any influence with his father?”

“Yes, some. The Prince doesn’t hold with most of the Sultan’s practices, though.”

“How so? Wait, don’t tell me, Nuan is allergic to diamonds, right?”

“Actually, he’s a simple man, drawn to nature to a large degree. He loves to hunt and explore. I met him in Torinth.”

"That's clear on the other side of the continent! What was he doing way up there?"

"Exploring, as I said. He was curious about the Pillars of Zor and wanted to visit the Union of Knights Errant in the city, to study their lore."

"I doubt his father has ever left Najal. He mostly just sits around and eats." Altira leapt up and sat on the hold cover. "In between bouts of drunkenness, that is, and cavorting around with his harem." She shuddered. "The world will be well rid of that man when he dies, that's for sure."

"Nevertheless, we must try reason, mistress. He hasn't done anything worthy of death—as yet."

"Oh, *really*? Have you talked with any of his subjects? He's a merciless tyrant. His taxes are almost more than they can bear, and if you fail to pay he will flog you without mercy. Why is that not sufficient reason to eliminate him?"

"We shall see." Danera turned toward the railings, apparently unwilling to argue the point. She stood, the wind whipping through her hair, staring into the sky. Altira jumped down and crossed to her.

"So where is your bird?" she asked, ducking to see behind the vessel's great mainsail. "I thought Companions and Guardians could never be separated. Doesn't it cause you discomfort or pain or something? Ooh, there!" She pointed upward. "Oh, wait, no, that's just a seagull."

Danera laughed lightly. "There's no discomfort, Altira. Erlini is in Anora`Fel, resting. If there is need, she can pass to me. We're relatively safe here, though, and without a convenient resting place she'd just have to circle overhead endlessly. Either that or perch on one of the masts, and that could be … well … somewhat detrimental to us remaining upright."

Altira giggled and leaned casually against the railing. She liked this Companion. Danera had a sense of humor—unlike the cursed warder—but maybe the seagull jokes were going a bit far. After all, the green bird had saved her life. "How did you ever become a Companion, anyway? How does that work?" she asked. "Did Erlini swoop down from the sky and pluck you out of the street or something?"

This time, Danera's laugh was boisterous. "Oh my, no, silly! She foresaw that I could serve and sent word to my father—I was but a child, back then. It was a long time ago."

"Just a child? That seems kind of strange—isn't being a Companion a pretty … oh, I dunno, a rather *serious* thing? I would think Erlini would have wanted someone older and more experienced, you know."

Danera became more serious. "Most Companions are called when they are very young. Hearing the Guardians is a unique ability, and when we grow older, our hearts are set more upon the things of the world; upon our families, our profession, our lives. The young still have an open heart and are willing to listen to the teachings of the Phorin`Tra. Very few who are older have the capacity to hear, and even fewer, the ability to serve as a Companion."

Altira watched the rolling, foam-tipped swells on the other side of the railing for a moment, deep in thought. "So when you decide to be a Companion, it's for life, then?"

Danera assented. "Yes, quite. Only once in recorded history has a Companion chosen to renounce his calling—and that was a very long time ago, and the circumstances unique. Of course, from time to time, Companions fall in battle. That's always very hard."

"Because of the bond with your bird?" asked Altira.

"Exactly. Finding a new companion can take years."

Altira turned from the railing and took a deep breath. "So what will happen when we arrive in Fu? Is the Sultan aware of our mission?"

This question brought Danera's wistful gaze back to Altira and she became more serious. "Yes. I met with the Prince. He'll greet us personally at the docks and escort us to the palace to avoid any … unpleasantness."

"Well, I hope you don't mind if I reserve my trust until *after* the treasure's been delivered and we're safely back out. I, for one, don't believe Al`Taaba's goodwill can be purchased so simply."

A cloud passed over Danera's normally serene features. "I have my doubts as well, I confess. There is much intrigue these days at the Fuan court … But we must try nonetheless."

"I just hope that in trying no one will be dying," Altira said quietly.

The only response she got was a dour look from the Companion. Danera turned once again to watch a lone albatross soaring across the bow and out to sea, high over the windswept swells.

THE DAY OF THEIR ARRIVAL WAS COLD AND DAMP. THE SWEEPING structures and pointed minarets of the Sultan's vast citadel seemed unusually subdued in the blanket of cold drizzle, almost as if they were hunkered down, like a huge gray panther preparing to strike. The gilded rooftops of the inner palace glittered dully in the morning's subdued light, not nearly as resplendent as they had been on Altira's prior visit. But then again, the last time she had been hiding in a too-hot attic, waiting for dark so she could sneak through the heavily guarded main gates. Altira

supposed this was a better way to enter, although by no means less dangerous.

The captain maneuvered the great three-masted schooner gently into place at the end of the capacious dock and the bow and stern lines were made fast. As soon as the gangplank was extended, a party consisting of several mounted Fuan regulars and an elegant carriage approached down the wharf. A tall man, dressed in silk finery and a blue turban, exited the coach and leapt lightly to the ground then crossed to the ship, the guards following at a respectful distance. It was Prince Al`Nuan, clearly, and Danera was the first down the gangplank.

The Prince greeted her with a brilliant smile and a bright twinkle in his deeply cobalt eyes. They embraced warmly and he then turned to observe the heavily banded chest being lugged down the gangplank by two Dwarven sailors, supervised by Tyke. Altira closely followed her treasure, not intending to let it out of her sight, but lingered near the railing on the ship, considering the docks narrowly. It would not do to be careless. She sent her vision ahead as far as she could, surveying the carriage, the soldiers, and the tops of the adjacent buildings for archers. She was trying desperately to detect the ambush she knew must be imminent. All seemed quiet though, at least at the docks.

"Come down, mistress. There is nothing to fear!" Danera called to her and separated from the Prince as the Dwarves lashed the chest to the back of the carriage. The Companion ascended the gangplank halfway and gestured for her. Altira said nothing, squinted at the Prince one last time, and then reluctantly descended.

"Altira ne'Senoli, may I present his highness Prince Al`Nuan of the Island Nation of Fu," said Danera, bowing slightly to the man in the blue turban.

"Welcome to our shores, mistress." The Prince's voice was light and pleasant and held not the slightest hint of subterfuge. "It is my hope that our differences of the past may be resolved soon as a result of the generosity of your sponsors. Please do accompany us to the palace. I personally guarantee your safety en route."

Altira considered him for a moment and then followed the Prince and Danera into the carriage, casting her sight about all the while, prepared to jump at a moment's notice. Tyke followed them in as Altira reclined stiffly in an elegant silken cushion, across from the Sultan's only son.

Danera intertwined her arm with the Prince's. "So how does your father feel about all of this, Nuan?"

The handsome man glanced at her for a moment, as if he was uncertain of Danera's motivation in asking the question. He considered her hand on his arm then looked out the window of the carriage. "He is not unaware of the importance of good relations with our Dwarven neighbors to the east. I'm sure he will be amenable to the arrangement."

"You're *sure*? You don't know?" Danera removed her hand, somewhat perplexed at his response.

"It is difficult to predict my father's temperament of late," said the Prince, still looking out the window. "Things have changed in Fu in recent moons."

A frown crossed Danera's brow. "What do you mean, Nuan? How have things changed?"

The Prince watched as his honor guard surrounded the carriage and they began to move toward the castle. "My father is not a well man, Dana. Some of his edicts have been—erratic. He has a new advisor, Zalfeer, from Xancata. He's a strange, melancholy man, and my father has abandoned his harem to spend long hours with him in his private chambers in study, which for my father is extremely disconcerting. On the few occasions we've met, he's seemed … unwell."

"Has the Sultan said anything about me?" asked Altira.

The Prince's steely gaze turned upon her. "Quite a bit, in fact, on more than one occasion."

A slight chill went down Altira's spine as she waited for him to continue, but the Prince instead turned back to the window to stare at the passing shops and the kneeling townspeople. Danera tugged at his arm again to draw his attention back. She nodded at Altira, encouraging him to continue.

"You have no idea the furor you created, mistress." He paused, as if choosing his words carefully. "The amulet you … obtained … was very significant. Its loss has caused us a great deal of difficulty."

Tyke, who had been sitting quietly beside Altira, spoke up at the mention of the pendant. "It was stolen from da Dwarmak in da firs' place, ya know. By all rights we shoulda kept it."

Danera scowled at the Dwarf, but his words didn't seem to faze the Prince.

"You have it with you, I assume?" Nuan asked Altira.

The Dark Elf sat forward and dodged the question. "You said it was significant, well how is that, exactly? And how did the Sultan come to possess it in the first place?" The Prince frowned, apparently unwilling to respond, but Danera urged him onward a second time. The Prince untwined her arm gently. "I cannot, Dana. For me to deny my father's wishes would be unwise at this time."

The Companion seemed hurt for a moment but quickly recovered. "Nuan, this is important. We need to know the truth, and the Dwarves do as well, for that matter. The amulet was entrusted to them, after all. We're not asking you to break any vows, just inform us of the situation. Surely that's in the best interests of Fu."

The Prince scowled and stared out at the serfs, who kneeled as the carriage passed. It seemed an eternity before he sighed and continued. "Very well, but if any of this gets back to my father it will be bad for you—for all of us."

Danera moved closer and took back his arm. The Prince smiled wanly and continued.

"The amulet is part of a covenant between my father and the Dar," he said. "Fel`Soon only recently learned of it and sent a squad of his most skilled infiltrators to pilfer it from the Dwarmak. His purpose was to destroy the talisman. Apparently it is somehow a curse upon the Dark Elves. But he could not destroy it, though he tried everything. It seems that it possesses some sort of ancient enchantment that is proof against all magic of the Alo`Dara. Numerous times it was cast into the deep, into bottomless pits, buried in the darkest part of the forest. Yet it always came back to haunt Fel`Soon, one way or another. Apparently many wizards and mages died trying to rid the Alo`Dara of its curse."

Altira smiled to herself. It was more likely those who found it were slain to ensure its secret would be kept hidden, but still it was encouraging that the amulet was so resilient. "So the Dar asked the Sultan to destroy it because he couldn't do it himself? Is it really that simple?"

"Yes, in return for his actions on our behalf and a substantial payment in gems. Our wizards tried every form of magic upon the item, to no avail. We finally sent to Xancata for one of the Dark Sorcerers as a last resort and Zalfeer came."

Tyke crossed his arms and sat back in disgust. "If da Dar had'n stolen it in da firs' place, dere'd be no problem—it was sittin' ignored in da deepest vault, an' da Dwarmak wasn' about ta go to war over a silly gem."

A confused look was Danera's only response. "So wait. This Sorcerer from the Dark Lord … did he actually test his powers against the jewel?"

"No, Altira took it before he arrived," said Al`Nuan. "He has since become my father's chief advisor."

This clearly surprised Danera. "A Sorcerer from Xancata is meddling in the affairs of Fu? That's unheard of."

The Prince grunted. "More than just meddling, Dana. Some say he has my father under some sort of trance. Things have been much worse in the palace since he arrived."

"Worse in what way?" asked the Companion.

"My father's directives and edicts have been erratic, even for him. He has recalled the border guards, for example."

"The coastal defenses have been abandoned?" Danera was clearly astounded.

"Quite. Never in the vaunted history of Fu have our shore cannon been forsaken, yet that's not the worst of it. He has dismissed the Minister of the Arcane, and the Prime Minister resigned in protest."

Danera jerked her arm free. "What?! But who is running the government? How can this be?"

The Prince shrugged. "The Sultan can do anything he wants. The administration has ground to a halt—except for the tax collectors of course. And my father sees no one. It's impossible to reason with him. We can execute no treaties of trade; without his edicts the judicial system has ground to a halt. Something dire is going to happen, I'm telling you, Dana, and all I can do is sit and watch it happen!" The Prince hit the cushioned side of the carriage with his fist in frustration.

"So what does this mean for *me*?" asked Altira. "Danera said we were going to meet with him. Why shouldn't I believe this isn't some kind of ruse to steal back the talisman and the treasure from Telfall? What assurances do we have?"

The Prince grunted. "None whatever. All I can guarantee is that you'll be conveyed safely to my apartments until you are granted an audience. After that, it's anyone's guess what will happen."

CHAPTER TWENTY-SIX

AL'TAABA

ALTIRA GAZED IMPLACABLY THROUGH THE WINDOW OF HER SUITE, thrown open to overlook an elegant inner courtyard of the great Palace of Najal. The rain of the previous day had relented, and the early morning sunlight reflected brightly off the golden minarets, visible over the tiled roofs to the east and north. The tall fig trees planted in the garden below swayed gently in the morning breeze and the slight zephyr wafted through Altira's raven hair. If you ignored all the intrigue, Fu would be a most excellent place to live. Too bad half the people in the country wanted her dead.

It felt really strange, in fact, to be sitting here, in the very hand of the Sultan. It was kind of like hunkering down in the midst of a vast hive of sleeping hornets—you didn't want to breathe too loudly for fear of rousing a nightmare. But that wasn't the half of it. Altira was visiting the palace as if she were some kind of vaunted diplomat, and not a former thief of state property. She couldn't shake the feeling that at any moment this travesty of a plan was going to blow up in her face. She needed to be done with this and get away as quickly as possible.

Seeming to echo her concerns, Tyke spoke from behind her, "Ya canna go in dere alone, Alti. Dere's no guarantee 'e won' jes kill ya and steal da amulet. An' besides, da Dwarmak made me responsible fer da gems. If da fat man's gonna take 'em, 'e'll have to do it past me own axe!"

Altira returned from the window and came to stand next to the Dwarf and the seated Companion. "You heard what Nuan said. I alone am permitted an audience with the Sultan. Don't worry, I can take care of myself. It's not like he could threaten me, really. Skies, he must weigh forty stone! It would take an army of servants to hoist him off his throne. I could outrun him carrying Erlini." She plopped down into a chair and put her feet up on the table. "But I do appreciate your concern, Tickles."

Danera had been entranced by the golden glitter of the minarets outside the window. She tore her eyes away with some reluctance. "It's not the Sultan I'm worried about, Altira, it's the Sorcerer."

"The mage from Xancata? Why would I care about him? No minion of the Dark Lord would ever attack one of the Alo`Dara—we're ancient allies."

"I think you may find Xanath Xak's opinion of the Dark Elves somewhat diminished as of late," Danera said. "You had best assume nothing as regards your standing with him. And furthermore, why is the Sorcerer still here? If he was called to destroy the pendant, and it was stolen by you, then why would he still remain in Fu? He must have a more devious intent. No, this whole thing smells of dead fish. I believe the time has come

to call Erlini, and perhaps Naroc as well. I'm with Tyke in this. You shouldn't go alone."

This assertion seemed to inflate the now well-equipped captain and Altira rolled her eyes as Danera continued. "In fact, we all should be there, or go not at all. There is protection in numbers, remember."

Altira dropped her feet to the ground and sat up. "And you think sauntering in there with a couple of Guardian birds, two Companions, and a pudgy Dwarf with an oversized tree-chopper is somehow going to be overlooked? That's crazy. I'm telling you, the best thing to do is to slip a sildar between the Sultan's ribs—"

"Hush!" hissed Danera, her voice edged with atypical severity. "You mustn't threaten Al`Taaba within the walls of the palace. There are ancient wards about. And as I told you before, violence in this case is the worst solution. It will only engender more conflict and turn Nuan against us."

"It seems to me that violence is *precisely* what we're about here," replied Altira. "It was violence that the Sultan intended when he hired the Cirrian and Jen`Tar in the first place. What, do you think they were trying to bore me to death with harsh language? And if that Sorcerer intends to steal the amulet, do you really think he's going to send us an engraved request via courier? No, magic will be afoot—dark and dire forces for sure."

Tyke grunted and crossed to the chest of gems placed near the wall. "Well, dis treasure is goin' nowhere near either the Sultan or dat Sorcerer wit'out me and da Companion, I'm tellin' ya. So jes git over the idea dat ye'r goin' in dere alone. It's all of us or none of us, as Danera says."

"Fine! You can keep your cursed treasure." Altira slid forward on her chair and judged the distance to the door, preparing to jump. "I'll deal with him in my *own* way, then."

Danera, discerning her intent, reached across and gripped her arm. "Wait, mistress, I've called Erlini, and she's just arrived. Please, let's consult with her before making any rash decisions. Also, Farthir and Naroc are ready to spring to our aid if the need arises. As you said before—safety in numbers."

Altira squinted at the Companion, considered the sincerity in her eyes, and wrestled with her anger for a long moment. Having both birds here would work to her advantage—they would be a great distraction. With the Fuans' attention drawn to them it would be much easier to kill the Sultan at her leisure. Also, there was a holy fortune inside that chest and Altira had no desire to give it all to Al`Taaba without at least a chance to pilfer a few of the larger baubles. She settled back into her chair and tried to pull her arm free.

"All right, fine, then let go. So what marvelous Guardian-hatched plan has Erlini concocted? Is she going to sing some magical song that melts the Sorcerer into a pile of lard? Can Farthir and Naroc intimidate him by encircling the castle in a ring of fire? I'm telling you, this isn't going to be solved with magic. The only answer to this is going to be blood, mark my words."

This seemed to disturb Danera greatly. She removed her hand from Altira's arm and sat back. "Well first, Erlini can shield us from any attack by either the Sorcerer or Al`Taaba's men, as long as she is close. She also has great experience in negotiation. The Phorin`Tra are ancient—"

A heavy knock on the door interrupted Danera. Before anyone could respond, it was thrust open by a well-armed soldier who then stepped back to permit Al`Nuan to enter.

Altira was struck again at how different the Prince was from his father. He held himself erect and walked with a purposeful step. He projected confidence and an assurance of control,

whereas the Sultan seemed to wallow in his own gluttony and thought only of wealth and how to acquire more. And there was a spark in the Prince's eyes, something alluring and revelatory of an intelligence and perception that was completely absent in his father.

The Prince didn't even glance at the others in the room, his attention focused solely on her. "Altira, come with me. Vizier"—he gestured over his shoulder—"have your people bring the chest."

A short man dressed in flowing yellow silken robes ducked around the Prince and swirled toward the treasure, assisted by two hefty slaves.

"Nay. Stand fast, there!" barked Tyke, his hand going to his short-sword. "No one touches da ches' but me, and where it goes I go, by order of da Dwarmak. You want da gems, you'll havta take me wit' 'em."

Al`Nuan raised a restraining hand, halting the Vizier. The Prince considered the stubborn Dwarf for a moment. "Very well, short one, but I doubt even you could carry that chest alone; it must weigh fifty stone. You can't guard it and carry it at the same time."

This caused Tyke some pause. He started to reach for the trunk but jumped back when the iron-banded chest rose from the floor, apparently of its own volition, to hover in midair. He whipped out his sword and cast about. "Who? Put it down or I swear—"

Danera smiled serenely and rose from her divan. She gestured and the chest moved toward the Dwarf. "It's all right, Tyke. I'll float it. Nuan, lead on. We'll all go together and pay your father a visit."

The Prince took a step, as if to intervene, then relented. "Very well, but I warn you, we may not all be granted entrance. But we shall see." He motioned for the Vizier and his men to leave and then led the group out. Danera followed closely with the chest, and Tyke walked alongside, his hand resting on one of the handles. Altira brought up the rear with several soldiers following closely.

They turned right and started down a long corridor with elegant carpets. Altira scooted around the chest and leaned close to Danera. "Where is Erlini?" the Dark Elf whispered.

"Here, circling above in the clouds, ready to descend at need. Naroc and Farthir will also arrive shortly. Let's hope they're not needed."

"Yes, let's do hope." Altira smiled crookedly and laid a hand on her long knife. This would be entertaining, at the very least.

They didn't have far to go; the great Hall of Inquisition was close. They walked down a second long corridor, this one lined with larger-than-life statues of bejeweled rulers perched upon gigantic steeds. Lush flowering plants and shrubbery adorned numerous sheltered alcoves and great white plaster pillars lined the corridor. The palace was certainly impressive, although Altira had to wonder how many peasants had starved paying for it.

They reached the end of the hall and stopped before a pair of huge golden doors festooned with flowing crimson silk. Two hulking sentries armed with gleaming scimitars barred entry. One of them gestured, palm outward, and spoke in a commanding voice. "Only the Elf be permitted entry by His Majesty. The rest must wait outside."

Tyke's hand drifted toward his axe but the Prince intervened quickly.

"Do you really think it wise to interfere with me, Calas?" Nuan said. "Should I mention this to your Vizier? The latrines in the south wing have been in need of a good cleaning for a month now. I'm sure we can find some more profitable employment for one with so little respect for authority." The Prince looked down upon the guard—for Nuan was nearly a head taller—and smiled as he laid a hand on his elegant sabre. "And further, how exactly is the Elf supposed to drag a chest into the hall alone when it weighs three times as much as you do? Tell me this."

An uncomfortable mixture of fear and befuddlement overcame the sentry and he dropped his hand, but still didn't move.

"Open those doors, now!" Nuan commanded, the softness around his eyes hardening in an instant, "and hold them while we enter. I *will* converse with my father, and you will stand aside. Now move!"

His barked command cowed the pair, who clearly hadn't been expecting a regal entourage. They pulled the doors open and the Prince strolled through, gesturing imperiously for the rest to follow.

Altira couldn't resist giving the two a superior look as she sauntered by. She was rewarded with a glare that spoke volumes.

They passed through several layers of flowing linen and silk and emerged into a great, circular enclosure bounded by elegant pillars of ivory-colored marble. A raised platform occupied the center of the area, surmounted by a throne carved from a single huge quartz crystal adorned with myriad gems. Above, a vast rotunda was perforated by numerous circular openings that admitted the late morning sun, casting shafts of brilliant light that reflected off the marble floor and glittered amongst the diamonds, rubies, and emeralds of the throne.

Upon the gem-studded seat, reclining against a score of elegant silken pillows, was surely the largest man in Salustra. In all her exploits, Altira had never come across a more corpulent example of humankind. She couldn't even guess his weight, but it would have taken one of the coal wagons from Telfall to move him. Al`Taaba, the 'beneficent' Sultan of Fu, wore a blindingly white chemise draped in garnets and sapphires. The sunlight hit the jewels, causing tiny crimson and blue rainbows to glitter against the pristine linen, making it difficult to focus upon him without blinking. By contrast, he was attended by a shadowy figure dressed in a deeply hooded charcoal robe standing immediately behind the throne.

"Good morning, Father," said Prince Nuan. "I believe you asked to see this Elf, and these are her friends and the ransom provided by the Dwarves. A kingly sum, if I may say."

The Sultan glowered and waved the Prince aside. His other arm gripped the throne and shook slightly, as if he was barely able to keep himself from sliding to the floor. "I did not summon these others. What are you doing here, Nuan?"

"My apologies, Father. I felt it was necessary in order to bring the treasure into your presence—it was much too weighty for the Elf to manage, so we assisted her."

The chest floated to the foot of the Sultan's dais as the huge ruler waved a dismissive hand. "Bah! We have slaves aplenty for such foolishness. What need have we of a Dwarf and since when do the Companions of the North deign to lug around chests of gems? What do you take me for, Nuan, a complete idiot? Now, get out. Our business is with the cursed Elf, not with all these others!"

Danera moved forward to stand beside the Prince. "As you say, sire, it is not usual for me to be here, and you know we do

not advise frivolously. Believe me when I say that it is in the best interests of the Fuan Nation to permit us to remain."

The Sultan shifted uncomfortably in his seat and the dark-cowled figure behind leaned forward to whisper in his ear. Altira nearly reached for a sildar but thought the better of it when she noticed a suspicious billowing in the draperies above the throne. She sent her sight upward and discovered two snipers secreted behind the crimson curtains, both armed with steel crossbows, arrows nocked and at the ready. Casting about the chamber, Altira was alarmed to discover ten more archers encircling the dome behind the curtains.

She sidled toward Danera. "How far is Erlini?" she whispered, her voice barely audible.

The tall Companion glanced down at her—she had been watching the interaction between the cowled figure and the Sultan with some alarm. "Sorry. What was that?"

"Your bird, how close is she?" Altira's annoyance at having to repeat herself was revealed in her hiss. "We're going to get skewered if we're not careful."

"Erlini is just above the rotunda, circling. She's causing some stir amongst the sentries atop the hall."

"She needs to get in here with us, and fast. I think—"

Altira was interrupted by the Sultan, who had finally leaned away from the Sorcerer. "We are not interested in the point of view of the Guardians," he said. "This is an internal matter involving the theft of Fuan state property. The Dwarf and the Companion will leave immediately and the Dark Elf will remain for judgment, with the chest."

Altira stepped forward. "Sultan, there is no need for discussion. Behold the treasure the Dwarves have offered." She motioned for Tyke to open the strongbox. The Dwarf fished out a key from around his neck and bent to undo the large padlock.

Altira spoke through clenched teeth. "Sultan, I am … sorry … for any inconvenience my prior acts may have caused. We are here to make amends. These gems …" Tyke finally threw open the lid of the chest to reveal its glittering contents. The sheer grandeur of the jewels stunned even Altira for a moment. *Skies! The Dwarmak was right—when Dwarves put together a ransom, they don't mess around.* She hastily continued, "These gems represent a hundred times the value of what I removed." The Sultan's eyes filled with avarice as he beheld the size of the diamonds in the chest—many were larger than Altira's fist. "As for the amulet, it seems the Dar stole it from the Dwarves. Since it was not his to give in the first place, I'm sure the beneficent ruler of the Fuan Empire wouldn't mind consenting that it should be returned to its rightful owner. Please accept these trinkets in return for any inconvenience—"

Al`Taaba grunted and leaned forward, reaching toward the chest. As he did so, the dark-cowled figure behind him raised three of the fingers on his left hand, formed a fist, and then thrust a pointed finger at Danera. Altira recognized the gesture instantly—it was Cal`Tali.

Before she heard the twang of the three crossbows, Altira passed upward, appearing behind the snipers on the hidden balcony encircling the chamber. She whipped out her long knife as the Prince below screamed, "No!"

Altira attacked before the soldiers had a chance to reload. First one, then the other—her ancient knife danced in her fist as if it had a will of its own. She skewered the second soldier and he tumbled from the balcony, ripping the drapes from the ceiling as he fell. The revealed scene below pierced Altira as

surely as any sabre: Danera was sprawled on the floor in the spot Altira had just vacated, a black-feathered shaft protruding from her chest. The Prince lay bleeding on the marble behind, an arrow embedded in his shoulder. Tyke was nowhere to be seen. Altira leapt to the balcony railing and finally spotted the Dwarf up top, at the far end, hewing through archers with his battle-axe.

In that instant, a horrific shriek sounded from above and a huge chunk of the roof was ripped from the rotunda, showering the Sultan and the Sorcerer with debris and bits of glass. This was followed by a second piercing cry as the rest of the gilded dome was torn away by a pair of golden-tipped talons.

Even as Erlini tore through the roof to get at her Companion, the Sultan himself, seeing his son viciously attacked, whipped out a bejeweled sabre from his robes and thrust it at the Sorcerer. Altira, however, was focused on Tyke—she was not about to let the Dwarf be overcome as a dozen archers turned upon him. Jumping into the Darkness, she bounced back and forth across the chamber, her knife dealing death at every passing. She managed three leaps before she was thrown to the wall by a tremendous explosion from below.

The talisman shielded most of the blast but smoldering bits of the crimson curtains rained down around her as plaster dust and the smell of burning flesh filled the air. Rising from the floor and wiping dust from her eyes, Altira stumbled to the railing of the balustrade. The remaining elegant draperies surrounding the upper railings were swirling to the floor in burning, smoking tatters. Erlini had somehow managed to descend to the throne-room floor—doubtless falling most of the distance, for there was no room to extend her wings inside the building—and a bright green bubble surrounded the

Phorin`Tra, her slain Companion, and the Prince. The Sultan lay crumpled against the base of the soot-singed pillar on the opposite side of the chamber. His corpulent body was charred, bloody and motionless.

The Sorcerer was nowhere to be seen.

CHAPTER TWENTY-SEVEN

PRINCESS OF TORINTH

IT WAS FARTHIR NOW WHO STOOD GAZING FORLORNLY OUT THE closed palace window, and not Erlini's Companion. Altira sat across the room near the fire while a somber Tyke perched on a stool near the door, absently stroking a whetstone down the razor-sharp blade of his battle-axe. The tall warder turned from the rain pattering against the windowpanes and came to extend his hands toward the meager blaze in the hearth.

"Miserable weather," he noted.

Altira nodded. "You'd think it would be warmer … this late in summer." It had poured all night and morning and she was beginning to wonder if the sun would shine upon her ever again.

Farthir sighed. "We should talk. Tyke, come and sit."

The Dwarf propped the handle of his axe against his stool and plopped into an armchair across from them. Farthir fished a poker from a stand next to the fire and tried to evoke some warmth from the smoldering wood in the hearth. His ministrations didn't seem very effective. He turned back to them and sat. "Mistress, I realize a lot happened during the fight, but can you remember how it all started?"

"Of course. I'll never forget that moment," replied Altira. "It was the cursed Sorcerer."

"He used some sort of spell?"

"No, he directed the archers to attack."

"Dat makes nae sense, Alti," replied the Dwarf. "How in da seven skies could some cursed Sorcerer from Xancata be orderin' roun' Fuan soldiers?"

"I've no idea. All I know is that he raised three fingers and then gave the signal to fire—in Cal`Tali. He specifically directed them at Danera."

Farthir shook his head in confusion. "I don't understand. He could have used magic to enthrall them I suppose, but why would Xanath Xak interfere with the Sultan? They're supposed to be allies. Al`Taaba had always been his best supporter in the south. Now he's made a bitter enemy of Al`Nuan. It's been my experience that when you don't understand the Dark Lord's purpose, you're in mortal danger. We must figure this out."

Altira squirmed in her chair and shifted her long knife out of the way. "I've got an even better question. Why strike down poor Danera at all? She wasn't threatening anyone; she was just trying to arbitrate—to make it better for me, to make it right with the Sultan."

"I think the archers were originally intended for you," said Farthir and she scowled in response. "But any minion of Xanath Xak will jump at the chance to destroy a Companion. They know how painful it is for the Guardian and how difficult it will be to replace Dana. Erlini is devastated."

"Where did she go?" asked Altira. The green bird had grasped her Companion's body and vanished from the hall before Altira could leap from the balcony.

"Erlini returned Danera to her father in Torinth, then retreated to Anora`Fel to mourn."

"Dana was from Torinth?" Tyke sat up, showing some interest. "Da city of da Knights?"

"Aye," replied Farthir. "She was the daughter of King Cestellan."

Altira's eyes went wide and she sat up. "Danera was a *princess?*"

"The one and only Princess of Torinth, yes. Cestellan has two sons but no other daughters. She was but a child when she was called by Erlini over fifteen anna ago, and well beloved by her father. It was perhaps the most difficult thing he's ever done—to let her go. But she was an exceptionally gifted Companion. She took naturally to the calling."

The three fell silent for a long moment as they recalled their friend and colleague. It was Farthir who finally broke the spell and his somber mood seemed to permeate even the feebly glowing embers of the fire. "She gave up everything for her Companionship. She loved Erlini so. She was an exceptional friend and will be sorely missed, not just by the Emerald Guardian, but by all of us who knew and loved her."

"She helped me when no others would," affirmed Altira. "If it wasn't for her I would never have had the chance to make things right with the Sultan. She talked to Al`Nuan—how is the Prince doing, by the way?"

"Miserable, as you can imagine. He and Danera were, well, close."

The meager flames in the hearth held Tyke's attention as well. "Ya, it was pretty clear dey liked each other. I guess he's da new Sultan now—assuming he survives his in'jry."

"It wasn't serious, just a shoulder wound," said the warder. "He took the shaft intended for Danera, I guess."

Altira started and tore her eyes from the fire. "But the Sorcerer commanded an attack on three. I saw his gesture. Danera and Nuan were hit … What happened to the other bolt?"

Tyke grunted and unbuttoned his tunic to reveal a silvery, glimmering undershirt. There was a tiny depression in the center of his chest. "Borin gave me dis elemail before I left Telfall. Wit'out it, I'd be lyin' next to da Prince."

A dawning realization descended upon Altira. "Wait a minute. If the archers were aiming at us, why did they hit the Prince?"

Tyke rebuttoned his shirt, his somber look deepening. "I saw it all." He paused a moment and glanced sideways at the Elf. "She was divin' to push ya out of da way, Alti. And the Prince was reachin' ta pull her back."

"Me?" A chill of revelation descended upon Altira like a plunge into icy water. "You mean, if I hadn't passed …"

"Ya," responded Tyke. "Well, dere was no way she would've known you'd 'scape so quickly."

"Oh no …" Altira hid her eyes with a hand. "No, no, no …" Was she really responsible for the death of her friend? Was her pitiful life worth such a price?

Farthir laid a gentle hand on her shoulder. "Do not lay upon yourself the blame for the Sorcerer's actions. You reacted instinctively, Altira, as did the Prince and Danera. There was no time to consider your decision. It's amazing you weren't all killed. It was clearly Zalfeer's intent."

"Dat's why he snuck in 'ere den, wasn' it? Ta kill Dana?"

"I don't know, Tyke. I interviewed the Ministers. He's apparently some lesser minion of the Dark Lord. I think originally, he was summoned just to destroy the amulet."

"Where is he, the scum?" A grim fury descended upon Altira. "He'd better put his affairs in order because he's going to regret the day he ever laid eyes on this Alo`Daran." She straightened her belt, wiped her eyes with the back of a hand, and crossed to the fire, her back to the two. For a moment, the only sound in the room was the plaintive pattering of the rain against the windows and the rustling of the palm fronds in the wind outside.

Farthir broke the silence. "No one knows, mistress. He seems to have vanished."

"That won't do him any good." Altira turned from the hearth and crossed to Tyke, pulling him to his feet by the arm. "Go find something of his—a comb, a brush, a piece of clothing …"

"Me? But Alti, I nae—"

"Enchantments will be made. No one can hide from me. Danera's death will not go unanswered, this is my solemn vow." She laid one hand on her knife and turned to look down at Farthir, her fury evolving into an iron resolve.

"Aye," agreed Tyke, retrieving his own glittering weapon. "And me axe will aid ja. Dat murderer will nae escape our vengeance by hidin' in some cursed desert!"

Farthir was not so easily aroused. "A Sorcerer of Xak is no one to be trifled with, my friends. He commands dark powers that are daunting and dangerous. Finding him will be one thing, killing him will be … harder."

"Farthir, don't you dare tell me—" cried Altira.

The Companion raised a hand. "Don't get me wrong. I feel as you do, but we need to ask ourselves, what is the most important task in front of us? Remember the amulet. Don't forget, it was the Dar that started all this—it was he who had it stolen from Telfall, it was he who sent it to Fu and requested it be destroyed, and I'm thinking, it was he who sent the second assassin to kill you, Altira. If it wasn't for him, the Dark Sorcerer would still be sitting in Xancata and Danera would still be alive."

Altira's fury was turned as she recalled the vision contained in the gem. That was all true. She should deal with Fel`Soon first. Otherwise she'd be dodging Jen`Tar's poison darts for the rest of her life.

"Fine," she said. "But when we finish with the Dar I'm telling you, wherever that snake is hiding, be it in Xancata or the deepest pit in Trellious, he's done for. He will feel my sildars slip into his heart."

A loud crack from outside the window was followed by a shuddering boom and the floor shook. Altira hastened to the window to behold one of the great palms, lying prostrate in the courtyard. A howling vortex of wind swirled around it, as if capering over its fallen foe. She set her jaw and imagined the tree as Zalfeer, lying below her.

The warder's voice interrupted the rumination and drew her from the window. "First things first, Altira. We need to enlist aid if we're going to expose Fel`Soon. He's too powerful in Nar`oo. Besides, the Alo`Kin need to know of the vision and Queen Shathira may have insight as to how to best address the issue of the Dar."

The prospects of journeying deep into the forests of Valinar were none too pleasant, but the warder was right. If anyone would know how to get at the leader of her former people it would be the Greenies. If traveling there meant she could answer, even in part, the death of Danera and the subjugation of her people by Fel`Soon, then she would put aside her oath of vengeance and her hatred of the Alo`Kin, at least for the moment.

"All right, fine, Valinar then. But Naroc had better come—him and that red bubble of his." Altira had the distinct feeling

she was falling behind in the battle for her life. "I don't want to end up looking like a green-quilled porcupine with a thousand Alo`Kin arrows in me before I can say hullo."

CHAPTER TWENTY-EIGHT

SHATHIRA

ALTIRA SQUINTED AGAINST THE WIND, AND TRIED TO SEE INTO THE forest far below. She clung tightly to Farthir for her very life as the air tore at her blouse. Still, the wind here was humid and warm at least, unlike the frigid blasts she had endured when they returned from destroying the Cirrian. This breeze was pleasant, even refreshing. The radiant afternoon sun shone on the cotton-puff clouds while below, the verdant green of the sun-kissed canopy beckoned. Naroc banked gently right and spiraled lower. These trees were very different from the forests of Nar`oo. Altira could almost hear a faint, melodious song drifting upward, as if the trees themselves rejoiced in the gloriousness of the day.

In spite of the compelling vistas and the woods' call, Altira's mind continued to worry over the death of Danera. She felt responsible, and that alone was surprising. Since she'd never cared for anyone or anything before, why would the demise of a Companion affect her so? She had tried to rationalize her actions in her mind many times, but it just didn't work. Even the prospects of finding the Sorcerer didn't seem to assuage her pervasive feeling of loss and guilt. She needed to talk with Tyke. What had he said after his sister died? Something about her being with her family in a better place? Altira needed to find that belief somehow.

Her mind snapped back to the present as Naroc angled toward a clearing carpeted with lush grass and bright patches of wildflowers. As they alighted, Altira was struck with the sheer vitality of the place. She could almost feel each blade of grass stretching toward the nurturing rays of the afternoon sun. She had always enjoyed the open green spaces of her home forest. These flowers, however, in vermillion, aqua, and gold, put the colorful denizens of Nar`oo to shame. They swayed in the gentle breeze swirling from the east as if dancing in unison to some ethereal melody. It was a day more marvelous than any in her memory.

Altira raised a hand against the brightness and surveyed the tree line over Farthir's shoulder, half a league to the west. "Where are we, then?" she asked the warder. "Is this the meeting place?"

"Yes." Farthir shifted his sword and leapt to the ground, then headed toward the forest terminus, striding through the ankle-deep grass as if wading into the ocean. Altira leapt from Naroc's shoulder and reluctantly jogged after him. Meeting in the open was one thing. Traipsing into the forest was quite another. Here things were under control, but standing in the middle of a thousand trees, well, a Dark Elf could have any number of mysterious "accidents" wandering around inside Valinar.

A huge gust of wind rippled through the grass as the great eagle took to the sky behind them, Naroc's cry as much a challenge as a farewell. Altira turned to watch with some alarm as the huge avian beat into the air. There was another bit of protection gone.

After gaining some speed, the great eagle banked sharply left as if he sensed something that altered his intent. Dipping a huge wing, he circled back to her high above. Altira watched in surprise as Naroc cocked his head in her direction, seeming to focus intently upon her for some reason.

"Patience."

Altira leapt forward in a crouch thinking some Greenie had snuck up behind her in the grass, but there was nothing. Who had spoken? The voice was definitely not Farthir's—the warder was a goodly distance away, gazing in confusion at his bird. Also, the tenor of the voice was strange. It was deep and low, impossibly sonorous, almost as if a giant had somehow snuck inside her head and was addressing her from the inside out. Altira glanced up at Naroc.

No, he couldn't. She very nearly called back to the crimson eagle, but that was silly. No shout could possibly reach so high up. Still, she swore she saw the bird smile before he broke from his orbit and headed for the edge of the clearing, gaining altitude as he went. "Wait, come back!" she called as the red eagle disappeared into the Darkness.

Altira stood, staring where the Guardian had vanished, trying to make some sense of what had just happened. What was going on in her life? Wasn't it enough to be burdened with guilt over the death of Danera and hounded all over Salustra by half a dozen factions, all of whom wanted her dead? Now she had to deal with going crazy and hearing voices. "What's next?" she muttered. "Babbling to myself like a crazy warder?"

"What did you say, mistress?"

Altira jumped again. The man had snuck up behind her.

"I couldn't hear you with your back turned. What was that?" he repeated.

"Oh, nothing, forget it." She glanced back at the clouds that had swallowed Naroc. "Just losing my mind is all."

The warder cocked his head in much the same manner as his bird. "Are you all right, Altira? Why did he return to you?"

"I have absolutely no idea." She sighed then rubbed her eyes with her palms, and leveled him with a steady gaze. "Okay, listen, when he talks to you, what does it sound like?"

Astonishment crossed the man's face as he gaped at her, his mouth open, unable to reply.

"Ya, that's what I thought," she said grimly. "When Naroc came back—when he was circling over me … Are you planning on standing there like that all day? A sparrow's going to nest in there if you're not careful." The warder slammed his mouth shut. "Look, never mind. The pressure is finally getting to me, I guess." She turned, dodged around him, and started toward the forest. Death from a Greenie arrow would be a welcome relief compared to the web of insanity her life had become.

"No, wait! Mistress, hold on a moment." Farthir trotted to her and touched her shoulder. "You heard something. Is that what you're saying?"

"I don't know what I'm saying. I don't know anything anymore."

"The voice of the Guardians seems different to each that can hear, but usually it manifests as a sound in your mind possessing great substance and weight. Is that what you heard?"

She didn't answer, just kept tromping toward the edge of the clearing.

"He said, 'Patience,'" Farthir blurted out.

The word hit Altira like a mountain of lead. She stumbled and very nearly fell to the ground, but managed to catch herself. She slowly turned on the warder, frightened in a way she'd never thought possible.

Farthir seemed just as off center, which was nearly as disturbing. "This is—well, I've never known of any Alo`Daran that could hear a Guardian. It's incredible. Not since the ancient days when your people were one with the Alo`Kin was such a thing even conceivable." He closed the distance between them, studying her intently. "You are truly a mystery, Altira ne Senoli` of the Alo`Dara. When we met you, you were dark, hidden, and closed. Now … well, it's amazing for you to even hear, but why Naroc would choose to speak to you—that's almost the greater mystery. He never does that without a purpose, without sensing some great portent in someone. This implies a unity that's astounding. That *you can hear him*"—he shook his head, a smile creeping across his lips—"it implies a great change in your heart, indeed."

"I'm not admitting anything, warder." Altira intently considered the grass swirling around her legs for a moment. "I don't have any answers, okay? I have no idea what's going on, either in my heart or in my life, but this is neither the time nor the place, all right?"

"Perhaps you will find answers with the Alo`Kin."

"Either that, or I'll discover a new way to carry a thousand arrows." She chuckled to herself and dodged around a clump of sedge, then pushed harder through the swirling grass. Her fear of the Greenies had somehow vanished, to be replaced by a surprisingly numb acceptance of her fate. It was clear she no longer had control over her life. Altira felt like she was careening down a great turbulent river, clinging desperately to a tiny bit

of flotsam, bobbing and pitching uncontrollably toward some unknown destination. She was no more capable of altering the path of her life than of changing the course of the mighty Calasta River. Her only option, it would seem, was to desperately try not to be forced under the surging waters swirling about. Perhaps some merciful Alo`Kin shaft would end her misery and she could join Danera in whatever place she had gone.

It wasn't far to the forest. The huge maple and birch trees—two hundred cubits tall at least—towered over them as they approached, walking side by side. The glorious residents of Valinar were twice the size of the tallest trees in Nar`oo, and Altira became dizzy trying to even glimpse the tops. To fall from one of them would be disastrous. The trees, however, evoked an unusual peace in her soul that was confusing. The closer she got, the better she felt for some reason, and this shouldn't be. She was Alo`Daran; Valinar should feel alien, foreign, hostile. But instead, the closer she got, the more the lost, panicked sensation that had followed Naroc's communication was suffused by a stillness in her soul. She felt a strange attraction to these trees, like she were returning home after a long journey, or perhaps as if they represented some part of her that had been hidden for a very long time.

Farthir was directly in front of her now, his back to her, and Altira nearly ran into him when he came up short.

"What—" She stepped around him and froze. Two Greenies stood just cubits away. Altira's first impulse was to flee. These were the Elves she had been taught to despise her entire life.

Farthir, sensing her discomfort, laid a gentle hand on her shoulder. "Altira, may I present Aanarain and Shathira of the Alo`Kin."

Altira stared at the two white-skinned Elves, not knowing what to do. These weren't just any two Alo`Kin, they were the leaders—the King and Queen of the people responsible for the death of her parents. What was she supposed to do now? Finally, she decided on a curt nod—the least deferential greeting among Elven-kind.

Shathira, on the other hand, stepped forward with a gentle smile and bowed deeply. Her flowing gossamer gown rippled in the summer breeze that whispered through the forest. "Ak`ta e`olith, Altira ne`Senoli. Long have we awaited this day, and grateful we are that it has finally arrived."

Altira took a step back, the Queen's deference almost a physical blow. There was really no way she deserved such esteem.

King Aanarain stepped forward as his companion finished and also beckoned toward Altira. "Be at peace, daughter of Senoli. We bear you no malice. Danera has informed us of your quest and need and we are here to assist. However …" he turned toward Farthir in some confusion, "… we had expected Erlini's Companion, and not the Phorin`Ala of Naroc."

The somber mood that descended upon the warder seemed to diminish the very light of the forest. "It is with great sorrow that I must report the loss of the Princess of Torinth and Phorin`Ala of Erlini. She was slain by the Dark Sorcerer Zalfeer in Najal not three days hence."

Queen Shathira gasped and would have fallen to the ground if her mate hadn't reached around her waist to support her. "I had feared this," he said. He held Shathira's hand tightly. "We felt a dark ripple in the cha`kri but had been unable to discern its source. All Elven-kind grieves for the loss of the benevolent Lady of the North and Companion of Erlini. We will send a

delegation to Anora`Fel forthwith to offer comfort to the Emerald Guardian."

"Thank you. I am certain she will welcome this."

Having recovered somewhat, Queen Shathira reached toward Altira. "Come, daughter. There is much to discuss, and I wish to understand your role in these dire events. Come visit those who welcome you as kin."

Altira gazed at her outstretched hand. Shathira's unnaturally light, nearly translucent skin seemed to radiate a warmth and vitality that was unreal. "Why do you call me 'daughter'? I am not of your people. I've never been here before. Why do you act like I'm coming home?"

A slight darkening of her open demeanor was the Queen's only response. "There is much that has been withheld from you, dau—Altira, and much here that will help you understand your past. Come now, let us retire to a more comfortable place to converse. I give you my vow that no harm will befall you in the blessed forest." She backed toward the trees, beckoning for them to follow.

Altira hesitated. Years of indoctrination were not so easily discarded. Was this all an elaborate trap to lull her into a sense of ease so they could leech from her the secrets of the Alo`Dara? The Queen seemed open enough, and her vow was sincere—the greeting Altira had been given could not be abused; it was magical and ancient. And there *were* a myriad of questions she had as well. Since she had been banished from Nar`oo, the Alo`Dara were technically no longer her people, strictly speaking, so perhaps she could glean some greater knowledge from this woman about her parents, her purpose, and her future in exile. And the amulet should protect her to some degree.

Altira cast about then reluctantly complied. Shathira led them into the sun-draped woods, arm in arm with her mate, down a well-kept path lined with tiny glimmering stones. Altira could sense a thousand eyes in the treetops above, but none were threatening—at least not as yet.

Altira picked at Farthir's sleeve, drawing him closer. "Where are we going?" she whispered.

"To Shathira's personal residence, I presume."

"What did she mean about much being withheld from me? What's that about?"

"I'm sure I don't know. Perhaps it would be best to let her reveal that in her own way. We will arrive soon, in any case."

Altira frowned. Typical—ask a simple question and get a half-answer. At least Farthir was consistent. There were a thousand quandaries now swirling within her, not the least of which was how she had heard Naroc. She had come to Valinar for answers, but thus far all she'd gleaned was more confusion and additional serious reasons to doubt her own sanity.

In spite of Farthir's meager assurance, it seemed an interminable hike to their destination. Altira continued to sense many watchful eyes above, but no one descended and none interfered. The distant, whispered chatter of a thousand hurried conversations in the forest canopy trailed her, and the farther they got inside the verdant forest, the more anxious Altira became. If things went badly she'd never escape. Even with her skill at passing and the protection of the amulet, she'd be hard-pressed to survive two seconds this far inside Valinar. She could not dodge a thousand Greenie arrows no matter how quick she was.

Altira laid her hand on her long knife and wondered if Naroc could pass into the middle of a forest. Probably not—unless there was a big clearing. She'd feel a lot better with a Guardian bubble around her, but that wasn't going to happen.

In due course they arrived at the largest oak Altira had ever seen. It was at least fifty cubits across and ascended through the canopy far above—it was impossible to see the top. There was no apparent way to ascend.

Shathira and Aanarain stopped and then gestured upward, implying the treetop as their destination. "Welcome," said the Queen.

Altira cast about. "Where are the stairs?"

Aanarain smiled, joined hands with his companion, and simply rose with her into the air, floating upward at a gentle pace.

Farthir watched them ascend for a moment and turned to Altira. "Can you levitate, or shall I help?"

"What am I, a cloud?" Floating had never been one of her strengths. "Why do we have to go all the way up there, anyway? Can't we just talk down here? For that matter, why couldn't we just have talked back at the meadow?"

"You'll understand once we're aloft. Come."

The warder took her arm, and Altira shrieked as they soared upward through the leaves, right into the midst of thousands of Alo`Kin.

CHAPTER TWENTY-NINE

TRUTHS REVEALED

"LEAVE OFF, FARTHIR! UNLEASH ME THIS IN–" ALTIRA LOOKED down and then yelped and gripped the warder's arm with both hands. They were *hundreds* of cubits up! If she yanked free now she'd surely fall to her death. This was much worse than walking off the cliff with the Cirrian. At least then she had control of her fate, and she didn't have to trust some horrid man not to drop her. *Why did you ever let yourself be talked into coming here?* she thought, chastising herself silently.

She cast about, desperately seeking some handhold. If she could reach the trunk she'd be fine—she could easily climb down. But they were too far away and there were no branches to snag this far below the canopy. Altira gritted her teeth, hung on for dear life, and silently fumed. She was going to have a talk with the infuriating warder about floating her all over Salustra. Oh yes, the time was well past to put him in his proper place.

Her mental tirade was interrupted by the approach of a huge branch of the oak, but again, just out of reach. They were floating through a great emerald tunnel now, surrounded by the tree's greenery. As the dense foliage embraced her, the tree's gentle, comforting nature stilled Altira's annoyance somewhat. It was difficult to be angry when surrounded by the sustaining, vital sensation emanating from the tree. They passed through the lower branches without incident and emerged into a cleared area. Farthir changed their direction, and they hovered to an extensive, pearlescent surface resting on the great radial branches of the tree.

They landed and Altira flexed her knees to test the footing. The surface was firm and resilient. It felt a lot like the floor in her pode back in Nar`oo, only a thousand times larger—it seemed to circle the entire tree. She bent to one knee and laid a hand upon the alabaster surface. It was slightly dimpled and tough, somewhat like ivory in color and strangely warm.

"What is this stuff?" she asked. "It's not wood. I've never seen anything like it."

"It's a resin," Farthir replied, "formed from the sap of the Nar`tal`aloin bush. It is called 'Nartala' in Elvish and is a most prized building material. The Alo`Kin construct most of their dwellings from it. Come this way."

She rose and Farthir led her around an intervening branch toward a large and elegant domicile hugging the trunk of the tree. Nestled among the branches and leaves, the building was constructed entirely of the same ivory material and extended upward for at least sixty cubits. It had numerous peaked windows with balconies and seemed to glow with radiated light and warmth. There were no edges in it; the walls gently curved around and upward to a pinnacle not unlike the gilded minarets of Najal, but with an alabaster roof instead of gold.

Queen Shathira stood to one side of the entrance. She beckoned to them and Farthir entered. Altira hesitated though, sending her mind into the building, trying to sense some attack. Shathira knitted her fingers and waited patiently.

After carefully searching, Altira could detect no danger and with some trepidation, she stepped through a shimmering veil draped over the entrance, into a spacious sitting room. Much of the furniture was made from the same substance as the walls and floor, giving the whole room an unearthly, celestial appearance that was more like standing in a cloud than anything else. The walls were translucent, allowing the light from the golden rays of the afternoon sun to penetrate from above.

"Come and sit," Shathira said. "There is much to speak of, and surely thou art weary from thy lengthy trip and the trials thou hast endured." The Queen gestured toward one of the elegant wooden chairs and Altira crossed to it, entranced by her surroundings in spite of its strangeness. The chair seemed to fit her perfectly, the pillows conforming themselves to her every curve.

Farthir retired to an ivory chair and the Queen sat across from them in a delicate chaise with canary and cerulean pillows.

"Altira ne`Senoli," said the Queen. "As I mentioned before, we have sought thee for many seasons. There is much about thy past that thou dost not know and much that still must be revealed."

Altira scowled slightly. "Why do you address me thus?" she asked. "I'm not of the house of Senoli. I've never heard that name before."

The Queen smiled warmly in spite of Altira's cross reply. "I shall explain, child. What dost thou know of thy father?"

"What business is that of yours? He died years ago. You should know better than I, you people killed him."

The Queen, unperturbed, continued. "And thy mother, what dost thou know of her departure from Nar`oo?"

At the mention of Antarra, the good mood and sense of familiarity that had enveloped Altira upon their ascension to the dwelling completely vanished. "*Departure?* What are you talking about? She was murdered! She left to gather berries one morning and never came back. Ac`Tan told me everything—how you lured her into the meadow, the sniper, and how you stole her body away. Don't deny it!" Altira nearly rose and stormed out the door, but something in Shathira's demeanor held her back. The Queen should be registering guilt or fear, or at least some form of anger after the accusation, but instead Shathira's serenity was unperturbed, her gentle smile undimmed.

Altira leapt to her feet. "Say something! It's true, isn't it? You killed her, didn't you? Admit it!"

The Elvish Queen folded her hands in her lap and gazed at Altira with infinite serenity. "Nay, child. This story is an untruth, as is much of the lore taught by the leaders of thy former people. Thy mother was slain by no one—in fact, she lived with us for many anna."

Altira's first reaction was to rail against this outright lie but instead she perched back on the edge of her chair and stared at the Queen, challenging her. Altira fully expected the leader of the Alo`Kin to cave under the intensity of her scrutiny. The Dark Elf cast her mind and senses forward, focusing every bit of her perception upon Shathira, seeing every line in the Queen's serene visage, every wisp of her golden hair, every twitch of her elegant, slanted emerald eyes, her raised eyebrow, her breath, her posture, her nature.

She was telling the truth.

The significance of this fact descended upon Altira like a leaden cloud. Her eyes grew wide and she found it difficult to breathe.

"Thy mother was *forced* to leave Nar`oo, child," the Queen continued. "She was magically barred from returning to the Dark Forest—and to thee—by the Dar, not by any act of ours. She returned here then, seeking shelter and comfort. We had no hand in her departure from thy home, little one. I have no idea why Fel`Soon would cleave thy mother from thee, but rest assured, it was not our purpose to cause this harm."

Altira sat back in her chair, stunned anew by the magnitude and the extent of the lies she had been living. Was this yet another example of the Dar's manipulation? Could her mother's disappearance fit into some gigantic puzzle that included not only Altira but the amulet, the Cirrian, and the Sultan of Fu?

Altira bowed her head for a moment, trying to master her emotions. "You're saying that my mother is still alive."

"This I do not know, daughter," replied the Queen. "She lived with us for a time, and tried on many occasions to return to the Dark Forest, and to thee. Apparently there were deep enchantments woven about her and the fields of thorn that surround Nar`oo. She was unable to breach this magic. She never returned from her final attempt. We know not of her fate."

"And my father?"

"He accompanied thy mother on their last attempt. He had hoped that his skill and knowledge of lore might help. But neither returned."

Altira considered this revelation, confused by the implications. "But that makes no sense. Why would a couple of Dark

Elves come here instead of going north, or to Xancata, or finding their own place in the world? That's just crazy."

"There is something else that must be revealed, and it is a most delicate issue." The Queen paused, considering her words carefully. "Art thou familiar, child, with the practice of Arborancy?"

"No, what is that? Something to do with trees?"

The Queen smiled warmly. "Yes, quite. It is an ability unique to the Alo`Kin. The `Dara have never possessed the aptitude to commune with the spirits of the ancients—it is not in their nature. We Alo`Kin alone among the Elven possess the skill to hear the song of the trees."

This confused Altira. What did trees have to do with the potential death of her parents? *Honestly, sometimes these Greenies …* "Look, I don't see how this could possibly have anything to do—"

"When ye did enter the forest, didst thou feel anything?" Shathira interrupted with a knowing look.

Skies, would everyone please stop sneaking around in the shrubbery! "Sure, I felt like I was about to become a pincushion for a thousand Greenie arrows."

The Queen laughed lightly. "No, daughter. I mean, didst thou sense a mood emanating from the forest?"

This gave her pause. "Well, sort of." Altira tried to remember her perceptions when she first entered Valinar. "It felt as if the trees were welcoming me home—which is silly, of course. I've never been here before."

"Exactly. The ancients have long sought the day when one of the Alo`Dara would enter their demesne with an open mind and heart." Altira's eyes snapped to the warder. His cursed smile was back again. The Queen continued, "Can ye hear the song even now? Close thine eyes and listen."

"Listen for what? What in the skies are you *talking* about?"

"Close thine eyes, little one. Extend thy mind toward the ancient that cradles this dwelling. What dost thou perceive?"

Altira looked at her crossly. "Look, I don't know—"

The Queen raised two fingers, cutting her off, and bowed her head. Clearly she wasn't going to brook any further prevarication. Altira was going to have to humor her in order to continue. Sighing, Altira closed her eyes and sent her mind toward the great oak embracing the house. There was, of course, nothing—just cold bark, branches, and leaves. And yet … as she became more centered and as her perceptions widened, Altira became aware of a sort of ethereal melody. It started as a windy whisper, something that swirled just beyond the realm of her perception, uncatchable, untraceable, insubstantial. Her mind soared with the song, trying to catch its essence, intertwining with its spirit, becoming one with the melody.

Slowly, as her stillness became complete, the song became a message. The tree *was* singing, and the music held distinct implications. It was the heart of the forest, the center of the verdant universe. It drew all life to it, all health, all power. It was old—incredibly ancient in fact. It had seen the genesis of all the races on Salustra. As a sapling it had watched as the first Elves stepped into the nascent, verdant forest, followed by the Dwarves, the men, and the other races that now foolishly tried to claim ownership of that which was unclaimable. It was connected to everything everywhere and knew the truth of all things that drew strength from the earth. It was vital, it was alive, and it knew of her, of her parents, and of the truth of all the Queen had revealed.

The whispered voice of the tree swirled through Altira's mind and spoke in a strange, ancient tongue. A word formed in her perception, unbidden, evoked by the song.

"Sath`a`laala."

Then the tree went silent.

Altira opened her eyes with a start and beheld the Queen considering her narrowly.

"Didst thou hear?" Shathira asked. "Didst thou perceive the ancient beneficent, the true greeting?"

"I think … it said 'Sath'—something. I've never heard the word before."

Shathira nodded solemnly. "It is an utterance that cannot truly be spoken by those of the flesh. It is an arborescent invocation—the original prayer of life in fact. It cannot be heard by any other than the Alo`Kin."

"Well, that's just crazy talk." Altira jerked a thumb Farthir's way. "I heard it and I'm about as Green as the warder here."

Farthir, who had been sitting quietly, observing their interaction, chuckled. "I think not."

Altira tore her eyes from the Queen to consider the smug Companion. "And what, exactly, is that supposed to mean?"

"That you may be somewhat 'Greener' than you think you are."

Altira nearly jumped to her feet at this insult but was interrupted by the Queen.

"Indeed. And how certain art thou, that thou art not Alo`Kin?"

Altira turned her ire back upon the leader of the Green Elves. "What kind of insane, insulting, ignorant question is that? Look at me. I'm *black.* I'm of Nar`oo. Are you blind?"

"I see more than thou might imagine, dear one. Although thy mother was a descendant of the line of `Dara, thy father was not. He was the son of Ana`de Senoli of the Alo`Kin. He was an honored teacher, a scholar, and the chief historian in the great Library of Valinar."

At first Altira could say nothing. Several witty retorts formed on her lips but she couldn't seem to gather the power to let them fly. Eventually the truth of the Queen's revelation settled upon her like a suffocating blanket. She gripped the arm of her chair and tried to breathe as the room began to turn about her. She shook her head and stared at the elegant Fuan carpet. "But … that's impossible," she said weakly. "I'm Alo`Daran. Look at me …"

"Much in thy appearance doth stem from thy mother, 'tis true," said the Queen, "but much in thy heart and nature comes from thy father. For this reason, thou hast always felt an outcast amongst those of the shaded glen. Is not this true?"

Altira couldn't find the strength to deny it.

"Thy mother …" Shathira paused, choosing her words carefully, "was a most enlightened `Daran. Were ye aware of her love of lore and history?"

Altira shook herself from the swirling confusion in her heart. "Well … yes, she spent hours reading in the library at Nar`oo, but how does that—"

"Were ye aware that she secretly journeyed to us as a young woman?"

"What? No."

"It was an event long foreseen by us. There was some alarm, as thou canst imagine, and it took tremendous courage for her to approach the borders of the forest—she was nearly slain by our defenders. But when her intentions were discerned, I granted her admittance to study with loremaster U`talain. She spent many moons here as a young Elf."

"She never said anything. But what does this have to do with me?" asked Altira.

"While she was here she met Eran, one of the seekers of history in the great house. They spoke often of the division of Alo`Kin and `Dara and shared a love of lore. They became … close."

A light began to grow in Altira's mind, like the sun peaking through the leaden clouds surrounding the storm that was her life.

"Eran was …"

The Queen smiled. "Thy father, yes. Thou wast conceived in this place, young one. Thou seest, thou art as much a child of the Alo`Kin as I."

"But … but why did she … why did my mother return to Nar`oo, then? Why was I not raised here?"

"Antarra never intended to make Valinar her home. She had many friends and family in the Dark Forest and sought, against my advisement I must say, to return to her former life. Thy father's heart bound him here, but because of his great love for thy mother he made the fateful decision to journey with her to Nar`oo in the hope of gaining acceptance among the Alo`Dara. Thou wast born nearly an anna later."

"So what happened to my father, then? When they returned to Nar`oo the first time?"

"Regretfully, he was an outcast from the moment he stepped inside the Dark Forest. The Dar became aware of thy mother's interests and the moment he learned of her relationship with thy father thy entire family was doomed. Thy mother discovered the truth of the division of the Elvish races, you see, and began to speak openly of Fel`Soon's treachery. This was very unwise."

"Wait—you *know*? You know about Fel`Dara and Sen`Tana and all of it?"

This startled Shathira for a moment. "It is surprising that thou wouldst know of this, being of the Dark Forest, but yes.

The truth of the separation of the races is common knowledge amongst the Alo`Kin. Among thy former people it is a closely guarded secret. How did you—"

"So, *the Dar* knows? He withholds this truth from all of us?"

"It was why thy mother was banished. He was afraid the truth would become widely known among the Alo`Dara. The presence of thy family became a testament to the treachery of Fel`Dara and a threat to the current leader of thy people. Everything that has happened in thy life has been about the Dar's dominion. The knowledge thy mother and father possessed was a direct threat to his reign. For the last three thousand anna, the Dars have enjoined their people to carve a place in the world using thievery, trickery, and deceit. As a consequence, as thou dost well know, thy race has been both feared and greatly maligned. This path has led to much unhappiness, and the Dar has used this to further ostracize and isolate Nar`oo."

"So *he* got rid of my mother?"

A great sadness came over Shathira. "He tried. He drove both of thy parents out of the Dark Forest. Thy father first by trickery, and then thy mother, bearing thee, was compelled to leave her home shortly thereafter by force and magic. She was abducted and would have been slain were it not for the propitious actions of one of our scouts. If not for him, ye truly would be an orphan."

The Dar, that cur! That murdering, sneaking, conniving tyrant! And his father before him and *his* father before *him,* apparently. *Enough!* A fierceness came over Altira that hushed even the ancient arboreal song of the Sovereign of Trees upon whose branches they rested. She rose from her chair and glared down at the leader of the Alo`Kin. "The rest of the Alo`Dara will see the vision in the amulet, this I vow. We must find a way

to return to Nar`oo and prove the truth to all my people. Fel`Soon doesn't deserve to lead us. He must be stopped!"

Shathira smiled thinly. "We have believed this for nearly a thousand years, *daughter*. Long have we awaited the moment forseen by the Prime Arborant, and it would seem that this time has finally arrived. But the question is, how can the truth be revealed to thy people?"

"By using the Dar's own trickery against him, by finding a way to sneak back into his city and showing everyone the vision in the amulet." She jabbed an assertive finger at the Queen. "*You* might not be able to sneak into Nar`oo; you're not Alo`Daran …" Altira's attention was drawn to her arm and her midnight skin. "But I *am*."

CHAPTER THIRTY

RETURN

"I DO APPLAUD THY SENTIMENT BUT ONE MOMENT PLEASE, DAUGHter," replied Shathira. "What is this amulet of which ye speak? And how would a mere trinket bear upon the truths we have discussed? How could an object, no matter how potent, convince thy people of the truth?"

Farthir touched Altira gently on the arm, drawing her gaze. The Dark Elf lowered her hand.

"This is the other reason for our journey, Aniki," Farthir said. "During Altira's mission into Fu, she discovered a talisman that bears upon the schism between the Elvish races."

"Mission?" Altira almost laughed aloud. Apparently smug Companions didn't mind bending the truth a bit from time to time.

"I see," Shathira replied slowly, her interest clearly piqued. "And how is this? Daughter, please be seated." She gestured Altira back into her chair.

Still fuming over the Dar's treachery, Altira scowled and sat. She tried to focus and managed to push most of the tempest from her mind. "The amulet. Yes … the Dar stole it from the Dwarves who were holding it at the request of an Elf named Talamar. Do you know of him?"

"Nay, but the loremaster might. Pray continue."

"In any case, the gem appears of Elvish make." Altira slid forward on her chair and reached into her blouse, extracting the talisman and lifting it over her head. The faceted jewel glittered in the light, casting tiny azure rainbows on her hand, its strange allure quite compelling.

Shathira drew a breath when she saw it and leaned closer, her eyes narrowing. She reached for the gem and Altira started to hand it to her but as the Queen's fingers drew near, the amulet began to hum ominously. Altira could feel the talisman drawing power into itself, as if it were about to defend from an attack.

The Queen snatched her hand away in amazement.

"It doth possess great magic, indeed," she said. "It is ca`taalan—I sense the power. The gem is bound to the Alo`Dara and cannot be touched by one of the Verdant Realm. Clearly, it is the blood of the `Dara within thee that permits thee to hold it, daughter. Of what significance is this gem? How didst thou come to possess such an ancient vessel of power?"

The hum from the gem diminished and Altira closed her hand around the jewel, sensing its power stilling. "The Dar sent it to the Sultan to be destroyed. I rescued it from his vault." She couldn't help giving the warder a smirk. They all knew what an Alo`Daran would be doing on a "mission" into the Sultan's treasury.

Shathira smiled knowingly.

"Can you join your sight to mine?" Altira asked the Queen. "Or Farthir, can you do what Danera …"

The invocation of the name of her friend caused a cascade of emotions inside Altira. She had managed to forget about Fu. Now the painful memories came back in a flood of feelings. It was all Altira could do to maintain control.

Shathira came to her aid. "I have the power to share what thou dost see, daughter. Why dost thou ask?"

Altira wiped her eyes with a back of a hand and perched on the edge of her chair. This was one of the main reasons she had come to the Green Forest. The revelations about the Dar had accomplished one thing at least—they had convinced Altira that the stories she had always been told about the Green Elves were lies. Shathira had been open with her, and the simple fact that a Dark Elf was still alive in the home of the Alo`Kin Queen was a testament that the Dar's assertions regarding the Greenies were part of the same pack of lies as the stories about being kicked out of the City of the Stars. Perhaps Shathira could help with the Dar. It was Sen`Tana, her ancestor, who was slain, after all. The Queen had a right to see the vision.

Glancing quickly at Shathira, Altira mastered her emotions and focused on the amulet. "Watch this …"

The Queen's presence drew near as Altira dove into the blue expanse of the crystal. Turning it in her hands, she found the right angle. She opened it and let the vision play. Altira could sense Shathira's growing excitement as the truth of the ancient schism between `Kin and `Dara was revealed. When Fel`Dara struck, Shathira cried in agony. The vision ended and Altira withdrew to discover the leader of the Alo`Kin visibly shaken, a tear descending her cheek.

"This … this is amazing, daughter. The loremaster must see it, and it must be shown to thy fellow Elves! The day of unity is nigh. We finally have the means to prove the truth to those of the darkened realm!"

ALTIRA NEEDED TIME. SHE SAT IN AN UPPER ROOM IN THE QUEEN'S apartments, trying to sort through the myriad emotions whirling inside her. The meeting with the Queen had redoubled her confusion along with her simmering fury over the abuses of the Dar. She especially needed time to figure out what to do with the amulet. Her expulsion from Nar`oo, overcoming the Cirrian, the Sultan, Danera, and now the news about her parents and her heritage—she felt like a helpless, useless wreck of bewilderment. She needed to go somewhere quiet, somewhere alone, so she could sort it all out in her mind and make sense of it—if such a thing was possible.

One thing was for sure. She needed to get rid of the cursed amulet. She wasn't ready to be the "instrument of great trial and pivotal change" that Naroc had predicted. If the pendant did indeed represent the means to free the Dark Elves from their enslavement under the Dar, then Altira needed to find someone in Nar`oo to bear that message and mission. She was done with those people and the Dark Forest. Done with being chased all over the continent. Done with being hated by everyone she'd ever known. Let someone else take responsibility for showing the world the vision. She just wanted to creep into a hidey-hole and sleep for a hundred anna.

One good thing had resulted from her journey here and her meeting with the Queen, though. She was finally coming to understand her place in the world. Altira belonged to neither of the Elvish races. She was an outcast from both and loved by neither.

So be it.

Altira would find her own way in the world, and she didn't need the Dar's approval. Or Shathira's, for that matter. She would rid herself of the burden of bearing the truth of Fel`Soon's treachery and find her own path. The vision in the amulet would get the Dar off her tail once and for all and give her a chance at a decent life somewhere. That was the only thing that mattered at the moment, and she needed it done as soon as possible.

She rose and went to find Farthir. He was sitting in the entry room, talking with Aanarain, who rose as she entered.

"Greetings, young one. I trust your rest was refreshing."

Altira nodded to the Alo`Kin monarch. "Yes, thank you. Farthir, we need to talk. I need to get this amulet to Nar`oo. The Alo`Kin cannot help with that, obviously—they can't even touch it. We need to figure out how to get back inside the Dark Forest and I need to talk to Ac`Tan."

The warder pondered this for a moment. "Getting you back into Nar`oo may be more difficult than you imagine."

"How surprising. Tell me what in my life isn't 'more difficult' than I imagine? I guess. Can we go back to Telfall, then? All my things are there and I'd feel better away from Elves for a bit—both dark and green." She smiled wanly and bowed to Aanarain. "No offense intended, Anoreth."

"None is taken, daughter. I understand thy feelings. Know, however, that thou art always welcome in our forest. Thou mayest return when ye feel the time is right."

"Thank you. Farthir, is there a place nearby—can Naroc come?"

"Yes, quite. We visit here often. There is a clearing not far to the south."

Altira turned back to the monarch of the Alo`Kin. "Please give Shathira my best wishes and tell her I will return when I am able." She bowed again, this time more deeply.

Aanarain returned the honorific and Altira left with the warder.

THE NEXT MORNING SHE ENTERED TELFALL'S AUDIENCE CHAMBER to find Farthir in his usual seat, perusing some sort of missive with an elegant seal of reddish wax. She was bathed, rested, and packed. She greeted the warder as she entered, crossed to the table, and plucked an apple from a bowl of fruit.

Farthir let her chew a moment. "So what have you decided?" he asked. "You can't stay here forever—eventually someone from Nar`oo will thwart the Dwarven defenses."

Altira grunted and plopped into the chair across from him. "They won't get the chance. I'm going to head back to the Dark Forest and deal with that cur of a Dar."

"And how do you intend to do that, exactly? You already said it was impossible. They'll be on the alert. Naroc can't take you. That would cause a considerable commotion, to say the least."

She smiled crookedly. "Can you imagine him landing in the Dark Forest? Every single arrow in Nar`oo would be loosed." She took another bite of her apple. "No, we need to figure some other way in."

"Perhaps the Dwarves could help, or your friend. The one you mentioned in Valinar. I forget the name."

"Ac`Tan?"

"Yes, perhaps he could aid us. Having someone on the inside is always good. If we showed him the vision, do you think he'd believe it?"

"Tan has an open mind, although he *was* the one who told me the lies about my mother …"

"Perhaps just repeating what he heard from the Dar."

"Maybe." Altira chewed thoughtfully. "I've never known him to intentionally mislead anyone—he's always been forthright with me. All of the seven Calis need to see the vision, though, preferably all at once. He could only help with our Cala—or rather, my *former* Cala."

"I'm not so sure about revealing it to the leaders of the Calas alone," replied Farthir. "Some of them may be in league with the Dar. There must be some way to reach all of your people directly without going through the Cali."

"Who we're going to tell isn't our biggest problem," Altira pointed out. "I can manage that. The problem is—how do we get inside? Fel`soon will know we've gone to Valinar—he has spies everywhere—and he'll suspect we've allied ourselves with Shathira. He'll have tripled the border patrols. The woods will be swarming with watchers. Short of a full-on battle, I don't see any way to get close to him. Even an assault by all the mounted legions of Torinth wouldn't get into the Dark Forest; the defenses are too well hidden. And even if we reached Fel`Soon, he's still devilishly hard to catch. Believe me, many have tried, and they ended up as mulch for the trees. No, we need to use some kind of subterfuge. We need to sneak up on him somehow, without him suspecting."

Farthir rose and paced to his Companion's empty roost, tapping it in thought. Finally he turned back. "Let me ask Naroc." The warder did his stare-into-space bit and Altira squinted and

tried to eavesdrop on the Guardian's thoughts. She heard nothing—which put her back into doubting her own sanity. Someday she'd have to figure out what exactly had happened back in that meadow—

"Ha!" exclaimed Farthir, returning to her. "I should have thought of it! Of course we don't *walk* into Nar`oo."

"We already agreed we can't fly—"

"We tunnel! Fel`soon will never suspect a subterranean approach!"

Altira opened her mouth in a reflexive action, intending to reject the absurd notion out of hand, but the longer she thought on it, the better the idea sounded. "It's true," she began, turning the concept in her head. "We live in the tops of the trees. We only descend when we leave Nar`oo. The roots and dirt are beneath us and not worth considering. No one would think of an approach from below. But it would have to be totally silent, and besides, how can you do it without the trees knowing? Surely they'll give us away."

"Ahh, but remember, the rest of the Dark Elves do not have your skill in Arborancy. The whispers from the trees will go unheeded, will they not? In fact, you could very well still their fears yourself, as you approach."

Altira at first brightened at the idea, then scowled. "No, wait a minute. It's nearly three leagues from the edge of the forest to the Dar's pode. There's no way in the seven skies we'd be able to tunnel that far—it would take moons, even for Dwarves. Nay, anna!" She tossed her apple core in the air, whipped out her long knife and caught it with the point as it fell. "It was an interesting notion, though. I'd love to pop out under the Dar's quarters and skewer him with a few sildars before he had a clue what was going on." She flicked the core into the fire.

"Don't give up so fast, now. Let's talk with Gentain. Or perhaps Tyke might know better—mages aren't generally involved in tunneling. I've seen the Dwarves do some pretty amazing things in the heat of battle. They seem to be able to pass through dirt like you and I walk through grass. And I'm thinking that the first thing we need to do, if we make it inside Nar`oo, is show your people the vision. If you kill the Dar right off it will set everyone on your tail, cause mass hysteria, and there'll be no chance to reveal the truth. It's hard to have an intelligent conversation with a thousand people chasing after you."

She tapped the point of her dagger on her chin. "Possibly," mumbled Altira. "If everyone knew of his treachery I can't imagine he'd last more than two seconds, anyway. We need to figure out some way to get him to call a Conclave."

"What's that?"

"A meeting of all the Alo`Dara. Usually he calls them when he wants to make some change to the law, or to publicly denounce someone. They had one when my mother left." The fire in Altira's eyes returned for a moment. "Yes, a Conclave. That would be perfect. We need to figure out some way to get everyone together and show them the vision all at once—with the Dar in attendance and unable to stop it. That would be truly priceless. I wish my parents could see that!"

"Assuming, of course, that we can figure out a way in."

"Oh, we'll get in." She sheathed her knife and stood. "Let's go find Tickles. We have a forest to tunnel under!"

CHAPTER THIRTY-ONE

INTO NAR`OO

THE DWARMAK PACED TO THE FINELY BEVELED WINDOWS IN HIS personal study and looked through the misted glass unhappily. “There is no way we can help, I’m afraid. It would surely be construed as aggression against the Dark Elves and I’m not willing to risk war just so the Alo`Dara can learn of some ancient treachery committed by the first Dar.”

Farthir steepled his fingers and watched as Balfor paced back to the table. “We certainly don’t want to worsen your relations with those of the shaded forest. But remember, if this mission is successful it will radically improve your position. We all know the prime instigator of the tensions between the Dwarves and the Alo`Dara has been Fel`Soon. Without his tyranny, and with a true knowledge of the duplicity that originally caused the schism with their Alo`Kin brethren, the Elves of Nar`oo may very well become a close ally against incursions from Xancata.

Think how much more stable things would be with Nar`oo as a friend. And we require only a handful of your countrymen—enough to construct a single tunnel. None will be asked to enter the forest, if that's your concern. Is not this a minimal risk compared with the potential benefit?"

One of the logs in the blazing hearth fell forward in a shower of sparks. Tyke rose from his chair and fetched an iron poker to adjust it, speaking into the flames. "An' don' forget dat assassin—what was 'is name, Jenta'?"

"Jen`Tar," supplied Altira.

Having fixed the log, Tyke replaced the poker and returned to his chair. "Right, 'im. 'E attacked our guards and nearly killed Daltra—one of yer own Dara`Phen, m'Lord. Methinks dat requires some response, don' it?"

The Dwarmak was clearly not happy that Tyke would side with these outlanders. "The retrieval of that cursed amulet has led to nothing but trouble," he said.

Altira squirmed a bit in her chair. "You have *no* idea."

Balfor was still not convinced. "Regardless of the potential benefit, and the recent attack on Telfall, I'm still not sanguine about attacking the Dark Forest. It will be obvious to everyone that we built the tunnel. Only the Dara`Kin can burrow through solid rock. Regardless of whether or not Dwarves enter the city proper, the Dar will know we helped, and dire repercussions may result."

"There is another question, though," suggested Altira. She sat up in her chair and brushed a stray lock of hair from her eyes, trying to concentrate. "The amulet was created for the Alo`Dara, that we know—it contains a vision of critical importance to us. How, may I ask then, did it come to be in your personal treasury, sir?"

"We already covered that. The true account of the acquisition of the amulet has been lost," Balfor replied gruffly. "It's been over three thousand anna since it came into our possession. All we have is lore, and that is sketchy at best."

Tyke had returned to his chair and was about to add something but was halted by a glare from the Dwarven leader.

Altira pressed on. "And what else, pray tell, does the lore reveal about the 'acquisition' of our amulet, as you put it, sir?"

The Dwarven chief pressed his lips together and stared at her through stubborn, bushy eyebrows for a moment, then seemed to relent. "There *are* some additional writings of the first Dwarmak, Callious, that *tend* to indicate that the amulet *may* have been delivered to us by a Dark Elf.. Callious writes that a refugee of 'shadowed birth' bestowed upon him a 'shield of crystal purity' for his use alone."

She raised an eyebrow. "That's it? That's all he wrote? There's nothing about its purpose, or its future?"

Balfor responded by raising his own bushy eyebrow. He clearly wasn't inclined to elaborate.

Farthir spoke silently with Naroc, in the audience chamber below them. He then addressed the group. "Surely if Talamar knew of the preciousness of the amulet, there would have been more recorded. Perhaps we should seek in the library in Valinar. I bet the loremaster could shed more light upon this."

Balfor sighed deeply. "Oh, all right. The writings state that the amulet was to be returned to the 'dark nation' when 'one of the evening strides from darkness into light,' whatever the skies that means."

The warder smiled knowingly. "I think it's pretty clear what it means."

Tyke, sitting on her other side, had been listening to the conversation, unwilling to interrupt in deference to the Dwarmak. "Sir, if da amulet was entrusted ta us wit' the promise dat it was ta be return' at a future date, well den, don' it make sense dat the first Dwarmak would have promised da Elves to help accomplish it? An' if dat's true, does'n dat pledge still bear force? Are we not den bound by dat agreemen'?"

"That's a lot of ifs, captain." Balfor raised a hand to keep Altira at bay. "All right, all right, mistress. It *may* be that Callious did make such a commitment, though there is nothing in our lore that would confirm it. But I will nonetheless permit the amulet to be returned to the Dark Elves and we will aid you in this by allowing you to use our tunnel, but no Dwarf is to enter the Dark Forest."

"*Use your* tunnel?" repeated Altira, with some outrage. "You mean to say you've already built it?!"

The Dwarmak ignored her query. "As I said, no Dwarf is to enter the forest—even underground, nor be seen by any resident of Nar`oo. Second, you must give me your vow, Altira, that if you succeed, whatever new regime may be installed in Nar`oo, they will not turn against us. And if you fail—no one must know of our assistance."

Altira returned the Dwarmak's steely gaze. "I am no diplomat, sir. I can give you no guarantees about the future. But I *can* promise to tell no one about the tunnel. I will perish before I do so."

Balfor considered her for a long moment then nodded. "Very well." The Dwarmak turned to Tyke. "Inform them of the tactical situation, captain."

Altira turned in surprise to the former burglar. "All right now, Tickles, what have you been up to? And how did you get to be an officer in the army, anyway?"

Her stocky friend nearly barked a retort then glanced quickly at the Dwarmak. He straightened, tugged on his leather jerkin, and managed to shake off his response. "Later, *mistress*." He refocused and continued, "Dere is indeed a tunnel constructed under da Dark Fores'. We finished it o'er three moons ago."

"Before I even got here? For what purpose?" She turned upon the Dwarmak. "You realize, *sir*, that this is a violation of our sovereign territory. How can you speak of not wanting to offend the Alo`Dara and at the same time be tunneling beneath the Dark Forest?"

Balfor was unfazed by her accusation. "You've been banished, remember? The residents of Nar`oo are no longer 'your people,' as you put it."

Altira bit her lip. There was a reason she wasn't a cursed diplomat. All the finessing of language, the backstabbing, the half-truths …

"In any case," Balfor continued, "the tunnel's initial destination wasn't Nar`oo at all. It was intended as a safe passage to the coast and onward, to Fairn. We were forced to build the subterranean thoroughfare because of *your* own bandits, mistress. Don't talk to me of violating sovereign territory when your own people have hijacked more than a score of our trade wagons bound for Fu."

Altira herself had looted one of the heavily burdened vehicles as part of her training. But she kept that tidbit to herself. "So if the destination of this tunnel was the coast, how in the skies did it end up under Nar`oo? Are you telling me your *expert*

Dwarven diggers *missed* their destination and just *happened* to wander under our city?"

"Hardly. When we tunnel for something we don't 'wander.'" The Dwarmak gestured for Tyke to continue.

"When da amulet was stolen from da Dwarmak it was decided ta mount a mission ta retrieve it. A side tunnel was created," explained the newly commissioned 'captain.'

Balfor paced back to the window then turned to them. "The motivation for the tunnel is immaterial. Suffice it to say, it exists. Do you wish to avail yourself of this access to Nar`oo or not?"

Altira was about to tell the stumpy man exactly what she thought of this invasion of her former home, but Farthir cut her off. "We are most grateful, sir, for your assistance." Altira scowled but remained silent as the warder continued. "All we require is someone to show us the way to the tunnel entrance."

The Dwarmak waited for a moment, but Altira wasn't about to give him an excuse to retract the offer. "Very well," the Dwarven leader allowed. "Tyke here has been assigned to help you. If you have any further questions, talk to him. I wish you luck in your endeavors." The head Dwarf left, closing the door behind him.

"And good day to you, too," Altira said to the closed door. Dwarves never ceased to amaze her. Altira stood and turned on Tyke. "And since when are you the Dwarmak's personal advisor, Mr. *Burglar*?"

Her friend smirked and moved toward the door leading down to the audience chamber then turned back. "Me cousin recommended me. After we did in da Cirrian an' all, apparently da Dwarmak felt 'e owed me sumfin', so 'e offered me a commission. Fer some unknown reason he seems ta think I'd be an asset to da nation or some such. It seemed like foolishness at first, but the more I thought on it, da more I realized it was me only option. I nae kin go back ta Caltra obviously, so's I agreed. 'Tis not too bad a life; ya gets as much ale ta drink as ya wan', and it's not really any more dang'rous den bein' a smithie. Especially when ye'r friends with Dark Elves n' such." He chuckled and bowed slightly toward her.

"Fine, so how did you learn about this mysterious tunnel into the middle of the Dark Forest, then? Happen to be wandering in Nar`oo one evening and fell into it, did you?"

Tyke didn't take the bait. "When ya went ta Valinar ta talk wit' da Elves, I was assigned ta 'elp wit' da defenses fer a bit an' I learned about da passage from the Chief Tunn'ler. I din' know it'd be importan' till now."

"So fine then, let's get on with it." Yet another tunnel to explore. Clearly she was doomed to live forever underground. "The sooner we get to Nar'oo, the quicker I can put an end to Fel`Soon and his lies. We'll see how he feels when he's the outcast—a *permanent* outcast at that."

CHAPTER THIRTY-TWO

AC`TAN LISTENS

WHY IN THE NAME OF THE FIVE LORDS OF THE FELSHAR DID THE stupid Dwarves have to make their tunnels so tiny? Didn't they realize that normal people couldn't fit in them? Altira bumped her head on the ceiling for the thousandth time and nearly kicked the pudgy Dwarf ambling in front of her.

The "main thoroughfare," as Tyke called it, was fine—large enough even for one of the massive coal wagons from Telfall and more than big enough for even Farthir to walk upright. But the passage to Nar`oo was a mole hole by comparison. The warder had tried to enter the dimly lit tunnel, all bent over, but was forced to give up after only a short distance, the coward.

"I'd only slow you down," he'd said. "And Naroc won't let me go in—it's too risky, now that we've lost Danera."

Handy excuse, but then, the warder wouldn't last two seconds inside the Dark Forest—he was probably right to defer.

So Altira and Tyke had gone on alone—and she was just about ready to shove a sildar in the back of the annoying dorf and leave him behind. The captain was even more smug and insufferable than the burgler, if that was possible. It was better when he was just a bumbling thief. At least then he didn't have the authority of the Dwarmak to throw around. Now, he seemed intent on beating her over the head with his superiority. It was all Altira could do to control her temper and keep up. If they didn't get to the end of this cursed rat hole soon she was going to do something she'd regret. Altira took yet another deep breath and pushed her anger away, focusing on the mission and trying to ignore the annoying Dwarf.

"Dey really did a good job on dis hole," Tyke mused as he bounded to the left to avoid a thrust of bedrock. "Nice work on da timbers, too. See dere?" He pointed to one of the large supporting pillars as he passed. "Excellen' joinery, dat. Done wit' oaken dowlin'."

"If you don't stop the—" Altira caught herself, took a deep breath, and centered. "Can we *please* get on with it? I'm starting to really hate this wretched burrow. How much farther is it, anyway?"

"Dunno. Never been down dis far."

"'Dunno'? And you call yourself an *officer?* Well, move along. I'd really love to get out of here by Michaelmas."

"All ri,' don' be getting—"

"—my britches in a bunch. Ya ya, I know."

The Dwarf stopped and turned on her, about to utter some further incantation of his superior commission from the Dwarmak. Altira simply drew her long knife and raised an eyebrow.

Tyke locked a thumb in his belt and feigned alarm. "Now, dere's no reason fer dat, missie. I'm goin', I'm goin'!" The Dwarf scurried away, muttering to himself. Altira sheathed her weapon and followed with a rueful smile.

The end of the tunnel turned out to be quite close. They had traveled no more than a few hundred cubits when Tyke halted at the base of a substantial ladder. He stood at the bottom, hands on hips, looking up, seeming rather let down.

"Well, I guess dat's dat. Accordin' to da eng'neer dis comes out in da midst of a pile o' rocks on da north side of the city. I assume ya can find yer way from 'ere?"

"Indeed. Thanks for the help." Altira placed a foot on the first rung and started up.

"If ya need me, jes' call an' I'll come ta 'elp."

Altira looked down at the little man. "You have no idea what you're saying. If you enter the forest you won't last two seconds."

"Ye'd be s'prised what Dwarves are capable of, and no one kin see me if I'm below da ground, can dey?"

Altira considered this for a moment. "Stay here. The last thing I need is for another friend to get killed. I don't need anyone's *protection*." Tyke grinned broadly as Altira realized her blunder. *Friend …* "Oh good grief … Enough." She turned away and called back as she started to ascend. "There's nothing more you can do, just go home."

The vertical shaft grew darker as the light from the glowspheres faded below her. Altira cast magisight and continued climbing. She hauled herself up the ladder until her legs began to burn. *This thing goes on forever!* They must have been *hundreds* of cubits below ground!

It was so dark magisight was nearly useless. A wisp of a breeze barely caressed her hair—she must be nearing the top. She took another step and almost rammed her head into the trapdoor at the top of the shaft. Placing her back against the heavy wooden slats, Altira shoved open the portal. It swung upward without a sound—at least the Dwarves knew to oil their hinges properly.

She emerged from the hatch into a tiny cave-like space. The dim outlines of several huge boulders delineated an area no more than a pace or two across. The peaked ceiling was equally low—her head just brushed against the damp roof of the rocky alcove. Taking no chances, she silenced the hinges magically and closed the lid of the tunnel.

Skies. How was she supposed to get out of this death trap? There was no door.

She cast about with her mind. She was buried inside a small hillock with no apparent exit. The Dwarves must have intended to dig their way out when the time came. Well, no matter. She could pass beyond the rocks easily enough, but where *was* this place? She sent her mind farther afield, looking for something familiar. It took some time, but Altira finally located a path some distance to the east and then a sentry outpost she knew. She was in the heart of Nar`oo. There were not many watchers here; most were at the periphery of the forest. The Dwarves had been cunning in their tunnel placement. If they wanted to invade Nar`oo, this would indeed be the perfect location for a subversive assault.

Her first objective was to find Ac`Tan. She cast about one last time and, sensing no one, she passed through the rocks to land softly on the moist loam carpeting the forest floor. She went invisible and headed south, toward Ac`Tan's pode.

It felt odd being back home. The song of the trees seemed strange, evoking a dissonant air of unease. It was several minutes before Altira realized what was wrong: The dark and aged residents of the forest were clearly not happy with the Elvish occupants of their domain; the trees whispered of rebellion and anger. Something was sorely amiss in this forest and it disturbed her greatly. Altira had lived here for as long as she could remember and she had never felt the dissonance. Was it something new within the forest, or had something changed within her recently, like Farthir and the Queen had said?

Or perhaps both?

Altira stayed at ground level—ascending to the rope bridges would be sheer insanity, as some of the highly trained watchers could see through invisibility. Nevertheless, it didn't take long before she reached her destination. There were a couple of sentries she had to dodge, but her journey thus far had been uneventful.

She located a stairway, carefully ascended into the still-sleeping city, and scurried over two intervening bridges to the front door of Ac`Tan's pode. Knocking was obviously out of the question. She put an ear to the door and listened a moment. `Tan was snoring somewhere in the back. Altira passed into the front room and padded silently to the equipment rack behind the front door. The First Aide's curved black sabre hung on a peg. *Let's just play it safe, why don't we?* She carefully wrapped the belt around the sword and placed it behind the couch near the wall. Only then did she creep across the rich carpeting and peek into his bedroom.

The divan was empty!

"Are you completely insane, you little guttersnipe?"

Altira spun around, her hand darting instinctively to her long knife. The First Aide stood just inside the door, his naked sabre directed at her heart with practiced precision.

"What in the seven skies are you doing in here, Tira?" His face was shadowed, but she knew his piercing hazel eyes tracked the hand she rested on the hilt of her blade. Altira's life teetered in that moment upon a razor's edge. `Tan crept forward, now

crouching slightly. "Have you lost your mind along with any desire to keep on breathing?"

She took a deep breath and went completely still. "The question of my sanity is debatable," she admitted, willing herself to calmness—Ac`Tan was one of the quickest fighters in the forest. "But my desire to breathe remains quite intact, thank you." She slowly lifted her hand and tried her most disarming smile. Ac`Tan froze in place, the tip of his sabre rock steady. She took a slow breath. "Look, things have changed, `Tan. There's something you need to know—"

"I know you were banished. I know if I sneeze too loudly, the watchers will slice you into petite ribbons before you can blink twice. I know the Dar is livid and about to instigate a lan`talla. I know he's offered ten thousand gold pieces for your capture—preferably dead."

"You know a lot, `Tan," she granted and her light tone seemed to reduce the tension in the room a notch. "But you don't know everything. Why do you think the Dar's all bent, eh? I took a couple of piddling rocks from the fat former Sultan of Fu. Why, in the name of the Five Lords of the Felshar, is all this effort being expended to do in one pitiful little Dark Elf who couldn't possibly pose a threat to Nar`oo?"

This finally broke `Tan's focus. He rose from his crouch. "*Former* Sultan?" The tip of his sabre dipped slightly. "What are you talking about? What's happened in Fu? What did you do to Al`Taaba?!"

"I didn't do anything. He was killed by some Sorcerer from Xancata. I told you—things have changed. That imbecile of a wizard tried to kill me, missed, slew Danera, nearly did in Prince Al`Nuan, and killed the Sultan. It all happened over a fortnight ago, now."

"What! How do you—no, wait a minute. Why in the skies should I believe anything you say? You'd lie to your own mother if it suited you. We all know your history. The Dar told us everything."

"And what makes you think *he's* any better at telling the truth than I am?" she asked.

This caused `Tan some pause and he lowered his sword entirely. She still couldn't see his face for the shadows. Altira slowly crossed her arms, keeping well away from the handles of her sildars.

"He's the Dar," `Tan said with firmness. "I don't need another reason."

"All right now, look. I've spent the better part of two moons running all over Salustra, trying to fix what happened in Fu. I don't have time to explain everything, but there's something you need to see and it'll prove I'm telling the truth. I'm not asking you to believe me, but if our friendship means anything, give me a chance to validate what I say. The Dar is a liar. All I ask is that you watch and listen. And put away the Dwarf-sticker, for pity's sake. I'm not going to attack you."

"It's the middle of the blessed night. What in the skies am I supposed to *watch*? What are you talking about? I'm not going to traipse around in the forest on the say-so of some banished Dark Elf with a life span measured in moments. You wouldn't get two strides outside this pode before you'd be skewered with a thousand arrows from the watchers."

"I made it this far, didn't I?" Altira fished the pendant out of her blouse and Ac`Tan raised his sabre to guard position.

"What is that?" he barked. "What are you doing?"

"It's not a weapon, silly. It's an ancient amulet that contains a vision. It tells the truth about the Alo`Dara and the Dars."

"How can a little blue trinket prove the truth of anything? You're making no sense, Tira."

Altira shifted to the couch and perched on the edge. `Tan followed, staying just out of reach.

"I don't see how—" he started.

"Hush," she said. "Now bind your sight and watch."

Ac`Tan squinted at her and apparently decided she was no imminent threat. He shoved his sword into its sheath, which was clutched in his other hand. "All right, but if you think I'm going to trust you just because you wave some stupid glowing trinket around, you're crazy."

"As I said, that's still up for debate. Now just sit and watch." She waited for her friend to settle warily into a chair on the opposite side of the room and then focused on the gem. She opened the sigil. It seemed only a moment before the vision completed this time. When Altira was done she looked up to discover the First Aide staring openly at her. He sighed and tossed his sword on the table in front of him.

"That's it? So what is that supposed to prove, eh? It's a fabricated lie, probably manufactured by the Greenies to sow discord amongst us. It can't be true."

Altira tucked the gem back inside her blouse and pressed on. "No, it can't be a lie, `Tan. It's not possible; didn't you see? It's enclosed in *Ver*. You know what that means—*Ver* cannot seal an untruth. The most ancient of magics assures it. One of our wizards could verify, but I'm certain the message is valid. Besides, I showed the amulet to an Alo`Kin. She couldn't even touch the thing—it nearly killed her when she tried."

"All right, now I know you're lying. How in the seven skies did you manage to show it to a Greenie? How could you possibly do that and live to tell the tale? You can't tell me you got anywhere near Valinar without being sliced into a thousand bits, admit it!"

"That's kind of not the point is it, `Tan? Who cares about the Greenies? The point is, if the vision is true then we've all been living a lie for a thousand anna. Further, it explains why the Dar is so incredibly intent on destroying me. It's not because I took some stupid gems from the Sultan. Others have done that with no problems. It's because I took the amulet, don't you see?" Altira leaned closer and lowered her voice, drawing him into her argument. She jabbed at her friend with a finger. "The Dar himself sent this talisman to the Sultan specifically for destruction because he couldn't do it himself, no matter how hard he tried."

"Bah!" `Tan snapped, and leaned back in his chair. "And just how are you supposed to know that? How do *you* know what the Dar is doing, when he never whispered one iota of any of this to me?"

"Because Nuan told me."

"The Prince? Since when are you on a first-name basis with the royalty in Fu? And why would the heir apparent to the Sultan be confiding in a Dark Elf? This is becoming tiresome, Altira. Now tell the truth!"

"Look, `Tan, I can recount the whole sordid story and we can be here for a week, but there's no time. The vision is true—you don't have to take my word for it; a wizard can prove it. But if I walk through that door and one of the watchers kills me, the truth will never be known and our people will never know the kind of Elf that leads us. If I'm lying, you still have nothing to lose in checking the vision. On the other hand, if it's true and we show it to everyone, it'll change everything. So tell me this—and be honest now." She tucked the gem back into

her blouse then looked her friend in the eye. "Which would be the better outcome for the Alo`Dara? Me dying with the truth, or revealing the Dar's treachery?"

The First Aide said nothing for an eternity. Altira started to wonder if she'd overestimated her friendship with him. "It would have to be a Convocation," he replied finally. "You'd have to show it to everyone, all at once."

Altira nearly leapt from her chair. "Yes! Exactly. So you believe?"

"Let's just say I don't *disbelieve* ... There are many in Nar`oo at the moment that are rather ... disenchanted about the way things have been going lately. You don't know about the situation in Xancata, Tira. Things are bad there."

She sat up at the mention of the great city of the Overlord. "What do you mean? What's happening with Xanath Xak?"

"He's either expelled or killed most of our people. Some say he's about to wage open war against the Alo`Dara."

"What?!" She'd been so focused on her own troubles lately, Altira had clearly been ignoring the rest of the world. "What have we done to deserve that?"

"No one knows. About two moons ago our people began to trickle in from the north. Apparently he's driving out all of the Alo`Daran officers and servants from the city."

"All the more reason to be done with Fel`Soon," replied Altira. "The crystal proves that most of what we've been told about the Alo`Kin are lies. They didn't kick us out of Anea`Na`Silithar; we were tricked into leaving by Fel`Dara. He lied to us and we're still paying the price for it. I'm thinking that everything the Dars have told us about the Green Elves for the last thousand anna has been designed with one thing in mind—to isolate us and keep us from learning the truth. If we can change that, if we can get the Greenies' help instead of fighting them all the time, then Xanath Xak will think twice before he makes war on the Dark Forest."

"You're dreaming, Tira. This is way bigger than you and your amulet. If we're sucked into some great battle with Xanath Xak, no pitiful bunch of Greenies is going to save our skins."

"Yes, but you forget that it wouldn't be just the Alo`Kin on our side. If we are allies with them, we have the Guardians and all *their* friends, and that's a force to be reckoned with. Right now we're all alone—and the Dark Lord will take advantage of that."

This prospect seemed to encourage and disturb Ac`Tan at the same time. "Perhaps. But we've got fifty thousand Dark Elves to convince. You think they'll suddenly change alliances and make nice with a bunch of murdering Alo`Kin because of an ancient amulet and a few muttered words? Altira, if the Dar or the watchers don't kill you, any one of those Elves could."

"I don't care what happens to me. And, frankly, I don't really care what happens to the rest of Nar`oo. I'd be happy to just run away and live in Finiath for the rest of my life, but we have to try, `Tan. I could never live with myself if I had the chance to save every Elf in the Dark Forest and threw the chance away because I was afraid. It's up to them whether or not they believe or reject what's in the crystal. It's up to us to show it to them or die trying."

CHAPTER THIRTY-THREE

KATHA

ALTIRA PEEKED AROUND THE SIDE OF AC`TAN'S PODE. IT WAS STILL dark, but she could just make out the tops of the trees to the east against the first charcoal hints of morning. Soon the shadows protecting her would be banished. Her friend was on the far side of the back bridge, scouting for sentries. Finally, he gestured for her to cross. Altira went invisible and scurried carefully over the dewy planking. Nar`oo's bridges were treacherous when wet, something she'd discovered more than once as a podling. If it hadn't been for her mother's alertness she could easily have slipped through the side-webbing any number of times.

Ac`Tan led on, but Altira's thoughts were forcefully drawn back to the events in Valinar. There were still a score of questions to be answered regarding her parents. Why had they left the safety of the Verdant Realm to return to Nar`oo? What had happened to them? Had the Dar finally succeeded in eliminating Antarra and Eran, or did they yet live? How could Altira find them in the vast expanse that was Salustra?

"Watch it, Tira!" hissed Ac`Tan as she collided with him near the edge of a platform. "Pay attention. Katha's pode is over the next bridge, but there are two sentries. You plan on stumbling into them, as well?"

Altira shook the ruminations from her mind and focused. "Sorry. Too many battles and too little sleep. Go on ahead, it's not far, I can pass to you on your signal."

He glowered. "This isn't the place for humor, you twit. You've been spending too much time with the Greenies. Remember, you're risking my life as well here."

"What are you talking about? What humor?"

"You can't jump all that way. It's impossible."

"Skies, `Tan, I've passed way farther than that before." She shooed him away with an impatient gesture. "Get on with it. Signal when it's clear."

The First Aide gave her a dubious look but turned and hastened over the final bridge nonetheless. He cast about on the far side for a bit then gestured. Altira popped over and landed right behind him, crouching low in the shadow of the wall. `Tan was still glancing back at her former position, clearly concerned that she'd apparently vanished.

"So Katha is the new Chief Wizard, then?" she whispered.

Ac`Tan nearly leapt off the platform. "Drat it! Stop doing that! Can't you land in front? What? Yes, Tanithar was sent to Xancata—and never returned. Probably never will."

"Kind of a strange choice for the head magic wielder isn't it? I've always thought Katha was a bit, well … you know."

"He's okay, I guess. He's just been studying magic by himself for way too long. Stay here. I'll check the door."

Ac`Tan didn't wait for her response but moved around the side of the Wizard's pode toward the front entrance, alert for sentries. He knocked once on the door, then again, and yet a third time before it was jerked open. Indistinct but clearly harsh words drifted to Altira on the gentle morning breeze, but she was too far away to make out exactly what was said. She was starting to get anxious. Crouching in the shadows behind a pode was hardly a safe position, even invisible. She needed to get going. Ac`Tan finally gestured for her to come. Altira renewed her invisibility then crept around the pode and through the door into a well-appointed parlor.

Katha was as Altira remembered. Tall—taller than a Dark Elf should be, really. And wiry, and unkempt. He looked more like a leafless willow after a tornado than an actual Dark Elf—he was missing one eyebrow and his hair was always disheveled. He wore an elegant black, silken robe but it was in desperate need of washing and smelled of stale wine and too many walnuts. What made the image worse was his bad mood—Katha was always as sour as a lemon, except when he was buried in one of the many leather-bound tomes in his library. His temper didn't improve any when Altira stepped into view beside Ac`Tan.

"What's the meaning of this intrusion, Counselor?" the Wizard snapped. "Couldn't it have waited till morning? I was three levels deep into an incantation. I very nearly turned my pode into so much dragon ash." He burped then brought a hand to his mouth. "And who is this podling? What is so all-fired important that you have to drag me from my studies? Do you realize what I've had to deal with this week?"

Exercising an impressive degree of control, Ac`Tan bowed deeply. "I do, and my apologies, sir, for interrupting. This Elf has discovered an object that may contain a message of crucial importance."

"Why couldn't this wait until a more decent hour? Oh, bother, well you're here and you've obviously destroyed any chance I might have of … of … What was it I was doing? Never mind, just come in, if you must, and do step away from there."

Tan and Altira moved toward the large curtained window and Katha impelled the door to slam shut with a wave of his hand. He brushed what looked like bits of walnut shells off his robe and sat across from them. "And who is this *person,* again?" He considered Altira's clothing with a degree of skepticism. Although she had chosen the most Alo`Daran-like garments in the Dwarven closet, her attire had originally come from Valinar and looked it. There was a hint of fire in the Wizard's eyes, as if he perceived a need to incinerate her in order to maintain the sanctity of his pode—although, from the look of it, you'd be hard-pressed to force a pack rat to live amongst the clutter, assuming of course you could find a place for one.

"She is an agent recently returned from Fu," said Ac`Tan. "She's extracted a pendant that needs to be examined. It's a matter of state security. Altira, give him the amulet."

"*Altira?*" Katha leapt from his chair and raised both hands defensively. "The traitor? How dare you bring her here, you idiot! Are you insane? Alert the sentries at once!" The Wizard executed a complex sigil and a translucent shield popped up around him.

Ac`Tan raised a hand, trying to assure the frightened conjurer. "There is no need, sir, I assure you. I have the situation well under control. I'm taking her to the Dar as soon as we finish here, but I need to verify this trinket first. Give it here, cur." He turned on Altira and gestured sharply for the amulet.

She hesitated a moment. This Wizard was, well, a bit tilted. Should she entrust him with her life and the fate of the entire

nation? Then again, what alternative did she have? Wizards were few and far between in Nar`oo, and Ac`Tan must believe. Altira lifted the glittering platinum chain over her head and handed `Tan the amulet. In truth, a big part of her was glad to be rid of the thing.

Ac`Tan proffered the pendant to the Wizard. Katha hesitated for a moment, then dropped his shield and accepted it. The moment his fingers touched the gem his entire aspect changed.

"Oh my. What is this? It feels … it's tingly. This is no ordinary trinket, Counselor." He moved to a nearby table stacked with scrolls and held the glittering jewel up to a lamp. He squinted over it in the darkness, then realizing what he was doing, waved a hand at the lamp and it jumped into luminance. He sat and turned the gem in his skeletal fingers. "It possesses some sort of aura." He bent closer and held the chain to the light. "Most curious. There has been an allural enchantment woven into the gem. And the chain—this linkage is of ancient design. One moment." He rose from his chair and disappeared through the door for a while. He returned with a heavy leather-bound book, which he propped on his knees, oblivious to his visitors.

It took the Wizard quite a while to find what he wanted in the tome. Finally he gasped, looked at the gem, then back at an illustration in the book. He considered Altira, disbelief clearly written on his face. "Do you know what this is? It's a talisman of the Ana`Ala. It's an infamous artifact, if I'm not mistaken. Where did it come from? Where did you get it?"

"I found it in the Vaults of Fu," Altira replied, "but it was originally stolen from the Dwarmak. Look inside."

"Inside?" Katha waved his hand and the lamp became still brighter. He turned and examined the jewel closely. "Oh, it's *Ver*. There is—is there?" An air of childish excitement came over him, as if it was Michaelmas and he had been given some new toy that none of the other podlings had. "Oh! Let me guess. There's a message within it, no?" He glanced up at her, expectation bubbling in his eyes.

Altira smiled. "Yes, have you turned it right?" She approached and bent over him and adjusted the amulet in his fingers. "There. Now it's aligned. Just use access—like you were opening a lock."

Katha frowned for a moment then his face lit up. "What? Oh! I see, yes. Did you know that messages enclosed in *Ver* cannot be lies?" He looked up at her, her old teacher returning for a moment.

"Yes, I know. Go ahead and view the message. We will wait."

The Wizard looked back at the gem and hesitated for an instant. "One moment. Why in the seven skies would this be sitting in some vault in Fu? It is an ancient Elvish artifact, unbelievably rare in fact. One would expect to find it in some deep cavern in Xancata, not in a Sultan's treasure chest."

Altira smiled again. He certainly did love to go on tangents, didn't he? "Let's talk about that later. You should see the vision first; it will explain a lot, and it speaks of Anea`Na`Silithar—the City of the Stars."

Katha's curiosity was instantly piqued. "Really? Excellent! Sit down somewhere over there and be quiet now. I need to focus. You can put those books on the floor." He gestured impatiently at a nearly buried divan below the window and bent over the amulet. Altira and Ac`Tan busied themselves clearing a place to sit as the Wizard made a complex gesture and stared into the depths of the gem. Katha seemed entranced for an eternity before he gasped and nearly dropped the talisman on the dusty carpet. When he finally looked up, he was speechless.

"This … we … do you realize what this *means*?"

Ac`Tan grunted. "It means we've been living a lie for the last three millennia—nothing too earth-shattering. Listen, Katha, I know how you feel about the events in Xancata. You have been a critic of the rule of Fel`Soon from time to time. We felt you would know how best to utilize this information."

"And you asked how it got to Fu," said Altira. "The Sultan had it because the Dar sent it to him to be destroyed." The Wizard gasped in horror and clutched the amulet to his chest. Altira pressed on. "He tried himself, but couldn't do it. Al`Taaba was slain by a Dark Sorcerer, sent by Xak to obliterate the gem."

"Inconceivable! And impossible, of course. If the Dar had deigned to ask *me*, instead of that ditherer Tanithar, I could have told him that. It cannot be shattered by any of the Alo`Dara, nor by any minion of the Overlord I might add, no matter how powerful. The deep magic prevents it. In fact, as long as it contains the sigil, the talisman will be nearly indestructible. It will protect itself by drawing power directly from the cha`kri."

A light suddenly dawned in Altira's mind. "Wait a minute. So, if some physical or arcane force threatened it—"

"It will defend itself as proof against its destruction."

"And if someone happened to be, say, wearing the talisman when they were attacked?"

"If the gem was in physical contact with that person, its protection would extend to the bearer. But the gem itself cannot be affected by anything but the most powerful of the ancient magics. It cannot be destroyed by physical force. It has to be unmade, and that skill has been lost from our lore and knowledge. Maybe one of the Guardians would know, but certainly not the Dar, nor any pitiful Sorcerer from Xancata."

Altira nodded. So the talisman hadn't been protecting her as much as it was shielding itself from attack.

Ac`Tan perched on the edge of the divan. "We must show this vision to the people, don't you agree? Can that be done? Can you project it so all can see the message in the talisman?"

"They would need to be physically proximate. It's not possible to share with that many people simultaneously over more than a few score cubits. The vision can't be shown to the entire city, for example."

"So if it was done at, say, a Convocation?"

The Wizard brushed his hair from his face and considered this for a moment. "Yes. That should work."

"So when is the next meeting?" asked Altira, a glimmer of hope sparking inside her.

"Tomorrow," said `Tan. "It's why I asked. The Dar wants to issue an edict of demise"—he paused and looked Altira straight in the eye—"for you."

"Me? It's tomorrow? Well …" Altira reached over and plucked a well-worn feather-topped hat from the sill of the window and set it on her head at a jaunty angle. She smiled ruefully. "So he's given up on Jen`Tar and the assassins?"

"You know about the contract?" asked the First Aide.

"I know about a lot of things, `Tan." She tossed the hat on the table and became more serious. "Far too many things, to be honest."

"Well, your pudgy little friends from Telfall did quite a job on Jen," `Tan said. "He was nearly killed by a company of the little cretins during his escape. He dragged himself back to the Dark Forest with an arrow through his shoulder and a hundred cuts, at least. Needless to say, he wasn't too happy."

A fire kindled in Altira's eyes. "Serves him right, coming after one of his own kind. I've done nothing worthy of death. I pilfered a piddling sack of gems and an innocent amulet from the overweight ruler of an insignificant island."

It was Katha's turn to chuckle. "Yes. An 'innocent amulet' that indicts every single Dar since Fel`Dara in a complicity to misdirect, dominate, and misuse every Dark Elf who's ever lived in Nar`oo for the last three thousand anna. Truly innocuous. My arcane abilities should be so impotent."

Altira graced him with a crooked smile. "Well fine, then. So what are we going to do about it? You can show the vision at the Convocation, but what then? How are we going to keep the Dar from just killing us all? If he learns I'm here, I'll be pushing up toadstools under some bramble bush on the outskirts of the forest."

Katha rose and returned the amulet. "You must remain here. I will weave protective wards about my guest chamber. Where did I put my hat?" Altira picked up the feathered cap from the table and held it out to him, but the Wizard walked right by as if he didn't see. "No one will be permitted to enter or detect either your presence or the power from the gem. This is not unusual for someone in my position. Ah!" He crossed to a well-stuffed chair and yanked a black, pointed fedora from underneath what looked like a pile of empty birdcages and shook it. "I often weave protections about my dwelling. The greater difficulty will be in getting you into the Convocation in one piece so that the contents of the talisman can be viewed."

He herded Altira into a back room without a word and closed the door. She listened to the retreating footsteps as perhaps the only two friends she had in the entire city left her to fend for herself. She tossed the hat she still held onto a nearby chair and sat on the bed. Only then did she notice that the hat's feather was huge, and green. It shimmered with the same emerald vitality as the Guardian of the same name. Was it somehow an omen of things to come?

CHAPTER THIRTY-FOUR

CONVOCATION

ALTIRA LAY ON THE BED, STARED AT THE CEILING, AND TRIED TO relax. It didn't take long before she began to sense movement in the city about her. The everyday bustle of the Elves—the slight noises that echoed just beyond the realm of normal perception—grew fainter and more distant. The people were congregating in the great amphitheater to the north; she could tell. It was the common gathering point for matters of great moment or spectacle. The time had come.

She surveyed the surrounding platforms with her mind, found them deserted, then cast below and passed through the floor, to the ground. Alighting in the thick carpet of leaves she started toward the center of the city. Afraid that one of the superior watchers would see through her invisibility, Altira passed the whole way, never treading on open space, never risking the snapped twig or the stone tumbling down the slope. The slightest rustle would alert those in the treetops. After a dozen jumps, she reached the base of a huge pine near the crest of the natural depression that formed the arena. The cacophony of a thousand whispered conversations drifted over the top of the rise, a hundred cubits away. Everyone was inside.

Altira crept now—there were no watchers here—and stole silently around the northern arc of the huge depression, invisible and alert for the random sentry, but found none. She made her way to the westernmost section of the vast stadium and located a tree of sufficient height. She climbed silently into the canopy and found a gap in the foliage. She could see the center of the great, circular amphitheater. On the raised platform were fourteen chairs and a huge, thick table. One seat, positioned in front, was for the Dar. The rest were for the leaders of the thirteen Cala—the great houses of the Alo`Dara.

Several of the chairs were vacant and Fel`Soon had not yet arrived, though the stadium was filled to overflowing. She judged the distance. It was too far to make it in a single jump, even for her. She'd have to pass to somewhere in the audience first, then pop onto the platform. That shouldn't be a problem—she'd only be amongst the crowd for a moment—and then she could jump onto the stage. The key would be to choose somewhere open. She didn't want to collide with anything.

A hush fell over the thousands of Elves as an entourage appeared near the far side of the arena. It was the Dar and the remaining Cali. They moved to the center and Altira strained to see. Yes! Ac`Tan and Katha were there, walking close together and slightly behind the Dar. She watched as the remaining Cali took their seats. The hush in the crowd became a vast silence that permeated the bowl like an ominous, oppressive vapor.

The Dar took his seat and motioned for Ac`Tan and Katha to stand behind. He gestured to his First Aide and primary Counselor, who bent his ear for a moment and then stepped to the front of the platform. His magically enhanced proclamation was quite distinct, even from Altira's remote position.

"Fellow `Darans," he said. "We come this night in Convocation for several reasons. Seldom is it that such a meeting is called, but our great leader, Fel`Soon the Wise, Primas and Leader of the Alo`Daran brotherhood, has invoked the right of assemblage. Listen now and hearken well, or suffer the consequences!" He then bowed to the Dar and retreated behind Fel`Soon, who arose and took center stage. The Dar paused for a moment, surveying the vast, silent assemblage of Elves, then spoke with a force Altira had never heard.

"My kin and brethren, we are threatened on every side. As many suspect, and I am here tonight to confirm it to you, the Dark Lord has decided that the Alo`Dara, after centuries of faithful sacrifice and service, are no longer the valued and trusted servants we once were."

A substantial murmur of speculation rippled through the crowd and Fel`Soon raised his hand for silence. "We know not what event or action has caused this shift in the Master's consideration, but rest assured, our diplomats are engaged in tireless efforts to rectify the situation and to reestablish the cordial relations with Xancata that have been the norm for many centuries. No one should assume that a state of animosity exists between us and Xanath Xak. Let me repeat that—no hostility exists between us. The Lord has simply decided for some reason to employ other servants in his continuing battle with the cursed Birds of the North for the moment."

The Dar shifted his belt, smiled, and continued. "On that note, diplomats recently returned from Xancata are pleased to report that the dread Emerald Guardian's Companion, the spawn of those treacherous knights of the north, Danera, was slain in a pitched duel with the great Dark Sorcerer, Zalfeer!"

This evoked a halfhearted round of applause from the crowd, which the Dar accepted graciously. Altira's rage nearly pushed her over the edge. It was all she could do to resist rushing the stage and unleashing all the pent-up fury she'd held inside against the liar in a hail of sildars, but the time was not right.

"Yes. Marvelous news, indeed, is that," continued Fel`Soon. "One fewer Guardian pawn is always welcome. However … there is a more dire report from our allies to the west, I'm afraid. I know that what I'm about to recount may seem inconceivable, given the close and affable relations we've always had with Al`Taaba, but it is with great sadness that I must report to you that one of our own number—yes, a former citizen even of this great city—has slain the Sultan of Fu."

Altira nearly gasped at this outright lie, a reaction that was echoed by more than half her countrymen in the assembled multitude. The Dar let the significance of his statement settle in for a moment then continued.

"Yes, I know. The loss of the fair and beneficent ruler of that island kingdom is a severe blow to all of us. That one of our own number, a fellow Elf, might commit such an atrocity is unthinkable, but the evidence is, I'm afraid, incontrovertible."

"Who was it?!" cried a voice from the crowd.

"Hunt him down!" yelled another Elf in the bleachers just below Altira.

"I will get to that in a moment," the Dar said, "but this is unfortunately not the only evil news I bear. Jen`Tar, come forward!"

The familiar assassin rose from the first row and trudged up the steps to the platform. His right shoulder was heavily bandaged and he was limping badly. The Dar, in an almost fatherly gesture, put his arm around the murderer and drew him close. The assassin winced.

"Jen, I believe I speak for all of us when I say I'm tremendously grateful that you survived the numerous injuries incurred in your valiant battle with the Dwarves." The assassin nodded to a scattering of applause from the crowd and the Dar released him and raised his hand for silence—none too quickly, in Altira's opinion.

"You might wonder why I chose this particular moment to acknowledge Jen's many acts of heroism in defense of our noble people. Many of you know that he was sent on a peaceful mission of diplomacy to Telfall to negotiate for the extradition of the traitor, Altira, so she could be tried before the council for her numerous crimes against Nar`oo. For those of you—and I cannot imagine there are many—who do not know, she was responsible for the theft of valuable state property, an assault on my own person, and for revealing many of our secrets to the cursed Guardians. It was *she* who betrayed Jen`Tar to the Dwarves and, incredible though it may seem, she actually *aided* them in their vicious and unprovoked attack upon our noble envoy, resulting in the injuries which you see. Jen, please be seated. I know you must be tired."

The Dar took the assassin's arm and helped him down the first step, then returned to his position before the seated council.

Altira was starting to wonder just how many more utter fabrications the Dar was capable of, but he had only just begun.

"We come now to the main purpose of this gathering. Most of you are aware of the dubious heritage of the cursed Elf, Altira of the Nathalic Cala. You know of the treachery of her mother, of her sympathies with the lying, despicable Alo`Kin. What you may not know is that her father was actually *one* of those sons of a liar! You do not know that because of some trifling service to a previous Dar, I at first granted her mother, Antarra, a place among us. This trust was betrayed when she attempted to break her promise and return to Valinar to reveal our secrets to the cursed Greenies." The crowd erupted in a cacophony of outrage. The Dar raised his hand to silence them. "Yes! And we dealt with her most severely. We must now deal with her traitorous daughter, it would appear."

This was answered by several angry shouts from the crowd for Altira's demise. The Dar smiled. "It would seem that you all feel as I do—"

"Fel`Soon!" Senalith, the leader of Altira's Cala, rose from his chair. The Dar hesitated, clearly annoyed, but at Convocation all on the dais were permitted to speak as equals. "This is all supposition!" Senalith was clearly agitated. "The only thing we know for sure is that Altira stole some gems from the Sultan. We also know that Al`Taaba hired the Cirrian—"

"Yes!" shouted the Dar, cutting him off. "I'm glad you reminded me, Cali Senalith, thank you." He turned back to the crowd. "As if all of her prior acts against this people weren't enough, she is also guilty of the murder of a blessed Cirrian, if you can believe that! Imagine someone killing one of the Lords of Light. That act *alone* would justify any means to guarantee her immediate execution!"

This last revelation drew fully a quarter of the Elves in attendance to their feet. Shouts of "death to the coward" and "skewer the traitor" echoed among the crowd. Senalith, seeing the utter futility of any further objection and having his own attempted defense turned against him, collapsed back into his seat. It was several moments before Fel`Soon was able to quiet the crowd enough to continue.

"Yes, yes, I agree, my friends. Thank you. So … as a result of crimes too numerous to mention, and as an act of support for the new Sultan of Fu, Al`Nuan, and in response to her murderous acts against the denizens of Cirrus, I call upon the Council of Calis, and indeed upon this entire assembled multitude, to enact an Edict of Demise. The cursed Elf Altira must be hunted down, rooted out, and terminated. Every Dark Elf here must make it their own personal commitment and responsibility to see this decree fulfilled to its fullest. The time has come to vote. What say ye, honored Cali?"

He turned and, one by one, each member of the thirteen Cala drew their ceremonial daggers, preparing to either lay them down or bury them point first into the pockmarked oaken Table of Final Derision. Altira's fate was about to be determined by a bunch of people listening to nothing but a pack of lies.

CHAPTER THIRTY-FIVE

REVELATION

ALTIRA'S SEETHING ANGER COULD EASILY HAVE REDUCED HER TREE to a stump of smoldering soot had her rage been expressed as arcane power. The Dar was lucky he was too far away for her to launch a sildar through his callous heart. It was all she could do to not fall off the branch she was perched upon. Gripping the sticky bark of the tree with white knuckles, Altira suffered through the wretched concatenation of deceit and half-truths, and she could only watch in rising frustration as the final vote commenced. Then there was Ac`Tan. That son of a narthak let Fel`Soon continue, stacking lie upon lie, and even let the Cali start the vote for her demise without giving the sign. She had agreed earlier that he would lay his hand upon his sword when the time came for her to act, but the First Aide seemed more interested in the drama of her trial than upon revealing the truth to the multitude.

Three daggers were buried in the surface of the judgment table. With each affirmation of her sentence of death, the roar in the stadium increased. At least her own Cali had his wits about him: when his turn came, Senalith laid his weapon down with great solemnity. The crowd jeered. He turned to the Cali on his right but his fellow's attention had been drawn to the Dar. Ac`Tan had stepped to the side of the beaming leader as a berobed Elf in the front row rose from his seat with the apparent intent of ascending to the platform. `Tan gestured angrily for him to sit down and—*laid his hand on his sabre!*

The sign! Altira jerked upright and sent her mind forward, located an open spot in the aisle, and passed. She popped out in the center of the walkway, facing toward the stage. The noise was deafening. She winced, refocused, and passed again, appearing on the platform just behind the Dar, who was reaching for Ac`Tan's arm.

A gasp of shock rippled through the crowd when she appeared. The Dar at first thought it was in response to one of his gestures and stepped forward to reassure the audience. It took him a moment to discern that the riveted gaze of the assembled multitude was not upon him. He turned and beheld Altira. A look of complete amazement overtook him, and for an instant he was speechless. Altira seized the opportunity.

"My fellow Alo`Darans!" She raised both arms and cried to the crowd, the magically embued stage amplifying her voice as it had the Dar's. "What you have just heard is nothing but a pack of lies!"

"Kill her! Protect the Dar!" yelled a warrior in the third row, clad in the burgundy armor of Fel`Soon's personal guard. He leapt to his feet and threw his long knife at Altira.

The blade only made it halfway. A bluish flash stopped it midair, and Katha stepped forward.

"No!" the Wizard shouted, his voice booming over the crowd. "No edict has been enacted. Any Elf here that violates the Dar's wishes will be dealt with most harshly. We *will* have order, or we will terminate this meeting. The Cali have not yet spoken. The accused has the right of self-defense. Altira will be heard." He then bowed toward a stunned Fel`Soon, shook back the sleeves of his voluminous satin robe, and glared at the crowd, prepared for further opposition. There was none. In fact, a shocked hush had fallen over the assembled multitude in the wake of his powerful arcane demonstration.

Altira smiled and touched the amulet under her blouse. Katha turned to her and nodded slightly. The Wizard was ready.

"Listen to me!" Altira stepped toward the crowd, keeping a good distance between her and the Dar. "I have something to say to you all. You can kill me afterward, if that's what you want, but every Elf here must listen. This"—she fished the amulet out and dangled it on its platinum chain—"is the reason I am here, not the rest of the lies Fel`Soon has just uttered. *This* is the reason the Dar wants me dead. This amulet was obtained from the Sultan's personal vault and it contains the truth about the heritage of the Alo`Dara!"

The glittering pendant drew the eye of every citizen in the audience as Katha stepped forward. But he never got close to her—Fel`Soon was not about to let Altira reveal the contents of the amulet. The Dar leapt at her, a wickedly pointed dagger filling his hand. His battle skills had been honed by innumerable duels with those seeking to challenge his authority, but that didn't matter—Altira never had a chance to react; her attention was on the crowd and Fel`Soon struck from behind.

Altira's involuntary grip on the gem tightened as he laid his hand on her shoulder, and she started to turn in an attempt to dodge the blade, but she wasn't nearly fast enough. The Dar aimed at her heart, his vicious upward jerk of the knife meant to stem her lifeblood at its source.

There was a brilliant flash of blue-white that momentarily blinded Altira with a feeling of intense cold. This was followed by a thud, shouts, and the sounds of wood being split behind her. Altira, still standing, wiped at her eyes and turned around. All thirteen Cali were on their feet. Several were rushing to the Dar, who lay sprawled on the stage some distance away, lying amidst the shattered remains of his chair. He was unconscious. The amulet had saved her yet again, and the force of its defense had tossed the Elven leader nearly a dozen cubits.

She whirled back to the crowd, realizing her opportunity. "Listen to me. LISTEN!"

The shouts and tumult subsided into a stunned silence as Katha joined her and yelled at the people himself. "Everyone *sit down*. Do it NOW!" He waited for obedience as most of the assembled multitude reluctantly took their seats, unwilling to challenge the Chief Wizard.

"As you can see," he said, his amplified voice commanding in a way she never would've expected, "Altira's amulet is more than it appears. It is, in fact, an ancient Dark Talisman. The amulet contains not only deep magic, but a message that is of critical importance to every single Elf—dark and green. Be silent, and behold the truth!"

Altira half expected some great arcane demonstration to punctuate Katha's statement, but it wasn't necessary. The crowd had been cowed into silence simply by his words. He nodded to Altira and she focused on the gem. They needed to get this done before Fel`Soon came to. She had expended her one chance at protection. Altira's heart pounded as she desperately

searched for the sigil. Her hands shook as she opened the mark and felt the Wizard's power drawing close.

"THIS IS NOT THE WAY OF THE LIGHT ..." Sen`Tana's booming voice, as recorded in the amulet, reverberated now over the entire assembled multitude, amplified by the magic of the dais. Altira looked up to behold the now-familiar vision, suspended in the air above the stage, revealed for all to see. They watched the argument. They watched the murder. They watched as Fel`Dara divided the Elves.

They finally knew the truth.

CHAPTER THIRTY-SIX

TIMBER!

SENALITH SLAMMED HIS CEREMONIAL DAGGER ONTO THE POLISHED reading table in his study, the pommel's large sapphire gouging a jagged trough in the beautiful wood. The leader of Altira's Cala tossed his cloak on a chair and turned on her. She was perched on the edge of a wooden bench across the room, with Ac`Tan lurking near the door.

"What in the fracas do you think you were doing, you little twit?" Senalith seethed. "What was that absurd vision supposed to prove? Do you *realize* what you've done? We're at risk on the west from Xancata, our envoys to Fu have been expelled, the Sultan—our former ally—is dead, the Greenies are skulking around the northern border, and in the middle of all of this, you threaten the rule of the Dar himself? Half of the Elves in Nar`oo believe they've been lied to for three thousand anna and the other half are ready to attack the Alo`Kin because they think it was all a fabrication, intended to sow discord amongst us, probably as a preface to war. You've made the whole thing a thousand times worse. Why didn't you come to me? I would have listened. Why didn't you show this to the council before exposing the Dar in front of everyone in Nar`oo? What in the skies do you think you were doing?!"

"I thought I was saving my own skin, you overweight excuse for a politician!" Altira leapt to her feet. "If you had the slightest care about the Elves you're supposed to be leading, if you had half the courage of a gnat in the deepest cesspool of Trellious, you'd have done what I did decades ago." She very nearly kicked her Cali in the shin, she was so finally done with all of it—the lying, the plotting, the backstabbing, the incompetence, and the murders. Enough of beating around in the shrubbery. The time had come to stare the dragon in the eyes. "And as far as sowing discord, Fel`Soon has done more than enough of that, thank you so *very* much. And I might add, done a much more masterful job than I ever could—and you know it. The vision reveals the kind of person he really is. The kind of person *all* the Dars have been, for that matter. A bunch of flaming, two-faced, self-important liars, the lot of 'em. There was never any expulsion from the City of Stars; we are not all outcasts; none of the lies we've been told about the Alo`Kin has the slightest basis in truth." She jammed at the rotund Elf with her finger, nearly impaling him with a nail. "I would think that instead of standing there, thinking about yourself and fussing over all the problems we have with our neighbors, you'd be focusing on how to prove the vision to all those twits in that cursed stadium who can't see the truth when it's staring them right in the face."

Senalith was stunned and tried to stammer a reply. "Don't for one instant dare tell me—"

"No! I'm tired of listening. You all can go jump into the deepest pit in Najarak, for all I care. I've done my part. I've shown you pitiful excuses for Elves the truth. Now is the time for you to get off your cushioned, all-too-comfortable buttocks and for once *do something*." Altira stepped back and took a deep breath. "The half of the Elves that don't believe must be convinced. We need to get rid of Fel`Soon and form an alliance with the Alo`Kin. They stand ready to unite with us against the Dark Lord, if it comes to that. And as far as all the drama in Fu, we're all much better off with that former pig of a man gone, I can tell you that for flaming certain. Skies, his smell alone would've killed half of Nar`oo! Nuan is Sultan now, and thank the Lords of Light for that. You send envoys back to Najal. They will be welcomed—and especially so when we've made allies of the Greenies. We just need to keep our heads about us. Everything will be all right."

Altira had lost a measure of her fire but it had only permitted the Cali to find his own.

"Keep—KEEP OUR HEADS?!" he yelled. "Have you gone completely insane?" Senalith raised both hands as if trying to keep his head from exploding outright. "Enough! Do you hear yourself? You can't just wave a hand and change the mind of fifty thousand Dark Elves overnight. There will be ten thousand questions, and the Dar will fight hook, tooth, and claw to keep his power. He will continue to weave his web of deceits around those who doubt. You have no idea how difficult this is. In fact, you may very well have guaranteed the end of Nar`oo."

Ac`Tan had been wisely keeping to himself, but finally stepped forward. "Cali Senalith, I sincerely doubt the revelation of a single vision, no matter how world-shattering it might be, would prove the destruction of the Alo`Dara."

Altira took in her friend's confident stance, realizing that for the First Aide to stand with her instead of with the Dar must have been one of the toughest decisions of his life. "Perhaps not, `Tan," she said, "but Nar`oo would be more than happy to see the end of me, that's for sure. Then they would never know the truth and the Dark Lord would wipe us out sooner or later."

Her Cali sighed deeply, then he clenched his teeth but said nothing, just leaned on the table with both fists. He looked old suddenly. Altira remembered the first time she'd been summoned to his office—she'd pinned a midnight bat to a tree from a hundred paces. The problem was, it was her instructor's pet bat, and the trainer was not entirely enamored of her skill. Senalith had always been fair in his pronouncements, though, in spite of the fact that he was a politician.

"All right," she said, breaking the silence, "let's say the Dar was ousted. What happens if the half that believes the vision gets their hands on him?"

The weary features of the leader sagged further. "Civil war, nothing short of it. The city would rip itself apart. Thousands would die."

"Krakas," Altira whispered. "This city hates itself nearly as much as it hates me." She stared at her hands, dirty from weeks on the road and calloused from anna of hard training. Hands that seemed good for naught more than basic survival …

Altira looked up suddenly. "There is only one option." She fished the amulet out, lifting the chain over her head, and offered it to her Cali. "Take it. Give it to Katha. He's probably the only one in Nar`oo who can protect it. You can reveal the veracity of the vision to the council in private, if that's what you want, and to any others that doubt. They won't believe me, that's obvious."

Senalith accepted the gem with a confused look. "What are you doing? Why are you giving this to me? You should show it to the council yourself."

Altira shook her head once then passed through the floor of the pode before they knew what she was about. She landed on the ground and cast about to get her bearings. The time had come to put an end to the madness. She was sick and tired of running, sick and tired of lies, sick and tired of Fel`Soon's tyranny. She started south at a jog. She didn't even bother with invisibility.

It wasn't far to the Dar's personal dwelling, and it was clear he wasn't intending to give up easily. No fewer than fifty of his personal guard clustered around the high pavilion on the platforms and on bridges in front and behind. She snuck to a hidden position behind a rise and considered the trees supporting the great three-story structure. The dwelling was much too far up to pass, even for her—Fel`Soon had designed it specifically to be inaccessible from the ground. But there was something strange about the two great trees supporting the house—they were silent. Altira squinted and focused more intently upon the great pillars, then gasped in shock. The bark had been stripped from the trees! That made it virtually impossible for anyone to climb—and it had doomed the majestic firs to a slow and painful death. The Alo`Dara as a race prided themselves in living in harmony with the forest. No tree was ever sacrificed to expand the city—it was a sacrilege. That their leader would kill two of the greatest members of the woods at the altar of his own protection was an outrage that could not be tolerated. It was yet another example of the disdain Fel`Soon had for everyone and everything.

Altira growled, hunkered down, and tried to think.

"Ya havin' fun yet, or are ya ready fer some 'elp?"

Altira whipped out her long knife and spun toward the familiar voice. "Tyke, what in the seven—you *imbecile!* What are you doing here?" Altira cast about. "How—"

"As I said afore, we Dwarves are pretty good at tunnelin'." The stocky little man hooked his fingers in his belt and smiled smugly. "I saw yer show at da stadium-place. Ya caused quite a ruckus dere, missie."

Altira shoved her knife back into its sheath. "Look, you little twit, I don't know what you think you're doing, but this is no walk in the woods. If you take a single step from this tree, you'll be skewered a thousand times. Dwarves aren't immune to arrows, I don't think. Look up there. See all those guards? There are a hundred more watchers in the trees above them, ready to spit you like a roast pig. Now go back down whatever hole you've come from and go home! I don't need any help. This is my fight."

"So da head feller is up in da tree house, in'he? Ya wan 'im down?"

"Of course, but look, I'm telling you, you can't—Tyke! Wait!"

But the Dwarf had already turned away and dropped from sight two paces from her, near the base of her tree. *Drat it, Dwarf!* Altira glanced up nervously then edged around the bole. There was a hole—a burrow barely wide enough for the little man, apparently made directly under the tree. Altira considered jumping in for a moment, but memories of her last excursion into Dwarven tunneling held her back. This was into raw earth—there would be no light at all. Her indecision was interrupted by a tinny voice emanating from her waist.

"Don' come down 'ere, missie. Jes wait dere. Ye'll know when ta act."

The faintly distant voice was coming from the gem perched on the pommel of her long knife—the Can`tie! She had completely forgotten about the talking stone. "Tyke!" she hissed into it. "Have you been eavesdropping on me this whole time, you little cur?"

His smug reply issued softly from the glowing stone. "Ya, well, no one said not ta, an' I thought ye might jes be in need of 'elp. 'Ang on. Git ready fer a real fracas."

"What in the skies are you going to do? *Tyke?*"

Altira shook her head in frustration and returned to the top of the rise. What was the fool about? She lay in the gently rustling leaves and peeked over the hill toward the pair of now-silent trees. Nothing happened. Then, softly at first, some of the leaves at the base of the closest pillar rose, as if there was a bubble forming beneath. A mound of dirt appeared. There was no sound. The mound grew larger, now at least two cubits in height. Altira nearly shrieked when a single, stocky arm emerged from the mound, followed shortly thereafter by Tyke's dirt-encrusted head. The Dwarf had somehow managed to tunnel from the top of her hill to the base of the Dar's pavilion—a distance of at least a quarter league—in no more than a few moments!

Altira glanced at the patrolling guards up top. The platforms hid Tyke's activities. The Dwarf slowly extracted himself from the ground and brought a hand to his mouth. His whispered voice crackled softly from her long knife. "Right. Now I'ma gonna fell dis tree right at ya. Be ready fer some fun."

"Fell what tree?" whispered Altira. "The support? It must be three cubits thick! It'll take you forever and it will make a horrible racket. You'll be discovered for sure, you idiot!"

"Na. It'd be hard if'n it was granite. Dis be easy, an' it won' take but a mo'."

Altira looked on in stunned silence as Tyke whipped his silvery, glowing axe from his back in a single fluid motion and

gripped the impossibly thin handle with both hands. He glanced at her then up at the pavilion, apparently judging the angle of the tree. It was at least a hundred cubits from the ground to the platform high above. He sidled right a bit then drew back the axe. Kneeling sharply, he executed a sweeping low arc that seemed to completely miss its target. Then he stood higher and made a downward-angled swipe that again seemed to cut nothing but air. There was no sound of steel cleaving wood, no chopping noises, no grunt of exertion, just a couple of missed swings. *Lovely. The stupid twit has missed.* Altira sat back on her heels, suddenly more tired than she'd ever been in her life.

But Tyke didn't seem fazed by his apparent failure. He stepped left and performed exactly the same two movements—low swing then high. From this angle it certainly looked like the blade penetrated the wood, but still there was no sound. The tree seemed undamaged.

"Ya ready?" came his distant, whispered voice.

"Ready for what? You gonna dance a jig for me now?"

"Ready for *dis*."

Tyke backed away from the tree, got a running start, then leapt into the air. He struck the trunk with both feet. There was a single loud crack as the tree spat out a huge, smiling wedge of wood from its base. Nothing happened for several moments as Tyke stood and dusted off his clothes. Then a staccato *snap-snap-snap* of splintering wood began.

"Skies!" Altira leapt up and pulled her knife out, shouting into it. "Tyke, run!"

The words had barely left her lips when a horrendous crescendo of exploding wood echoed through the forest. The Dar's pavilion was ripping itself in half. Four guards fell from the nearest walkway to the ground, and the rest scrambled away as the planking surrounding the edifice erupted into the air and fell. Altira ducked behind her tree. Bits of roof and shingles flew high, impelled by the shattering of the roof's supporting timbers. They snapped like toothpicks as the falling tree tore the dwelling apart. The great fir began a slow, arcing fall to the earth, heading right at Altira. The leader's great pavilion disintegrated into a shower of planking, furniture, dust, carpeting, and personal effects. The remaining half of the elegant dwelling, missing its companion for support, also began to fall apart, scattering the floor of the forest below with debris.

The whole thing happened in slow motion. Altira watched in amazement as the greatest of Alo`Kin construction was decimated in a matter of moments by a single Dwarf with an axe. A score of the Dar's personal guard dangled midair, clinging to the remnants of the two rope bridges, trying desperately to climb to safety. It would take them forever to get down. The nearest stair was at least a ten-minute walk—Fel`Soon had designed it specifically to ensure his safety. No one ever expected that the massive supports could be cut out from under the house.

Altira's attention was quickly drawn to the rubble on her right. Sounds of scratching were followed by a hand emerging from what must have been a bedroom of some sort.

"Tyke?" she called out, stepping forward. But the arm was black and grew longer as the hand reached upward. It was no Dwarf.

A mattress was thrown off, and the Dar himself arose from the remains of his house, dusty and scratched, bloody and furious. How he could have survived the fall was a mystery.

But that was the least of her worries.

CHAPTER THIRTY-SEVEN

CONFRONTATION

THE DAR HELD UP HIS HAND TO SHIELD AGAINST THE CHOKING rain of dust still billowing down around him. The massive cloud of gray swirled toward Altira, engulfing her and the forest in a thick, suffocating blanket. She ducked behind her tree for a moment, covering her nose and mouth with a hand, desperately trying not to cough. She finally was able to clear her throat and, crouching near the base of the tree, she extracted her knife. She wiped off the talking stone and held it close.

"Tyke!" she whispered. "Are you okay? Get the skies out of there—the Dar survived. He'll see you for sure. Quick, tunnel or something!"

A loud cough emanated from her dagger. "I kin nae see a thing. Where are ya?"

"At the top of the rise, you little fool. Now get going!"

"Can't. Da tunnel is buried unnerneath all dis stuff."

Altira growled, wiped her eyes, and crawled back to her vantage point. The air was clearing somewhat. She could barely make out the Dar now through the yellow mist, searching amidst the remains of what must have been his bedroom. He tossed a shredded mattress aside and yanked on his weapon-belt, buried underneath a pile of trash. It came free, and Fel`Soon whipped the sword from its scabbard and spun around.

Altira searched in the murkiness for the Dwarf. There he was! The idiot was stumbling around in the remains of the tree, apparently looking for the entrance to the tunnel. She hissed into the talking stone, "Tyke, get out of there. Don't worry about the stupid tunnel! Dig a new one somewhere. Fast! He sees—"

She saw the Dwarf look in her direction. Tyke spotted Fel`Soon through the dust and raised his hand to his mouth. "I kin nae dig wit'out tools, can'a? Dey inna hole."

"Well, then, run or hide or some.... Skies!"

The Dar passed. Altira leapt to her feet and followed, jumping wildly into the Darkness, desperately hoping she didn't end up inside a tree. She popped out at least a cubit too high and in front of Tyke. Fel`Soon, however, had misjudged his passage even more badly and wound up at least a stone's throw away. The huge Elf growled, brandished his double-edged sword, and swaggered toward them, sure of his advantage.

Altira crouched, knife at the ready, and gestured behind with her other hand. "Tyke, get out of here. He wants me, not you. Get to the other tunnel, fast!"

"Nae, missie." Tyke started rummaging wildly in the debris. "Methinks I'll be hangin' roun'. Ya may need da 'elp. Where's me axe?"

"Altira! You two-faced, traitorous little pinkie!" the Dar screamed as he moved in.

Altira backed toward the Dwarf. "Tyke, stop messing around! Get out, now! Remember the Dwarmak. You can't be SEEN. Now GIT!" She stepped forward, palmed a sildar, and threw in one motion at the Dar as she heard her friend backing around the stump of the tree.

Her blade never reached its target, though, for Fel`Soon swatted it out of the air with his blade as if it were nothing more than a fat June bug.

"You'll have to do better than that, you little guttersnipe," he growled, then halted, just out of her reach. "I've been waiting for this for quite a while. Time to squish you like the slime you are."

She knew what he would do. It only took a moment for him to vanish into the Darkness. Altira leapt forward and spun. She was right—Fel`Soon reappeared behind where she was and tried to skewer her. Prepared, she spun low and caught the side of his calf with her blade.

The Dar grunted, but being a cagey fighter and well experienced in hand-to-hand combat, he spun away at the moment of impact, diminishing the force of her strike. He ignored the scratch and leapt forward, aiming a backhand slash at her, trying to hew her down like the tree that had supported his former home.

But it was an uninventive move. His blade found nothing but air as Altira passed to the top of the hill behind him and then jumped again. She ended up behind the Dar, crouching low. This time she managed a wicked jab into his off shoulder before he leapt into the air—but again she was not quite fast enough to score a crippling blow. Altira didn't wait for him to counter. She passed immediately, this time to the far side of the fallen tree. Fel`Soon spun around, seeking her with his mind. He bent and wiped the blood from his leg then stood, looking in her direction.

And then he smiled. It was a sight to chill her blood.

The Dar vanished, and without a second thought Altira also passed, ending up at her original position, at the top of the rise, near her tree. She could hear some sort of faint scratching coming from underneath, but she had no time to investigate. She turned and sought her quarry. The Dar was near the stump where she'd last stood. He had apparently thrust at her and missed. He'd stumbled into the tree and was pulling a wicked splinter from his off hand. Clearly she was the better passer, but he was much stronger. Her greater skills would be an advantage only so long as she kept guessing his moves before he thought them up. Thank the Lords of Light she had watched nearly every one of his challenge matches. The moment she hesitated, the moment she displayed any doubt, he'd have her.

The Dar threw the bloody shard of wood to the ground in anger, cast about, then passed again, right at her. She vanished.

He passed a second time, and she vanished again.

"Altira, you little scat! Get back here and fight with some courage!" he shouted before passing yet again.

This cagey battle of wits continued for the better part of three leagues. Altira would jump and the Dar would follow, trying to gain some tactical advantage. His ineptness at passing surprised her more each time, but she couldn't let down her guard, for that would be certain death. They rapidly moved through the deepest part of the forest, away from the city and toward the eastern terminus. It turned into a moonless night and even with her magisight, it became nearly impossible to see. Altira was getting tired. Each jump became a strain, and she wasn't sure how much longer she'd be able to dodge Fel`Soon's blade. She stepped into the Darkness for what surely must be the last time

and fell to the ground. A twig snapped to her left and she spun, breathing heavily, her knife in her hand.

She squinted into the darkness. She could just make out his shadow, silhouetted against the thick underbrush behind.

"I've got you now, you little …" he growled, breathless. He crouched and crept forward, preparing to strike. "There's nowhere left to jump. You've surrounded yourself with brambles, you little pissant. If you pass, you'll be skewered."

Altira cast about and discovered he was right. They stood at opposite ends of a small, circular clearing on the edge of the great eastern thorn field. The shoulder-high thistles bristled with wickedly pointed barbs—it was the forest's vast defensive perimeter, designed specifically against the Alo`Kin. It was impenetrable and deadly. Each needle was hollow and contained a venom that could easily kill someone twice her size. Altira crouched and held her long knife at the ready, trying to draw the strength to jump around the Dar. She could really use Naroc right about now.

The huge Elf shifted slightly left, seeking the best advantage. "So it comes to this, does it? You run and you jump like a scared little podling but when it comes down to it, you're no better than either of your parents. You're a traitor and a liar. You think your pitiful little attempt at revelation with that amulet means anything? As soon as you're dead, I'll have it and every traitor that helped you obliterated. Come on, you spineless little whelp. Let's see what you've got."

He was trying to get her angry, trying to make her strike first, but Altira knew him well enough to know that if she got within reach, she was done for. She tried to still her breathing and force herself to calmness. She might be able to run, but there was little hope she could best him hand to hand. She needed to find some natural advantage. Her ponderings were shattered as he leapt at her. Altira spun as fast as she could, but he scored a cut on her arm nevertheless. She almost screamed but bit it back—she would not give him the satisfaction. She knew he'd eventually slice her to ribbons like this, one bit at a time, but at least he'd pay dearly in the process.

"All right, enough dancing," he said. "Time to finish you and reclaim my dominion."

Altira backed toward the forest and cast about, but she wasn't sure she had the strength for another jump. "You're a cursed liar, Fel`Soon. A tyrant and a conceited imbecile who's ruined the lives of everyone in Nar`oo. You deserve to be thrown into the deepest pit in Najarak."

"An excellent notion!" he replied. "You'll see Najarak's pits soon enough—or rather your corpse will." He extracted his own long knife from the belt slung over his shoulder and prepared to attack two-handed. Altira's arm was throbbing and she could feel the blood trickling down the back of her wrist. She didn't have much strength left. He could outdance her now, let her bleed and then simply slice her up like a spitted boar. So this was to be her end? After all she had gone through.

Not while there's a single breath left in my body! She lunged forward but the Dar jumped nimbly back.

He laughed. "Enough, you pitiful excuse for a fighter. You're done, and you know it." He rose from his crouch and stepped casually in her direction, happy to let her wither. "What a complete waste of `Daran skin you are."

Altira glanced at the Can`tie on her knife. *At least Tyke escaped,* she thought. At least she hadn't been the cause of his death, too. Maybe this was right, after all. Maybe this was the only way to pay for Danera's death.

Standing there, blood dripping from her fist, a strange sensation caressed her heightened senses. The faintest whisper came to her from behind Fel`Soon. At first she thought it was the wind whistling through the naked branches and spikes of the bramble field, but the more she focused, the more it sounded *alive*. Suddenly she realized—it *was* the brambles! They were murmuring at her. And oh, they were livid. They didn't possess words as such, but they clearly knew of the Dar, knew of his desecrations, knew of his disdain for the living denizens of the forest, knew of his arboreal murders. They bore great malice for Fel`Soon, the Destroyer of Trees.

Altira stretched forth her bloodied and shaking hand as if she were reaching for the grain in an infinitely convoluted tree. The Dar backed up and raised a warding arm, uncertain as to her intent. He was at the very edge of the clearing now, his back to the brambles. Her action was obviously not something he expected or understood.

Tears welled in Altira's eyes as she finally understood. "My friends," she murmured, beckoning to the brambles. "Help." Exerting all of her remaining power, she invoked her arboreal ability, asked for their aid, and unleashed the wrath of the woods.

Fel`Soon, deciding her gesture was an impotent feint, leapt at her, his sword raised in a final, deadly swipe as Altira collapsed to her knees. But midway into his attack, a tangle of roots burst from the ground and clutched his husky form, midair. Altira gasped and fell back to one elbow.

The squirming Dar was dragged backward, his feet and legs tightly snared. "What? You swine!" he cried. "How dare … unhand me. Leave it!" The Dar rolled to his right and slashed wildly at the grasping roots, but the instant he hit the ground, a hundred more vines erupted from the dark grass. He sliced through scores of the curling, clutching fingers of death but for every five he severed, ten more wrapped themselves tightly around him. The Dar was lifted, thrashing, into the air. Somehow he managed to continue to hack at the roots with his sword arm for a time, but eventually a bramble-root got one of the quillions on his sword. "No—" His deep-throated cry was swallowed by the brambles, a pointless yelp from a now irrelevant tyrant. Fel`Soon the Magnificent, the Primas of the Alo`Daran Nation, was finally at the mercy of the forest.

Squirming like an upended cockroach, the wide-eyed Elf was lifted high into the air and then unceremoniously yanked into the thousand glistening daggers of the bramble field, his blood required in payment for his innumerable offenses against Elves, Nature, and the Dark Forest of Nar`oo. He spasmed once then went still. His heavy body sank to the ground, the brambles clutched him more tightly, and he disappeared into the twisted, grasping mass of piercing vegetation.

The Dar was done.

CHAPTER THIRTY-EIGHT

AWAY

ALTIRA GRIPPED HER THROBBING ARM AND FELL BACKWARD, FINALLY releasing the knife from her stiff and bloody fingers. All that remained of the Dar now was a thick, coffin-like heap of intertwined brambles. The clouds shrouding the midsummer moon parted, revealing the landscape and the glistening barbs of the thorn field in a shimmering quicksilver light. It was over; she was finally free. Altira sighed, relaxed into the welcoming grass, and just stared into the starry expanse of the heavens.

For a while the only sounds were the murmuring of the brambles about her. They seemed satisfied with their judgment of the Dar. She felt an acknowledgment from them, coupled with a strange sensation of kinship and camaraderie. They were outcasts, as was she. They were alone, as was she. And they survived, as did she.

Altira lay amongst the tickling blades of grass for a long time, recovering her strength, then sat up and reached for her knife. The blade glistened in the moonlight. As her hand gripped the hilt, she hesitated—the Can`tie!

Holding the talking stone close to her mouth, she spoke in a hoarse whisper. "Tyke, are you out there?"

It took several long moments before the familiar, gravelly voice of her friend emanated from the stone. *"Aye, Alti. Are ye al ri'? Ja need me 'elp?"*

"No, everything's fine, at last, thanks. Where are you, did you get out?"

"Aye. I'm in da big tunnel. We've sealed the way ta Nar`oo. I thought it bes' ta sit 'ere fer a bit. What about da Dar? 'E seemed pretty bent, back there."

Altira glanced at the former leader's prickly bower. "He's not going to be doing any more bending ever again."

A distant grunt echoed from the stone. *"Well, good riddance den, and good work. I'm glad ye'r safe—I knew ya could do it. So, whatcha gonna do now? Go back ta da city?"*

"No, I can't return to Nar`oo. It would just stir up a hornet's nest. Katha has the stone and he knows what to do with it, I think. We need to let them use the vision."

"Ye'r always welcome in Telfall, ya know."

Altira sighed. "I know, but I can't, Tyke. It's not me. I need to find somewhere … above. No offense."

"None taken, missie. Well, I guess I'll be headin' back den. Ya take care, and if'n ya need 'elp, jes use da stone!"

"I will, and Tyke?"

"Yes'm?"

"Thank … thanks for everything. You don't know … you just …" Altira tried to find the words to express her connection

with her valiant friend, but the feelings swirling inside her were too new.

"'S all ri', missie." The Dwarf paused for a moment. He seemed to be likewise struggling for words. *"Ya know, I'm glad I tried ta get dose shanks, way back in Caltra. Otherwise I nae woudda had da chance ta know da great Skymistress. You take care, now."*

"And you, my friend. Be well."

Altira returned the knife to its scabbard and pushed herself dizzily to her feet. She checked the cut on her arm. The bleeding had stopped at least, but she was still weak and exhausted. No way could she remain here. The last thing she needed at the moment was to be discovered by some overzealous watcher.

She wiped her hands on the grass. The glistening dew-wet blades seemed to lend her some strength. She rose and turned toward the center of the forest for a moment, toward the remnants of the Dar's pavilion, toward her former home, and then turned away and paced to the edge of the brambles. They parted for her, revealing a safe path away from the forest. She started walking north.

With the thorns' acquiescence, it didn't take long to cross the great bramble field. When she reached the stubbly grass of the northern plain, she turned to survey her trail, afraid for a moment that someone might follow. But there was no path evident through the vast field of wickedly pointed spikes. The brambles had closed ranks behind her, preventing anyone from discovering her departure.

She turned and trudged into the plain, not sure at all where she was going, just needing to put some distance between herself and the past. The moon rose higher, casting the gently rolling hills in welcoming silvery light. Altira pressed on for as long as she could, but the stress, the battle, and everything she had endured in the recent past had sapped too much of her energy. After about a league, she collapsed under a lonely alder tree, the only cover she could find amidst the rolling landscape.

She was thirsty, but thinking about it was pointless. She had no supplies at all—nothing to drink, no food, not even a blanket to ward against the chill, just her weapons and a bloodied silken blouse that was sticky and far too thin for the chill breeze from the top of the rise. She needed to keep moving or she'd freeze.

Grunting, she levered herself to her feet and began to wade through the knee-high grass encumbering the backside of the hill, trying to remember if there was a stream somewhere on the north side of the Dark Forest. Movement in the sky above the plain on the northern horizon drew her attention. Something was flying toward her in the moonlight, and it was moving fast.

Pushing her exhaustion away for a moment, Altira scampered back up the hill to take cover behind the tree. Whatever it was, it was coming closer. As the speck drew nearer the thing resolved itself into a winged creature. It was a bird—a really big bird. It looked like—no, it couldn't be. No Guardian would be so foolish as to approach the Dark Forest; they'd be skewered in an instant. On the other hand, Altira had been walking for a goodly time, and the north was sparsely populated. Most believed the brambles were impenetrable.

She watched a moment more. It *was* a Guardian. In fact, it looked like the green one—Erlini, Danera's former bird.

Altira remained hidden, still uncertain as to why a Companionless Phorin`Tra would be flying around near the Dark Forest. Perhaps some strange mission to gather information? The great eagle seemed confident about her course, however—she was headed right at Altira's tree.

Erlini swooped over the far hill, soared into the small valley below Altira's position, flared, and alighted delicately at the bottom of the rise. The great green eagle gazed implacably up at her tree, as if seeing right through it.

"Come down, little raven. Ye need not fear, we be safe in this place."

Altira's jaw dropped. She recognized the words instantly—it was just like the voice she'd heard in the clearing outside Valinar, when Naroc had spoken to her, except this one seemed to exude comfort instead of power. Either Altira had now gone entirely insane, or she had somehow managed to acquire the ability to hear Guardian-speak. Throwing caution to the wind, she rose from her hiding place and came down the hill. The closer she got to the bird, the bigger it seemed. She came up short, in the grass, a stone's throw up the hill, uncertain how to respond.

"Thy heart has indeed changed greatly in the last catch of wind, little one. A bright future lies ahead of thee."

What do you say to a Guardian? "Um, thanks, I guess, but what are you doing here? Isn't it dangerous? I thought you were way up north, in the Guardian city?"

"I was there for a time, little one, but felt thy need and flew. Where goest thou? This seems a solitary nest for one with such a vaunted tale in life."

There was a strange, peaceful comfort in Erlini's words. The Dark Elf crouched wearily in the grass and then sat, encircling her legs with her arms in a vain attempt to try to keep warm. "I honestly don't *know* where I'm going, or what to do. Somewhere far away, I guess. Somewhere no one will look for me. I've had more than enough of amulets and intrigue and wars and politicians and all."

The bird smiled. *"Come then, little one, let us fly. Ye will be needed in the north. It is there I will take thee."*

"To Anora`Fel, you mean?" Altira almost laughed, her first real laugh in ages. "I hardly think they will welcome a Dark Elf in your city, much less *need* one. Where in the north would I go?"

Erlini considered this for a moment. *"Ye speak with the truth of the wind, little raven. It was indeed my thought to bring thee to my own nest, but perhaps ye be right. The time is not yet ripe for that to occur, though the need will be great anon. We will find a place for thee. Come, climb up and we will fly."*

Altira hesitated. "Wait a minute. What do you mean, 'the need will be great'? What need? All I want is to find a place that's quiet, and away from everyone and everything. I've had quite enough of 'helping,' thank you very much."

The great bird cocked her head. *"The Dark Lord weaves an all-encompassing web, little one. It ensnares many and is difficult to avoid. Ye have freed thy people from one snare, but in so doing ye have revealed thyself to the Master at Xancata, and have also shown him the weakness of one portion of his plan. His next endeavor will be more devious and more deadly. I cannot foresee it all, but I sense it will commence in the north, and that thy particular talents will be required. That is all I can say at the moment, raven."*

This was disconcerting on many levels, but Altira simply did not have the energy to resolve it all at the moment. In any case, it was clearly best to put as much distance between herself and the Dark Forest as possible, and the bird was offering the perfect escape. Altira rose and took a step toward Erlini. She had ridden Naroc, of course, but it had always been with Farthir. She wasn't at all sure she was comfortable soaring around, thousands of cubits above the ground on a Guardian, all by herself.

"Fear not, little one, I will show thee how. Here, grasp my feathers and sit above."

The eagle dipped her huge emerald wing. Altira approached with some trepidation, then grabbed a fist of feathers and heaved herself to Erlini's back.

"Now, lean forward and grasp me tightly around the neck. Yes, that is right."

Erlini's down seemed warm and comforting. An evening zephyr caressed Altira's hair and she looked back at the gentle hill with the lone alder crowning it like a fertile monarch. The tree swayed gently in the breeze, and its calf-length, sheltered grasses rippled as if bidding them farewell. She smiled, turned back, and intertwined her own fingers in the bird's velvety vanes. With the grace born of an eternity of departures, Erlini leapt into the heavens, circled once, and vanished into the Darkness.

ACKNOWLEDGMENTS

BOOKS ARE LIKE SYMPHONIES. THE COMPOSER MAY CREATE THE music, but it isn't fully realized until the conductor and the orchestra perform it in a way that is sonorous and stirring. Though these words are mine, the book you hold in your hands was a synergistic effort involving many great artisans. I bow in deference to my superb editor, Deborah Halverson, and to Tamara Dever, Erin Stark and the fantastic folks at TLC Graphics, whose excellence in the publishing world is without equal. I am continually amazed at how much has been added to my humble beginnings in an effort to make our offering truly excellent, not the least of which is the marvelous art contained herein and on the cover. It is my hope to return to this oasis of creativity many times in the years to come, and I am grateful to all those who helped make Dark Talisman a reality.

— *Steven M. Booth*